NEW YEAR'S BABY

ABOUT THE AUTHORS

JoANN ROSS is the author of over fifty novels. JoAnn wrote her first story—a romance about two star-crossed mallard ducks—when she was just seven years old. She sold her first romance novel in 1982 and now has over eight million copies of her books in print. Her novels have been published in twenty-seven countries, including Japan, Hungary, Czech Republic and Turkey. JoAnn married her high school sweetheart—twice—and makes her home near Phoenix, Arizona.

ANNE STUART has been writing for more than two decades, a great deal of that time for Harlequin. She has won every major award in the business and, as she says, "prides herself on being a model of decorum at all times."

MARGOT DALTON is a top-selling author who has written more than twenty contemporary romance novels. She has been writing since she was able to read, and completed her first book at the astounding age of eleven. She received the *Romantic Times* Reviewer's Choice Award for her novel *Daniel and the Lion*, and her books make regular appearances on the Waldenbooks romance bestseller list. Her novel *Another Woman* was recently made into a television movie and aired by CBS. Margot lives in British Columbia, Canada.

JoAnn Ross
Anne Stuart
Margot Dalton

NEW YEAR'S RESOLUTION:
BABY

Harlequin Books

TORONTO • NEW YORK • LONDON
AMSTERDAM • PARIS • SYDNEY • HAMBURG
STOCKHOLM • ATHENS • TOKYO • MILAN
MADRID • WARSAW • BUDAPEST • AUCKLAND

HARLEQUIN BOOKS
225 Duncan Mill Road, Don Mills,
Ontario, Canada M3B 3K9

ISBN 0-373-83320-2

NEW YEAR'S RESOLUTION: BABY

CHAMPAGNE AND MOONLIGHT
Copyright © 1997 by Joann Ross

A MIDNIGHT CLEAR
Copyright © 1997 by Anne Kristine Stuart Ohlrogge

LONNIE'S SECRET
Copyright © 1997 by Margot Dalton

CONTENTS

JoAnn Ross

CHAMPAGNE AND MOONLIGHT

Prologue

They could have been cherubim, looking down from a celestial mural painted on the gilded ceiling of a Renaissance cathedral. Two plump, stunningly beautiful babies—a boy and a girl with chubby pink cheeks, rosebud mouths and intelligent, thoughtful faces—sat side by side on the puffy white cloud, arguing, as they had been for what seemed an eternity.

"So what's the holdup?" the baby boy complained. "We've been hanging around here forever."

"This isn't such a bad place to be," the baby girl said, pointing out what she'd already told him time and time again.

"It was fun in the beginning. Flying around and playing hide-and-seek in the clouds." His rosy mouth pouted. "But New Year's Eve's coming, and I'm going to make a resolution."

"We don't make resolutions."

"But mortals do. So, that's my resolution. To be mortal."

It was, she admitted secretly, a wonderfully appealing resolution. "These things take time." Unfortunately, in their case, an extraordinarily long time. She couldn't even count the number of children who'd passed them by and were now living happily with their new parents.

"That's what everyone keeps saying. But I'm tired of always being reminded to polish my wings. And my halo's too tight."

"That's because it's crooked. Again." With a sister's tolerance, she straightened the gleaming band of light.

"On earth a guy doesn't have to worry about any stupid halo," he grumbled.

"On earth a boy can't fly."

"I know." Sunlight glinted blindingly off his short wings as he shrugged, giving her that point. "But there's lots of other neat stuff to do. Like playing baseball, and riding bikes, and going camping—"

It was her turn to make a face. "Camping's dirty."

"It's fun."

"There are bugs and snakes."

"That's what makes it fun, silly." He sighed and shook his head, which resulted in the halo tilting askew again. "I don't understand why we have to keep hanging around up here. How long can it take to find us parents?"

"Our mother's already been selected," she reminded him in that superior way little girls often adopted when speaking to lesser beings—boys.

"But before we can be born, we need a dad." It was her turn to sigh. "Unfortunately, it's taking longer than expected to find him."

The sad truth was that Shiloh Beauregard had horrendous luck with men. The one last summer had run over her cat. Unfortunately, it had not been an accident. The man before him—an express mail pilot—had conveniently neglected to mention he had a wife and three children tucked away in a two-story brick house in suburban Des Moines. And the one before that . . . well, the girl didn't even want to think about him!

"So what's wrong with the guy our mom's dating now?" the boy argued. Like his earthly young counterparts, patience was not his strong suit.

"He's not right for her."

"I think she's being too picky."

Pale blond curls bounced as she shook her head in frustration. "As usual, you just don't understand. . . . Here. See for yourself."

With a single wave of her chubby little hand, the girl parted the white cotton-candy clouds, allowing them to look down on the physical world they were both so eager to join.

Chapter One

The scream, torn from the woman's throat, reverberated through the night. A full white moon cast a ghostly glow on the Louisiana bayou, illuminating Shiloh Beauregard as she raced through the murky swamp, her long hair streaming behind her like a gilt flag.

"Damn, damn, damn!" The flowing skirt of her nightgown had caught on a low branch, holding her hostage. Frantic, Shiloh ripped it loose, leaving behind a swatch of ivory silk as she took off running again.

Close behind her, she heard branches breaking, the insistent pounding of feet, the harsh breathing of a man capable of chasing her to hell and back.

No! She couldn't die! She was too young. She still had too much living to do. And although she'd been running too late this morning to check her day planner, Shiloh was absolutely certain that dying had not been on the agenda. Besides, her horoscope assured her that today was a day of changes. A day when she'd receive an unexpected surprise. A day that would change her life.

Thinking about it, Shiloh realized that being chased through an alligator-infested swamp was definitely a surprise. And wouldn't dying change her life? Like in a major, permanent way?

Distracted by that unpalatable idea, she tripped over the moss-covered roots of a century-old oak and went sprawling. A heartbeat later, her pursuer caught up with her.

"No!" Shiloh's anguished scream caused a flurry of wings as night birds took to the inky sky.

She scrambled to her knees, breasts heaving beneath the lace bodice of the nightgown. Her cornflower blue eyes were wide with horror as she stared into the face of the man she'd loved. Although the night was hot and steamy, she was ice-cold and trembling.

"Please, Damian. You don't want to do this!"

"Sorry, my love." His teeth flashed in a deadly smile that made a mockery of the drawled endearment. "But this is exactly what I want to do."

She could not understand how such a seemingly gentle, caring soul could have turned into such a monster overnight. For a man who was always fastidious about his appearance, his beard was thick and rough. And as he ran his hand down her cheek, Shiloh could have sworn that his palm felt oddly furry.

"But why?" she asked.

When he gave her another of those dangerous smiles, she wondered why she'd never noticed how large his teeth were. And how sharp. They glinted in the cold white moonlight like jagged steel saw blades.

"Because it's my nature, of course." He twisted his hand in her golden hair, tilting her head back. "You see, my darling, I'm a werewolf."

She was still desperately struggling to process that horrifying, impossible statement when his shaggy head swooped down. Razor-sharp canine teeth clamped down on her throat, causing crimson blood to gush forth as if from a geyser.

And as the life drained from her limp body, the man on whom Shiloh had pinned all her romantic hopes tore into her, growling as he fed on her tender, perfumed flesh.

"Cut!" the director called out.

"Cut!" the assistant director echoed.

"That's a wrap, boys and girls," the director said with obvious pleasure. "And right on schedule."

Shiloh leaped to her feet and hugged the director. "Thank you, Brandon. You're a darling." She'd been so hoping they wouldn't end up shooting over the Christmas holidays.

"You're not so bad yourself, kiddo." Brandon O'Roarke tousled her hair, dislodging fake leaves. "I've never known a woman with your lung power."

"That's 'cause she's got great lungs." Michael Davis, her werewolf lover-killer, cast an exaggerated leer at her remarkable breasts, so dazzlingly displayed in the lace-and-silk nightgown.

Shiloh laughed, taking no offense. She knew she owed her successful Hollywood career to the generous gene pool that had gifted her with beauty and a *Playboy* centerfold's body.

"It's a tough job, playing the soon-to-be-dead bimbo," she said with self-deprecating humor. Her voice was warm and rich with the flavor of the South. "But somebody's got to do it."

The crew laughed as she gathered her belongings and headed to her car. Everyone liked Shiloh. During her years in Hollywood, she'd earned a reputation for being genuinely nice, treating everyone from the producer to the lowliest grip with the same natural friendliness. As a bonus, she always came to work with her lines memorized and didn't agonize over character motivation like those prima donna method actors.

She understood that the horror movies she worked on—most of which were destined to go directly into the video market—didn't have excess retake funds built into the budget, and was known in the genre as "One Take Shiloh."

And then, of course, there were the gift baskets of peanut-butter fudge and home-baked Christmas cookies she'd handed out this morning. She'd baked the sugar cookies last night, after Kenneth Patterson, the man she'd been dating for six months, had called, complaining of a migraine that forced him to cancel their date. Secretly, Shiloh hadn't minded missing his faculty Christmas party at the University of Malibu.

She understood that her less than stellar acting career wouldn't garner a great deal of respect from his colleagues in the literature department. But the last time she'd attended a cocktail party for a visiting lecturer, Kenneth's graduate assistant—a young girl with stick-straight hair and a figure to match—had been openly hostile.

Well, Shiloh would see Kenneth tonight. She twisted the dial on the car radio until she found a station playing carols. After making a quick stop at a store, she was merrily singing along to "Winter Wonderland" and pulling into the driveway of her rented bungalow, located in funky west Hollywood.

"In the lane, snow is glistening," she sang as she carried the treats she'd picked up on the way home into the compact kitchen. She took two champagne flutes from the pine hutch in the corner, and digging around in the back of a cupboard, she found a frosted crystal plate decorated with bells for the glistening black caviar she couldn't really afford.

"But it's a special night," she said to herself. Not only had *Swamp Wolf* wrapped on time and under budget, Kenneth had received notification that the Ph.D. dissertation he'd been working so hard on all these months was going to be published.

She carried the champagne and caviar into the living room, dimmed the lights and turned on the Christmas tree. As an actress, Shiloh knew the importance of setting a scene. She was bending down to turn on the stereo when she noticed an envelope bearing the return address of the University of Malibu that had been pushed through the mail slot in her front door. The note was brief and to the point.

After skimming the few lines quickly, hoping against hope that there was a reasonable explanation for this, Shiloh read it again. Then she sat there for a long, silent time.

The room was draped in deep purple shadows when she opened the bottle of champagne. Impossibly expensive, imported from France, it opened with a discreet pop. She poured it into a flute, debated tossing the other against the wall, then decided Kenneth Patterson was not worth shattering good Waterford over.

She took a long swallow of the sparkling wine, which was a lot more fizzy than the supermarket vintage she usually drank. Since she honestly preferred the cheaper kind, she decided this was yet more proof that she wasn't really cut out for stardom.

"I should have saved the money," she muttered as she tuned the radio to a country station, scooped up some caviar and began to celebrate Christmas Eve as she had so many others.

Alone.

* * *

It was the same every Christmas. The bright and cheery waiting room was overflowing with patients who'd fallen prey to the risks of a busy holiday season. There were the usual cases of cold and flu, along with tummy aches from overindulging in gingerbread Santas and frosted sugar cookies. Three toddlers had decided to add tinsel to their diets, there were various cuts from broken glass balls and a nip from a Christmas puppy who'd found an exuberant four-year-old a bit too much to deal with his first day in a new home.

Now a mother had dragged her twelve-year-old twin boys in, horrified to discover they'd downed an entire punch bowl of spiked eggnog she'd prepared for her Christmas Eve open house. Dr. Matt McCandless entered the waiting room to find two green-at-the-gills kids and a distraught mother.

"Suffering a bit from too much Christmas cheer, are we, boys?" he asked easily.

The boys exchanged a bleak look. Their complexion, a mossy hue somewhere between gray and green, paled. Before either of them could respond, they both threw up—in unison—over Dr. Matt's new ostrich cowboy boots.

Having experienced far worse during his years as a family physician, Matt grinned at their mother, who began blurting out embarrassed apologies. "Guess that cures that medical emergency." He proceeded to give the boys a friendly but stern lecture on abstinence.

"Dr. Matt is so great with kids," the boys' mother said later to Millie Gardner, who worked as Dr. Michael McCandless's receptionist. "It's a shame he doesn't have any of his own."

"He'd make a natural dad, that's for sure," Millie agreed robustly. "But the way he's successfully dodged all the Mrs. Dr. McCandless wannabes, I don't see that happening any time soon."

"I'll say this for you, Millie," Matt said from the doorway leading to the suite of examining rooms, "when you're right, you're right."

Millie tossed her dyed red head. "Your father was already married with you on the way when he was your age," she reminded him pointedly.

"Ah, but my father was fortunate to meet the perfect woman while he was still in high school," Matt returned. "If I ever meet a girl like the sweet old-fashioned girl who married dear old Dad, believe me, Millie, I'll get down on my knees in a shot."

Before Millie could respond, the phone rang. Muttering that he was too damn picky, Millie turned to answer it.

"I have good news, children." Bathed in a shimmering light, the angel's wings glittered like polished gold. "After exhausting research, and more than a few less than perfect candidates, I've managed to locate your father.''

"You have?" the little girl and little boy answered in unison.

"Who is he?" the little girl asked. "Is he nice? Does he like kittens?" When she allowed herself to dream of a mortal life on earth, those dreams invariably involved a fluffy orange kitten.

"Guys like dogs," the boy argued.

"Kittens are fluffy. And they purr."

"Dogs play fetch. And roll over. And play dead."

"Why would any dog want to play dead?"

"Children, children," the angel interjected. "There's no need to argue. Dr. McCandless will be a perfect father, whatever his preference in pets."

"May we see him?" the little girl asked.

"Of course." She parted the clouds, allowing them to look down at a dark-haired man dressed in jeans, a plaid shirt and boots.

"Oh, cool," the little boy said, bouncing up and down with exuberant glee. "He looks just like a cowboy."

"Dr. McCandless looks very kind," the little girl said, watching as he managed to soothe a toddler's tears after an injection.

"He is certainly that," the angel agreed. "I think you'll be very happy."

"I know we will." The little boy wondered if the cowboy doctor had a horse he could ride. "So, can we go now?"

"Not quite yet. He and your mother still have to meet. But don't worry," she said, her smile absolutely beatific. "It will happen very soon. And when it does, it's going to be magic."

As those strong, gentle hands wiped the tears from the small patient's wind-chapped cheeks, both children exchanged pleased, knowing grins.

This time things were going to work for their long-suffering mother-to-be.

This time it would be magic.

Chapter Two

"I knew he was just like the others," Savannah Beauregard Dallas muttered.

"You only met him once."

"That's all it took to see his beady little weasel eyes."

"They're not beady," Shiloh corrected automatically, already wishing she hadn't been quite so forthright with her twin sister. "They're merely a bit close together."

"They're beady. Why, the moment I saw him, I told myself, damn, my baby sister's gone and done it again. Gotten herself mixed up with another loser."

"You are only four minutes older than me, Savannah, which doesn't exactly make me your *baby* sister. And he wasn't a loser."

"What would you call a man who allows you to practically support him while he writes his doctoral dissertation, then runs off with his graduate assistant?"

When Shiloh didn't answer, Savannah softened her tone. "Honey, it doesn't take a shrink to see that you keep choosing men who are the opposite side of the coin from the General."

After a sterling military career that included several years working in the upper echelons of the Pentagon, their unbending, autocratic father had recently accepted the post of commandant of a Southern military academy. Shiloh didn't envy the teenage would-be soldiers under the General's charge.

"There's nothing wrong with a man who doesn't spend his life leaping out of bed at a five-thirty reveille," Shiloh said, filling her champagne flute.

"Of course not. But the problem is, sweetie, you're foolish enough to expect happily ever afters from these guys."

"I can't help it if I believe in happy endings. And besides, you're a fine one to talk. The men you date aren't all that dependable, either. Like that no-account count you're jet-setting around with these days."

"He's not a count. He's an earl. Or a duke. I always get those stupid titles mixed up. Oh, well, it doesn't matter. The point is, honey, I *know* these men are unreliable. I also know that some of them, like Bertran, are more than a little attracted to the fortune I won in my divorce from that philandering playboy son of a Texas oil tycoon, Samuel T. Dallas."

"Doesn't it bother you?" Shiloh asked. "That they're unreliable?"

"Of course not. The trick is to play the game for fun, not with any idea of a future. I use men the same way they use me. And when it's over, we each go our own way. Without looking back. And without regrets."

Shiloh truly loved her sister. But she couldn't imagine having such a cold attitude toward romance. "I know I may be a bit naive and old-fashioned—"

"A bit?"

Since there was good-natured laughter in her sister's tone, Shiloh didn't take offense. "All right, I'm a lot old-fashioned. But I still believe it's possible to find a man who'll love me for who I am. And who'll want the same things I want."

"Diamonds and chinchilla are always nice."

"I was talking about love. And marriage. And children. I know it's a fantasy," Shiloh admitted softly. She felt the sting of tears behind her lids and blamed it on the champagne. "But sometimes I can actually envision them—a little boy and a little girl."

"And a vine-covered cottage with a white picket fence," Savannah said, her good-natured gibe hitting remarkably close to home. "Let's toss in a dog while we're at it, why don't we? How about a taffy-colored cocker spaniel?"

Shiloh laughed, as expected. But deep down inside she didn't think there was anything so wrong with the life her sister had just described. Maybe by next year she'd find a guy. Maybe she'd even be a mother....

"Look," Savannah said. "How about coming to my place in Aspen? I'm having a New Year's Eve party and there'll be scads of rich, eligible unattached males there. Believe me, sweetie, it'll be like shooting ducks in a barrel."

"I'll think about it." But as she hung up, Shiloh knew she wasn't going to do it. Last year, while returning from a location shoot in Wyoming, the jet the film company had chartered had gone down in the Grand Tetons. Although no one had been killed, and the only injury had been the pilot's broken leg, she hadn't gathered up the courage to board another plane. Especially one bound for a ski resort in winter.

But after a sleepless night spent tossing and turning, rerunning her conversation with her sister in her mind, Shiloh made a decision. She still wasn't ready to try flying again. But there was no reason she couldn't drive.

Although it was not her nature to fret, the baby girl was worried. "There are going to be lots of eligible men at the New Year's Eve party," she reminded the angel as they watched Shiloh making her way higher and higher into the rugged Rocky Mountains. The snow-covered peaks glistened as if they'd been sprinkled with sugar crystals. Fat white flakes drifted down from a silvery gray sky. "What if our mother meets the wrong man again?"

"That's not going to happen." The angel patted her benevolently on the head, then waved a graceful hand over the scene, causing the wind to pick up. The snowflakes began to fall faster and harder against the windshield of Shiloh's car. The first blizzard of the season had just hit Colorado.

"I can't believe this!" Shiloh stared in frustration at the barricade closing the highway. After driving all the way from Los Angeles, her trip was coming to a standstill a mere forty-five minutes from her sister's Aspen condo.

"I'm sorry, miss," the state trooper guarding the roadblock said. His tone was properly official, even as he allowed his eyes to register masculine approval of the blond beauty behind the wheel of the fire engine red Mustang. "But I'm afraid no one's getting over that pass tonight."

"But I've come all the way from Los Angeles. And I'm a very good driver, Officer," Shiloh assured him. "And I had some very expensive snow tires put on in Durango."

He shook his head. "Sorry."

Snow was flying in through the open window. Although the heater was blasting away inside the car, outside the temperature had to be in the low teens. Shiloh was beginning to shiver. She also knew when she was licked.

"Do you have any idea how long the road will be blocked?"

"That's hard to say. In the meantime, you're going to have to turn around and go back to Paradise."

Her pout was not feigned. "If you've been sending people there all day, there won't be a hotel room left in town."

"No problem. Just go to the Silver Nugget and tell the lady working the reservations counter that Fletcher told her to give you the governor's suite."

"How do you know it's not already taken?"

"Trust me, it'll be available." His grin, while remarkably attractive, failed to pluck a single feminine chord in Shiloh.

Realizing she had no choice, she turned around. Shiloh could only hope he knew what he was talking about.

The Silver Nugget was a large brick building situated on a corner lot on the main street. It boasted copper chandeliers, gleaming plank floors and a hand-stamped tin ceiling. Despite her frustration at having her plans ruined, Shiloh was charmed.

"So, Fletch told you to ask for the governor's suite?" the gray-haired woman behind the reception desk inquired.

"Yes, but I don't really need a suite," Shiloh was quick to assure her. "Any room will do."

"Every room in the hotel is booked, thanks to this storm. Even the broom-closet-size one next to

the elevator.'' The woman, who'd introduced herself as Dorothy Brown, pulled a card from a
wooden box. ''But Fletcher's right about the governor's suite being free. I like to keep it open in case
he drops by. It's good for business.'' She made a
notation on the card. ''But I figure he won't be
needing it, since he's basking on the beach down in
Hawaii.'' She looked out the window at the driving
snow. ''Lucky guy, our governor.''

''I like snow,'' Shiloh offered.

''Actually, so do I,'' the woman confided with a
quick, oddly familiar smile. She handed over the
registration card for Shiloh to fill out. ''Except
when it gets nasty, like tonight. Then I worry about
my boy bein' out on those icy highways.''

Shiloh suddenly recognized the warm smile.
''You're the trooper's mother.''

''Got that right. Fletcher's third-generation Colorado cop.''

''That's admirable.''

''We're big on tradition here.'' She took the card
back and filed it away. ''Speaking of which, there's
going to be a party tonight in the bar.'' She tilted her
head in the direction of a dimly lit room named the
Silver Nugget Saloon. ''It's been an annual event
for the past century, and nearly all the locals show
up. Of course, hotel guests are invited, too. No
point in a pretty girl like you spending New Year's
Eve alone in her room.''

Shiloh accepted the old-fashioned brass key, considered her options and decided that if she couldn't be with her sister, at least attending a party here in the hotel would keep the holiday from turning out to be a total bust. And then there was that ridiculously overpriced dress she'd originally planned to wear to seduce Kenneth. The same dress she'd tossed into her suitcase at the last minute to wow all those supposedly eligible men in Aspen.

Refusing the gregarious woman's offer to ring for help with her bags, Savannah took the old-fashioned gilt-cage elevator to the governor's suite on the third floor. She tried to call Savannah in Aspen to let her know about the change in plans, but a recorded voice informed her that all circuits were busy and suggested she try her call again later.

"You *will* have a good time tonight," she scolded herself as she ran a bath in preparation for what Dorothy had promised would be a gala occasion. "You will *not* think about Kenneth, the overeducated, unfaithful louse. You're on the brink of a new year. A fresh start. A year that could change your life."

As she poured a generous splash of perfumed oil into the water, Shiloh had no way of knowing exactly how prophetic her words would turn out to be.

She was, without a doubt, the most stunningly gorgeous woman Matt had ever seen. She was not all that tall—eyeing her in a very undoctorlike manner, Matt guessed her to be about five foot five—but the legs showcased by that scandalously short skirt seemed to go on forever. The scarlet cashmere dress hugged curves that belonged on the cover of a swimsuit issue. Her hair was a rippling gold waterfall, tumbling down her back, her blue eyes were wide as the Western skies, and her crimson lips reminded him of ripe strawberries.

Matt had no idea who she was. But she was the closest thing to a goddess he'd ever seen. Unfortunately, stopping by the Chambers place to check on Jamie Chambers's croup had made him late, and it was obvious that Fletcher Brown—looking disgustingly macho in his state trooper uniform—was in the process of posting No Trespassing signs all over that magnificent female body.

Squaring his shoulders, Matt forged his way through the crowd. "Happy New Year, Fletch." Although his words were directed to the hovering cop, his gaze settled on a face that belonged on a fifteenth-century madonna and seemed oddly out of sync with the body built for sin. "Shouldn't you be out keeping drunk drivers off our highways?"

"Nobody's going to be drinking and driving tonight, Matt," Fletcher Brown assured him. "Not in weather like this."

"You never know. I remember us doing some pretty crazy things when we were younger." He flashed a smile at Shiloh. "Since Fletcher seems to have forgotten his manners, let me introduce myself. I'm Matt McCandless."

Matt McCandless was handsome enough to have gotten work as George Clooney's stand-in. However, because Shiloh had spent the last six years in Hollywood, where a plethora of gorgeous hunks waited tables, parked cars and delivered pizzas while waiting for their big break, good looks didn't impress her. As a rule, she found handsome men horrendously self-centered.

Like the average guys aren't? that obnoxious little voice in her mind piped up. Kenneth had been short, with a rapidly receding hairline.

As she looked into eyes that possessed the sheen of buffed pewter, Shiloh felt a spark of attraction jolt through her like lightning hitting dry timber.

Oh, no! This couldn't be happening. Not now!

"Hello, Matt McCandless." Years of acting lessons kept her from revealing that every nerve in her body had begun to hum. She involuntarily glanced at his left hand, noting he wasn't wearing a ring. Which didn't necessarily prove he was single, she reminded herself, remembering the cheating pilot. "I'm Shiloh Beauregard."

Matt told himself that it was merely a trick of light, gleaming down from the brass-and-copper chandelier overhead, that made her look like a vision from another world. But he didn't really believe that. Not for a minute.

They stood there, Matt looking down at her, Shiloh looking up at him, for a long, extended time.

"Matt is Paradise's doctor," Fletch finally said grudgingly.

"How interesting." *Talk about typecasting!* Once again she considered how much he resembled *ER*'s resident hunk.

"In fact, thinking about it, shouldn't you be out making house calls?" Fletch asked. "What with flu making its rounds."

"I've already checked on everyone who needed checking on," Matt said easily.

He would have had to have been deaf not to hear the male aggravation in his best friend's tone. It reminded him of a time, back in the ninth grade, when he and Fletch had come to blows over pretty little redheaded Peggy Sue MacGregor.

Unfortunately, sometime during the fisticuffs that earned them both a month's detention for fighting on the school grounds, Peggy Sue had gone off with Walter Kendrick, the baseball team's hotshot pitcher. Of course Peggy Sue, as delightful as she'd been, couldn't hold a candle to this woman.

"So," he continued, "unless Carla Lawrence goes into labor, I'm free for the night." He bestowed another of those irresistible smiles on Shiloh. "What Fletch neglected to mention is that I'm also mayor of Paradise. As such, it's my job to play host to visitors." He held out his hand in an unthreatening gesture that unnerved her nevertheless. "So, Ms. Beauregard, may I have this dance?"

His voice was as deep and rich as molasses. Even as Shiloh tried to steel herself against its warmth, she couldn't help being entranced by the way it curled around her name, caressing it with smooth tones. The small spark that had flickered deep inside her flared dangerously.

Not wanting this overwhelmingly masculine man to think that she couldn't handle a small-town Lothario, deciding that it was time to rattle him back a bit, Shiloh flashed him her most seductive smile.

"Why, thank you, Dr. McCandless. That sounds lovely." Her melodious voice, singing with all the charm of the South, was the same one Vivien Leigh had used to charm the Tarleton twins.

As he led her through the throng of party-goers, Shiloh was aware of the eyes watching them with undisguised interest. When they reached the middle of the dance floor, he drew her into his arms with an easy grace that suggested he was extremely comfortable with the opposite sex.

"This is going to sound like a horrendous cliché," he said, "but you look awfully familiar."

"I've made a few movies," she murmured into his sweater.

Recognition instantly struck. "You're the cocktail waitress in *Night Bites*."

She tilted her head and looked at him, clearly surprised. "You actually saw *Night Bites*?"

It had been a campy vampire movie that had not called upon any of the skills she'd struggled to learn in drama class. All the young director had asked of her was heaving breasts and the ability to feign orgasmic pleasure while the star—a part-time valet parking attendant at Planet Hollywood—sank a pair of blatantly false fangs into her neck.

"My nephews were staying with me while my sister and her husband were on a second honeymoon in Kauai. They rented the tape one night. You were great." He decided, for discretion's sake, not to mention what her performance had done to the boys' teenage hormone levels. His own levels, he recalled with chagrined amusement, had soared into the stratosphere.

"That movie took five days to film," she revealed. "And amazingly ended up in the top fifty earning movies this year."

"I'm not surprised. Mike and Danny sat through it five times. They're convinced you're a shoe-in for the Oscar."

"Not until they add a category for swooning." The boneless faint had been her sole artistic contribution. Everyone had agreed it made her scenes much more riveting.

"The swooning was the best part." Especially since there was always that chance that her dangerously low-cut nightgown might just slip down a tad bit more, revealing nipples already visible through the filmy white silk. Matt had held his breath, right along with his nephews, waiting for that silk to slide.

"By the end of the weekend, they'd decided to buy the video. And your calendar."

"That was my manager's idea." Since the calendar featured still shots from her movies, she hadn't even had to pose for the pictures. "He said it would get me exposure."

"It certainly did that." The January shot of her, draped in seaweed, could have easily melted all the snow in the Rockies.

Shiloh sighed. She didn't have to be a mind reader to know exactly what he was thinking. In each photo she was, of course, scantily clad. The most ridiculous one, and the one she'd recently learned had been responsible for the most sales, had been the shot of her in the flesh-colored bikini, draped in kelp, from *Revenge of the Cheerleaders from the Black Lagoon.*

"It's a long way from being art," she admitted. "But it paid for a new car."

"Art—like beauty—is in the eye of the beholder. And personally, I think *your* calendar is a lot more decorative than the Audubon one with all the mallards one of my patients bought me for Christmas this year."

Shiloh laughed, and when he drew her closer, she twined her arms around his neck and surrendered to the magic. "I was so frustrated when the highway to Aspen was closed,'' she murmured. ''But now I'm glad it was.''

''Me, too.'' He nibbled on her ear. ''Remind me to thank Fletcher. In the morning.''

His words suggested that she'd be spending the night with him. Which was, of course, out of the question. She may play a woman of loose morals in the movies, but she was, after all, a general's daughter. And General Stonewall Jackson Beauregard's little girl did not sleep around. Well, perhaps Savannah did. But Shiloh had never been that reckless.

She was about to warn him that if he was expecting to get lucky tonight, he ought to go looking for another dance partner, when she made the mistake of looking into his eyes. She was suddenly reminded of a dangerous, storm-tossed sea, and felt as if she was drowning.

''You realize that every man in town is dying for a chance to dance with you,'' he said.

''I think that's probably an exaggeration.''

''Not at all. And the annoying thing is, I'm probably going to have to let them.''

''That's not exactly your decision to make,'' she felt obliged to point out.

He captured her chin between his fingers—long fingers that could have belonged to an artist if they hadn't been delivering babies or suturing up wounds—and held her gaze to his.

''Isn't it?''

"I think this is where I tell you that you're not really my type." Having thought about it a great deal since Christmas Eve, Shiloh had come to realize that Savannah was right about her being fatally attracted to irresponsible men.

"That's okay." He played idly with the ends of her hair as he smiled at her. "You're not my type, either." What she was, Matt warned himself, was trouble. With a capital *T.* "But that doesn't really seem to matter tonight, does it?"

"I don't even know you." Her voice, capable of belting out a scream that could shatter glass, was little more than a whisper.

"We can take care of that. Let's find ourselves some private corner and share stories. I'll tell you how Lilabeth Long broke my heart in the first grade, and you can tell me about your first kiss."

"There have been so many," she said flippantly. "I'm not certain I can remember the first one."

"He must not have been that good a kisser." He ran the back of his hand down the side of her face, causing roses to bloom on cheekbones sharp enough to cut his mother's prized crystal. "Mine will be a great deal more memorable."

His outrageous masculine arrogance should have irritated her. But since every instinct she possessed suggested he was not exaggerating, Shiloh didn't argue the point. *You are purely pitiful, falling for a smooth line from a backwoods pickup artist.*

Her gaze had just drifted to his lips when Fletch appeared beside them. "Mom says there's a call for you, Shiloh. From your sister."

Having tried to call Savannah three more times before coming downstairs, Shiloh was relieved her sister had somehow located her. She was also more than a little grateful to have that strange, almost hypnotic mood broken.

"Thank you, Fletcher." She looked at Matt. "I'd better take that."

"I'm not going anywhere," he assured her. Nothing short of plague hitting Paradise would make him leave the Silver Nugget tonight. "I'll be here when you get back."

The two lifelong friends watched her make her way through the crowd.

"Fast work," Fletch murmured.

"Sometimes things click." Actually, Matt felt as if he'd been poleaxed.

"So I noticed."

"It's that obvious?"

Fletch laughed at that. "I doubt if there's a person in this place who didn't notice that the two of you were somewhere off in your own little world. You've got the devil's own luck, pal." He flashed a wicked grin rife with suggestion. "Looks like I won't have to worry about you driving on icy roads tonight." He patted Matt on the shoulder. "If you need protection . . ."

Matt laughed at the offer. It was the same one Fletch had made the night of that long-ago Winter Wonderland dance when Matt had been determined to lose his virginity with his then steady girlfriend, Connie Underwood.

"I'm a doctor, remember. I know the risks. And I recall enough from my Boy Scout days to be prepared."

What he didn't say was that he'd put the condoms into his wallet at the last minute this evening in a halfhearted acknowledgment that perhaps this might be the night he gave in to Connie Underwood Warner's frequent suggestions that they get together "for old times' sake." The newly divorced former Winter Wonderland queen had been actively pursuing him since they'd danced together at Octoberfest.

Since he'd been celibate for a lot longer than that, and had always liked Connie, the idea had become more than a little agreeable. Until he'd walked into the Silver Nugget and come face-to-face with an angel.

Chapter Three

"As relieved as I am to hear you're all right, I hate the idea of all these rich, gorgeous men going to waste," Savannah complained. "I hate you being alone tonight even worse."

"I'm not alone."

There was a slight pause. "Oh, Lord, don't tell me. You've met another loser."

"He's not a loser. He's a doctor."

"Undoubtedly a quack, under censor from the medical board."

"He seems to be very well thought of in town."

"So was Dr. Jekyll. And don't forget what happened to the women who ended up in bed with Mr. Hyde."

"I have no intention of going to bed with him."

"Where have I heard that before?" Savannah asked dryly. "Ah, I remember. I said it last night, right before I left a party with a former Mr. Universe turned celebrity bodyguard."

"I'm only flirting a little," Shiloh insisted. "After being dumped, it feels good to have a man want me."

Kenneth had held off consummating their romance, professing he didn't want her to think he was only interested in her body. Plus, his mind was so wrapped up in his work. And then there were the convenient migraines. Thinking back on it, Shiloh realized that in his own strange way, he'd been trying to remain faithful to his snippy little graduate assistant who wasn't capable of providing the financial support Shiloh had.

"Look in the mirror," Savannah drawled. "Any male still breathing would want you. But whatever happens, Happy New Year, baby sister."

After hanging up, Shiloh returned to the saloon. As she stood in the doorway, searching for Matt in the crowd, she felt a tingle at the back of her neck. Turning around, she saw a tall, gangly boy she guessed to be about fifteen staring at her.

"Hello." She smiled.

He immediately dropped his eyes to the floor and mumbled what sounded like hi.

"Nice party," she said.

He mumbled something that could have been an agreement and took a sudden interest in the toe of a size-twelve hiking boot that seemed determined to rub a hole in the pine plank floor.

"The band's good, too," Shiloh said. "I like country. It's the only music left that tells a story."

Another mumble, less coherent than the others. Deciding this wasn't going anywhere, Shiloh was about to give up when he suddenly blurted out, "You were wonderful in *Night Bites,* Ms. Beauregard. I think you should get an Oscar."

"Why, thank you. You wouldn't happen to be Dr. McCandless's nephew, would you?"

"I'm Danny—uh, Dan—Bannister," he said, managing to almost look her in the eye. "Matt's my uncle."

"And you have a brother named Mike, right?"

"Yeah. How do you know that?"

"Your uncle told me the three of you had watched the video."

"Five times."

Her lips quirked at his enthusiasm. "That's what he said. And thanks for buying the calendar."

"It's a cool calendar! Even better than Claudia Schiffer's. I especially like January."

"Yes, that seems to be a popular month." A little silence settled over them. "Would you like to dance, Dan?"

"Dance?" His Adam's apple bobbed furiously as he swallowed. "With you?"

"I love this song," she said as the band began wailing away on an Alan Jackson favorite. "It seems a shame to just listen while everyone else is enjoying themselves."

He looked as if she'd offered him the keys to a shiny new four-by-four pickup. "Oh, wow, Ms. Beauregard, I'd love that. But I'm not that good a dancer."

"Neither am I," she lied. "But together, we should do fine."

Although his palms were sweaty, and he tripped over those oversize feet a time or two and stepped on her toes once, they managed quite well. However, once she was seen dancing with the star-struck teenager, it was as if a dam had burst, and soon Shiloh found herself facing a continual stream of partners.

By the time the clock in the lobby chimed eleven, she figured she'd danced with nearly every male in Paradise, including Danny's equally star-struck brother, Mike, Matt's father, Dr. Michael Mc-Candless, Horace Tyrell—"owner of Tyrell's Feed and Fuel," he'd proudly informed her—and Reed Kavanaugh, publisher of the *Paradise Weekly Sentinel*. She even danced two slow numbers back-to-back with Fletcher Brown, who seemed openly amused by Matt's resultant glower.

And although she was enjoying herself immensely, when she found herself back in Matt's arms, she felt as if she was finally right where she was supposed to be.

"I knew I was going to have to share you," he muttered. "But I never counted on my own nephew opening the floodgates."

"He's sweet. So's Mike."

"You haven't seen either of them in a major teenage funk. It was nice of you to ask Danny to dance." Matt had watched the exchange, surprised by her apparent understanding of a young man's delicate ego.

"I suppose I could have waited for him to ask me. But I think we'd still be standing there this time next year."

Matt laughed at that and drew her a little closer. "You know, speaking of next year, it's almost midnight. And we still haven't had any time alone together."

"I know." She twined her fingers together behind his neck. "I suppose it's too cold to go outside."

"Unless you want to risk hypothermia." Which wouldn't be all that bad, Matt thought, as he considered all the ways he could warm her up. "As a physician, I wouldn't advise it. With the windchill, it's probably ten below zero out there."

"And I doubt we could find much privacy here."

"Not an iota." Unable to resist the lure of her sultry mouth, he traced a finger around her lips. "I think, if we really want to be alone, we've got two choices.''

Her lips parted beneath that feather-light sensuous touch. ''What are they?''

''Number one, we can blow this joint and drive to my place.'' The pad of his index finger had picked up a smear of crimson lip gloss. With his eyes on hers, he seductively licked it off. ''Which is, even in decent weather, twenty minutes away.''

''And choice number two?''

''We can go to your room.''

She knew she should say no. But as she watched his tongue gather in that scarlet smear, Shiloh felt on the verge of swooning. And this time she wasn't acting. Reminding herself that things would only go as far as she'd let them, Shiloh made her decision.

''I think I like choice number two.''

Matt had always prided himself on being a careful individual, the kind of man who considered all the possible consequences of his behavior. After making the decision to follow in his father's footsteps the summer of his twelfth year, he'd set out planning his future with the same unwavering attention to detail NATO generals used when planning invasions.

With the exception of a fling with a sexy young soap opera starlet during his medical student days at UCLA, his love affairs had always been born of long-term relationships with women he knew well and admired. Women of his own world, with whom he shared views and values. The relationships usually lasted from four to six months, and when they ended, he and the woman easily went back to being friends.

And although he'd always thoroughly enjoyed sex, he'd never, ever, been driven by rampant hormones. Until tonight.

Settling his hand on her waist in an openly possessive masculine way, he led Shiloh out of the saloon, pausing at the bar only long enough to buy a bottle of champagne.

"It's not French," he apologized, "but it's not bad."

"Since you brought it up, I prefer inexpensive champagne. Not that I have many occasions to drink it."

His brows lifted in obvious disbelief. "Don't tell me a gorgeous woman like you isn't part of the party crowd?" He could see her, a bright butterfly, flitting from actor to actor, flirting with Val, dazzling Mel, teasing Stallone to distraction.

"Now you sound like my manager. He's constantly trying to set up dates with hunks of the month, but to tell the truth, I'm pretty much a homebody." She gave him a dazzling smile. "Which is why tonight is so special."

She sounded amazingly sincere, which just went to show that the lady was a better actress than he would have guessed from watching her in *Night Bites*. Matt was almost tempted to believe her.

During his short-lived affair with the soap actress vixen, he'd hung out for a time with the Tinseltown crowd. From what he'd observed, actresses tended to be self-absorbed and relentless when it came to furthering their careers. It wasn't easy getting ahead when every waitress and salesclerk was a former beauty queen from towns like Topeka, Tucson and Texarkana hoping to become the next Sandra Bullock or Kim Basinger.

As good as Shiloh Beauregard looked in that tight red dress, Matt already knew she looked even better out of it. She obviously had no qualms about shedding most of her clothes in her movies, which made him wonder how many she'd shed in producers' offices to win those roles over other wannabe starlets. Putting that unpalatable thought aside as they entered the old-fashioned elevator, he drew her into his arms.

"Cold?" He lowered his head until his mouth was a whisper away from hers. The question wafted across her lips.

"Hardly." She laughed, a silky sound that crept beneath his skin. Although the champagne bottle was cold against her back, his body was hot against her breasts, stomach and thighs, causing her to tremble. "I know it's freezing outside, but I can't remember ever being this warm."

And he couldn't remember being this hot. He pressed her against the back wall, enjoying the way her soft, feminine curves melded so invitingly against him.

"I have a feeling it's going to get a lot warmer before the night is out."

His eyes gleamed with wicked seduction that a sensible woman would resist. This was Savannah's territory, Shiloh reminded herself. Even now, her twin was probably flirting her way through a crowd of male admirers. Even as she'd driven toward Aspen, Shiloh had known that despite her sister's of- fer of all those eligible men—and despite her own vow to drive nails into the coffin of her failed romance with Kenneth by dazzling them—she'd be sleeping alone. Shiloh never indulged in one-night stands.

But then the blizzard had hit and fate had landed her in Paradise. In the arms of the only man who'd ever possessed the power to make her breathless.

"Do you realize we've known each other nearly three hours?" he asked.

"That's not very long."

"It's a lifetime," he corrected. "And to think I haven't even kissed you yet."

He hadn't exactly propositioned her. But the glint in his eyes spoke volumes. ''Just because I'm letting you come up to my suite doesn't mean I'm going to sleep with you.''

''Did you hear me say anything about sleeping?''

''Please don't play word games with me. You know what I mean.''

''Yes. I know exactly what you're getting at.'' Reminding himself that he'd always been an infinitely patient man, Matt brushed his lips against her cheek. ''Just a simple kiss, Shiloh. The kind of kiss strangers share every New Year's Eve. How dangerous could that be?''

How dangerous indeed? she asked herself as his mouth created a trail of sparklers up the side of her face. ''Just a kiss,'' she echoed.

As his lips switched sides to create that same tingling havoc on her right cheek, Shiloh began to realize that there was no such thing as a simple kiss where this man was concerned.

''I knew it.'' His tongue cruised a hot, wet path along the line of her lower lip.

''Knew what?'' How was it that she was already breathless?

''That you'd taste as good as you looked.'' A thoughtful, thorough man in all things, Matt took his time, his mouth savoring hers with seemingly infinite patience.

The moist sumptuous kiss went on and on, making Shiloh wonder if he intended to kiss her endlessly. Gradually, it grew deeper. Darker. And infinitely more dangerous.

By the time the elevator reached her floor, stopping with a discreet little ding that reverberated like a carillon in the suspended silence, the flavor of him had seeped into her until she was nearly drunk with it.

"Well." Matt was shaken and determined not to show it. "That was certainly pleasant."

Pleasant? Shiloh was unable to believe he could remain unaffected while her entire world had been turned upside down.

"It wasn't bad," she agreed numbly. "For a simple kiss."

"Want to push the button for the lobby and try it again?"

"As delightful as that sounds, perhaps you ought to go back to the party," she suggested. If there was one thing that kiss had shown her—other than the fact that it was, indeed, possible for blood to boil— it was that there was absolutely nothing safe about this man.

"And leave you to toast the new year alone? What kind of mayoral ambassador of goodwill would that make me?"

"I find it difficult to believe you kiss every visitor to Paradise like that." She was, thank heavens, beginning to get her equilibrium back.

"You're right." His grin was as easygoing as ever, but this time Shiloh wasn't fooled. "I only kiss gorgeous blondes who can scream the house down in horror flicks. Other visitors get the standard chamber of commerce packet." He bent toward her again and kissed the tip of her nose. "But I gotta tell you, sweetheart, this was a lot more fun."

She couldn't deny it. "Contrary to the impression you may have of people who live in Hollywood, I'm not into one-night stands."

"That's wise," he agreed. His smile didn't waver.

"Yes... Well." It was not like Shiloh to be at a loss for words. For the life of her she couldn't think of a single logical-sounding reason she should send this man downstairs to the party. Alone.

"I'm not going to pounce on you, Shiloh." He ran the back of his hand down her cheek in a gesture she supposed was meant to reassure, but did just the opposite. How was it that such a seemingly innocent touch could make her nerves hum? "We'll turn the radio on, dance a little more, drink some champagne, share some conversation, a traditional New Year's kiss at midnight, then I'll leave.

"And tomorrow the roads should be clear and you'll be on your way to Aspen and we'll both have memories of an enjoyable snowbound New Year's Eve."

"All right. But no dancing."

He followed her out of the elevator and down the hall. "I like dancing with you."

"And I like dancing with you. That's precisely the problem."

"Okay," he agreed, deciding he could always change her mind later. He took her hand in his, lacing their fingers together. "No dancing."

As they entered the suite's living room and she heard the quiet click of the door behind her, Shiloh hoped she hadn't made the biggest mistake of her life.

Of course she hadn't. It was ridiculous to worry, she reminded herself firmly. She'd been introduced to the doctor by a state trooper, for heaven's sake. His own parents—along with half the town—were downstairs. He may be dangerously tempting. But he wasn't dangerous.

He opened the champagne with a flair she admired, poured the sparkling wine into two of the glasses sitting on the tray atop the mini bar and handed one to her.

"To the new year," he said.

"The new year," she echoed, thinking it couldn't come a minute too soon. She was definitely ready for a fresh start. She took a sip of champagne, enjoying the way the bubbles danced like laughter on her tongue.

Given the spark of attraction that had flared between them at the beginning, Matt was amazed when they were able to actually talk. He told her about life as a small-town doctor. She told him about shooting the werewolf movie. When she described the race through the swamp, including how her nightgown had ripped on a tree branch, he decided Danny, Mike and half the male population would undoubtedly cause the film to top even *Night Bites* when it came to video rental revenues.

She told him about her sister, too, and how growing up with the General had made them both able to adjust to new surroundings. He surprised himself by admitting how homesick he'd been during his student years in Los Angeles.

Growing more and more comfortable with him, Shiloh found herself telling how her mother, chafing under the General's need to control his wife and children as he did the troops serving under his command, had run away before Shiloh and Savannah had celebrated their third birthday. In turn, Matt told her how his own mother had been his father's office nurse until her retirement three years ago. A retirement that coincided with her hus-

band's, the plan being they'd get in all that traveling they'd always wanted to do.

"It took them three months to realize that they
didn't like traveling," Matt said with an easy laugh.
"I think it'd take dynamite to get them out of Paradise now."

"It seems like a nice town." And friendly, if the
people she'd met tonight were any indication.
"Your mom and dad seem happy." She'd witnessed the couple exchanging a tender kiss during a
slow dance, and Shiloh had experienced a guilty
twinge of envy that two people could still be so obviously in love after so many years together.

"They're as nuts about each other as they were
when they were high school sweethearts."

"That's sweet." It was also exactly what she
longed for for herself.

Her soft sigh told Matt it was time to change the
subject, so he launched into a highly edited account of how, his first night as a resident in the ob/
gyn service, he'd ended up delivering triplets.

"You must have been frantic," she said.

"At the time I probably would have sold my soul
for another pair of hands. But now, looking back
on it, I can definitely see the humor in the situation."

Suddenly, bells started ringing all over town,
from the melodious carillon of the Good Shepherd
Church at the end of Main Street to the mellow
chimes high in the redbrick tower in the town

square. Horns blared, and people shouted out greetings to the new year.

"It's midnight." Matt's hand cupped her cheek. His eyes met hers.

"Yes." The witching hour. Never before had she realized how accurate that description was. Of course, never, not once in her life, had she ever felt so bewitched.

"I'm going to kiss you now, Shiloh." The simple statement of intent was spoken with a grave seriousness that caused her heart to take a painful little lurch.

"Oh, yes." Her smile, which only wavered slightly, was as beatific as any woman ever shared with any man.

He bent his head until his mouth brushed hers. "Happy New Year."

Her lips parted on a rippling little sigh of pleasure. "Happy New Year," she whispered back.

His lips claimed hers in an explosion of pent-up desire. His hands tangled in her hair, rough, possessive, as he held her to a kiss that ignited her blood like a thousand flickering flames.

She clung to him breathlessly, her avid lips raining a blizzard of kisses over his face as he scooped her up and carried her into the adjoining bedroom.

Chapter Four

P assion ruled, desire overwhelmed. There was no time for gentleness or finesse. Matt thought he'd go mad if he didn't touch her. Shiloh dragged his sweater over his head, desperate to experience his hard body against hers.

Hands that could deftly stitch up a slice in a lacerated scalp suddenly turned clumsy as he fumbled with the buttons down the front of her dress. She would have helped him, but her own hands were yanking at the stubborn metal buttons of his jeans.

"I hate these things," she muttered.

"I'll buy a pair with a zipper the minute the stores open in the morning," he said, groaning, conveniently forgetting she'd be leaving town in the morning.

Success! He peeled the dress from her, then, taking no time to appreciate her scarlet bra and panties, he stripped them away, as well. She hadn't managed to unfasten his jeans, but it was just as well. Matt knew that all it would take would be the touch of her hands on him, and this would all be over.

As his mouth raced over her furnace-hot flesh, kindling fresh fires while feeding those already ablaze, heat suffused her, making her forget she'd ever felt the need for caution. No one had ever taken her with such passion. Never had she experienced lovemaking so furious, so fast, so abandoned. It was terrifying. It was thrilling.

Ravenous for more, she arched against him and breathlessly pleaded with him to take her, now, before she went mad.

"Not yet." His lips blazed a wildfire path across her quivering stomach. "You're not nearly there yet."

Her flesh was flaming, and she was burning from the inside out. Surely there couldn't be more! "Not where?"

"Where I want to take you."

Her stockings ended high on her thigh, held up with a lace band at the top. He lifted one leg in the air, nibbled his way from ankle to lace, then repeated the sweet, sensual torture on the other leg.

Matt left her only long enough to strip off his own clothes. And although he resented anything coming between them, he took the extra time to sheathe himself. Then he was back, pulling her against him, heat to heat, flesh to flesh. As they rolled over the bed, bathed in the silver glow of moonlight streaming through the window, there was no hesitation, no holding back.

Her arms and legs wrapped around him like warm silk. Shiloh could feel his heart pounding against his ribs, its rhythm synchronized with the wild, out of control beat of her own. Matt tasted her hunger on her soft, avid lips.

He lifted his head and looked at her. Their eyes met and held. Yesterday spun away. Tomorrow seemed a lifetime away. All that mattered was now. And then, in that shimmering moment of suspended passion, Matt did something Shiloh knew she'd remember for the rest of her life.

He smiled. A slow smile that lit up his eyes with tender emotion. Transfixed, she watched as he lowered his head again and kissed her with a gentleness that made her want to weep.

"Now," he murmured against her lips.

"Now." She sighed as their breath mingled.

Then he plunged into her, driving her deep into the mattress, taking her higher and higher into the flames. When he heard her cry out his name and felt the rippling waves of her climax, Matt surrendered the last of his control. With one last mighty thrust of his hips he filled her completely, giving in to his own release.

He could still feel her inner tremors as they lay together on the tangled sheets, pulses of life flowing between them.

"I wanted this," he murmured, stroking her damp hair away from her face. "I wanted you. From the first minute I walked into the Silver Nugget and saw you."

"I know." Shiloh smiled even as she sighed. "I wanted you, too. Even if it was crazy."

"Insane," he agreed. Her eyelids fluttered closed as he kissed her. "Want to know what's really nuts?"

"What?" She felt the mists clouding her mind again as his tongue traced a slow, erotic circle around her parted lips.

He ran a hand down her moon-gilded flesh. "I want you again. Already."

She opened her eyes and smiled, a slow, shy siren's smile. "Me, too."

This time he'd do it right, Matt assured himself as he gathered her into his arms. This time he'd take things nice and slow. He'd made her burn and he'd made her fly. This time, he vowed, he'd make her float.

And he did. All night long.

"Hey!" the little boy complained, "who turned off the lights? It's dark in here!"

"Well, of course it is, silly," his sister said. "Didn't you pay attention when Gabriel told us how it happens?"

He held a pudgy little hand in front of his face, frustrated when he couldn't see it. "I remember something about magic," he muttered, unwilling to admit that he'd been too excited about becoming a real boy to listen to the details.

"Actually, it's more like a miracle. And miracles take a while."

"How long? Geez, we've already been waiting an eternity."

"Not hardly." The little girl, who watched the comings and goings around her with more interest than her brother, knew exactly how long an eternity could be. "And we've only got a few more months."

"How many months?"

"Nine. Give or take a couple of weeks either way."

"Nine?"

"Nine. And don't whine." She reached out, unerringly patting his head in the close, dark space. "You'll see. The waiting will be over before you know it."

The little boy sighed. Nine months sounded like forever.

* * *

When she woke to find the bed empty, Shiloh's first thought was that Matt had left, creeping away like a thief in the night.

What did you expect? Going to bed with a man you didn't even know? She closed her eyes and wondered what flaw she possessed that had her continually zeroing in on the wrong men, like iron filings pulled toward a powerful magnet.

On the other hand, she considered, desperately trying to find a bright side to all this, with him gone, she wouldn't have to try to make awkward, morning-after conversation.

She crawled out of the rumpled sheets that still carried the evocative scent of their lovemaking and stumbled into the adjoining bathroom, where she brushed her teeth, showered and washed her hair. Usually the feel of suds streaming over her body gave her a wonderfully sensual feeling, but this morning her mind was too filled with self-recriminations to enjoy it.

She'd been out of her mind last night, she scolded herself as she turned off the water and reached for the white robe hanging on the hook on the back of the door. From now on, she was definitely staying away from champagne. Obviously, it made her crazy. Remembering that her hair dryer was in the other room, she left the bathroom and came face-to-face with Matt.

"I'm sorry," he said, when she let out a surprised little yelp that embarrassed them both. "I knocked, but you didn't hear me. I guess you were in the shower."

Although she'd been as intimate with this man as a woman could be, in the cold bright light of this January morning, Shiloh felt unreasonably uncomfortable at having him see her looking so disheveled. She looked at him looking at her and decided he was trying to figure out what had happened to the glamorous movie star he'd bedded last night.

She couldn't have been more wrong.

Matt had known she was gorgeous. But now, seeing her with her hair wet, engulfed in those voluminous terry-cloth folds, without an ounce of makeup on her well-scrubbed face, he realized he'd underestimated her true beauty.

Obviously, on some subconscious level, he'd attributed her appearance in her films to expert lighting and makeup designed to create the illusion of beauty. But in the bright mountain light streaming through the window, the truth was undeniable.

Shiloh Beauregard was absolutely exquisite. And as uncomfortable as he was with this situation, as he took in the beads of water on her exposed skin,

Matt was struck with a sudden need to lick them off. And that was just the beginning.

"I thought you'd left," she admitted softly.

He grimaced at the veiled hurt in her eyes, the faint accusation in her tone. "I was calling down for breakfast. I didn't want to wake you."

"Oh." The way he was staring at her was making Shiloh decidedly uneasy. She drew the lapels of the robe more tightly together. "That was very thoughtful of you." She decided this was no time to mention she never ate breakfast.

An uncomfortable silence settled over them. Shiloh was the first to break it. "Well," she said, dragging a hand through her wet, tangled hair.

"Yet another deep subject." When she simply stared uncomprehendingly at him, Matt shrugged and jammed his hands into the pockets of his jeans. That's what he got, for breaking his lifelong tenet about one-night stands. He couldn't ever remember feeling this uncomfortable after a night of unbridled sex. Actually, he couldn't recall ever having a night of such unbridled hot sex, but that wasn't the point.

"It was a joke," he explained. "A bad one, obviously."

"Oh." Her eyes widened with comprehension. "I get it now." Her smile was obviously forced. "It's funny."

"Not really." He was dying here. "I'll let you get dressed." He left the bedroom, shutting the door behind him with a decisive click.

"Well," Shiloh repeated softly, staring at the closed door.

The General had taught his daughters that everything came with a price. That being the case, Shiloh supposed she shouldn't be surprised that the cost for the most thrilling, exciting night of her life would turn out to be the most disastrous morning of her life.

She reminded herself that she'd certainly survived far worse than Matt's obvious discomfort. And by the time she'd blow-dried her hair into its usual smooth blond slide, she'd convinced herself that she could, indeed, survive breakfast with Matt McCandless.

The table from room service was waiting when she exited the bedroom. The television was on, tuned to the Rose Bowl Parade. He muted the sound but kept the picture on as she sat down.

"The sun's out," he announced into the well of silence that had surrounded them again. *Terrific, McCandless,* Matt blasted himself mentally. *As if the lady can't see that for herself.*

"Yes." She took a sip of too hot coffee and burned her tongue. On the screen a pair of ice skaters was spinning around on a Plexiglas lake surrounded by orchids.

"With any luck, the pass'll be clear and you'll still be able to spend New Year's Day with your sister."

Who would, Shiloh considered glumly, undoubtedly have a major league hangover. At this point, Shiloh would gladly trade the mother of all hangovers for this strained conversation.

"I suppose so." She pretended vast interest in a pink-and-purple polka-dot pig wearing a tutu and dancing to "Swan Lake."

Last night Shiloh Beauregard had behaved as if he were the most scintillating conversationalist in the world. This morning he couldn't even compete with Willard Scott describing a float covered with roses.

"Want me to turn up the sound?"

That same dark velvet voice that had murmured such wonderful words in her ear all night long was now edged with aggravation. "No, thank you," she said politely.

He watched her fingers tighten around the handle of the cup and realized she was every bit as tense as he felt. Having never been one for beating around the bush, he decided to tackle the problem head-on. "Shiloh. Look at me."

She did. Reluctantly. He reached across the table and took her hand. He was about to try to let her know last night had been special when a knock at the door caused her to jump.

"Who is it?" Matt barked in a way that made her cringe.

"Fletch."

Hell. "I'd better see what he wants."

She nodded.

Biting back a pungent curse, he stood up, tossed his napkin onto the table, strode over to the door and flung it open. "What's up?"

Fletcher Brown's expression was as smooth as the ice that had coated the road last night. "I thought Shiloh might like to know the pass is clear. We're removing the barricades."

"Thank you, Fletcher." Matt couldn't help noticing that her smile was a lot warmer than the one she'd given him. He also noted her obvious relief. "That *is* such good news." She sounded, Matt thought with renewed aggravation, like a condemned woman who'd just received a pardon from the governor.

"I always like bringing people good news." Fletch touched the brim of his trooper's hat. "Happy New Year, Shiloh. Have a safe trip to Aspen."

"Thank you, Fletch." She flashed another genuine smile his way. "And Happy New Year to you, too."

Fletch glanced over at Matt. "Happy New Year."

Matt grunted, in no mood for pleasantries. What kind of woman could scream her head off with orgasmic pleasure with one man, then turn right around and toss gilt-edged feminine invitations at another the next morning? The Hollywood kind, he reminded himself.

It didn't take Fletcher Brown's investigative police skills to correctly read the situation. "Well, I'll leave you two to your breakfast," he said. "Before it gets cold." Warning Shiloh to drive carefully, he left.

"I suppose I'd better settle my bill and be on my way," Shiloh said.

Conveniently forgetting he wasn't interested in a long-term affair, Matt was nevertheless irritated by her obvious desire to get out of town as soon as possible.

"That'd probably be a good idea." He glanced out the window at the blinding bright sun. "The weather's tricky up here in the mountains. Another storm front could blow in."

If the sun was any brighter, she'd think they were in Hawaii. He was obviously eager to get rid of her. Shiloh tried to tamp down the disappointment she felt when he didn't at least suggest she consider staying on in Paradise a few more days.

Their parting outside the lodge, as he put her suitcase into the back seat of her car, was as awkward as their earlier conversation. Wanting to recapture of bit of last night's magic, he leaned into the driver's window to kiss her goodbye. Unfortunately, she chose that minute to turn her head, causing his lips to hit her eye.

After muttered apologies on his part and assurances from her that she was fine, Shiloh drove away. Out of Paradise. And out of his life.

If her vision hadn't already been blurred with tears, and if she'd dared look in her rearview mirror, Shiloh would have seen him standing alone on the sidewalk, hands thrust into the front pockets of his jeans, looking every bit as forlorn as she felt.

Chapter Five

"There's got to be some sort of mistake!" Shiloh stared at Dr. Karen Silvers in disbelief.

"You shouldn't be that surprised. Since it's the same answer your home test kit gave you."

"I figured it was a false positive. I mean, things like that happen all the time, right?"

"They happen. But not this time. You're definitely going to be a mother, Shiloh." The doctor grinned. "It must have been one hell of a New Year's Eve."

Shiloh had met Karen Silvers at the health club where she worked to keep her voluptuous curves under control. And although they'd become friends, she could have done without the enthusiasm. "It's certainly turning out to be memorable."

"Who's the father? And please don't tell me it's Kenneth." Shiloh had shared the story of her abandonment over pineapple freezes in the club bar after one of their workouts.

"I thought you liked Kenneth."

"I only pretended because you were so determined that he'd turn out to be Mr. Right. Personally, I thought he was a weenie."

Having come to the same conclusion, Shiloh managed to laugh. Then she immediately sobered as her mind returned to her dilemma. "Kenneth and I never made love."

Karen arched a brow. "You're kidding."

Shiloh sighed. "I managed to convince myself that he was saving himself for our marriage." What he'd been doing, she realized, was indulging in a little harmless foreplay with her, then rushing off to his skinny, sharp-tongued assistant. "So, to get back to your question, there isn't any father."

"Unless you recently received tidings of great joy from some angel you forgot to mention, I'm not buying that story." Karen folded her arms across the front of her white lab jacket. "So, what are you doing for the next thirty minutes?"

"Other than having a nervous breakdown, I didn't have anything planned. Why?"

"Obviously you need a refresher course on how babies are made. Perhaps I should get out the animated video showing all those cute, energetic sperm swimming up to woo mama egg."

"I'm on the Pill," Shiloh reminded the doctor. She'd wanted to be ready for the day Kenneth succumbed. "And he wore a condom." Although she'd admittedly gotten carried away with the romanticism of the champagne, the moonlight, the midnight hour, she hadn't been foolhardy enough to forgo protection.

The gynecologist whistled. "Talk about hitting the jackpot. Perhaps you ought to buy a lottery ticket on your way home."

"I'm glad someone's enjoying this," Shiloh muttered.

"I'm sorry." Karen's expression immediately sobered as she switched from friend back to physician. "I take it this isn't good news?"

"I don't know." Shiloh dragged her hand through her hair. "I've been thinking about how much I'd like children someday—"

"From your lips to God's ears," Karen interjected quietly.

"Surely you don't believe in divine intervention? What about those spunky little swimmers you mentioned?"

Karen turned thoughtful as she made a brief note on Shiloh's chart. "There's biology. Then there's fate. And miracles. During the ten years I've been practicing, I've witnessed all three." She folded her hands on the top of the desk. "If you don't want this baby, you should make the decision soon."

"This baby might not have been planned, but I intend to keep it."

"Fine." Karen nodded. "Then we need to set up a schedule of appointments." She scribbled onto a prescription pad. "Meanwhile, you should begin taking vitamins. Do you have any questions?"

"I don't know." Shiloh felt shell-shocked.

"They'll come to you when the idea starts sinking in. You should make a list, since people tend to forget things once they walk in the office door." She gathered up a few brightly colored folders from the credenza behind her desk. "Here's some basic information on what you can expect over the next few months. And a list of recommended books. And, of course, you can always call me any time between appointments."

"Thanks." Shiloh took the folders, rose to her feet on wobbly legs and managed to somehow converse long enough with the nurse to make an appointment for the following month.

A baby. The words reverberated through her head as she drove to her bungalow. She was going to be a mother. A *single* mother, she reminded herself. Because despite Karen's quip about visiting angels and eager sperm, her baby didn't have a father.

"Of course the baby has a father," Savannah insisted that evening when Shiloh called with the news. "Obviously you need to contact the doc and have him live up to his responsibility."

"I believe shotgun weddings have gone out of style."

"I'll bet the General would disagree with that."

"Oh, my God." Shiloh quit pacing her compact living room and sank down onto the couch. "I didn't even think about his reaction."

"The Gulf War was probably less explosive," Savannah said with what Shiloh considered inappropriate cheer. "But I wasn't talking about making the guy marry you, honey. I was talking about him living up to his financial responsibility."

"I don't want to take any money from Matt."

"Terrific. Go ahead, be independent. And while you're doing your 'I am strong, I am invincible, I am woman' act, you want to tell me how you're going to pay for pablum when you're not working? Granted, I don't know a great deal about the movie business, but I would guess that there's not a huge demand for pregnant women in horror films. Even if they can scream and swoon on cue."

The idea that she'd soon be unemployable stayed with Shiloh all during a sleepless night. By the time the sun had risen, she'd made the decision to go back to Colorado. Although she was still uncomfortable with the idea of asking Matt for money, at least he deserved to know that he was going to be a father.

Damn. Six weeks had gone by without so much as a word from Shiloh Beauregard, and although he'd tried to convince himself that she hadn't been as gorgeous, as sexy, as terrific as he remembered, the moment she walked into his office, looking like the siren who'd been haunting his dreams, Matt knew he was sunk.

"Hello, Shiloh." He managed to keep his tone matter-of-fact. "It's good to see you."

"I hope you mean that." Suddenly horribly nervous, facing this controlled man who seemed such a stranger across the room, Shiloh twisted her fingers together behind her back.

"What do you think?"

"You didn't call." She hated how needy she sounded.

"You never gave me your number," he reminded her mildly. "And you're not in the book."

"You called information?"

"Three times." He'd kept hoping he'd get an operator capable of being charmed into giving him the information he'd so desperately wanted. He hadn't. "I also called the studio. But apparently they're used to strange men professing to know you. The dragon lady who answered the phone told me in no uncertain terms that if I wished to communicate with you, I could send fan mail to the studio post office box."

He'd tried to call her! Hope fluttered its fledgling wings inside Shiloh. "I'm sorry about that. I wish I'd known."

He shrugged. "*You* could have called *me*."

"I know." She sighed. "But you didn't seem all that happy to be with me the next morning—"

"I don't recall either of us being exactly scintillating conversationalists that morning."

"About that night . . ." Words failed her.

Because it had been too long since he'd touched her, Matt stood up, went around the desk and ran his palms along her shoulders, soothing her tense muscles. He found the idea that she was nervous around him more than a little endearing.

"About that night," he coaxed. Her pink angora sweater was as soft as a cloud. Matt knew from experience that her skin was even softer.

His eyes were warm and inviting. His caress, meant to soothe, did just the opposite. Shiloh bit her lip and tried again. "Speaking of that night," she repeated quickly, eager to get the words out before she lost her nerve, "I'm pregnant."

His fingers tightened just enough to reveal his shock. "What?"

"I'm pregnant," she repeated. Her shoulders sagged beneath his palms. "You're going to be a father, Matt."

Pregnant. Father. The words reverberated in his head. "That's impossible." He cringed when he felt her stiffen and mentally blasted himself for responding so bluntly. "I mean, we used protection." She'd even put the condom on him the second time. Or was it the third?

She gave him a faintly censorious look. "You're a doctor. You should know they're not one hundred percent effective."

"True. But I seem to recall you mentioning you were also on the Pill."

"I am. Was." She'd stopped taking the little pink pills the minute she'd gotten the results of her home test kit.

Matt's first thought was that women had been trapping men in just this way since the beginning of time. His second thought was that there was no reason a Hollywood actress would want to trap a country doctor whose yearly income probably didn't equal what she spent at the hairdresser's.

"I also seem to recall something about your boyfriend having just dumped you."

The question hovered unflatteringly between them. "Kenneth and I never . . . I mean, he didn't really want to, and—"

"What was he, dead?"

Despite her discomfort, Shiloh almost smiled at that. "Actually, he was sleeping with another woman."

"So he wasn't dead, just crazy."

This time she did smile. "Thank you. And it really is your baby, Matt, but of course, I'll understand if you want tests—"

"Let's jump off that bridge when we come to it." He dragged his hand through his hair and considered his options. "Obviously we've got a lot to discuss."

"I'd say that's an understatement."

This was definitely not a conversation to have here in his office, where he suspected Millie was poised outside with her ear to the door. And the restaurant at the Silver Nugget was definitely out.

"Why don't we go to my place? I'll throw a couple steaks on the grill. Then we can come up with a plan."

Relieved at how well things were going, Shiloh agreed.

Although the mood was definitely more strained than the last time they were alone together, as he tended to the steaks and she put together a salad, they managed to exchange small talk without a great deal of discomfort.

It was later, after he'd put the dishes in the dishwasher and they'd moved into his study for coffee, that things began to fall apart.

"I want you to know," Matt assured her, "that although legally it's your decision, I'd have to fight an abortion."

"That was never an option."

Matt let out a breath he was unaware of holding. "Okay. So, we already agree on something." This might, he considered, go more smoothly than he'd first feared. "I fully intend to live up to my responsibility."

"I appreciate that."

"I also understand that you're in a unique position. You probably won't be able to work once you start showing."

"There's not a lot of demand for pregnant women in my line of work."

"That's what I figured. So, it only makes sense that I support you for the next few months."

"You don't have to—"

"It's my child you're carrying, Shiloh," he reminded her. "You're the one who's going to suffer morning sickness and swollen ankles and backaches. This is the least I can do."

"Can you afford it?" She glanced around his

cozy log home, which, while extremely comfortable, was far from ostentatious.

"Unless you get a sudden yen to set up housekeeping in Beverly Hills, I can manage."

"It took two of us to make this baby. I'll want to earn my share of expenses."

He waved her offer away with an impatient hand. "That's not necessary."

"Yes. It is."

For the first time since she sprang the news on him, Matt looked honestly aggravated. "Are you always this stubborn?"

"I prefer to think of it as being independent." The General, having no patience with slackers, had raised both Savannah and Shiloh to stand on their own two feet.

As frustrated as he was by the turn this conversation had taken, Matt couldn't help noticing that she was awful cute when she was being earnest. The way she jutted her chin forward made him want to kiss her. Reminding himself that's how he got into this predicament in the first place, he resisted the temptation.

"I thought we'd agreed that you're not going to be able to get any work."

"Not acting, perhaps. But I'm not exactly helpless. I happen to have a college degree."

That came as a surprise. "In what?"

"Theater arts. With a minor in music," she admitted reluctantly. She decided this wasn't the time to mention her failed singing career. Or the songs she kept sending to Vince Gill, Kathy Mattea, Reba McEntire and other country stars, hoping someday someone would recognize her potential.

He folded his arms across his chest in a knowing way that made her want to smack him. "I rest my case. Let's move on to working out a visitation schedule."

"Isn't that a little premature? I'm only six weeks pregnant," she reminded him. "Do you always plan things out so far in advance?"

He'd always prided himself on considering all sides of an issue before acting. Except for that New Year's Eve. And look how that had turned out.

"I take it you have something against an orderly life?" Even as he said it, Matt hated how stiff and stodgy the words made him sound.

"Not at all. Although I've always preferred to go with the flow, I can appreciate that some people might feel more comfortable planning ahead. But orderly is one thing. Monotonous is another."

The accusation he heard in her voice stung. "I don't remember you being bored on New Year's."

"No." A soft, reminiscent smile touched her eyes. "I was many things that night. But bored definitely wasn't one of them."

He felt it again, that age-old stir of a male for his mate. He resolutely pushed it down. "Getting back to the subject of visitation, obviously, the child will live with you in Los Angeles during the year. But I'd like to request summer vacations. And perhaps half the holidays."

She hated the way he was making this sound like strictly a business arrangement between strangers. After all, if they hadn't gotten extremely personal, they wouldn't be having this discussion in the first place.

"Like New Year's?" she asked pointedly, reminding him of a night Matt knew he'd never forget.

He could tell she was angry, although about what, he couldn't understand. Matt figured he was being a lot more accommodating than most men in his position. Reminding himself that her out-of-control hormones were bound to contribute to mood swings, and eyeing the faint purple circles beneath her eyes that suggested she hadn't been getting enough sleep, he decided they could continue this conversation another time.

"You're right," he said. "We've plenty of time to hash out the details. Why don't I take you over to the hotel, and we can continue this discussion tomorrow morning?"

It was more than a little obvious that he couldn't wait to get rid of her. "Fine," she agreed, refusing to let him know how badly his curt attitude hurt.

Neither spoke on the drive into town. But by the time she'd checked back into the governor's suite and had several cups of tea in the hotel restaurant, Shiloh was more than a little dispirited.

"He's definitely not my type," she mused aloud as she stared into the cup, as if hoping to find some solution to her dilemma in the dark amber depths. Matt McCandless was strong and dependable without being overbearing. He was passionate, but tender. He was, in so many ways, the man she'd been dreaming about all her life. The man she hadn't truly believed existed.

Despite a disastrous track record when it came to men, Shiloh knew that a lot more had happened on New Year's Eve than two people sharing a mutual attraction and making a child together. She desperately wished life was like a book, so she could skim ahead and discover the ending. Since it wasn't, she was just going to have to do the next best thing.

"I can't walk away without seeing how things turn out."

That much settled in her mind, Shiloh swallowed the last of the cooling tea, paid her bill, then went to the reception desk, where Dorothy Brown was chatting with Fletch. "You wouldn't happen to know if there are any jobs available in town, would you?"

Dorothy revealed not an iota of surprise as she considered Shiloh's question. "I'm afraid not. This being the ski season, all the good jobs were filled weeks ago."

"What about the not-so-good jobs?" Shiloh wasn't proud. She had, after all, worked as a dog beautician her first year in Hollywood. In fact, she'd gotten her first acting job when she'd shown up at a producer's house in Bel Air to shampoo his Airedale.

"Well, there is one." Dorothy shook her head. "But it's not for you."

"Why don't you let me be the judge of that."

Dorothy's expression was definitely less than encouraging. "The night cocktail waitress in the saloon eloped on New Year's Day with a ski bum who got stranded in town when Fletch closed the highway. Since he turned out to be the millionaire owner of a computer software company, I doubt if she'll be asking for her old job back anytime soon. The day girls have both been taking turns doing double shifts, but it's starting to wear on them.''

"I'll take it," Shiloh said without hesitation.

"You sure you want to do this?" Fletch asked, entering into the conversation for the first time.

Shiloh nodded. "Absolutely."

Mother and son exchanged a quick look. Then Dorothy shrugged. "The job's yours." She named a salary just above minimum wage. "And you may as well keep the suite."

"What if the governor shows up?"

"He had his chance and he blew it. So, the way I see it, he's flat out of luck. When can you start?"

"How about tonight?"

Dorothy immediately agreed. After Shiloh had gone upstairs, she turned to her son and held out her hand.

Cursing good-naturedly, he dug into his pocket, pulled out a ten-dollar bill and placed it in her outstretched palm. "How did you know she'd be back?"

"Never bet against a sure thing, darling. Anyone with eyes could see that Matt was a goner the minute he walked into the Silver Nugget. And she was lit up from the inside like a Christmas tree." She folded the bill and stuck it in her pocket.

"Feelings that strong don't go away when the sun comes up."

Discretion—she was, after all, his mom—kept Fletch from arguing that point. But as he went out to resume patrolling the lonely stretch of highway, he thought back on how Matt had so uncharacteristically thrown caution to the wind, and how ever since Shiloh left town, his longtime, normally good-natured pal had been acting as angry as a grizzly who'd gotten his paw caught in a bear trap. Fletch decided that in this case, Mother just might know best.

Chapter Six

Matt was in his study, staring into the fireplace, trying to absorb Shiloh's bombshell, when his doorbell rang.

The minute he saw Fletch standing on his porch, fear shot up his spine. "What's wrong?" He immediately pictured Shiloh's sporty red Mustang overturned in some snowbank.

"Not a thing. I just got off shift and was thinking about having a beer down at the Silver Nugget. Thought you might want to join me."

Matt didn't hesitate. "Let me get my jacket."

Although he wasn't about to admit it, the possibility of seeing Shiloh again was the reason he'd taken Fletch up on his invitation. And, just as he'd hoped, she was the first person he saw when he walked into the Silver Nugget Saloon. Of course it would have been impossible to miss her, dressed the way she was.

The red-and-black satin dress, styled like an old-fashioned dance-hall costume, was cut low enough in the front to make a leg man reconsider his choice. Not that her legs, encased in black fishnet stockings, weren't damn fine, too. She didn't look like any expectant mother Matt had ever seen.

"What the hell do you think you're doing?"

No one in Paradise had ever heard Dr. Matt roar like that. The bar suddenly went quiet. Even the band stopped playing.

Shiloh had known Matt would find out about her decision to stay in Paradise. But she'd been hoping to break the news to him tomorrow. In her own way. Refusing to let him see how his disapproval stung, she managed to keep her head high as she walked across the room with a tray of margaritas, handed out the drinks to the party of four with a feigned smile that didn't waver even a little bit, made change and returned to the bar.

"I'm talking to you, Shiloh."

"Really?" She placed the empty tray on the bar, gave the bartender the money for the drinks and slipped the hefty tip into the pocket of her full skirt. "Sounds to me as if you're yelling, Dr. McCandless."

"I asked what you think you're doing."

"I'm working." They'd definitely garnered everyone's attention. Heads began to swivel between them, like spectators at a tennis match.

"Here?"

He made it sound as if she'd taken a job in a brothel. She glared at him. "Surely you don't have anything against good, honest work?"

"Of course not. But this isn't any kind of job for a pregnant woman."

Shiloh would have thought it impossible for the room to get any quieter. She was wrong.

She felt the color flood into her face and watched as the same scarlet flush rose from Matt's collar. Obviously, this was not something he'd planned to blurt out in public. They stood there, on opposite sides of the room, looking at each other, while everyone else looked at them.

Dorothy was the first to break the suspended silence. "Shiloh," she said mildly, "why don't you take a little break? I can handle things here."

Shiloh gave her a look of heartfelt gratitude. "Thanks, Dorothy. I promise I won't be long."

"Take as much time as you like, honey." She turned toward the band. "I'm not paying you guys to stand around and gawk at the help."

As the band resumed playing, Shiloh walked past Matt and out of the saloon. Cursing beneath his breath, he followed.

Neither of them saw Dorothy pause beside one of the tables. "You gotta put out that cigarette, Floyd Jenkins." She plucked the Marlboro from between his lips and ground it out in an ashtray shaped like a cowboy boot. "This is a nonsmoking establishment."

"Since when?" the grizzled seventy-year-old rancher challenged.

"Since I hired a pregnant cocktail waitress. Everyone knows smoke's bad for the baby." She put both hands on her ample hips. "You got any problem with that?"

His eyes, accentuated by deep lines earned from a lifetime of working out in the elements, turned as hard as agates as he stared back for a long moment. Then he caved in. "Guess not," he muttered.

"Glad to hear that," Dorothy said robustly, clapping him on the shoulder. "And for being so agreeable, the next beer's on the house."

"You realize, of course," Matt said with what he thought was extraordinary patience, "that this is ridiculous."

Shiloh hated his attitude. "What is? Me working here? Or you telling half the town that I'm having a baby?"

He dragged his hand down his face. "I'm sorry about that."

"You should be. I was hoping to have a chance to fit in before everyone found out that Paradise's newest citizen is a woman of loose morals."

"No one would think that."

"Oh, no?" They were in her suite, but the mood was definitely a great deal different than the last time they'd been together in this room. "Have a lot of unmarried mothers in town, do you?"

"More than you'd think. And a lot more than I'd like."

"Well, now there's another." She crossed her legs with a swish of scarlet crinoline. "And I'm afraid your sterling reputation just got a bit tarnished, as well."

"I'm not worried about my reputation. I'm worried about you."

"That isn't necessary. I'm healthy as a horse."

"And stubborn as a mule," he muttered.

"As a doctor, you, of all people, should know that pregnancy is a perfectly natural condition. There's nothing wrong with me working. Besides, what would you have me do, sit home for the next seven and a half months and knit booties?"

He knew he was being out of line. But some basic protective instinct had clicked in, making him want to wrap her in cotton batting until her baby—their baby, he reminded himself with a renewed sense of shock and wonder—was born.

"I don't suppose you'd consider doing just that?"

"Sorry. I don't know how to knit."

He gave up on that argument, planning to come back to it when he'd had time to gather more ammunition. "Why here?" he asked.

She shrugged her bare shoulders. Her fragrant flesh looked like porcelain. Matt remembered it being a great deal warmer.

"Why not? As you pointed out, I can't sign on for another movie right now. And I like Paradise."

Like a wild animal catching the scent of a trap, Matt narrowed his eyes. "You're not thinking of marriage—"

"Of course I'm not," she said quickly. A bit too quickly, he feared.

Damn. He didn't want to hurt her feelings. But he felt he owed it to her to lay his cards on the table. "That's good. Because as great as things were between us, sex isn't a firm foundation for marriage."

Personally, Shiloh thought it wasn't such a bad start, but understanding what he meant, and appreciating what he was trying to do, she opted not to argue.

"I didn't come here expecting a proposal, Matt. I came because I thought you deserved to know that you were going to be a father. And, to be perfectly honest, because I could use a little financial help. Although I've always made enough to support myself in a fairly comfortable life-style, I'm definitely not in Sandra Bullock's or Nicole Kidman's tax bracket.

"After the baby's born, I'll return to Hollywood and go back to work. But for now, the idea of spending the next few months in Paradise, away from the Hollywood gossip mill and tabloid reporters, is enormously appealing."

Matt had forgotten about the publicity angle. The idea of having his personal life played out on the front pages of tabloids in supermarkets all over the country was horrifying.

"When you put it that way, it makes sense."

He tried telling himself maintaining his privacy was the only reason he found her decision to stay so appealing. That and the fact that this way he'd be able to look out for her. Make sure she was taking her vitamins, getting her rest, having regular prenatal checkups . . .

That thought brought another to mind. "We'll need to get you a doctor."

"What's wrong with you?"

"It'd be better if it were someone not so close to the situation."

"Oh." Shiloh was momentarily disappointed, then decided that it was probably for the best. Those ugly paper gowns were unflattering enough, even if a woman didn't look like the Goodyear blimp.

"There's a good obstetrician in Aspen," he said. "Susan Lucas. I think you'll like her."

"Fine." That settled, she stood up. "Well, now that we've had our little chat, I'd better get back to work."

"Do you have to?" He wasn't ready to let her go yet.

"Dorothy was nice enough to give me this job. Along with this suite. I wouldn't want to take advantage of her."

Matt gave her a long look, different from the ones she remembered that fateful night. This time, instead of looking *at* her, Shiloh felt as if he was looking *into* her.

"No," he said finally. "I guess that wouldn't really be right."

They went downstairs together. When Shiloh returned to work, Matt found Fletch waiting for him.

"You knew, didn't you?"

Fletch's face revealed his regret. "I knew she'd come back to town. But I didn't know about the baby, Matt. And I'm really sorry about springing her new job on you that way. As practical jokes go, this one definitely bombed." His voice turned as sober as his expression. "Anything I can do?"

"Yeah," Matt said, frowning as he realized how the neckline of that ridiculous costume drew attention to Shiloh's breasts. Before, they'd been merely wondrous. Now, already more voluptuous from pregnancy, they could probably be declared a natural wonder. "You can hang around and drive me home after closing. Because I'm going to sit here, watch all those bozos looking down the front of the mother of my child's dress, and get very, very drunk."

Shortly after her arrival in Paradise, morning sickness hit with a vengeance, making Shiloh extremely grateful she had a night job. If she'd been required to move before noon, she never would have made it. She was staggering back to bed from the bathroom, when a knock sounded at her door.

"Come on in, Dorothy," she managed to call out weakly. Matt had recently vanished, without explanation. Fletch's mother, bless her heart, had taken Shiloh under her wing, delivering tea and dry toast the past five mornings in an attempt to ease Shiloh's discomfort.

"It's not Dorothy," an all too familiar voice called back.

Remembering the gruesome sight of her reflection in the bathroom mirror after she'd managed to brush her teeth with only minimum gagging, Shiloh wasn't about to let Matt in. Vaguely, she wondered where he'd taken off to.

"Go away."

"Not on a bet. Dorothy says you've been under the weather."

"It's only morning sickness. Surely you've heard of it, Dr. McCandless."

"Sarcasm's good. It shows spirit. Now, are you going to open this door or am I going to have to go downstairs and get the master key from Dorothy?"

Cursing beneath her breath, she flung open the door and nearly groaned as she viewed him standing there, looking like a movie cowboy hero in a shearling jacket, jeans and a black Stetson. He was holding a tray with her tea and toast, a covered bowl and a familiar box of crackers.

"I thought the good guys wore white hats," she muttered.

He arched a brow. "Who says I'm one of the good guys?"

"Anyone who brings me saltines is one of the good guys." She moved aside, letting him in.

He took a slow, judicious, medical perusal from the top of her head down to her bare feet. Her hair was piled precariously atop her head, and her toenails had been painted a brilliant scarlet. That was the good stuff. Unfortunately, the purplish shadows beneath her eyes had deepened since the last time he saw her, marring her delicate skin like bruises. And she was too pale. And beneath the oversize cotton nightshirt, she appeared to have lost about five pounds.

"You look like hell."

She tossed her head, then wished she hadn't as her aching head conspired with her stomach and sent it into a series of flip-flops. "If you'd been so complimentary on New Year's Eve, I wouldn't have danced with you, let alone let you come up to my room, so I'd look a lot better right now."

"You want false flattery, go back to Hollywood. I was merely giving you my medical opinion."

"You're not my doctor," she reminded him. "And instead of handing out opinions, how about giving me a couple of those crackers?"

He put the tray down on the table, opened the box, then the cellophane wrapper and took out a stack of the saltines. As she nibbled tentatively, he poured the tea. "Sugar?"

"Two. Make it three," she decided on an afterthought.

"It's a wonder you have any teeth left in your head," he murmured as he tore open a third package.

"It helps settle my stomach." She took the cup from him, holding it with both hands like a child. "Most of the time, anyway."

He watched her sip the oversweetened brew, her expression suggesting it was some mythical nectar from the gods instead of ordinary Constant Comment. The faint bit of color remaining in her face faded, leaving her complexion the color of ashes. She shoved the cup into his hand and took off running.

"You know, this isn't necessary," he said, standing in the doorway of the bathroom watching her retch. Since she'd already thrown up, she was down to painful dry heaves.

"Could you please give me some privacy?" Her head was spinning like an out-of-control carousel. She leaned against the tile wall and closed her eyes.

She sure didn't look like any sex goddess right now. She looked small and fragile. "I'm a doctor," he reminded her as he ran some cool water into the sink. Squatting beside her, he ran a wet washcloth over her face. "I've seen a lot worse." And because he wanted to see her smile again, he told her about the eggnog twins.

It worked. "Thank you," she said in a soft little voice tinged with that unexpected shyness he'd caught glimpses of before.

"For what?"

"For making me laugh." She sighed and dragged her hand through her hair, causing it to tumble over her shoulders. "I can't remember the last time I laughed."

Matt could. It was on New Year's Day, sometime before the sun had come up, bringing with it that strained realization of what they'd done. He'd gotten the idea to try out new ways to drink the last of the then warm champagne, and when he'd tipped the bottle, dribbled it into her navel and began lapping it up, she giggled and wiggled beneath his mouth, and pretty soon they were tangling the sheets again, laughing and kissing and . . .

And making a child. As he thought back on that night, Matt experienced a sudden need for physical and emotional space. He stood up and carefully hung the cloth on the plastic ring beside the mirror. The sight of her sitting on the floor, her arms wrapped around her bent knees, brought a flood of renewed guilt and responsibility. Along with a faint stir of some emotion he couldn't quite recognize.

Uncomfortable with the intimacy of the situation, he said, ''I'll wait for you in the living room.''

His tone was so distant he could have been talking to her from Kansas. Shiloh felt the sting of tears at the back of her lids and resolutely blinked them away.

''Thank you,'' she said again. But she said it to his back, and he didn't respond.

As she brushed her teeth again and changed into a pair of leggings and a scarlet sweater she hoped would add some much-needed color to her cheeks,

Shiloh reminded herself that she was not some weak-kneed, marshmallow-spirited Camille. She was Shiloh Belle Beauregard, daughter of General Stonewall Jackson Beauregard and descendant of General Pierre Gustave Toutant Beauregard, victor of the first battle of Bull Run. The blood of generations of warriors ran in her blood. She could handle this pregnancy. And she could handle Dr. Matt McCandless.

Returning to the living room of the suite, she found that Matt had taken off his jacket and was sitting on the couch that held too many memories.

Without saying another word to him, she drank the tea, ate the unbuttered toast and even polished off the cinnamon-spiced oatmeal he'd added to her Spartan breakfast.

"I don't normally eat breakfast," she said, looking with some measure of surprise at the empty bowl.

"That's why you've been getting sick. You should keep some crackers by the bed and eat them before you get up. Do you have asthma?"

She blinked at the seemingly swift change of subject. "No."

"Good." He pulled a pad out of a pocket of his denim shirt and began scribbling out a prescription. "These should help, too." He put the piece of paper on the coffee table in front of her, along with some sample blister packs of medication.

She frowned at the small blue capsules. "I don't want to take any medication."

"That's commendable. But you're not helping the baby when you can't keep anything down. They won't hurt you."

"You don't know that. For certain."

"Nothing's for certain, but—"

"I'll try the cracker therapy." She smiled politely. "I'm sure that will do the trick."

He shook his head, eyeing her with a mixture of frustration and admiration. "You really are one stubborn lady."

"I prefer to think of it as tenacious."

"You argue a lot, too."

"That's funny, most people consider me charming. And agreeable."

"Is that so?" He gave her another long look, then shrugged. "Maybe it's the hormone swings."

"Or maybe it's because I don't respond well to men trying to boss me around," she countered sweetly. Although she had to admit that looking at him in those snug Wrangler jeans and denim shirt made her want to have her way with him—to drag him into the bedroom, or onto the floor for that matter—he really wasn't her type. In fact, she informed him haughtily, he'd even begun to remind her of the General.

He laughed at that. A rich, deep sound she liked more than she could comfortably admit. He sat down beside her on the couch again.

"I just got back from a medical convention in Sydney, Australia," he said.

"Oh?" So that's where he'd been. Although she'd throw herself off the top of nearby Mt. Elbert before admitting it, Shiloh had been miffed by his disappearing act.

"People I hadn't seen since last year kept asking me what was new in my life." A ghost of a smile twitched at the corner of his lips. "There were a couple of times I was tempted to tell them that I'd met an angel and was about to become a father."

The compliment, spoken so casually, should not have made her feel so good. But, heaven help her, it did. "I'm hardly an angel."

"I'm finding that out for myself," he agreed easily. "But I gotta tell you, sweetheart, you sure looked like one that night."

Sweetheart. Even as the lifelong romantic's heart quickened at the drawled endearment, the General's daughter sternly reminded herself that it was merely a word to Matt. She'd heard him address at least three women—one who had to be in her eighties—the same way the night of the party.

"My parents were at the convention, as well," he continued conversationally.

"I thought your father was retired."

"He is. But he was there to receive a humanitarian award."

"Oh, that's nice."

"Mom thought so. Pop was underwhelmed, but he's never set much store in things like awards and trophies. He always said doctoring was a people business and they should save the plaques for insurance salesmen and car dealers."

This time her smile was as warm as he remembered it. "He sounds sweet."

Matt considered that for a moment. "I don't know about sweet. But he's a pretty good guy." He took a breath and decided the time had come to drop his own little bombshell. "He's also pretty keen on becoming a grandfather."

"You told him about me? About us?"

"I didn't have much choice, since you've decided to stay in Paradise," he pointed out. "Besides, I would have told them anyway."

"Terrific." She leaned her head against the back of the couch and closed her eyes. "I can't wait to see them again." She could just imagine how they must feel, discovering that the mother of their new grandchild had once played the role of a vixen possessed by the devil.

"I'm glad to hear that," Matt said, conveniently overlooking her sarcasm. "Because you're invited to Sunday dinner tomorrow afternoon."

Her eyes popped open. "Tell me you're kidding."

"Believe me, Shiloh, I wish I were." He shook his head. "I'm not that eager to undergo my grandmother's third degree, either."

"Grandmother?" Her voice rose several octaves. "Your grandmother knows, too?"

"She didn't when our plane landed this morning. But I'd bet that by now she's been filled in on the situation."

Shiloh tried to remember if they had earthquakes in Colorado. She could really use one right now to swallow her up. Anything to avoid being put on display at a McCandless family dinner.

It was ironic, she thought, after Matt had left. After six years of playing the scarlet woman in movies, tomorrow she'd be playing the part for real.

The thought made Shiloh want to throw up again.

She needn't have worried. Matt's mother and father were as warm and friendly as they'd been when she'd first met them on New Year's Eve. Within minutes of her arrival, Shiloh found herself alone in the kitchen with Catherine McCandless.

They exchanged small talk for a brief time, then Catherine got down to brass tacks. "How are you feeling?" she asked as she began peeling potatoes.

"I'm fine. Really," Shiloh insisted when Matt's mother gave her a disbelieving, sideways glance.

"Then you're lucky. I was sick as a dog with Matt."

"I've been a little nauseated."

Catherine laughed at that. A bright, breezy sound that reminded Shiloh of silver bells. Although her memories of her mother were admittedly faint, she couldn't recall ever hearing Margaret Beauregard laugh. "More than a little, I suspect, if you're carrying a McCandless. My husband's mother, Augusta, insists she had morning sickness the entire nine months. She even threw up on the delivery table."

"You've no idea how that depresses me," Shiloh said glumly.

"I felt the same way when Augusta told the story to me." Catherine handed her a plastic bag of carrots and a peeler with a casualness that made Shiloh feel even more welcome. "But they have wonderful drugs now to take care of that."

"Matt gave me some samples. But I don't want to take anything."

Instead of arguing, Catherine merely nodded. "It's your child. You need to do what you feel is best. But remind me to give you some ginger tea before you leave. It's wonderful for morning sickness."

She smiled at Shiloh's obvious surprise. "I have tremendous faith in the McCandless men and their miracle pharmaceuticals. But I've also studied alternative herbal medicine, and believe me, dear, our ancestors were no slouches when it came to healing."

"Matt wasn't real thrilled when I turned down his prescription," Shiloh admitted.

"I'm not surprised. If you don't mind a personal observation, everyone is immensely relieved that you've come back to town. My son has always been remarkably even tempered, but ever since you left town on New Year's Day, he's been decidedly out of sorts."

Shiloh smiled. "Thank you for sharing that."

Catherine smiled back. "You're welcome, dear."

As they worked together in the cozy, sunlit kitchen, Shiloh, who'd never experienced anything as ordinary as sharing cooking duties with her mother, found the experience more than a little enjoyable.

Matt's grandmother arrived precisely as the golden roast chicken was being placed on the table. "You're a stunningly beautiful woman, Shiloh

Beauregard," she announced to one and all. "I can see why Matt finally took the tumble."

"Tumble?" Shiloh asked.

"Grandmother," Matt said at exactly the same time.

Augusta McCandless ignored his veiled warning. "There have been more women than you could shake a stick at trying to get my grandson to the altar. But he's managed to dodge them all. Guess he was saving himself for you."

An embarrassed little silence settled over the table. Catherine and Michael exchanged a brief look, Matt pretended a sudden interest in buttering his Parkerhouse roll, and Shiloh began tracing the floral design on the lace tablecloth with a fingernail.

"So," Michael finally said, with a little too much enthusiasm, "that's an interesting name you have, Shiloh. It's like the battle, right?"

She could have kissed the man for changing the subject. "That's right. My father is a Civil War buff. I've got a twin sister named Savannah."

"Such pretty names," Catherine said smoothly. "And original. Like their owners." Once again the warm reassurance in her eyes settled Shiloh's nerves. And her stomach.

"I've seen all your movies," Augusta announced.

"You have?" all the people at the table responded in unison.

Augusta nodded her dark head. "I get one hundred seventy-five stations with my satellite dish. You'd be amazed at how many of them you show up on," she told Shiloh. "You're a pretty good actress. And you sure can scream the house down."

"She's a pretty good swooner, too," Matt said. Shiloh knew she was in deep, deep trouble when the simple words of praise caused a rush of pleasure.

"That was the best part of *Night Bites*," the elderly woman agreed. "But my favorite movie was *Gentlewoman from Another Land*. Where you played the seal woman."

"You played a seal?" Matt looked at her with renewed interest.

"A *silkie*," Shiloh elaborated. "From Celtic myth. They supposedly become partly human."

"Of course, they're so gorgeous and mysterious, the men want to keep them," Augusta continued the explanation, "so the husbands hide their skins so they can't return to the sea. The woman in the movie discovered hers after she'd given birth to twins." She turned to Shiloh. "You did a bang-up job showing her dilemma of whether to return to her family in the sea, or to stay with her human one. Had me bawling like a baby."

"Thank you." Shiloh beamed at the praise for the one performance she'd hoped would catapult her into the role of a serious actress. Unfortunately, the distribution had been so limited that the film had gone unnoticed by the Hollywood elite.

The ice broken, the conversation flowed easily, allowing Shiloh to learn a lot about Matt. She discovered he'd been a junior rodeo bareback riding champion, which, she supposed, was part of the reason she kept thinking of him as a cowboy. She also learned he was valedictorian of his high school and made the dean's list every semester in college, while playing shortstop for the UCLA Bruins baseball team. His favorite dinner was steak, his favorite dessert apple pie, and he preferred beer to champagne.

"Although," he said, slanting Shiloh a wicked, sideways grin, "under the right circumstances, champagne can taste pretty good, too."

Remembering him licking the wine off her body made her turn scarlet, and once again Shiloh was more than a little relieved when his mother changed the subject.

"Shiloh," Catherine said thoughtfully, "I just had an idea I'd like to run by you. But I want you to feel free to turn me down."

"All right." Shiloh worried where this might be leading.

"I'm chairman of the local preservation society. We've been struggling to raise money to save the old Orpheum Theater, but it's difficult to find something that will draw people from outside Paradise. What would you say to us putting on a Shiloh Beauregard film festival? A two-day event, perhaps—"

"It's going to take more than two days, if you're going to show all her movies," Augusta broke in.

"Three days, then," Catherine said, switching gears easily. "And perhaps you could give a short dinner talk about life in the movies? I realize you'll need to think this over, but—"

"I think it's a wonderful idea." Shiloh grinned. *Eat your heart out, Woody Allen.* "And I'd love to do it. Especially if it will help save a theater."

"Of course she will," Augusta said. "The girl's got community spirit. Just like all the McCandless women." She gave Shiloh a stern look that included Matt, who was sitting beside her. "I expect a beautiful, brilliant baby from you two."

Matt didn't exactly smile. But his lips twitched at the corners. "Yes, Grandma." He took Shiloh's hand beneath the tablecloth and squeezed.

Shiloh didn't speak on the way to the hotel. She just kept reliving the surprisingly enjoyable dinner in her mind. When she'd first learned she was pregnant, she'd thought of the baby as hers alone. Then she'd broadened her view to include Matt. But now she realized how many lives were being touched by her pregnancy. The baby she was carrying would be a McCandless. It would come into this world with warmhearted grandparents and a wonderful, forthright great-grandmother waiting to love it.

But it would also have Beauregard blood running in its veins. Which meant that it was time to call the General and break the news that he was going to be a grandpa.

Chapter Seven

Shiloh was relieved when she called the military academy and was told that the General had taken the senior cadet corps on a training exercise off the coast of Florida. Three weeks' breathing room wasn't much, but she'd take anything she could get.

Having grown up in the military, Shiloh was accustomed to fitting into new places, and she soon began to feel as if she'd lived in Paradise all her life. After she'd been working at the Silver Nugget for a month, she mentioned, during a conversation with the head guitarist for the band—Fletch's brother, Kevin—that she'd written some country music. Immediately interested, he'd asked to see her work, and before she knew it, she was moonlighting as a songwriter for the Outlaws.

Rather than being standoffish, the people of Paradise welcomed her with open arms—a fact she attributed to Matt's popularity—although she'd overheard more than one patron of the Silver Nugget grumble that Matt ought to just "marry the girl and make an honest woman of her."

Not that Matt wasn't proving supportive. He dropped by the hotel every evening to check on her, and on those nights when she wasn't working, he'd buy her dinner in the hotel restaurant. He made the appointment for her with Dr. Susan Lucas, then surprised her by not only insisting on driving her to Aspen, but accompanying her into the doctor's office to discuss her pregnancy. On the day of the ultrasound exam, Matt was also at her side.

"Looks as if it's a boy," the doctor said.

Matt leaned forward. Experienced with ultrasound images, he recognized the vital parts immediately. "It sure is."

"A boy?" Shiloh squinted, trying to make out what the other two were seeing.

"Right here." Matt was holding her hand. He used his free one to point out the baby. "See?"

"Oh!" Shiloh murmured, "Is that a—"

"It sure is," Susan agreed. "And quite a nice one, too."

Matt grinned wickedly. "Of course it is. We McCandless men have always been known for our—"

"Oh, my," Susan interrupted him. "Look at this."

Matt whistled. Shiloh felt his fingers tighten around hers. "What?" she asked, suddenly nervous. What if something was wrong with her baby?

"We've got a little girl."

"Instead of a boy? But I thought—"

"Not instead," Matt said.

Shiloh's mouth went dry as comprehension sunk in. "Twins?"

"Got it on the first try." Matt smiled down at Shiloh, his eyes filled with that same tender warmth she remembered from their night together. "We're having a son *and* a daughter, Shiloh."

Tears sprang to Shiloh's eyes. This was too, too much.

Later, as they sat in Matt's truck in the medical building parking lot, he turned toward her, his arm resting along the back of the bench seat, his fingers playing with the ends of her hair.

"Feeling better?"

Embarrassed at having wept at the news, Shiloh looked straight ahead out the windshield and nodded stiffly.

"You know, it's not the end of the world," he tried again. "Granted, twins are going to be double trouble, but people manage. And so will we."

"It's not that," she murmured, still not looking at him.

He put a long finger beneath her chin and turned her head to his. "Then what's wrong?" Other than the fact that she was now about to be an unwed mother of two, Matt thought, mentally blasting himself for being so insensitive.

"Nothing. No, really," she insisted at his disbelieving look. "It's just that all my life, whenever I thought about having children, I envisioned a little boy and a little girl. And now it's coming true. Just as I dreamed." Of course, in the dream, there'd always been a husband.

Matt watched the shadow drift across those expressive eyes, read the thought that was emblazoned on that lovely face and felt lower than a snake in a rut.

"So why don't you just marry the girl?" everyone had been asking.

Although he knew that he had lots of legitimate answers to that question, right now, he couldn't think of a single one.

When she'd first discovered she was pregnant, seven months had seemed very far off, but Shiloh was amazed at how fast the time flew. Of course, she was keeping busy, working with Catherine's preservation society during the day and serving drinks at the Silver Nugget at night. She was also attending childbirth classes with Matt, who, running true to form, had insisted on being her coach, never mind the fact that Susan Lucas predicted he'd pass out in the delivery room.

"I'm a doctor," he reminded her, obviously affronted. "I've delivered babies."

"You've never been a father," she returned. "I'm betting you'll hit the floor before we get the first baby into Shiloh's arms."

He harrumphed at that, much to the amusement of both women.

Shiloh was amazed and more than a little relieved when her father didn't blow up at the news of her pregnancy.

"It's not that weak-kneed professor, is it?"

"No, Daddy. Matt is a doctor. In Paradise, Colorado. He's very well thought of by everyone in town."

The General muttered something she couldn't quite hear. "So, is he taking good care of you?"

"Very good care." Just when she thought she was off the hook, he asked, "Do you love this man, Shiloh?"

He was the first person to ask her that question. "I don't know. Sometimes I think I do. But then I'm afraid that I only want to love him, and—"

"Well," he interjected, in that deep, gruff voice that had terrified her as a child, "I raised both you and your sister to stand on your own two feet. I'm sure you'll do just fine."

With that he professed a need to get back to the parade ground, where the seniors were rehearsing their graduation drill formation.

Promising to keep him apprised of her condition, Shiloh hung up, feeling both relieved and a little let down. Although he'd never been a demonstrative person, and she understood that he'd been uncomfortable with her revealing her feelings, she'd expected him to show his concern—and his paternal love—by yelling. When he hadn't, she was forced to wonder if perhaps he really didn't love her as much as she'd always hoped.

Sighing, she went back to work on a song she'd been writing that morning. As she wrote the lyrics, she poured out all the feelings she'd been keeping bottled up inside her. By the time she was finished the song—the ballad about a woman's unrequited love—she was weeping again.

Trust Matt to choose that moment to show up for his daily visit.

"It's hormones," she assured him when he expressed concern over the tears.

"Are you sure?" The way she was scrubbing at the moisture on her cheeks with the backs of her hands reminded Matt of an unhappy child. He wanted to take her in his arms, hold her close and tell her everything would be okay.

"Positive." It was definitely hormones, she told herself. That was all she would allow it to be.

* * *

Watching Catherine putting together the film festival, Shiloh realized where Matt had come by his proclivity for in-depth planning. Not only was the woman a whirlwind, she was the most organized individual Shiloh had ever met. And having grown up under the roof of a man who'd subjected his daughters to weekly room inspection, that was really saying something.

Still, Shiloh was surprised when the festival not only proved a local success, but drew fans from all over the country, as well. Including a famous producer-director who'd come down from his ranch in Utah.

"I've been working on a project I think would be perfect for you," he said as he handed her his card.

"You're working on a story about a two-ton bimbo?" she asked with the smile that had lit up the Orpheum's screen for the past three days.

"Actually, it's about a widowed young woman struggling to keep her family together when they lose their farm during the thirties dust bowl."

He was talking about a real role! Where she wouldn't wear a ton of makeup, where she'd wear ugly clothes and look drawn and serious. It could, Shiloh thought, do for her career what *The Burning Bed* had done for Farrah Fawcett.

"As I said, we're still in the development stages," he said. "Why don't you give me a call when you're ready to get back to work?"

Promising him she'd do that, Shiloh was floating on air when another festival attendee suddenly appeared in front of her.

"Dad?" She stared at him. "When did you get here?"

"I showed up in time for the seal movie." Furrows gathered in his forehead as he took in her expanding body, but blessedly, he didn't bring up her now-obvious pregnancy in this public setting. "You were very good." His tone revealed his surprise.

"She was better than good." Matt's deep voice slipped beneath her skin, warming her blood. "She was great." He put his left arm around what remained of her waist and held out his right. "Good evening, sir. You must be General Beauregard."

The General ignored the hand thrust his way. Beneath an ultrashort military haircut, his eyes were as hard as agates and his lantern jaw jutted out. "And you must be the son of a bitch who got my little girl in the family way."

Matt didn't flinch. He met the General's gaze with a level gaze of his own. "Yes, sir, I am."

"We need to talk," the General said. It was an order, couched in stone.

"Yes, sir." Matt's tone remained as mild as his expression.

"Daddy, please—"

"It'll be okay, sweetheart." Even as he reassured her, Matt worried about the sudden pallor he hadn't seen since her first trimester.

He turned to the General. "If you don't mind waiting, sir, I'd like to ask my parents to drive Shiloh to the hotel."

The General's response was a harrumph that Matt took as consent.

"Please, Daddy," Shiloh begged when they were alone again, "don't do anything to embarrass me."

"Seems you've already done that for yourself," he grumbled. "I don't understand you, Shiloh. I might have expected this from Savannah, but you've always been my good girl."

Taking affront at that—for both her own and Savannah's sakes—she lifted her chin. "I made a mistake, granted. But I'm accepting responsibility for my actions." She pressed her hands against her belly in an unconscious gesture of maternal protection. "And to tell you the truth, now that I am pregnant, I can't regret it. Because I'm too happy about becoming a mother."

"An unwed mother. Dammit, Shiloh—"

"Shiloh, dear," a blessedly familiar voice interrupted smoothly, "you haven't introduced me to your father." Catherine held out a well-manicured hand. "You must be General Beauregard. I'm Catherine McCandless, Matthew's mother. Shiloh has told us all so much about you, it's a pleasure to finally meet you in person."

Shiloh watched in amazement as her father's rigid, at-attention posture eased right in front of her eyes. "It's a pleasure to meet you, Mrs. McCandless." Stunning Shiloh further, he enclosed her slender hand in both of his. "I can see the resemblance. Your son has your eyes. But they're a lot prettier on you."

While Shiloh continued to stare openmouthed, Catherine laughed in a musical way designed to charm. "I've heard about you Southern gentlemen," she scolded lightly. "I'm so relieved to discover that your charm is not exaggerated."

While the General actually blushed, Catherine went in for the kill. "We're having a little brunch tomorrow morning. Please tell me that you'll come. I'd love to have you meet the rest of the family. Since we're going to be related, in a way, by our precious grandchildren."

"I can't think of anything I'd rather do than have brunch with you, Mrs. McCandless. And, of course, your husband," he added on an afterthought.

"I'm so pleased. We're getting together around eleven. Shiloh can show you the way." She turned toward Matt, who'd just returned. "Darling, the General has agreed to come to brunch tomorrow. Isn't that wonderful?"

Although he'd rather have been told that they were going to be visited by plague and pestilence, Matt forced a smile. "Sounds great."

It was at that moment that Shiloh admitted what her heart had been trying to tell her for weeks. She loved Matt McCandless. Madly, truly, deeply.

"How did you do that?" Shiloh asked as she watched her father leave the auditorium with Matt. "I've never seen my father behave so—I don't know—like a real person."

Catherine laughed. "You're not the only actress in the family. I don't like to boast, but I was lead scary tree in my third-grade production of Hansel and Gretel."

Laughing, Shiloh almost stopped worrying about what was happening between her father and the man she loved.

It was much, much later when Matt showed up at the hotel. Worried about her working too hard, Dorothy had given her the nights of the festival off, which left Shiloh with nothing to do but pace the floor of the suite, waiting for his arrival.

Recognizing his knock after all these weeks, she flung open the door. "Oh, my God." She stared in disbelief as she reached up and touched the darkening circle around his beautiful gray eye. "I can't believe my father hit you!"

"He's got one hell of a right hook for an older guy," Matt said, rubbing his chin where another bruise was blossoming. "His left isn't bad, either."

"I'm so sorry." Even as she was aghast at her father's overly macho behavior, another, more horrible thought occurred to her. "You didn't... I mean, I'd understand, but... you wouldn't..."

"Slug him back?" Matt shook his head. "Geez, you should know me better than that by now. In the first place, he's at least thirty years older than me, which I'm not sure in his case really means anything. Your father is in amazing shape."

"He's always prided himself on being able to do more one-armed push-ups than his men."

"That figures. But even so, age should count for something. And besides, I had to agree with his reasoning."

"You think he was right to hit you?"

"Of course."

"I can't believe this!" With the exception of the strong sense of responsibility both men shared, Matt was nothing like her father. He was sweet, good-natured and demonstrative. He was not the kind of man to get into a fistfight.

"If some jerk got our daughter pregnant, I'd want to punch his lights out, too," Matt explained.

"I can see wanting to," Shiloh admitted. "But you'd never do it." When Matt didn't answer, she said, "You wouldn't."

He shrugged, trying not to wince as he felt a sharp pain in his rib. Fortunately, the General had been content with three shots. Unfortunately, they'd all hit right on the mark. "Let's hope we never have to put it to the test." He sank down onto the couch. "I don't suppose you have any ice?"

"I'll get it right away." She hurried over to the apartment-size refrigerator, took out the tray and dumped the cubes into a towel.

"Thanks, sweetheart." He laid his head back and pressed the towel against his eye.

"What did he say to you?" Shiloh asked tentatively.

"Mostly what you'd expect a man in his position to say. That if I didn't marry you he'd cut out my heart and feed it to a pack of hungry coyotes."

"My father threatened to cut your heart out?"

He opened his good eye. It was filled with humor. "He didn't say that in so many words. But I got the drift."

"What did you say?" she asked, unable to stand the suspense any longer.

"The typical things. That I was truly sorry, that I respected you more than any woman I'd ever met, that I had every intention of living up to my responsibilities, that I was a skunk, a scoundrel, a—"

"No. What did you say about marriage?"

Silence immediately settled over them. A pregnant silence, Shiloh thought. He sighed, took the towel from his eye, put it on the coffee table and turned toward her. "Shiloh, you have to understand my position. I'm the fourth generation of McCandlesses to go into medicine in Paradise."

"So?"

"So, my roots go deep in the Rockies."

"I never thought you'd turn out to be a snob." She stood up and walked over to the window. Although it was now officially spring, it had begun to snow. Illuminated in the yellow glow of the old-fashioned streetlights, the fat white flakes looked like drifting feathers.

"A snob?" He stood up and crossed the room to stand behind her. "Where did that come from?"

"Well, I realize that I've never really stayed in one place very long, but it wasn't my fault. I mean my father was in the military, and—"

"Shiloh." He turned her around. "That wasn't what I meant. What I was trying, apparently poorly, to say is that I have lifelong ties to Paradise. Responsibilities. I couldn't leave, even if I wanted to. Which," he admitted, deciding it was time to be absolutely honest, "I don't."

Shiloh didn't know which was hurting more. Her pride or her heart. "Did you hear me asking you to?" she asked, afraid he'd think she was begging but unable to keep her feelings to herself any longer. "I understand you belong here, Matt."

"The same way you belong in Hollywood," he reminded her gently.

"That's not necessarily true. I've been happier here than I've ever been in my life. I can't imagine going back to that rat race."

"Of course you will," he insisted. The eye that wasn't rapidly swelling shut was shadowed with sadness. "Once the novelty of small-town life wears off, you'll be dying to get back into the fast lane."

"I always hated the fast lane. And I was getting tired of acting, anyway. Really," she insisted when he arched a brow. "I'm not getting any younger, and I know I'm never going to be Meg Ryan or Sandra Bullock—"

"Personally, I think you're better-looking than both of them put together."

"Thank you. But that's not even half the battle in Hollywood. Everyone's good-looking. Talent counts."

"And I suppose this is where you tell me that the producer who was here gave you his card because he thinks you're the most untalented actress he's ever seen on the silver screen?"

"Actually, he did mention a part," she admitted, remembering how only a few hours ago she'd been so excited by that small but oh-so-important recognition.

"See?" He brushed her hair from her face with a touch both tender and full of regret. "This time in Paradise, as good as it seems, is like a part you've been playing, sweetheart. You've got a real life waiting for you outside these mountains."

It had been months since he'd held her like this. Weeks and weeks since he'd kissed her. Despite the seriousness of their conversation, desire stirred. She twined her fingers together around his neck and went up on her toes, until her mouth was a whisper away from his. "What if I want to make a life here? In Paradise? With you?"

Didn't she realize what she was doing? Of course she did, Matt knew. She was trying to seduce him. And, dammit, it was working. And why not, since he'd been having hot, sexy dreams about her for weeks.

"Shiloh, this isn't a good idea." His hands slipped down, holding her hips, pressing her closer even as he struggled for emotional distance.

"Kiss me and tell me that." She brushed her lips against his. "Let me kiss you, then tell me that you haven't been going as crazy as me."

When she traced a ring of fire around his grimly set lips with the tip of her tongue, Matt remembered, all too vividly, how crazy he'd felt that night. And why. "You know I can't."

Greed and hunger twisted together in his gut. And lower. His hand tangled in her hair, pulling her head back to allow him to feast. She opened for him, instantly, eagerly. Matt felt her relieved breath leave her body on a ragged sigh. Her lips were parted and moist and receptive as he thrust his tongue between them, deep into her mouth. A moan, born of harsh need, was wrenched from deep in her throat. Matt thought it was the sexiest sound he'd ever heard.

He was about to rip her top from her when he felt something inside her suddenly move.

"My God," he breathed, "is that—"

"One of the babies," she confirmed. Her breathing was still fast and labored, but her calm smile belonged on the Mona Lisa. "I'll bet, from the way you were kissing me, that it's the girl."

He stood rigid as a stone, waiting. Seconds later, he felt the movement against his groin. Sexual hunger diminished, replaced by a primal feeling even stronger. And, he feared, more dangerous.

"I know it's a cliché, but that's truly amazing." He'd felt innumerable babies kick before. But none of those babies had been his. And that, Matt discovered, made all the difference. "Would you do me a favor?"

"Anything," Shiloh said instantly. Truthfully.

"Would you take your top off?"

She only hesitated a moment, then, seeing the reassurance in his eyes, she lifted the cotton top over her head.

Her maternity bra was not what he'd been expecting. "Black satin?"

She blushed like a schoolgirl. "It's from my sister, Savannah."

"Remind me to thank her." As his eyes moved over her full breasts with all the impact of a caress, Shiloh began to tremble.

"I will," she whispered. From the way he was looking at her, like a starving man suddenly presented with his own private smorgasbord, she thought he was finally going to make love to her. But instead, he surprised her by dropping to his knees in front of her and running his hands over her taut stomach.

"It's so hard," he murmured, as his palms skimmed over the pale, blue-veined flesh. He knew that at this stage in her pregnancy, her uterus would have expanded to her navel, yet somehow, because it was Shiloh, it all seemed new.

"I'm getting stretch marks," she complained.

He trailed a fingertip over a faint white mark, then pressed his lips against the flesh his touch had already warmed. "Badges of courage," he corrected, before proceeding to kiss every mark, until her flesh was as hot as a summer sun and her legs were trembling. As if stimulated by her tumultuous emotions, both babies began to kick.

"Amazing," he repeated. He spread his hands against her hard belly, enthralled by the movement beneath his fingertips. Looking down, Shiloh found the contrast between his dark hand and her pale skin incredibly sensual.

When the tumbling finally stopped, Matt looked at her. "I've tried not to complicate things. But I want you, Shiloh. I have from the beginning."

"I want you, too." It was only a whisper. But it vibrated with pent-up emotions. "So much it hurts."

"I can identify with that." Sighing, he kissed her stomach one last time, then stood up. "The last time we rushed into bed. This time I want to do things right."

"We've already waited months," she pointed out.

He laughed at that, a rough, humorless laugh. "You don't have to remind me. But as much time as we've spent together, going to the doctor, to the childbirth classes, dinners at my parents, movies with Gram, we haven't had a real date."

"I don't mind."

"Ah, but I do." He trailed his hand down her face. "I've already seduced you, Shiloh. Now I want a chance to woo you."

She felt the tears welling up in her eyes again. "It's hormones," she insisted, as he tenderly wiped them away. "Really."

But they both knew it was a great deal more. Just as they knew they were going to have to deal with these feelings they'd both been trying to ignore. But not tonight.

Although his intentions were absolutely honorable, as he kissed her again, slower, deeper, Matt knew that if he didn't get out of here now, he'd be sunk. Again.

"We've got brunch with your father and my parents tomorrow morning," he reminded her. "If we survive that, I'll pick you up at six tomorrow night," he said, brushing his lips lightly against hers. "And make sure you wear that bra."

Unwilling to release her quite yet, he plucked at her lips with his. "I don't suppose your sister sent panties to go with it?"

"Two pairs." He could feel her smile beneath his mouth. "Bikinis."

"I believe," he murmured happily, "that your sister and I are going to become very good friends."

He gave her one final quick, hard kiss that took her breath away. Then he left the suite. As she sank down onto the couch, Shiloh took in the ice that had melted all over the coffee table and laughed.

Chapter Eight

Thanks to Catherine running interference, the family brunch went amazingly well. Shiloh was not surprised when the General and Augusta hit it off right away. They were both no-nonsense, forthright individuals. The two fathers talked golf, and she was more than a little relieved that although her father obviously still wished she was married, he seemed to have come to the conclusion that Matt was at least more worthy of his daughter than the other men she'd dated.

Later that afternoon, as ridiculous as it felt to primp for a date at this stage in her life, Shiloh spent a long time getting ready for Matt. She even tried to take a nap so she wouldn't conk out by nine o'clock, but she was too giddy and excited to sleep.

She took a long soak in a bubble bath, refilling the water twice. Then, after toweling herself off, she smoothed lotion over her body. She followed up by dusting herself with powder. As the soft bristles of the brush flicked over her fragrant flesh, she imagined they were Matt's hands, touching her breasts, stroking her belly, skimming across her shoulders.

Her mind was filled with him as she stood in front of the full-length mirror and made a ruthless appraisal of exactly how much her body had changed since the last time he'd seen her without clothes. Would he find her girth a turnoff?

No. Shiloh smiled. Not Matt. Last night she'd had no doubt that he wanted her just the way she was. But wanting was easy. Tonight she hoped he'd begin to realize that he loved her, as well.

She'd put on the black bra and panties and her hair was up in big blue Velcro rollers when there was a knock at the door. She cast a quick glance at the clock. It was only five-thirty!

"Go away," she called out. "I'm not ready."

"It's Kevin, Shiloh. I just wanted to tell you the good news."

Sighing, she put down the mascara wand, slipped into the terry robe and padded barefoot to the door. "What is it? And please, make it fast because I'm trying to get ready to go out."

"With Matt." The leader of the Outlaws grinned at her. "He's taking you out on a real date."

"You know?"

"Everyone knows. We all think it's cool. Dorothy's even started a pool, so we can bet on when you'll get hitched." His smile turned as warm as his brother Fletch's. "I don't suppose you'd consider tomorrow? About five in the afternoon?"

"Sorry, Kevin." She patted his bearded cheek. "You lose." Deciding there was no point in being embarrassed about everyone in town knowing her business, she said, "So, what's up? I'm guessing you didn't drop by to remind me of my date."

"No. I wanted to give you the great news. It's finally happened, Shiloh."

The light in his eyes could only mean one thing. "The Outlaws have been offered a recording contract?"

"Well, not exactly. But close. We've finally gotten an agent to come out here from Nashville to watch our act. He's going to be here sometime in the next couple weeks."

"Oh, Kevin." Shiloh threw her arms around his neck and gave him a big kiss.

"If you don't let go of my woman, Brown," Matt growled from behind him, "I'm going to have to throw you through a window."

Kevin released Shiloh as if she'd suddenly turned into a flaming torch. "Hey, Matt," he said, holding up his hands, "it's not how it looks. Shiloh was just congratulating me on—"

"Kevin," Matt said quietly, "if you know what's good for you, you'll go downstairs. Right now."

"Good idea." The guitar player let out a relieved breath. "See you, Shiloh. Have fun tonight, you two."

Shiloh was too furious with Matt to even attempt to defend herself. How dare he catch her looking like this? "You're early."

"I know. I just couldn't wait."

"Tough." She pushed him into the hall and shut the door. "Come back at six."

Matt stared at the closed door in front of him, then he laughed.

Thirty minutes later, Shiloh still wasn't amused by the incident.

"I don't understand," Matt complained, as he drove away from the hotel, "you're all the time telling me that I'm too rigid. I figured you'd appreciate some spontaneity."

"You thought I'd like my date catching me looking like a pregnant bag lady?"

"Actually, I thought you looked kinda cute."

She muttered a curse.

"Really. Those curlers made it look as if you were trying to pick up satellite reception from outer space. I was thinking about seeing if we could get ESPN on the TV."

"It's not funny." She slapped his arm even as her mutinous lips twitched. "I wanted to look nice for you."

"You always look beautiful to me, sweetheart."

As he patted her knee, Shiloh melted. "I've decided to forgive you."

From her haughty tone, she could have been Catherine the Great dismissing an errant footman. Matt loved it. "Thank you," he said with what he hoped was an appropriately humble attitude. "I appreciate your generosity."

This time her smile broke free. "You haven't seen anything yet."

"That idea is precisely what had me showing up early in the first place," Matt informed her.

She relaxed and began to enjoy herself. "Where are we going?" she asked as he headed out of town.

"A little place I know in Aspen."

"Aspen? We're not eating at your house?"

"I told you, this is a date. I wanted to take you somewhere special."

Drinking in his smile, Shiloh certainly felt special. She was also glad she was wearing a dress Savannah had sent her from Paris. Although the flowered silk was definitely overkill for Paradise, she'd wanted to look her best tonight.

"By the way," he said, proving they were on the same wavelength, "I didn't get a chance to mention that I love that dress."

She ran her hand down the silk, where brilliant poppies bloomed on a black background. Cut tunic style, to allow for her expanding stomach, it featured a deep scoop neckline and a short, flirty skirt. It was ridiculously sexy for a pregnant woman. Which is exactly why Savannah bought it, Shiloh knew. It was also exactly why she loved it.

"Savannah bought it in Paris."

"I didn't think it looked like something you could pick up at Masterson's Mercantile." He cast a sideways glance at the soft globes of her breasts, so enticingly framed by that flowered silk, and felt the heat flooding into his groin. "You're just lucky I've promised myself to be a gentleman tonight. Otherwise I'd probably end up dragging you beneath the table before we finished our entrées."

Even though she knew he was joking, the sexual suggestion caused her tummy to flip in a way that had absolutely nothing to do with the twins.

Later, Shiloh would be certain that the dinner—served in a lovely restaurant with a charming country French decor and a dazzling view of the Rockies—was superb. But all she could remember was how his long dark fingers curled around the handle of his fork, or the way his throat moved when he swallowed his wine, or how his voice wrapped around her like a warm velvet cloak on a snowy night.

After dinner, they danced, but only to the slow songs, and even then it was more swaying than dancing. When his lips brushed her temple, she sighed happily. When her fingers stroked the nape of his neck, he felt as if she were branding him with her tender touch.

And then, too soon, they were in the elevator at the Silver Nugget, creaking their way up to the third floor. "There ought to be a plaque," he murmured.

"A plaque?"

"Commemorating the first place we ever kissed."

"Perhaps we can commemorate it in our own way." Her heart was shining in her eyes as she looked at him.

"Funny you should mention that. Since I was thinking the same thing." He drew her gently to him, framed her face in his hands and as his mouth touched hers, Shiloh realized that this was the kiss she'd been waiting for all of her life.

Her breath escaped unevenly as she put her arms around him and held on tight, expecting him to take them rocketing into the mists. But his lips remained gentle, making Shiloh marvel at the tenderness beneath the strength. Growing up on military bases, she'd known many men like her father—autocratic, opinionated, tough as nails. And later she'd known too many of the other kind—weak, aimless, content to go wherever life's currents led them. Men who took what they wanted, then moved on, with no thought to the shattered lives they were leaving behind.

But Matt was like none of those men. He was absolutely unique, the best of both kinds. Which was why she'd fallen in love with him.

"You are so soft," he murmured against her throat. "So sweet." His hands slipped beneath her top and caressed her breasts. "I don't think I'll ever get enough of you."

"There's certainly enough of me to get."

Understanding that she needed to be reassured, he ran his palm over her stomach. "All the more to love."

She tensed at the word she'd been longing to hear.

"Shiloh?" He looked at her, concern etched into every line of his handsome face. "Is something wrong?"

"No." Belatedly understanding he meant it in the physical sense, she tried to keep her disappointment to herself. "I'm out on a date with the sexiest man in Colorado, whose kisses can curl my toes. And whose touch can make me burn. What could be wrong?"

He gave her a long look, not quite trusting her answer. But it was difficult to think with her fragrance surrounding him and memories of the last time they'd been together like this shimmering in his mind.

Deciding he was imagining things, he lowered his head and kissed her again. A deep, dark, passionate kiss that took both their breaths away. When the elevator reached her floor, he surprised her by lifting her into his arms.

"Matt!" She was shocked by his behavior. Shocked and thrilled. "I'm too heavy."

"Would you stop fixating on your weight?" he asked as he strode down the hall, carrying her with an ease that suggested she weighed little more than a pillow of feathers. "I think you're great. Better than great. You're perfect."

He managed to unlock the door without even having to shift her in his arms, then carried her into the bedroom, where he laid her on the bed. This time, when he undressed her, he did it slowly, thoroughly, arousing her with butterfly touches and long, drawn-out kisses that made her skin warm and her heart swell. And when they finally came together, it was as if it was the first time for either of them, ever. And it was wonderful. It was, Shiloh thought, as she lay wrapped in his arms the next morning, heaven.

She spent the next two weeks in a romantic fog. All she could think about was Matt, and if there were times she mixed up a drink order or two, people were understanding.

"All you have to do is look at those two," Dorothy told Catherine, "to smell orange blossoms."

Catherine smiled at the idea. "McCandless women always have August weddings. I've already booked the Aspen Club for the reception. Now all we have to do is wait for my supposedly intelligent son to get a clue."

"Don't worry," Dorothy said, watching the couple seated at a corner table during Shiloh's break. Matt's eyes were on Shiloh's as he kissed each of her fingers, one at a time. "If that's not a man in love, I'll eat Fletch's trooper hat."

It was an unabashedly romantic scene. The two women sighed in unison.

Lost as she was in the depths of Matt's gray eyes, Shiloh didn't hear the band stop playing. Nor was she aware of Kevin coming to their table.

"Shiloh," he said, "I gotta talk to you. Alone."

"Kevin, Kevin," Matt said with a long-suffering sigh. "I thought I'd already warned you about staying away from my woman." He didn't take his gaze from Shiloh's face. Her lovely, lovely face.

"It's important. Please, Shiloh? I just need a minute."

Shiloh heard the honest distress in his tone. She dragged her gaze from Matt's. "I'll be right back, Matt," she promised.

"You'd better be. Or I'll come looking for you. And Kevin will go flying through the nearest window."

Ignoring the threat, she took hold of the guitar player's arm and dragged him into the stockroom. "Okay, what's wrong?"

"He didn't mean that, did he?"

"What?" she asked, impatient to get back to Matt.

"That thing about throwing me out a window. He wouldn't really do that, would he? I mean, it's against the law, and—"

"Of course Matt wouldn't throw you out any window, Kevin." Shiloh's frustrated sigh ruffled her bangs. "He's the sweetest, kindest, most gentle man I've ever met. He'd never hurt a flea."

"He sure sounded like he meant it."

"It's a joke. Honest." She folded her arms over the front of her satin dress, which had acquired more and more camouflage draping as the weeks had gone by. "Now, are you going to tell me what's wrong?"

"It's the Nashville agent."

"He's canceled?"

"No. He's coming here tonight!"

"So?"

"So, Dinah has laryngitis. She can't sing."

"Oh, Kevin." This was truly a blow. "I'm so sorry."

"Do you really mean that?"

"Of course." Her expression of surprise at the question turned to suspicion. "Why?"

"During your film festival, I saw that movie where you played a country singer on the Grand Old Opry who was stalked and killed by a psycho deejay."

"Country Morning Maniac," she said. It was not one of her better roles. But she had gotten to sing. Comprehension hit like a neutron bomb. "Oh, no. Don't even ask—"

"Did you do your own singing in that movie?"

"Of course I did. There wasn't enough in the budget to dub in a real singer, but—"

"Then can't you help us out, Shiloh? Just this once? Our entire careers, all we've worked for since the first day we got together in Jimmy Johnson's garage when we were thirteen is on the line here. This is our one big shot, and you're the only one who can save it for us."

"Dammit, Kevin." She raked a hand through her hair. "Isn't there anyone else you can get?"

"Not on this short notice. Not anyone who knows our songs like you do."

That was because she'd written most of them. She leaned against a wall of beer cartons and closed her eyes, trying to think this all out. It hadn't been easy convincing Matt that she wasn't the glamorous Hollywood sexpot he'd first taken her for. Like so many people, he'd confused her movie roles with reality. It especially hadn't been easy when he had to watch her sashaying around in this satin saloon girl dress every night. And now, just when he'd begun to believe that there actually might be a homebody lurking beneath her former cover-girl exterior, Kevin had to put her in this spot.

"All right," she said with a deep sigh. "I'll do it. But don't blame me if the agent takes off running. In case you didn't notice, I can't carry a tune." She'd worried about that when she'd made *Country Morning Maniac*, but the director had assured her everyone would be so busy watching her in those skintight sequin dresses, no one would notice she couldn't sing.

"You'll be great!" Taking hold of her shoulders, he leaned forward to kiss her. Then, remembering Matt's warning, he dropped his hands. "Thanks, Shiloh. I really owe you."

"You sure do. Big-time." She shook her head, still unable to believe she was agreeing to this. "Just let me explain to Matt and—"

"There's no time."

"What?"

"The agent's already here. I told the guys to start the intro right about now."

As she heard the familiar chords—chords she'd written!—Shiloh was sorely tempted to throw Kevin through a window herself.

"Please, Shiloh?" He was looking at her with big brown eyes that reminded her of a whipped cocker spaniel.

"If I lose Matt because of this, you're going to have to marry me so my babies have a father," she warned. Then, taking another deep breath, she ran out the door and up onto the wooden stage. There was a moment of shocked silence. Then applause from everyone in the saloon. Shiloh had no choice but start belting out the lyrics to "Honky-Tonk Angel."

Matt couldn't believe it! Who the hell did Shiloh think she was, belting out the raucous country song like Patsy Cline? Every time she took a breath, her breasts practically popped out of that ridiculous dress, and although she'd had to give up the high heels for ballet slippers, her wraparound legs still gave a man wicked ideas as she strutted across the stage, her red petticoats swishing. Although Matt was all too aware that tongues were hanging out all over the saloon, he managed to tamp down his knee-jerk jealousy and enjoy the show with the rest of the crowd. After all, he reminded himself, he was the man she was going to go home with.

He didn't know how many songs she sang, but when she perched on the tall stool that had suddenly appeared on the stage, crossed her legs and, bathed in a soft blue light, crooned a bittersweet ballad about a man and a woman trying to make conversation after a one-night stand, he realized how she'd been suffering that morning.

His ego may have been pricked, but her heart had been wounded. And he was the one responsible for that. She was a sweet, warmhearted, incredibly hardworking, independent, generous woman, and although he certainly hadn't meant to, he'd ended up treating her like some woman purchased for a night on Sunset Boulevard.

Marveling that fate had given them a second chance, Matt vowed to make that morning up to her. If it took the rest of their lives.

The thunderous applause, like cannon fire, jerked him from his thoughts. She was sitting there on her stool, the microphone in her hand, looking straight at him. He viewed the naked worry in her eyes and knew he'd been the one responsible for putting it there.

He weaved his way through the tables and jumped onto the stage, took the microphone and handed it to the keyboard player.

"I can explain," she began in a faltering little voice that pulled at a thousand unnamed chords inside him. He liked it better, he realized, when she was arguing with him.

"You don't have to." He pulled her gently off the stool and into his arms. "You were magnificent."

"I was out of tune."

"I didn't notice." He brushed a tendril of hair away from her frowning face. "No one noticed. We were all too caught up in the songs. They're really good."

A smile shone on her face, like a rainbow after a summer storm. "You really think so?"

"You bet. And even more important, the guy in the Western-cut suede suit sitting at the table in the back of the room seemed to think so, too." Not caring that they were bathed in a spotlight, he bent his head and brushed his smiling lips against hers. "There's something I've been meaning to tell you."

"Really?" Her heart suddenly felt so light, Shiloh feared it would float away. "What?"

"Hey, Shiloh," Kevin said, breaking into the conversation. "Guess what!"

Neither Shiloh nor Matt looked at him. "Go away," they said in unison.

"But we got the contract, Shiloh. The guy loved your songs. He loved us."

"Kevin Brown," Dorothy's voice called out from the back of the room, "would you please leave those two lovebirds alone?"

The room burst into laughter. Everyone but Shiloh and Matt, who were in their own little world.

"You were saying?" she asked breathlessly as she twined her fingers around his neck.

"I love you, Shiloh. I think I've always loved you, probably even that first night, but I was too stupid or scared to realize it. So, if you'll have me, after the fool I've made of myself taking this long to propose, I want to marry you."

"I told you," Catherine murmured to her husband, who'd arrived with his mother during Shiloh's second number.

"So you did," he agreed with an answering smile.

"It's high time," Augusta said, nodding her satisfaction.

Shiloh smiled at Matt. "I think I've loved you forever, Matt. Of course I'll marry you."

The wedding was held two weeks later in the Silver Nugget. Savannah had flown in from Monte Carlo to serve as maid of honor, and Shiloh had been amused—and hopeful—at the immediate attraction between her sister and Fletcher Brown.

"It's not serious," Savannah insisted. "My God, it can't be. He's a small-town cop."

"He's also like no one else you've ever met," Shiloh pointed out. Like Matt, Fletch possessed that rare combination of strength and tenderness.

"That's true," Savannah admitted with a rippling sigh as she fussed with Shiloh's diaphanous white veil. "Who would have thought it was contagious?"

"What?"

"Love, dammit."

Shiloh grinned, enjoying the idea of her sister living in Paradise with her. The smile gave way to a grimace as another cramp gripped her abdomen.

"What's wrong?" Savannah asked quickly. Before Shiloh could answer, realization kicked in. "Oh, my God. How long have you been having pains?"

"Since this morning." Exactly eight hours and twenty minutes ago. Shiloh had been keeping track.

"This morning?" The General had arrived at the suite. Soon, he'd walk her down the aisle. Shiloh watched in amazement as this man who'd marched bravely into battles all over the world turned chalk pale. "You're not even due for nearly three weeks."

"Try telling that to the babies," she suggested dryly. "Obviously they're impatient to be born."

"Why aren't you in the hospital?" the General demanded.

"Because it took me months to get Matt to the altar. And I'm not going to risk him changing his mind."

"He won't, if he knows what's good for him."

Since Shiloh understood her father's threat was spoken out of love for her, she didn't argue. "There's one more reason. I want to be married before I become a mother. So please," she implored them both, "don't say anything. I promise, as soon as the ceremony's over, I'll go straight to the hospital."

Father and sister exchanged a frustrated look. "Anyone ever tell you that you're damn stubborn, Shiloh Belle Beauregard?" the General said finally.

Shiloh laughed. "I think I've heard it mentioned before."

Moments later, as Matt stood beside Fletch, watching his bride walking toward him, he couldn't believe his luck. She was the most beautiful woman he'd ever met. Men all over the world fantasized about Shiloh Beauregard. And she was his!

When Savannah whispered something in the minister's ear, he cast a quick, alarmed grin Shiloh's way, then proceeded to whip through the ceremony in record time.

"And do you, Matthew McCandless, take Shiloh Beauregard to be your lawfully wedded wife, to love, honor and cherish for the rest of your lives?"

His smile was as warm as the August sun shining outside the Silver Nugget. "I do."

As he witnessed Shiloh suddenly bite her lip, the minister went into overdrive. "And do you, Shiloh Beauregard, take Matthew McCandless to be your lawfully wedded husband, to love, honor and cherish for the rest of your lives?"

Her heart in her eyes, Shiloh answered, "I do."

And then, as the minister proclaimed them husband and wife, Shiloh doubled over.

"I knew it," Savannah said. "My niece and nephew are going to end up being born in a bar."

In the end, the babies were born in the same hospital where Matt and his parents and grandparents before him were born. The mother remained absolutely calm throughout the births. The father was a basket case.

Matt survived the first birth, just barely, but as he watched his son come into the world, his legs folded beneath him and he landed, facedown, on the delivery room floor.

"I knew it," Dr. Lucas muttered as the nurse knelt and waved the ampoule of ammonium carbonate beneath his nose.

Holding both her babies in her arms, Shiloh watched the man she loved struggling to his feet and laughed with wonder. She was truly the luckiest woman in the world.

Epilogue

It was New Year's Eve in Paradise. Down at the Silver Nugget, the annual party was in full swing, but Matt and Shiloh had chosen to celebrate this special anniversary at home.

"I never believed in destiny," Matt mused as they sipped champagne in front of a crackling fire. He turned toward Shiloh, his expression immeasurably solemn. "Until you." He reached behind the sofa pillow, where he'd stashed the gift earlier in the evening.

Shiloh opened the gray velvet box and gasped at the dazzling pavé diamond heart. "Oh, Matt," she breathed. "It's stunning."

"I wanted you to remember, while you're in Oklahoma, that you've taken my heart with you."

The producer she'd met at the film festival had called. And when she'd been offered the starring role in his movie, Shiloh had hesitated. But Matt had insisted, pointing out it was the opportunity of a lifetime.

"I'll only be gone four weeks," she reminded him.

Four weeks—that would seem a lifetime. Matt reminded himself that after having paid her dues in all those B-movies, she deserved to reap the rewards.

"I know." He rubbed at the worry lines in her forehead with a tender finger. "And your husband and children will be home, waiting for you."

Her husband. And children. Shiloh had never heard sweeter words. She lifted the heart from its bed of white satin and held it out to him. "Would you put it on me, please?"

He fastened the clasp, then sat back, gazing at the sight of her, dressed in the white satin nightgown, with his gift nestled between her breasts.

"I want to make love to you. Here, in front of the fire, with you wearing only that diamond heart."

Reading the desire in his eyes, Shiloh was infused with a heat that had nothing to do with the crackling orange flames. "Right after we check the babies."

He ran his hand down her cheek, thinking he'd never met a more natural mother. "It's a date."

As they stood beside the matching cribs, Shiloh gazed down at these beautiful children she and Matt had made together and felt her heart swell.

"They're like tiny miracles," she whispered.

He brushed a kiss against her temple. "That's because we're a match made in heaven."

She smiled up at him. "Or Paradise."

As they left the nursery, closing the door behind them, the babies turned toward one another. And smiled.

* * * * *

Anne Stuart
A MIDNIGHT CLEAR

Chapter One

It was a cold day at the end of December. Kelly Malone huddled deeper into her canvas jacket, glaring at the control panel of her Aunt Edie's old pickup truck. Obviously the aging Ford had as little notion of just how cold it could get in New Mexico as Kelly had. When she'd accepted Aunt Edie's post-Christmas invitation—in fact, jumped at the offer—she'd foolishly assumed she was going to a semitropical climate. After all, the only time she'd spent in New Mexico was one summer and fall, long ago, and the heat had been high and dry.

It was cold and dry now, with the brilliant azure sky overhead, surrounding her and filling her with fresh awe as she continued her trek along the dirt road toward Samuel Watson's ranch. Aunt Edie had given her strict instructions to take the back way, and the scribbled map that lay beside her on the cracked vinyl seat was blessedly straightforward.

Kelly wasn't in a particularly good mood. She'd run away to New Mexico, there was no other word for it, to escape her family's smothering, post-

Christmas concern and helpful suggestions. She'd wanted to stay holed up in Aunt Edie's old house, helping her out while the old lady recovered from a fractured ankle, cooking and reading and eating and sleeping, at least until she had to return to her job in Boston in the New Year. She hadn't even meant to bring her medical bag, but something at the last minute had made her toss it in with the baggy sweats and faded jeans that constituted her wardrobe. She would have been better off with thermal underwear, she thought grumpily. Besides, it was still technically illegal for her to practice in a state where she wasn't licensed.

Still, a woman in need was a call she couldn't ignore, legalities be damned. Someone out at Samuel Watson's remote ranch was nearing her term, and Kelly was a nurse-midwife with a lot more up-to-date knowledge than the half-senile Dr. Winslow, who'd been practicing in the little town of Seville for more than fifty years. She wouldn't have to do anything, just check on the woman and see if she needed further help.

Aunt Edie had been surprisingly uncommunicative when the call came through, hurrying her out the door before Kelly could ask more than a question or two. She still didn't know if it was Samuel Watson's wife who was expecting a baby. She couldn't imagine a woman fool enough to marry a man like him.

Except that women did have a tendency to be blinded by a man's looks, and if Samuel was anything like the sullen, gorgeous bad boy he'd been at seventeen then he probably had women lining up from three counties, whether he was pleasant or not.

Even Kelly hadn't been immune to his sulky beauty, though she'd done her best to hide it. And mostly succeeded. At seventeen Sam Watson had a chip on his shoulder the size of the Rocky Mountains, and no one, with the possible exception of Edie Malone, could get through to him.

She'd heard all the stories during that summer she'd spent in New Mexico. They'd been just the kind of stories to make a fourteen-year-old swoon with the drama of it all. Samuel Watson's full name was Samuel One-Horse Watson. He was one-quarter Hopi Indian, and his heritage was clear in his silky, jet black hair that he always wore defiantly long, in the high cheekbones and hawklike nose, in the animal grace of him. He was an orphan—his father had died when he was in his early teens, his mother had disappeared years ago. He lived alone on his grandfather's run-down ranch off of Route 14, and all the social workers and teachers and children's aid people couldn't get him to stay longer than a few days at any of the foster homes they found for him.

The only person he liked was Edie. As far as young Kelly could see, Edie might have been the only one who really liked Sam Watson in return. She looked out for him, steered the social workers in the wrong direction when they were on the hunt for him, made up excuses and generally did her best to see that he was left alone, the way he needed to be.

He may have liked Edie, but he had no use for her eastern niece, a gawky, oversized creature desperately aware of her height, her breasts, her glasses and her foreign, eastern ways. And Kelly had no use for a teenage rebel who treated her like she was a major irritant.

Aunt Edie never knew she'd taken that picture from her scrapbook. The one of Sam, shirtless, his long black hair blowing loose as he held one of Aunt Edie's quarter horses, and Kelly in the background, staring at Sam with a hungry look that still pained her. She always told herself she'd taken the picture because she didn't want anyone to see her when she looked so vulnerable. But it was Sam she looked at when she pulled the picture from the hiding place in the back of her journal. Sam she dreamed about until she finally reached the advanced age of eighteen and started to think about other things. Other boys.

She didn't know where that picture was—creased and folded, it was probably back in her old room in Brookline, along with the treasured dolls and the worn-out teddy bears, the unstrung tennis rackets and the half-finished patchwork quilt. All remnants of a childhood long past.

She'd forgotten what he looked like. He probably hadn't aged well, and that surly disposition would have made a dent on that pretty face of his. He probably had half a dozen kids by now. Maybe he had even mellowed.

Not that it was any concern of Kelly Malone's. She was just doing what she was trained to do, answering a call, and if doing her moral duty meant going into the lion's den, facing the once secret center of her adolescent dreams, then so be it. She'd grown up. They'd all grown up. There was no time for dreams anymore.

She almost didn't see the gate. She slammed on the brakes, coming to a skidding stop that brought the nose of Edie's old truck within kissing distance of the rusted fence with its shiny new lock. She sat in the truck, staring at it in dismay. Maybe she'd made a wrong turn somewhere. Maybe she hadn't followed Aunt Edie's scribbled map as well as she thought she had. Maybe she'd been too busy rehashing her past....

He appeared out of nowhere, looming up beside the truck window like a wraith, startling Kelly into a muffled scream. He was bundled up in a shearling coat, his cowboy hat pulled low to shield his face from the icy wind. But she could see long, silky black hair whipping in the breeze, and she had the depressing thought that Sam Watson hadn't changed as much as she'd hoped.

"Open the door!" His voice was muffled by the wind, the collar of his coat and the tightly closed door, and for just a moment she considered slamming the truck into reverse and getting the hell out of there.

There were several very good reasons why she couldn't do just that. Number one, someone needed her, and even if the woman's husband was still a sour-souled stud, that shouldn't have any influence on her. Number two, Aunt Edie's clutch was notoriously temperamental. There was a good chance the gears would grind and the damned truck would just stall out, leaving Kelly feeling *really* stupid.

And number three, she had her pride.

She pushed open the door, after remembering to unlock it, almost slammed it into the man looming over her. He moved in time, unfortunately.

"Who are you?" he demanded as she slid down from the high seat. "And what are you doing on my property?"

"Who are you?" she responded with spurious sweetness.

She still had a stray, vain hope that it was someone other than Sam Watson. He pushed the hat toward the back of his head to glower at her, and there was no mistaking those icy blue eyes. "I'm Samuel Watson, and this is my place. I don't take kindly to trespassers, sightseers, reporters, environmental do-gooders, nosy parkers or tourists on the make."

"It doesn't sound like there's many people you do make welcome," she said. "I'm not here to see you. I'm Kelly Malone. My Aunt Edie sent me out here. She said there's a pregnant woman needing my help. If she's married to you I can see why she would."

If she'd hoped to shock him she got her wish. He stared at her for a solid minute, letting those icy blue eyes run from the top of her tousled head to the rough work boots she'd had the sense to bring with her.

It took all her willpower not to try to smooth her flyaway hair. Nothing short of her family's best, most expensive efforts was going to turn her into a sophisticated beauty, and she had no earthly reason to want that kind of life again. She knew her assets and her defects. She was too tall for a woman—just a hair over five foot ten without her shoes on, and she usually wore shoes. She had a strong, rawboned body, with big shoulders and hands, a mop of long, shapeless hair that was halfway between brown and blond, a big mouth, small nose and plain brown eyes. The khakis, flannel shirt and heavy sweater hardly added a touch of elegance to the ensemble, and she expected him to sniff disparagingly.

"Edie's niece?" he said after a moment in a slightly less hostile voice. His eyes narrowed. "Do I know you?"

There was absolutely no reason why it should sting. After all, he'd been three years older, lost in the angst of teenage rebellion. Why should he have noticed a lovelorn adolescent who watched him from afar?

"I stayed with Edie when I was younger. You might have been around," she said with a splendidly casual air. "I'm a nurse-midwife. Aunt Edie said someone out here needed my help. I assume it's your wife."

He was still looking at her in a slightly odd way. "I'm not married. It's... someone else."

So he wanted to be as mysterious as Aunt Edie. So be it. "Do you want to open the gate for me?"

she said patiently. "Or am I supposed to walk to your house?"

He hesitated for a moment, then seemed to come to some kind of decision. "I'll unlock the gate, and then you can give me a ride up there. I was just checking the fences when I saw the cloud of dust you were bringing up. You drive awful damned fast for these roads."

"I was in a hurry to get here."

He made a noncommittal sound that sounded like a grunt as he unlocked the heavy gate, pushed it open and waited for her to drive through.

She really wasn't looking forward to having him climb into the cab of Edie's truck. It was a big, old one, but Samuel was a big man, and she had the unpleasant feeling she was going to be dwarfed.

He shoved her bag aside as he climbed in, slamming the door after him and taking off his hat. His hair was still ridiculously long, still untouched by any gray. Kelly had found her first gray hair when she was twenty-three—she looked at the teeming black with jealous disapproval.

"Don't you think you're carrying this security thing a little far?" she said as she put the truck into gear again, only to have it grind, cough and die ignominiously.

She stomped on the clutch and turned the key again, offering up a silent prayer that the temperamental beast would start. It made haphazard groaning noises but no encouraging growl. She wouldn't look at her passenger as she cranked the key, though she could feel his eyes on her.

"You're going to flood the engine," he said mildly enough.

"Not if this truck wants to live," she muttered. Obviously the truck heard her threat, for a moment later the engine turned over and began rumbling noisily.

"Don't stall it again," he said as she popped the clutch and they bounded forward across the dusty road. He didn't give her time to respond, which was probably a good thing. "As for the security, I'd say that was my business, not yours."

"No one else around here seems to need an armed fortress."

"No one else is in my kind of trouble."

Oh-oh. She should have known it wouldn't be that easy. She knew Aunt Edie well enough to realize something was behind her insistence that Kelly rush out to Sam's ranch house. "Trouble?" she echoed.

"Edie shouldn't have sent you," he said, sliding down in the seat and staring out the pitted windscreen. "I could have handled things myself."

"She said I was needed."

He glanced at her, but it was too quick for her to read the expression in his eyes, and his face wasn't giving anything away. "Maybe," he said. "And maybe your Aunt Edie's worrying too much. Right now you just walked smack dab into my own personal mess, and I can't be certain I can get you back out again before all hell breaks loose."

She took a deep, calming breath. This was the West, after all. The land of guns and range wars and rattlesnakes and lawlessness. "You want to explain that?"

"After you've seen your patient. Unless you want to leave right now? Before you get in any deeper. It's okay with me—I told you, I don't like to be beholden to people. I can handle things on my own—I always have, and I like it better that way. You go back to your Aunt Edie and tell her I said thanks for the help, but no thanks."

"I can't do that."

"Why not?"

"Because someone needs me, and I took an oath. There's a woman having a difficult pregnancy who's near to delivery, and I'm someone who knows how to help. I can't turn my back on it because her husband got himself into some kind of mess."

"I told you, she's not my wife."

"Well, her significant other. Will that do?"

For a moment a wry smile lit his dark face, and Kelly nearly drove off the road. No wonder she'd been ablaze with passion for him when she was fourteen—anyone who could smile like that could rule the world if he wanted. Or at least the hearts and minds of any gullible females within forty miles.

"I guess at this point you may as well call her my significant other," he drawled, still obviously amused.

Kelly wasn't. He might not care about the women who got knocked up by his randy seed, but she'd seen enough fatherless children and heartache in her practice to have developed an alarmingly conservative set of values in certain areas.

"Pull up beside the ranch house and I'll get you a cup of coffee before we check on Blanche."

"I don't want any coffee," she said, pulling up beside the rambling old building. It was a two-story ranch house, weathered and weary, though she could see telltale signs of fresh lumber, replacement roof shingles where someone had been fixing it up. She turned off the engine, wondering if maybe Samuel Watson wasn't as tough as he was pretending. Maybe he was fixing the place up for his family, for the new baby coming....

"I do. And I'm not taking you to see Blanche until I get some."

She followed him out of the truck, dragging her bag with her. She had long legs, but she had to hurry to keep up with him as he strode up the front porch and into the house.

Inside the place was clean, cluttered, smelling deliciously of wood smoke and coffee. It was a man's place, though—no curtains on the windows, and through the doorway she could see the big, shabby easy chair smack dab in front of the television. The stairs were in one corner, and Kelly took a step in that direction.

"I can find her myself. You go ahead and have your coffee. . . ."

He caught her arm, turning her around and heading her back to the kitchen before she could protest or resist. "She's not in the house," he said. "And I'll take you to see her when I'm good and ready." He took the medical bag from her, set it on the floor by the scrubbed kitchen table and proceeded to push her into one of the chairs. Kelly was too bemused to protest. He hadn't been rough, he hadn't hurt her. He'd simply made her do what he wanted by putting his hands on her and moving her.

It was an unnerving sensation.

"Milk and sugar," she said, since he was already pouring two mugs, ignoring her refusal.

He set the mug down in front of her, pointed at the lumpy sugar and nondairy creamer at her, and sat down opposite her, his hat still shielding his face.

The silence that ensued was long and uncomfortable, and after two minutes Kelly couldn't stand it any longer. "Do you and Blanche live here alone?" she asked in her best social voice. "It seems a pretty big place for two people to run."

"I have help."

Another bout of silence, this one lasting three minutes. The coffee was so strong Kelly could feel her stomach twist in protest, but the alternative was to sit there and stare at him. "Do you?" she said finally.

"Do I what?"

"Have help?"

"What's it to you?"

"I'm trying to make polite conversation," she said testily, giving up the effort.

"I'm not interested in empty social pleasantries."

"That's obvious. Why don't you tell me about my patient?"

He hesitated. "What do you want to know?"

"How old is she? Is this her first child? How much weight has she gained? What kind of prenatal care has she had? How's she feeling?"

"Fine," he said.

"Fine?"

"She's feeling fine. Eating well, peaceful and contented."

"You make her sound like a cow."

A fleeting look of amusement crossed his face. "She puts me in mind of one, every now and then."

"She better not hear you say it," Kelly warned.

"I don't think she'd mind. As for the rest of it, I don't know how old she is. Young, I'd guess. I think this is her first, and I imagine she's gained about a hundred pounds or so. And she hasn't had any prenatal care."

"A hundred pounds? Do you realize what kind of strain that can put on the mother?" Kelly demanded.

"She's doing just fine."

"Then why am I out here?"

"Beats me," he said, taking his hat off and sending it flying across the room to a kitchen countertop. "It was Edie's idea. She worries too much, but as far as I know there's no problem with Blanche. She'll just let nature take its course, and she doesn't need any fancy East Coast midwives to get in her way."

She found herself wishing he'd left his hat on. Other women might have found his features too harsh, his eyes too bleak, his mouth too uncompromising. As a matter of fact, she was of just that opinion.

But it didn't change the fact that when she looked into Samuel Watson's face, she felt dizzy, like an adolescent with a sudden rush of hormones. Sentiment, she told herself sharply. Childhood memories flooding back. She wouldn't touch him with a ten-foot pole, even if he was offering, which he clearly wasn't. Besides, there was poor, portly Blanche to consider.

Beauty was only skin deep. Pretty is as pretty does. There were a thousand other aphorisms, but nothing changed the fact that when levelheaded Kelly Morgan looked into Samuel's cool, enigmatic face, she felt her insides turn to quicksand.

"Something wrong?" he said, eyeing her doubtfully. "You look like you've seen a ghost."

She gave herself a brisk shake. "Not a thing," she said firmly. "But I'd like to see my patient and then get out of here. You don't seem inclined to tell me what kind of trouble you're in that you need to live in an armed fortress, and I don't really care. I just want to see Blanche, make sure she's doing all right, and then get back to Aunt Edie's."

"Good thinking," he said. "She's out in the barn."

"She's working? In her condition? Are you crazy?"

He rose, and despite her best efforts not to notice, her eyes traveled up the length of him, the long legs in the faded jeans, the silver-studded belt, the faded shirt. He belonged on the cover of a romance novel, she thought grumpily. And when she got back to Boston she was going to stop reading the damned things. That was probably why she was so vulnerable.

"I'll take you to meet her," he said, pouring himself another mug of coffee and heading for the back door, leaving her to follow.

Follow she did, scampering after him as she bit back her annoyance. They crossed the wind-swept, hardscrabble yard to the barn, which was in better shape than the house, the new roof shining under the bright New Mexico sun. She followed him into the warmth and darkness, past empty stalls, heading toward the back.

He halted and she barreled into him, spilling his coffee over both of them. Apart from a muffled curse he said nothing, but there was a grin on his face that was both devastating and utterly annoying.

"Kelly Malone, meet Blanche," he said.

And Kelly found herself face-to-face with a very large, very peaceful, very pregnant creature that could only be a buffalo.

Chapter Two

"I suppose this is your idea of a joke," Kelly said. "I must say I don't consider it to be particularly funny."

"No joke. And I wasn't the one who asked you out here, remember? It was Edie's idea. I know enough about animals to figure Blanche will give birth when she's ready. Buffalo aren't that different from cattle when it comes to obstetrics, and since this is a cattle ranch I've been around plenty of calvings in my time. But you know your aunt—she worries."

Kelly looked up at Samuel Watson for a long, considering moment. Aunt Edie did more than worry about pregnant buffalo—she also worried about her recently jilted niece. It wasn't like her to matchmake, but Sam Watson had always been a special favorite of hers, just as Kelly was. It might not have been conscious on her part, throwing the two of them together. But it wouldn't do to underestimate Edith Malone.

"Why haven't you had a vet out here, just to set your mind at ease? They'd know a lot better than me what's normal in a buffalo."

Sam leaned against the barn wall, cradling his mug of coffee in his big hands as he took a leisurely sip, playing for time. "I'm afraid things aren't quite that simple."

"Why not?" She hadn't noticed the other resident of the stall. Curled up, almost hidden by Blanche's thick brown bulk, was a large white dog, one that was slowly rising to its feet, an intent look in its blue eyes. There was something eerily intelligent about the dog as it surveyed her, as if it were considering whether she was to be trusted or not.

"Because I don't believe Blanche is going to give birth to just any ordinary buffalo calf. Neither does Pete, and I trust his instincts."

She was still staring at the dog. "Who's Pete?"

"The wolf who's giving you the once-over."

"Wolf?" She stepped back hastily, unnerved.

"What did you think he was, a German shepherd?" he scoffed.

"Isn't he dangerous?"

"Only when he wants to be. Right now he's mainly concerned about protecting Blanche. If he decides you're to be trusted, then he'll protect you, as well."

"I don't need protection."

"We all need protection, at least at some point in our lives."

"You included?" She tossed the question off almost absently as she held out a hand for the wolf to sniff. He looked like a dog—she might as well treat him like one. He sniffed her hand delicately, consideringly, and she forced herself to relax. Animals sensed tension and fear and reacted accordingly.

"Me included," Sam said.

Kelly passed inspection. Pete licked her hand, then returned to his spot in the straw, curled up next to the somnolent buffalo. "What do you mean, she's not going to have an ordinary calf? You think she's carrying twins?"

"I think she's carrying a white buffalo."

She sank to her knees in the straw, putting gentle hands on the peaceful creature. The wolf watched her carefully, his long muzzle resting on his front paws.

"How could you guess that? Why should you think she'll give birth to an albino...?"

"The calf won't be an albino."

She glanced back at him. "You said she was going to have a white calf...."

"But not an albino one. White buffalo are very rare. As far as I know there have only been a handful born in this century, and each one is special. They come for a reason. We don't always know what that reason is...."

"Are you crazy?" she demanded flatly. "What you've got is a pregnant buffalo who should be out roaming free, and you're spouting stuff that makes me think you've been around too many farm chemicals."

"Native Americans believe white buffalo to be sacred," he said with surprising patience. "I won't bore you with the details—you wouldn't be interested. Let's just say I think Blanche is going to give birth to a very rare creature, and I want to make sure that baby stays alive."

"Why wouldn't it?"

"Because of where she comes from. Blanche and Pete used to live about a hundred miles away, on a ranch owned by a man named Brody. It was a hunting preserve, where his rich friends put down their money and got to kill anything they wanted. The rarer the better. White wolves were prized. A white buffalo would be the coup of a lifetime."

Kelly ran a hand over Blanche's soft fur, and the animal looked up at her out of peaceful, liquid eyes. "No one's going to do that."

"Enough people are going to try. I don't have any legal claim to these animals. When the federal marshals shut down Brody's little operation, most of the animals were taken to game preserves, to keep them safe. But Blanche and Pete got loose and found their way here. I figure they're here for a reason, and I'm not about to let anyone take them away. No matter how many court orders they have, no matter how many of them get together to try to storm this place, they aren't taking Blanche out of here."

"You think they'd do that?" she asked quietly.

"They've already tried. Why do you think I've got the gates locked? We've got a lot of rough characters around here, including the Gonyaw boys. They're my neighbors. They've never had any particular fondness for me or for wolves, and they'd sure as hell like a white buffalo hide to show off. Locked gates aren't going to keep the Gonyaws from coming across my land, but if they cut the wire they'll be trespassing, and they know I've got the right to shoot them on sight. Most people around here know I wouldn't hesitate."

"What did I get myself in the middle of, a range war?" she asked faintly.

"I warned you. You're safe enough. They're not going to force the issue. Not yet. Not until they're sure it's worth fighting for. In the meantime, Edie's got some lawyer working on it, trying to get the courts to agree that I've got legal rights to the animals. It ain't gonna happen, but it's keeping things at a standoff. For now."

"For now?"

"Until Blanche gives birth. For the time being, they're just making sure I can't leave. This place is under siege."

She sat back on her heels in the straw. "What's going to happen?"

"It depends on what happens with Blanche. If the calf is brown then we have no problem. The ranchers around here know there's no sport in shooting buffalo, and Blanche and her calf will be safe. If the calf is white, we've got a major problem."

"Why do you think it will be white?"

For a moment he didn't say a word, and she figured that like the white wolf lying so peacefully nearby, he was deciding whether he could trust her or not.

His decision wasn't as favorable as Pete's. "Instinct," he said flatly. "How does she look?"

Kelly turned back to the huge creature. She was resting comfortably, her heartbeat steady, her eyes clear and peaceful, her breathing regular. "As far as I can tell she's absolutely fine. Did you have any reason for thinking she'd be having a difficult time?"

"Nope. It was Edie's idea."

Edie the matchmaker. "I'll bet," Kelly muttered under her breath, rising from the straw. "You don't want to have the vet out?"

"He won't come. He's too scared of the Gonyaw boys to risk everything for three wild animals."

"Three?" she echoed.

"Blanche, Pete and me."

He didn't look that wild to her. A little untamed. A little rough. A little more honest than most people could tolerate.

"What about the police?"

Sam shrugged. "They're staying out of it. The Gonyaws have made a lot of threats, but no one's done anything. So the sheriff is having a wait-and-see attitude."

She looked at him. "This is crazy. You know that, don't you?" She shook her head. "As far as I can see Blanche is fine," she said finally. "If you think I can help, if you need me to come back, you just have to call Edie and let me know."

"I don't think that would be a good idea," he drawled. "You're lucky you were able to get in and out this time. If they think you're helping me they won't let you back. I told you—I'm under siege out here and they're trying to shut me off from any outside help."

"That reminds me, there's a couple of boxes of food in the back of the pickup truck. Aunt Edie thought you might be needing it."

"She was right." He leaned over and placed his hand on Blanche's head, and Kelly stared, unwilling, at the long brown fingers kneading the soft coat. Instinctively she arched her own back. How long had it been since she'd been caressed like that? Maybe her entire lifetime.

The wolf rose when Kelly did, following them from the barn at a steady pace, his blue eyes clear and watchful as Sam lifted the big box of food from the back of the pickup. "That's odd," he said. "Pete doesn't usually leave Blanche's side."

Pete came up to Kelly and pushed his nose against her hand, whining quietly. "Maybe he's hungry?" she said, squatting down to rub his head in unconscious imitation of the caress Sam had given Blanche.

"He's not that interested in food." Sam was already heading into the house. Kelly reached for the smaller box, the one with the apple pie Edie had asked her to bake, and followed him, Pete close on her heels.

"You probably better get going. I'd offer to let you use the phone and let Edie know you're on your way back, but they've cut my phone lines." He set the box on the counter and turned to her.

"I brought my cellular phone. I can call her from the truck." Pete was sitting beside her, leaning against her leg, whining softly.

Sam had an odd expression on his face. "That's funny," he said.

"What is?"

"Pete's never come in the house before. He never leaves Blanche."

"Maybe he likes me better," she said lightly.

"I don't think so."

The kitchen was suddenly still and quiet. The wind had picked up outside, and it was already growing darker in the midafternoon. They weren't that far away from the shortest day of the year, and even with the big New Mexico sky, darkness could fall quickly.

She didn't want to leave. She wasn't quite sure why. Maybe it was the smell of that horribly strong coffee he'd given her earlier. Maybe it was the bleak emptiness of the house. Maybe it was the wolf pressing against her, trying to tell her something. Maybe it was Samuel Watson and an adolescent passion she'd long outgrown.

Whatever it was, she wasn't giving in to it. She was getting out of there, and when she got back she was going to give Edith Malone a piece of her mind.

Except he was looking at her, across the shadowy kitchen, an odd expression on his face. She couldn't even begin to guess what he was thinking—he had always been a master at hiding his thoughts and emotions. But he was looking at her and thinking something.

Probably what an overgrown mess she'd turned into, she thought, shoving a hand through her shaggy hair.

That wasn't what she wanted him to be thinking. She wanted him to look at her the way he'd looked at that pregnant buffalo in his barn. She wanted warmth and affection. She suspected that he wasn't the kind of man to give it to anything on two legs. Not easily.

"I'll tell you what," she said brightly, forcing the odd, mournful thought away from her. "I'll leave you the cellular phone. You need to plug it in to keep it charged, but that way if something comes up and you need help, you can reach me."

"The power was cut a week ago, and the electric company gave up on trying to fix it. Besides, you'll be lucky to get home without any trouble. They're not likely to let you back here."

"If I'm needed, I'll come," she said firmly. "I don't abandon my patients."

"Who do you abandon?"

The question hung in the air, odd, quiet, and she found herself thinking of all the people who'd abandoned Samuel Watson during his life.

"No one," she said.

He didn't believe her. His expression didn't change, he didn't say a word, but he didn't believe her. And she had the oddest urge to cross the room, reach up and pull his head down to her breast, to smooth the long, tangled hair away from his bleak face and soothe his angry soul.

"I'll get the phone from the car," she said.

"Don't bother. I wouldn't use it."

She believed him. "Not even if Blanche needed help? You'd let your pride get in the way of her needs?"

He had no answer for that one. "Just go away, Kelly," he said wearily, and it might have been the first time she ever heard him use her name.

She shrugged. "I can't make you see reason," she said, and turned toward the door.

Pete was blocking it. He lay in front of it, staring up at her with his wise blue eyes, making no effort to move out of her way when she approached him.

"I'm leaving, boy," she said. He thumped his tail.

She started to step over him, and he rose quickly, coming up under her long leg, throwing her off balance. She moved around him and had walked halfway to the truck when she was brought up short.

Pete had the hem of her thick jacket in his strong, fierce teeth. He growled softly, in the back of his throat, but his eyes were still gentle.

"Let go of me, Pete," Kelly said. "Good dog. Er... good wolf. Let me go now."

He didn't even blink. Sam had come to the kitchen door, silhouetted against it as he watched the battle between wolf and woman.

"He doesn't seem to want to let me go," she said, yanking at the hem of her jacket.

"So I noticed. Come here, boy. Leave Kelly alone."

Pete ignored him, his teeth still tight in the canvas jacket.

"All right," Kelly said. "Take the damned jacket." She yanked it off, shivering in the chill winter wind, and sprinted toward the truck.

Pete was ahead of her, the jacket discarded in the dust. She had her hand on the door when his massive jaws clamped around her ankle, effectively trapping her.

She stared down at him in shock. There was absolutely no pain—he was holding her very lightly, like a hunting dog who's learned to fetch his prey without damaging it. His huge teeth rested against the denim of her jeans like a velvet-lined trap.

"Damn it, Pete," she said, pulling. When she pulled, the jaws tightened, just enough for her to know how much he could have hurt her. He whined, wagging his tail. But he wouldn't release her.

"What the hell's wrong with you, Pete?" Sam towered over them, his voice grim. "Let her go, boy. We don't need her around here."

Pete seemed inclined to disagree. He just kept whining, his jaws holding tight to the leg of her pants, trapping her.

"Can't you get him to let me go?" Kelly demanded, trying to keep the breathlessness out of her voice. She was freezing without her jacket, and Sam was uncomfortably close. Close enough to unsettle her, not close enough to warm her.

"I've got a shotgun inside," Sam said. "I can always shoot him."

"No!" she shrieked in horror, then realized he hadn't meant it. He was testing her. She didn't like being tested—she always failed, sooner or later. "Hey," she said in a calmer voice, "I can just stay out here with his mouth clamped around my leg. Sooner or later he'll get hungry."

"I don't think that's the answer. He might decide to see whether you taste as good as you look. You know what they say about how dangerous wolves are."

"I know that wolves have an undeservedly bad reputation," she shot back.

"You sure fell for it. You looked like you'd seen a ghost when you saw him in the stable."

"I'm not used to wolves."

"Maybe Pete's not used to women. Maybe he wants a little taste."

The blast of cold air blew down her neck, and she shivered. "Do you suppose you could get me my jacket? Maybe he'd rather bite that?"

"I think he has some stupid notion about you staying here," Sam drawled.

"You know how to read a dog's mind?"

"It's easy enough to know what animals are thinking. People, too, if you stop long enough to listen."

You better not be able to tell what I'm thinking, Kelly thought edgily. Even she wasn't too happy with the odd tenor of her thoughts—she certainly didn't want the object of those faintly erotic fantasies to be privy to Sam and Pete, as well.

He stripped off his own shearling jacket and threw it over her shoulders. She tried to shrug it off, but his hands were hard, holding it around her, and it was warm, from him. Like being wrapped in a lover's arms, surrounded by warmth and strength and touch and scent and . . .

Pete released her leg. Sam was running his hands up and down her arms in an absent attempt to warm her, but it was closer to a slow caress, one that unsettled her even more. She swayed toward him, unable to help herself, and she wondered what it would be like to kiss that wide, unsmiling mouth. And whether she could ever make him smile.

He stared down at her, his eyes intent. He'd left his hat inside, and the cold wind ruffled his long, silky hair, tossing it against the finely chiseled bones of his face. He was looking at her as if she were some strange, inexplicable creature who'd appeared out of nowhere, and she felt him draw her imperceptibly closer, closer, and she knew he wanted to kiss her as well, wanted to taste her....

Neither of them even heard the old pickup approach, which was astonishing, considering it was even more of a relic than Edie's, until it pulled up beside them with a screech of ancient brakes and the smell of ripe exhaust. Suddenly, it was as if they'd never been standing together beneath the bright New Mexico sky. Pete had already left—she saw his white body heading back toward the barn, and Blanche.

Sam was already yards away from her, and she might have imagined that strange, breathless moment when it seemed as if he might kiss her. Except she could still feel the strength of his hands as they'd rubbed her arms beneath the shearling coat, she could still feel the warmth of him. She turned her attention to the newcomer.

''Hey, Sam.'' The man who climbed out of the pickup was elderly, brown as a berry and wrinkled, with thick gray hair and eyebrows. "We got trouble."

"No sh—fooling, Ramos," Sam drawled. "What else is new?"

"She is, for one thing," Ramos said, grinning at Kelly. "Where'd she come from? I thought you didn't like gringo women except for old Miss Malone."

"This is Miss Malone's niece."

"They don't look much alike," Ramos observed, his dark eyes assessing her. "Welcome to Rancho Desolado. How'd Sam manage to get you out here?"

"Sam's trying to get her home," Sam said testily. "That fool wolf decided he didn't want her to leave."

"Pete's smart," Ramos said. "He knows better'n me when there's trouble."

"What kind of trouble?" Kelly asked.

"Take your pick, miss," Ramos said cheerfully. "We've got Animal Protection Services breathing down our necks, we've got the Fish and Wildlife Service out for blood, we've even got the BIA ready to scalp Sam here."

"So what else is new?" Sam muttered.

"That's not the real problem. Bureaucracies take too damned much time to do anything. Leave it up to them and they'll take Blanche away when she's dead of old age. It's the Gonyaws who are the problem. They've set up a roadblock. No one's getting in or out of here. Sheriff Jackson isn't going to stop them—he knows he's up for reelection this year and he's not about to risk getting shot for the sake of a buffalo. He's leaving it up to us to defend ourselves, and folks like the Gonyaw boys don't give a damn about the law, anyway. They want both the animals, and they're not about to wait around till you're forced to give 'em up.''

"Hell and damnation," Sam muttered.

"What does this mean?" Kelly asked, leaning against the cold steel side of Edie's pickup truck.

"It means that for the time being, you aren't going anywhere," Sam said. *"Mi casa es su casa."*

And somewhere in the distance, Kelly could just imagine the grin on Aunt Edie's face.

Chapter Three

"Don't be ridiculous," Kelly protested. "I'm not staying out here."

"They're watching every gate," Ramos said. "All we have to do is unlock one of them and they'll be swarming through here. The Gonyaw boys never had much use for Sam or for me, either, and I'm sure no one would have any problem if either of us happened to catch a stray bullet."

"This isn't a John Wayne western," Kelly said.

"Nope, but the Gonyaws wish it was." Sam reached past her, into the truck, and took the keys that were dangling from the end of a plastic cactus key chain. "And as long as the people shooting at you think they're still living in the Old West, you play by their rules or you'll end up dead."

"I never did like playing cowboys and Indians." Kelly held out her hand. "Give me the keys."

"Sorry." He didn't sound the slightest bit regretful as he tucked them into his jeans pocket. There was no way she was going to reach for them there. "I was afraid something like this might happen, and now it's too late. You don't even get to choose which side you're on."

"I'm on Blanche's side," she said. "Which means, I suppose, that I'm on yours." She kept her voice deliberately cool. "When do you think I can get back to Aunt Edie's?"

"A couple of days if we're lucky."

"A couple of days?" she shrieked, feeling real panic. "I'm not staying out here that long. What will Aunt Edie do without her truck?"

"She's got a broken ankle, remember? She can't drive, anyway."

There was nothing more annoying than a good-looking man who had an answer for everything, Kelly thought. "Well, then, what's she going to do without me to drive her places?"

"She'll make do. There are plenty of people to look after her. She didn't really need you to come out here, she just..." He let the words trail off, as if he'd realized too late that he'd said too much.

"What do you mean by that?" Kelly demanded.

"Nothing." He reached into his pocket and tossed the truck keys to Ramos, who caught them easily. "Stash the truck in the barn. We don't want to give those boys a target."

Kelly wasn't about to give in. "But what..."

"It's getting late," he said abruptly, "and I've got to do something about dinner. Unless you want to."

"I don't even want to be here, much less cook for you," she shot back.

"Suit yourself. My talents and larder run to spaghetti and meatballs. Though we may be out of them by now."

"There's a casserole in the box of food Edie sent along," she said grudgingly. "And an apple pie."

"Lord deliver us," he groaned. "Edie never could bake worth a damn."

Kelly wasn't about to inform him that she'd made the pie, and the casserole as well, any more than she'd offer to wash his dishes. She didn't want to go into that house, into that kitchen with him. She certainly didn't want to take off her clothes and try to sleep under the same roof.

Not that he would even notice. He hadn't been aware of her when she was a kid, and right now he viewed her as an irritant, not a possible bedmate. Which was a relief, she reminded herself. Her own reaction to Samuel One-Horse Watson was far too complicated already, and along with resentment and a reluctant admiration there was a totally mindless lust that brought her back to those desperate days of adolescence. If he were to touch her, want her, she'd probably fall like a dead sequoia.

Not that she'd ever even seen a sequoia, she reminded herself. In her twenty-six years she'd had exactly two sexual partners, the first being her high school boyfriend, who'd finally managed to deflower her after two and a half years of trying, and the second being her erstwhile fiancé, Dr. David Mallory, obstetrician, gentleman, scholar, and no man for the likes of her. A man who didn't want children, and in the end didn't want Kelly Malone for a wife, no matter how impeccable her lineage. Because of that she was well and happily out of the arrangement. If only she'd been the one to break free.

The fact of the matter was, she felt sex was greatly overrated, and nothing she'd heard from the pregnant teenagers and welfare mothers who populated the clinic where she worked had managed to give her any alternative view.

If two men who had insisted they loved and cared for her hadn't made sex more than faintly enjoyable, why should a wild, sullen renegade be any different?

But a dangerous little voice in the back of her head said, Wouldn't you like to find out?

He was making fresh coffee, not bothering to wash out the pot, and Kelly shuddered. "Let me do that," she said, taking it out of his hands. He let it go, willingly enough, and took a seat at the kitchen table, stretching his long legs out in front of him. If she wasn't careful she'd trip over them and go sprawling.

She could feel his eyes on her back, and she stiffened it automatically. She had no idea what was running through his head, but she doubted the thoughts were complimentary. ''What did you mean by that?'' she said when she finally had a fresh pot started.

''Mean by what?''

She turned to face him, leaning against the kitchen sink. ''You said something about Aunt Edie not really needing me. You started to say something about why she invited me.''

''You're imagining things,'' he said, not moving.

''I don't have a very good imagination. You said she didn't really need me, she just... She just *what?*''

He waited for a moment, considering. ''She thought you needed a break from your family. She said they were eating you alive, making you turn into something you didn't want to be. And she said you'd been dumped by your rich, handsome doctor fiancé.''

''Aunt Edie's developed a gossipy streak. It's a good thing I can't get back to her,'' Kelly mused. ''It's not nice to beat up on old ladies with broken ankles.''

''She was worried about you.''

''Fine. She didn't have to tell you about it.''

"She knew I didn't give a damn why you were coming. She was just making conversation."

"You get by on your charm, don't you?" Kelly said with false sweetness. "I just don't happen to like having my private business bandied about to anyone, including sullen cowboys who could care less."

She must have imagined the glint of amusement in his blue, blue eyes. "You forget—I'm an Indian. One of the bad guys."

"Depends on how you look at it," she said. "Where am I sleeping?"

"In a bed," he shot back. "Top of the stairs. You'll find sheets in the hall closet, or I can lend you my sleeping bag."

That was all she needed, to be cocooned in Sam Watson's covers. "Sheets will be fine."

"I'll find some clothes you can use. You're big for a woman, so you'll probably fit my stuff. The jeans will probably be too tight, though." He looked so bland when he said it that she couldn't be sure whether he was taunting her or not. She wasn't going to rise to the bait, whether it was being offered or not.

"Fine," she said in her coolest, most Brookline voice. "Call me when dinner's ready."

"Yes, ma'am," he said meekly. "I'll do that."

And Kelly had the cheerfully wicked thought that the Gonyaw boys might end up being the least of his problems if he continued to taunt her.

Sam watched her go. A moment later he heard her stomping up the stairs, and he let a faint grin cross his face. He was really managing to piss her off royally, a good thing, considering.

Considering that she was the sexiest thing that had been in his house in over a decade. Hell, maybe in his lifetime. She was big and strong and gorgeous, and he had to keep his hands shoved in his pockets to keep from touching her, seeing if she was as sleek and strong as she looked.

The smell of the dripping coffee was overriding the smell of her perfume, and as much as he loved coffee, he found he regretted it. She didn't smell of anything too fancy—just fresh air and soap and some really light, flowery scent. Just womanly enough to send his hormones into overdrive.

Hell, he shouldn't be that horny. He'd broken up with Susie Law more than a year ago, and he'd gotten over the need to have a woman. And Kelly Malone wasn't his kind of woman.

Except that was a damned lie. She was exactly the kind of woman he needed—brave, tender, and not about to take any crap from the likes of him. No one had dared call him sullen for the last fifteen years. It had taken Kelly Malone to make him see he was still acting like a sulky kid.

He remembered her from long ago. She'd been flat-chested and skinny back then, still wearing glasses, and her hair hadn't had much more shape to it. She'd watch him, and it made him nervous. At seventeen he was already used to having giggling girls watch him, and he knew half of what they were thinking about, because he was thinking about the same things.

But Edie Malone's gawky, fourteen-year-old niece from back East couldn't be thinking those things, and she made him uncomfortable. Because every now and then he found he was thinking those things about her.

He'd outgrown the rampant randiness of being seventeen. Except, for some reason, Kelly Malone was reminding him of it all over again. And he wondered what it would be like if he threaded his fingers through that mop of hair and kissed her.

Not in this lifetime, he reminded himself, lighting the gas oven and tossing the match into the sink where it sizzled. He was in enough trouble as it was with the Gonyaw boys breathing down his neck, not to mention every bureaucracy in the state wanting a piece of him. All because of one ordinary-looking buffalo.

He needed to get Blanche safely out of here. He needed to get Kelly out as well, but for the time being, no one was going anywhere. And sleeping under the same roof as that leggy, mouthy woman was going to drive him straight out of his mind.

Maybe he'd curl up with Blanche and Pete. Maybe they could keep his mind off what lay beneath her bulky layers of winter clothing. And the thought of her body lying between the same cool white sheets he slept in.

The upstairs of the ranch house was as neat and bare as the rest of the place. There were four bedrooms—two were empty, one held a narrow iron bed and chest of drawers, the other clearly belonged to her reluctant host. There was a stack of books by the huge old bed, discarded clothes over the back of one chair and an old pair of boots leaning against each other in a corner.

She stared at that bed for far too long. It was very old, made of carved wood, the kind of bed to found a dynasty in. The covers had been pulled together, the white sheets rumpled, the patchwork quilts piled high for a winter night. It looked like the softest, warmest place in the world.

She turned on her heel and went in search of her own bed linens. If she didn't get a ride out of this place soon she'd end up walking. This was a dangerous place for her state of mind. And the state of her heart.

She made perfect hospital corners on the narrow bed. She pulled the sheets so tight a quarter would bounce off them. And then she turned to find Sam standing in the doorway, watching her out of his enigmatic eyes.

She didn't want him looking at her while she stood next to a bed. Not that he cared, but her own usually staid mind seemed weirdly obsessed with sex. She'd stripped off her heavy sweaters while she worked, but now she was cold in just her T-shirt, cold as he looked at her.

"Dinner's ready," he said. Not moving.

"I'm not hungry," she said. A blatant, outright lie, and her stomach betrayed her by growling loudly.

His faint twist of a smile didn't do much for her peace of mind. "Ramos is down there, so you'll have company. Besides, this is probably the only decent meal you'll have while you're stuck here. While Edie's one of creation's worst cooks, I'm even worse, and from now on you'll be relying on my cooking skills."

She grabbed one of her sweaters and pulled it over her head, shaking her hair free. He was still watching her, and she would have given fifteen years off her life to know what he was thinking.

"I'm not going to be here that long. I only came to visit Aunt Edie for the week. My flight leaves New Year's Day, and it's the nonchangeable, nonrefundable kind. I'm just going to have to cut short your hospitality."

His long, slow grin would have tempted a saint. "Trust me, Kelly. You'd like the Gonyaws even less than you like me."

"Hard to imagine," she said, moving past him and heading down the narrow flight of stairs. Except that he didn't move far enough out of the way, and the entire side of her body brushed against him as she went. She was acutely conscious of him, the hardness of his body, the warmth, the strength of it, all in that brief touch, and by the time she made it to the kitchen she was practically breathless. *I have to get out of here!*

Ramos was already sitting at the table, eating contentedly enough. Which left two seats, uncomfortably close to each other. He looked up at her, and there was the hint of a smile in his old eyes. "You think you don't like Sam much, do you?"

"I don't think, I *know*," she replied, sitting down and helping herself to the casserole she'd made hours earlier, never suspecting she'd be trapped into eating it herself.

Ramos wheezed with laughter. "Then again, you might be wrong," he said.

There wasn't much chance for protest with Sam coming into the room and taking the remaining chair. They ate in silence for long minutes, and it was all Kelly could do to concentrate. Ramos was eating contentedly enough, his eyes darting back and forth between Kelly and Sam in obvious enjoyment. Sam concentrated on his food, staring down at his plate while he dutifully shoveled it in his mouth, ignoring them all.

"Your aunt's cooking has improved dramatically." His voice was so unexpected she almost choked on her dinner.

"She can rise to the occasion," Kelly said.

"Not when she has a broken ankle." There was almost an accusatory tone in his voice. His plate was absolutely bare, and he'd heaped it high.

"All right, I cooked it," she said with mild exasperation. "I cooked the pie, too. Just because I come from Massachusetts doesn't mean I'm entirely helpless in a kitchen. Don't worry, it won't cast a magic spell on you."

"It's cast a magic spell on me," Ramos said with an appreciative smacking of his lips. "Will you marry me?"

"Ramos is already married," Sam drawled. "His wife is visiting their grandchildren until this all dies down."

"Too true," Ramos said sadly. "Then maybe you'd just better marry Sam here."

Kelly choked on the piece of chicken she'd just swallowed. Ramos pounded her back, doing more harm than good. When she was finally able to speak she had tears in her eyes and her voice was raw.

"Don't worry about it," Sam said wryly. "Your cooking isn't *that* good."

Kelly pushed away from the table. "I've had enough," she said with determined politeness, declining to say what it was she'd had enough of. "I'm going to call Aunt Edie on the cell phone, and then check in on my patient."

"You sure don't look like a vet," Ramos said. "Are you a people doctor? You're a sight prettier than Doc Winslow. Isn't she, Sam?"

Sam made a humph noise in his coffee.

"I'm not a vet, I'm a nurse-midwife."

"You know anything about pregnant buffalo?" Ramos asked.

"No."

He shook his head, grinning. "I think we're going to have us an interesting time out here the next few days."

"I'm not going to be here the next few days," Kelly said firmly. "I'm getting out of here as soon as I can."

"Mebbe," Ramos said. "Mebbe not."

Astonishingly enough, the day went from bad to worse. The sun had set by the time Kelly found where they'd stashed the truck, and the cellular phone's already weak battery was almost gone. There was just enough power to call Edie but not enough to give her a much deserved scolding.

"I won't worry about you, then," Edie's voice came over the line, faint and crackly as the signal faded. "Sam'll take real good care of you."

"I don't want Sam to take care of me!" she'd practically shrieked into the phone, but the only response she got was a dry chuckle before the connection dissolved.

The barn was still and quiet as she made her way past the empty stalls to the back, where Blanche lay in maternal splendor. Pete was curled up next to her, for all the world like a lapdog. He sensed her presence before Blanche did, lifting his head to stare at her out of sharp eyes, then dropping his head back down on his front paws, accepting her.

It was warmer back in that corner, out of the wind, and Kelly sank down in the straw next to the animals, putting a soothing hand on Blanche's massive head.

"How are you doing, my lady?" she whispered softly. "For some reason I can't quite call you a girl. How's that baby coming? Is she kicking? I bet she is. Probably pressing on your bladder. Except that I don't know where in the world your bladder is—maybe it's nowhere near the baby. You look peaceful enough, don't you.''

Blanche's dark eyes were deep and soothing as she looked up at Kelly, and a strange sense of peace washed over her. The tension of the day began to drain away as she stroked Blanche's shaggy fur. "I wonder why he thinks you're going to have a white calf?" she murmured. "He said this was your first calf, though I'm not sure how he knows that. I'm not sure how he knows anything, or if he even does." She tried to work up a smidgeon of irritation, but the feel of the soft fur beneath her hand made it impossible to get angry.

"Maybe you told him," she murmured. "I wouldn't be surprised. You're a wise lady, you can probably tell me a thing or two. Like why I'm getting so worked up over something that can't be helped. Like why I'm feeling like a helpless fourteen-year-old."

An almost surreal calm emanated from Blanche, rising into the stall and enveloping Kelly in a warm cocoon of comfort. She accepted it, even as she distrusted it, and Pete looked up at her, thumping his tail in agreement.

Kelly leaned down and rested her head against Blanche's side, listening to her steady heartbeat. She could feel the solid bulk of the calf, moving beneath her, and once again the wonder of birth washed over her. Whether it was a teenage runaway or a buffalo in the middle of a New Mexico winter, a middle-aged wife conquering years of infertility or a newlywed with an unexpected pregnancy, they were all miraculous.

She closed her eyes, breathing in the rich, clean smell of the barn, the scent of Blanche's fur. She could see the calf in a dream, creamy white and perfect, with Blanche's dark, liquid eyes. And she let go of everything, falling into a deep, peaceful sleep.

Chapter Four

Dreams were dangerous things as far as Kelly was concerned. When she was awake she could be strong, resilient, in charge of her life. When she was dreaming all her secret longings could break free, flooding her with an aching need that lingered throughout her waking hours.

She dreamed of a white buffalo woman, walking through the forest. In her arms she held a very young baby, and neither of them made a sound. Kelly was seated cross-legged beneath a tall, dark tree, and she watched them, too filled with grief and need to call out.

But she didn't need to. The woman knelt in front of her, and the infant looked like Samuel Watson. She put the child in Kelly's arms and the baby opened its eyes. He had her eyes.

And the woman began to transform, turning into a huge white buffalo. And around them a light snow began to fall, the first snowfall on the first day of the year.

She didn't want to wake up. There was such peace, such a strange combination of serene contentment and wild joy, and she wanted to hug it to her as she held the baby to her breast. Despite the snow falling all around them, she was warm, the child was warm, and Samuel Watson sat and watched them, an abstracted, tender expression on his dark face.

She opened her eyes unwillingly. She was in the barn, cradled against the sleeping Blanche, and Pete lay curled up beside her, keeping her warm. And sitting across from them, his long legs stretched out in front him, was Sam. Watching her.

There was no way she could guess what he was thinking. If tenderness had been any part of it, that was gone now. His face was shuttered down, all expression wiped clean from it, as he watched her.

"It's warmer in the house," he said, his voice low.

She knew she should probably jump up, try to tame her tangled hair with her fingers, try to gather some of her defenses back around her. She didn't move. "I doubt it," she said. "Pete and Blanche are better than an electric blanket."

"They probably have fleas."

As a taunt it was ineffective. Kelly shifted lazily. "Nope," she said.

"How do you know?"

"The same way you know Blanche is going to have a white calf."

He seemed amused. "I doubt it."

"How *do* you know, then?"

"She told me."

It was an effective conversation stopper. The problem was, she believed him.

"Dr. Doolittle, eh?" she said, trying to lighten things.

"I wouldn't know. My childhood didn't have time for reading."

Unbidden, the memory of his bedroom came back to her. The huge old bed. And the piles of books all around. "You've obviously made up for your childhood's shortcomings." The moment it was out of her mouth she knew she'd made a mistake.

"Why do you say that?" It was lazy enough, but she'd learned not to trust him when he sounded laid-back. Like a rattlesnake, he could strike when you least expected it.

"The...uh...piles of books in your bedroom."

"And what business did you have in my bedroom?" Lazy and dangerous.

"I was just...exploring. Curious."

His eyes were narrowed in the dimly lit barn. "Did you call Edie and tell her where you were?"

"She didn't sound the least surprised. The battery was low and it ran out before I could give her hell."

"Why would you give her hell? Not that I can imagine anyone getting away with giving a tough old bird like Edie a hard time."

"She set me up."

"Why would she do that?"

She was too tired to watch her tongue. Besides, being circumspect had never been one of her particular gifts, and honesty might at least clear the air between her and Sam. Might make it a little easier to get along with him.

"She probably figured you were exactly what I needed," she said bitterly.

He didn't move. "She knows me better than that." He sounded faintly bitter, and she couldn't figure out why.

She shrugged. "Well, if she's not matchmaking, maybe she wanted to throw us together so I'd get an idea of what I should look for in a man."

"Is it working?"

"I'm learning what to avoid."

He laughed then, a soft sound that both enchanted and annoyed her. "Maybe I'm good for something, then." He rose, tall and straight and sexy as all hell. "It's cold here. You'd better come inside and get some rest."

She stretched, without thinking what she was doing, then realized he was still watching her with that unreadable expression on his face. There was an odd, breathless air of sexuality lying between them, as she lay on the bed of straw and he towered over her.

She scrambled to her feet, too fast. She stumbled, and he caught her, his hands strong, holding her inches away from his chest. "You do that on purpose, Kelly?" he drawled.

She was having trouble catching her breath. "No."

"Seems a little convenient if you ask me," he said. "Maybe Aunt Edie isn't the one who was matchmaking. Maybe you decided to go for a little walk on the wild side since your rich doctor boyfriend dumped you."

"You have a way with words, Sam." Kelly managed to find some dignity. "But I think I'll forgo the honor."

"That's probably a good idea." His face was cool, distant, but his long fingers were slowly caressing her upper arms, kneading them. "Then again, I've never kissed a woman from Massachusetts."

She could feel a slow burning in the pit of her stomach. "You aren't about to start now."

"You don't think so?"

She didn't even resist as he brought her body the last few inches, up against him. It was a strange sensation—she'd never been plastered against such solid strength.

He slid one hand behind her neck, beneath her tangled mop of hair, and she just stood there, feeling him against her, waiting. Feeling like a doomed martyr facing the lions. Feeling like a cat in heat.

His kiss was nothing like those of her previous boyfriends. Neil had been partial to wet, slobbery kisses, Richard was dry-mouthed and tight. She'd expect Sam to use his strength, to force a grinding, punishing kiss on her to prove his mastery.

He didn't. He brushed his lips against hers, gently, teasing them, and for a moment that was all she expected. Then he brought his mouth back, tasting her lightly. His teeth captured her lower lip, oh so gently, and she felt herself soften, all over, her mouth, her legs, her arms... her brain.

Somehow her arms had gotten around his waist, and she was holding on to him, melting against him as he deepened the kiss, slowly, using his tongue. Some distant part of her brain told her he was very good at kissing. She'd never considered it a particular art before, but Samuel Watson was an artist. And this particular kiss was a masterpiece.

When he finally lifted his head to look down at her she realized she'd forgotten to breathe. At least, that must be the reason why she felt like passing out. His mouth was damp, and so was hers, and yet it was nothing like the wet, messy kisses her first boyfriend had given her.

His eyes were narrow, intent, as he looked down at her. She was still holding on to him, afraid she might sink into the straw if she didn't have something to cling to, afraid of what might happen if she did. Afraid he'd follow her down into that sweet-smelling bedding and do exactly what she wanted him to do. And was frightened of him doing.

He let his thumb trace the side of her dazed face in an absent caress. "You know," he mused in a soft voice, "when I was a kid all the girls in school used to watch me, and I knew why. They'd flirt with me, and giggle, and then run away. But they wouldn't go out with me. Not until they were safely married to some white-bread businessman and then they could have their fun with the half-breed bad boy without having to lower their standard of living. I slept with a few of them before I realized what was going on, and then, because it felt so damned good, I slept with a half-dozen more.

"But then I decided I didn't want to be someone's sexual fantasy. And I decided to stay away from blond-haired, blue-eyed white women looking for a fling."

"My hair isn't blond," she said, still dizzy from his kiss.

"Close enough. But you know, Kelly Malone, you tempt me more than anyone I've met in a long time. And I'm thinking that maybe I'll just take you upstairs to my bed and give you the ride of your life."

He slid his hand between her legs, a shockingly crude, blatant caress that was so instantly arousing she yanked herself away from him and slapped him.

Or she tried to. He caught her wrist before she could connect. "Then again," he murmured, "maybe not."

He released her, and she was half-tempted to try again. But she wasn't a woman who hit people, no matter how much they deserved it. And she was afraid to touch him.

She knew her face was flaming, but there was nothing she could do about it. "Yeah," she said. "Maybe not." And she stalked from the barn without a backward glance.

He sat back down with a weary sigh, running his hand through his long hair. The white wolf was staring at him, Blanche was looking reproachful, and Sam felt like the worst piece of crap in the world.

"Think I was too hard on her?" he asked the wolf.

Pete just looked at him, making him feel worse.

"Well, it was for her sake as well as mine. I figured out long ago that women like her weren't for the likes of me, and just because she's out here, invading my house, my kitchen, my damned dreams, doesn't mean I'm going to change my mind.

"Yeah, I know, it's not her fault. It's Edie Malone's fault. She knew this could happen, probably wanted it to happen. Kelly's right about that. Edie's always had a soft spot for that particular niece, and she's always had a soft spot for me. I would have thought she'd be smart enough to realize that throwing the two of us together would only cause trouble, but then, Edie's never been one to shy away from trouble. Particularly if it's in a good cause.

"But she's got to be crazy if she thinks there's any future for that upper-crust amazon and me. I need a real woman. Someone who's not afraid to work, not afraid to get her hands dirty."

Blanche lifted her head, looked at him and snorted.

"Okay, well maybe that's a little too harsh," Sam conceded. "I guess I'm talking about her background, not who she is. But I don't want to know who she is. I don't want her anywhere around here. She's distracting me, and I've got too damned much going on right now. I want her to go back to the East Coast and find some other rich doctor to marry and leave me the hell alone!"

The white wolf rose, stalking toward him. When he got within reach he pushed at Sam with his long nose.

Sam grinned reluctantly. "I know what you're trying to tell me, boy. You're saying, *smarten up*. I can do that. You do me a favor. Tell Blanche to have her damned calf. Then we can move the three of you somewhere safe.

"In the meantime, I guess I can resist Kelly Malone's siren allure." He chuckled to himself. "Hell, I've never had a problem resisting women before. There's no reason why she should be any different."

The two animals just looked at him, as if to say, wanna bet? But Sam had had enough.

"There's bad things and good things about talking out your life problems with animals," Sam said, rising. "On the one hand, they can't talk back.

"On the other hand, you never know whether you're trying to convince them, or yourself." He ran a hand over Pete's big head, then leaned over and rubbed Blanche. "I know you guys like her," he said in a softer voice. "But you aren't going to be here. And neither is she."

He walked back across the yard to the old ranch house. The kerosene lamps sent a bright, warm glow over the frosty night. He looked up and saw a light in Kelly's room. He'd left some clean clothes for her and a spare toothbrush, and he wondered if she'd changed. If right now one of his old T-shirts was pressing against those breasts that had pressed against him.

"Hell and damnation," he said out loud, trying to banish the thought from his mind. She wasn't his type. His mind was fully aware of it, even if his body was trying to play tricks on him.

He wasn't quite sure if he still had a heart. He had a gloomy suspicion that he did, despite all his best efforts. And he was scared half to death that his heart was siding with his body, not his brain.

Two days before the New Year. Blanche would have her calf on New Year's Eve, he knew it as surely as if he had a say in the matter. And then things would be settled, one way or another.

He wished to hell he could get rid of Kelly before then, but he knew it was a lost cause. Besides, if Blanche had any trouble it would be just as well if an expert was around.

Pete probably wouldn't let her leave. The thought came to him, out of the blue. If Pete hadn't made that sudden scene, grabbing on to her jacket with his huge jaws, she would have been out of there before Ramos got back.

And he was spending too damned much time thinking a couple of animals had more brains than he did.

The night was clear and cold. It was near midnight—when he'd first realized Kelly was nowhere around he'd panicked, thinking she might have been stubborn enough and foolish enough to try to walk out of there.

Instead, she'd been lying curled up next to the two animals, her pale face flushed, her hair a tangle, her long, lush body looking impossibly sexy in her baggy jeans.

And he'd wanted to take her in his arms and roll with her on the straw-covered floor. He'd wanted to strip off her clothes and kiss every inch of that gorgeous body of hers. He'd wanted to kiss her mouth until she kissed him back.

That was as far as he'd gotten. The kiss, and the feel of her arms as they went around his waist, holding on to him as if she needed him. She wasn't a woman to play tricks, he granted her that much. She wasn't out for a literal roll in the hay with an Indian stud before she went back to her safe life. He knew that much about her.

But she didn't belong out here, even if she looked like she did. Even if some stupid, irrational part of him wanted her to.

It was getting colder, and he was being a fool, standing out there in the yard, staring up at the house. She was walking around the room now—he could tell by the movement of the shadows. And he wondered whether she'd come to the window and change her clothes. For that he'd be willing to freeze his butt off awhile longer.

But then the light went out, the room was dark, and he knew that was one particular temptation that fate had chosen to spare him. Instead, he'd have the dubious joy of his own imagination, picturing what she looked like.

Hell, he didn't have to see. He knew she had soft, smooth white skin. Wide hips, full thighs, a small waist and breasts that would be pale in the moonlight.

From somewhere in the distance he could hear a coyote baying at the moon. And it was all he could not to add his own mournful voice to the call.

By the time she came down the next morning the kitchen was deserted. The sludgelike remains of coffee in the bottom of the pot were undrinkable, so she threw it out and made fresh, scrubbing a couple of centuries of coffee oils off the coffeepot while she was at it.

They'd had the pie for breakfast, she noticed, amused at this small sign that men were men the world over. They'd left her a piece, which was a good thing, considering there wasn't much else to eat in the place except spaghetti and jars of sauce. She piled the dirty dishes on the counter, which was as far as she intended to go, and then sat down with a mug of fresh coffee and the remnants of the pie. She breathed a silent sigh of relief when it turned out to be Ramos's footsteps in the hallway and not Sam Watson's.

"You're up early," he said cheerfully, helping himself to the coffee.

"Later than you."

"Ah, but you didn't have cattle to feed." He took a deep, appreciative swallow. "I love Sam like a son, but the boy never did learn to make decent coffee."

"How's Blanche?"

"The buffalo? She's just fine. She and that wolf are cozy as two peas in a pod. No sign of her getting ready to pop, though, which'll piss Sam off. He was sure she was going to give birth on New Year's Eve."

"I'd forgotten it's New Year's Eve."

"It sure is. Of course, Sam's got other things driving him crazy apart from that buffalo. But I don't expect you know anything about that." He chuckled to himself.

"Why should I?"

"Can't say. I just know I've seen that boy in every state of mind imaginable, known him for most of his life, and I ain't never seen him in such a condition."

"He's worried about Blanche."

Ramos's ancient grin was knowing. "There's that," he agreed. "But something else is driving him crazy, and I think it might have something to do with you."

"He finds me inconvenient and annoying."

Ramos snorted. "He finds me inconvenient and annoying, and I still don't see him looking at me the way he looks at you. Good thing, too. Leonora is a jealous woman." He wheezed in amusement.

"He doesn't look at me any particular way." She denied it, but she could still feel the way his eyes burned through her clothing, the endless, breathless kisses, the shocking arousal of his hand between her legs.

"If you say so. Any more of that pie left?" he asked mournfully.

"Nope."

Ramos sighed. "Back to spaghetti again. I'll be glad when this is all over and we can eat Leonora's cooking again."

"And when will it be over?"

"When the calf is born. When they find out if it's white or not. If it isn't, no one will care and they'll leave us alone. If it is, we'll have a lot to deal with."

"Why? And why do people think she's going to be white?"

"Why do you think it's going to be a girl?"

Kelly shrugged. "Instinct."

Ramos nodded. "There's a lot of that going around. You ask Sam about it. He'll tell you."

His voice came from directly behind her.

"Ask Sam what?"

Chapter Five

"Hi, boss," Ramos said cheerfully. "Have a decent cup of coffee for a change. You could take lessons from Kelly here. Her coffee's as good as her pie."

"I've got more important things to worry about," he growled, refusing to look at her. He poured himself a mug of coffee, anyway. "We've got trouble. Someone cut the fence over on the northeast side. I think the Gonyaw boys have gotten tired of waiting."

Ramos's reaction was immediate and profane. Since it was in Spanish, Kelly couldn't understand it, but she could imagine what he said.

"Exactly," Sam said grimly. "We've got about twenty head of our best cattle wandering over on the Gonyaws' spread, and if we don't do something about it, fast, those cattle are gonna disappear. I can't afford to let that happen."

"So we go after them."

"Leaving Blanche alone and unprotected," he added.

"Do we have a choice?" Ramos countered. "And what about Kelly?"

"Your lack of concern for my well-being is truly touching," she said to Sam. "But at least I can look out for Blanche."

"No, you can't. You're getting out of here now," Sam said.

"I thought I was trapped here?"

"The Gonyaws will either be too busy waiting for us on the northeast border, or trying to get in here across their land. They won't be watching the main gate. You can get back to town and see if Edie's made any progress with that pet lawyer of hers."

"Don't you think she'd let you know?" Kelly protested.

"How? No phone, no truck, and, anyway, she's in no shape to drive."

"I don't think I should leave," she said stubbornly.

"I don't give a damn what you think. I want you out of here, out of harm's way."

"Who's going to look after Blanche?"

"Pete will."

"They'll shoot him!"

"Probably." Sam drained his coffee and slammed the mug down on the counter. "But I can't see you holding the Gonyaw boys at bay with a shotgun. The best place for you is someplace where I don't have to worry about you."

The thought of Samuel Watson worrying about her was both unlikely and emotionally disturbing. The thought of leaving the ranch, leaving Blanche and the wolf without any kind of protection, was even more disturbing. As for the thought of leaving Sam—she wouldn't even allow herself to consider her reaction.

He tossed her keys on the table, the plastic cactus glistening brightly in the late-morning sun. "Get out of here, Kelly," he said. "Now."

"I wish you'd make up your mind," she muttered, rising before she could think better of it. "First you tell me I'm trapped here, then you tell me to get the hell out. Don't worry, I don't stay where I'm not wanted."

She grabbed the keys and was halfway to the door when she heard his muttered comment. "I want you."

She whirled around to stare at him in shock, but he had his back to her, on purpose, as he poured himself another mug of coffee. She looked at Ramos, but the old man seemed oblivious, and she realized most of her conversation with him had been carried on at a half shout. He was half-deaf, and if Samuel had said anything so shocking, he certainly hadn't heard it.

But Kelly wasn't going to let it pass. "What did you say?"

He still didn't look at her as he spooned sugar into the mug with the concentration of a doctor performing brain surgery. He'd never had sugar in his coffee before. "Nothing."

"You said . . ."

"I said I want you to get the hell out of here," he growled, glaring at her.

He meant it, all right. She just wasn't entirely certain why he wanted her gone. At that point there was nothing she could do about it. He had other things to worry about.

She plastered a bright, phony smile on her face. "Well, I won't say this has been a treat, because it hasn't. Since I'm flying out of here tomorrow afternoon I don't suppose I'll see you again. Maybe Aunt Edie could let me know how Blanche makes out. Whether she really gives birth to a white calf."

"Sure," Sam muttered, turning away again. "Have a nice trip."

My, my, she did want to hurt him. But he was the one who was adept at hurting, whether he knew he was doing it or not. "Bye, Ramos," she said, tossing the keys in her hand. "It was nice to meet you."

"See you soon, Kelly," Ramos replied, a faint twinkle in his eye.

Not if Sam can help it, she thought.

He didn't say a word when she left, letting the door slam behind her. She half hoped the wolf would come out to stop her again, but Sam must have thought of that. The barn door was tightly closed, and beyond it she could hear a faint, angry whine.

It took five tries before the elderly engine in the old pickup decided to turn over. She tore out of the yard with a satisfying spurt of dust, but there was no sign of a tall figure in the doorway, watching her leave. He'd already forgotten about her.

She almost made it as far as the gate before the truck died on her with a loud, horrifying clunk that sounded permanent. She'd never heard an engine seize up before, but there was a first time for everything, and she suspected this was just one of too many new experiences.

She kicked the truck. She tried praying. She tried crying. And then she pulled her canvas jacket tightly around her and set off back down the track to the ranch house, cursing under her breath.

It was late afternoon on the last night of the year by the time she made it back to the ranch, and the place was deserted. The barn door was still shut tightly, but not locked, and she could hear Pete's soft bark of greeting as she opened the door.

The two animals were fine. The afternoon sun slanted in through the old boards, sending a halo of light around Blanche's huge, shaggy head. The effect was eerily serene, like a medieval nativity scene, with a huge buffalo in the place of a Madonna.

If Blanche was going to give birth before midnight she didn't show any signs of it. She allowed Kelly to touch her swollen belly, and beneath her hand she could feel the same gentle movements she'd felt before.

"I guess you're not in any particular hurry, my lady," Kelly murmured. "And if Sam's wrong about that, he's probably wrong about everything else. At least I hope so. If you're carrying a white calf it sounds like a huge mess of trouble. Better for everyone if it's just plain brown."

Blanche didn't contradict her. She simply looked at Kelly with those soulful eyes of hers, as if to say it wasn't up to her.

Kelly's feet were killing her from the long hike back to the house, and she was half tempted to curl up beside Blanche and stay there. For some reason she always felt strangely peaceful when she was around the wolf and the buffalo.

Still, it wouldn't be very wise to underestimate the danger of the Gonyaws. Samuel Watson wasn't the kind of man to overreact to a situation, unless it involved her.

There must be some kind of weapon in the house. Something she could use to keep any wandering bad guy at bay. The very notion still seemed like something out of a John Wayne western, and she couldn't quite see herself as the staunch little prairie woman, holding off marauders.

But she also couldn't see herself standing by and doing nothing while someone decided it might be fun to kill a buffalo and a white wolf.

"You watch over Blanche," she told Pete, rubbing a hand through his thick fur. "I'll go see if I can find something to eat, and maybe a machine gun while I'm at it."

Pete rose with his usual majestic grace, trotting along beside her as she headed for the barn door. When she got there he stopped, making a low, distressed whining noise, and she knew without words that he was considering clamping on to her jacket once more.

"You need to stay, Pete," she said firmly. "And I need to go." She whipped outside the door before he could stop her, closing it behind her. She could hear his scrabbling at the door in sudden desperation, followed by a long, mournful howl that sounded eerily like a warning.

"Hush, Pete," she said urgently. "I told you, I'll be right back."

She didn't waste any time back in the deserted ranch house. Grabbing a couple of blankets from her unmade bed, she headed into Sam's room, hoping there'd be some sort of weapon she could use to defend herself, bizarre as that notion seemed. The huge bed was torn apart, as if he'd tossed and turned all night, and the books were scattered on the floor beside it, as if he'd tried to read and been unable to concentrate.

He must have been more concerned about Blanche than he let on. That, or something else had been driving him crazy.

She knew the feeling. Looking at that big, rumpled, unmade bed, she suddenly had the strong, almost desperate need to lie in that bed. With him.

It was absurd, of course. Crazy, when he seemed to view her as an annoyance and she considered him a sullen throwback. She couldn't imagine anyone further removed from her safe, productive life in the Boston clinic.

Unless it was herself. She didn't belong there, and she knew it. She didn't belong here, either, despite the totally illogical sense that she did. She was too young to be going through a midlife crisis, and yet she felt adrift, with no home, no place to belong. It must be that strange sense of alienation that made her long for this beaten-down little ranch in the back of beyond.

Besides, Sam didn't want her. He didn't need anyone, he'd made that abundantly clear.

Except for that whisper, when she'd left. "I want you," he'd said, she was sure of it. Or was it just wishful thinking?

She had to get out of his bedroom, out of his house, before she started believing she belonged there. She headed downstairs, planning to find something remotely edible. She was starving, and she didn't fancy spending the next few hours curled up next to Blanche with a growling stomach. Particularly since it was always possible that Blanche would suddenly get in the mood to deliver her calf.

She was in the kitchen, staring pensively into the refrigerator, when she heard him come in. She froze, every instinct working overtime. "Did you stop the Gonyaws?" she asked, not allowing herself to turn around.

"Not 'zactly."

She whirled around in sudden panic. He was surprisingly young, with long, greasy blond hair and a stubble of pale blond beard. His eyes were slightly bloodshot, his clothes and his entire body could have used a generous helping of soap, and his mouth was unpleasant. But he didn't seem to be carrying a weapon.

She'd had years of training. She pulled herself upright, smoothing her rumpled hair and bestowing a glacial smile on the kid. "I don't believe we've met," she said calmly. "I'm Kelly Malone. And you're...?"

"You can bet your ass we haven't met," he said, moving into the room with a faint swagger. He smelled of beer as well as unwashed clothes. "I woulda remembered. I'm Tommy Lee Gonyaw. You probably heard about me and my brothers."

"Not much that was complimentary." She kept her voice particularly calm. He didn't seem all that dangerous, unless you looked into those bleak, soulless eyes.

"There're nine of us. I'm the baby in the bunch, though most people say I'm the most dangerous." He grinned, and Kelly was not reassured. "You must be Edie Malone's niece. I didn't know you were screwing old Sam. I guess you eastern women don't have no sense when it comes to injuns."

"Injuns?" Kelly echoed, her outrage coming out in amused horror. "I don't know what you're talking about."

"Samuel One-Horse Watson. I tell you, these guys are a pain in the butt when they start getting into their roots. Most of 'em just decide to be an Indian because they want a piece of the gambling action. Not to mention cheap cigarettes."

"Sam doesn't smoke," she said stiffly.

"Doesn't gamble, either. He's an all-around saint, that boy is. 'Cept when it comes to the ladies. He oughtta know he needs to stay away from white women.''

Kelly just looked at him. ''You're an idiot, aren't you?'' she said with some asperity.

It was, perhaps, not the wisest choice of words. She'd already noticed he had mean eyes. Those eyes narrowed, until they looked downright dangerous.

''I'm thinkin' you need a lesson,'' he said, half to himself. ''You need to learn a little bit about respect. And I bet it wouldn't do you no harm to find out what a real man is like.'' He started toward her. The late-afternoon sun slanted through the kitchen window, and Kelly held herself very still. She was no wraith, and she was strong enough, but compared to the hulking brute who was stalking toward her, she was thoroughly outmatched.

She wasn't that far from the hallway. She'd noticed another door at the end of it, seldom used, and with her luck it would be locked. She wouldn't know until she tried.

She started to back away from him, trying to look casual about the process. ''Look,'' she said in the same placating voice she used with some of the overwrought boyfriends and husbands of her pregnant patients. ''You don't want to hurt me and you know it.''

''I ain't talking about hurtin', ma'am. I'm talking about screwing.'' He was already unfastening his thick leather belt. "'Course, I came over here to kill that damned buffalo, but I figure she can wait. My stupid brothers ain't doing a damned thing about this here situation, so I figured I'd take care of it myself."

"What are you talking about?" she said, making it into the living room. He still followed.

"Who woulda thought my brothers would turn out to be wusses?" Tommy Lee demanded of the world in general. "No way I'm gonna pay attention to some court order, even if they do. That damned sheriff oughtta be ashamed taking Watson's side over ours."

"And what is your side? You want to kill a buffalo and you think you have the right?"

"Hell, we got as much right as Sam does. He thinks he's so damned hot, messing with our women, making his own rules. Those animals don't belong to him, they're fair game, and I intend to bag 'em myself. Not a hell of a lot anyone can do if they're already dead."

"He can put you in jail for violating a court order," she said, eyeing him warily. He was pulling his belt loose from his grubby jeans and she had the unpleasant notion that the court order wasn't the only thing he was planning on violating.

"Hell, we Gonyaws got enough power around here to keep from going to jail." He began unfastening his shirt. "Hold still. I'm not gonna like it if I have to chase you."

"You're not going to like it if I have to hurt you," she said, standing her ground, suddenly very calm.

He hooted with laughter. "Lady, you're a ripe handful of woman, but you ain't no match for me. Don't you know what they say—if there ain't nothing you can do about it you might as well lie back and enjoy it. My girlfriends do."

"You rape your girlfriends?" she said sharply.

"Let's just say I convince 'em."

He unsnapped his jeans, and at the same moment Kelly's temper snapped. "Take one more step toward me," she said, "and you'll wish you hadn't."

He made the mistake of laughing. He made the even greater mistake of lunging for her.

She flattened him in two seconds.

He lay on the floor, clutching himself, groaning, as he stared up at her in shock and fury. "Bitch!" he managed to choke out.

"I work in a very bad neighborhood, and some people occasionally mistake us for an abortion clinic," she said. "I learned to be prepared."

Not prepared enough. He surged to his feet with a bellow, and her reaction was pure instinct. She reached for the nearest thing and brought it crashing down on the top of his head.

This time when he went down he stayed down, and the ugly, cactus-shaped lamp lay in shards around him.

She knelt down beside him and checked the pulse at the side of his neck. Steady and strong. She checked his eyes beneath the closed lids. Pupils the same size. She could only pray they'd stay that way.

He was strong as a bull, and he lay there breathing heavily, almost snoring. She'd just knocked him out, nothing more, she told herself. He'd wake up in a bit with one hell of a headache, but by that time she'd have him tied up.

She noticed her hands were shaking when she went into the darkened kitchen. She couldn't seem to get the match to light, and in the gathering gloom she wouldn't be able to find any rope to keep Tommy Lee Gonyaw from settling the now-major score.

She heard the truck roar into the yard and slam to a stop in front of the ranch house. She barely had time to fumble in a drawer for some kind of weapon when the door flew open and a tall figure stood there, silhouetted against the dusk.

"What the hell are you doing here?" Sam demanded with his customary warmth. "And what have you got in your hand?"

She looked down at the dull paring knife she was clutching like a lifeline. It wouldn't make much of a dent in anyone's hide, and she had no good reason to stab Sam. Even if she wanted to.

She let if fall from her nerveless fingers with a clatter as Sam lit the kerosene lamp, then paused to stare at her more closely. "What are you doing here?" he asked in a softer voice, and the menace was gone. "Are you okay?"

"The t-truck broke down." At least, that's what she tried to say. For some reason she was stuttering. "It was c-closer coming back here than walking to the highway." It took her minutes to get the words out, and he watched her, still and silent. "The animals are all right—he didn't touch them."

Sam froze. "Who?"

"He s-s-s-said his n-n-n-name was Tommy Lee G-Gonyaw."

"Where is he?"   The rage was pure and implacable, and for the first time Kelly was glad she'd been the one to flatten the intruder. If she'd ended up killing him, at least it would have been by accident. Sam was looking as if murder was a very good notion indeed.

"In the l-living room," she stammered.

She watched him go, clutching tight to the kitchen counter, afraid that if she let go she'd collapse.

Wimp, she called herself, but it didn't help. There was no way she could go back into the room and stare at her victim, no matter how much he'd deserved it.

Sam stalked back through the kitchen to the door. "Ramos!" he called. "Get your butt in here and bring some rope. We got some garbage to get rid of."

Ramos appeared a moment later, and Kelly turned, plastering a smile on her face. Ramos stared at her curiously, but at some sign from Sam he kept his distance.

"What's up, boss? Whose pickup is that outside?"

"It belongs to the youngest Gonyaw kid. Apparently he didn't like the fact that his older brothers decided they didn't want to risk their ranch just for the pleasure of killing a couple of wild animals, and he came here to kill them himself."

"They're all right. I just checked on them."

"Kelly took care of him."

Ramos grinned at her. "You kill him?"

"Shut up, Ramos," Sam growled. "We'll tie him up and you can take him back to his brothers. Then you better head on into town and call Leonora. Tell her she can come back home now. It's all over. Wish her a happy New Year for me."

"I'll tell her, boss," Ramos said. "You gonna be okay out here? Want me to give Kelly a ride into town while I'm at it?"

Sam didn't even look at her. "I don't think she's up to riding in a pickup with Tommy Lee Gonyaw. I'll take care of her."

It was a nice thought. She'd been so busy taking care of everyone else that no one had had the chance to take care of her when she needed it. She needed it very badly right now, but she doubted Sam knew it. She watched, still clutching the kitchen counter, as he and Ramos trundled Tommy Lee's unconscious body outside. The muscles in her arms were cramping, but she couldn't let go.

She should make herself move. A comatose Gonyaw was safer than an alert Samuel Watson, and if she had any sense she'd let go of the counter and get in that damned truck.

She couldn't move. She heard Ramos drive away, and still she stood, knees locked, fingers clutching the wood.

The oil lamp sent out a pool of light, and when Sam stepped back into it he shut the door behind him. Locking it. He was huge in the darkness, and there was no way she could see his face in the shadows as she watched him strip off his shearling jacket and gloves.

He came right up to her, pried her hands off the counter and pulled her against him, holding her tight, letting her absorb some of his heat and strength. She realized then she was trembling, shaking all over with delayed reaction, and the feel of his body against hers was leaching it away, draining it from her, leaving her limp against him.

He put his hand behind her neck, tilting her face up to his. "I'm taking you to bed," he said.

"I'm n-n-not tired." The stammer hadn't gone completely yet, and stray tremors racked her body.

A faint smile curved his usually grim mouth. "I'm taking you to my bed," he said. "Unless you have some objections."

She thought of that wide, rumpled bed upstairs. She thought of his strong, warm body wrapped around hers. "No objections," she said.

And he kissed her.

Chapter Six

She was no featherweight, but Sam was used to hauling things around. Kelly weighed less than a newborn calf, and she helped matters by putting her arms around his neck when he scooped her up. He wasn't particularly interested in succumbing to the romantic gesture of carrying her up to his bed, but she was still shaking so hard he was afraid she wouldn't be able to make it on her own. And he needed her there, quite badly.

He'd known something was wrong when he and Ramos had started back to the ranch. His instincts were working overtime, but he'd told himself that Kelly was safely out of there, back with Edie. There was no way she could get into trouble.

He should have known better. Kelly Malone had been put on this earth to drive him crazy, and no amount of common sense could convince him his troubles were over. He'd taken one look at her through the window of Edie's battered old pickup two days ago and known he was doomed.

She wasn't his type, he told himself as he knocked her knee against the wall as he carried her upstairs. He liked his women petite and dark—he wasn't interested in a Junior League Valkyrie from Boston. Except that she wasn't some overbred socialite, much as he wanted to convince himself she was. She had the same blood in her veins as Edie Malone, and if Edie were forty years younger he would have been sorely tempted.

He'd been tempted by Kelly Malone since she'd first set foot on his land. He'd been tempted by her when she was fourteen years old and too young to realize what kind of thoughts she was rousing in his mind.

He'd had a long, hard day, and he was about to give in to that temptation. And to hell with the consequences.

She'd looked like holy hell when he'd first walked into the kitchen, and he hadn't known what to think. She was in some kind of shock, but it didn't look as if Tommy Lee had gotten around to putting his hands on her. Lucky for him, or Ramos would have been taking pieces back to his brothers.

He set her down on the floor by his bed, lit the oil lamp on the table, then looked down at her. She didn't look all that much better. She was pale, but the shaking that had racked her body had finally left. "You did a pretty good job on old Tommy Lee there," he said, half-surprised at how gentle his voice sounded.

She shuddered, keeping her face down. "I warned him," she said in a muffled voice. "They made sure everyone who worked in the clinic knew how to protect themselves. I was one of Master Dee's best students."

"But that's the first time you ever had to use it," he said. She nodded, still not meeting his gaze.

He looked down at her, at the bowed shoulders, the mop of tangled hair, and he knew it was too late. He'd never thought he could be vulnerable to a woman, particularly a woman like Kelly Malone. But it was too late. He'd already lost his heart.

He knew he was taking a step there'd be no retreating from. He threaded his fingers through her hair and tilted her face up to his. "Do you want to go to bed with me?" he asked her, deliberately blunt.

She eyed him warily, as if expecting rejection. "Yes."

He wasn't going to ask her for anything more. Tomorrow she would leave, go back to her wealthy family and her big city and forget about him, and he'd start to forget about her. If he could just count on Edie to keep her mouth shut.

He'd been hearing about Kelly this and Kelly that for the last ten years. He'd heard about the jerk who was going to marry her and then dumped her, he'd heard about the way her family treated her, alternately ignoring her and then trying to "improve" her.

And he would look at the photographs Edie kept scattered around the place, and he'd remember the long-legged, shy eastern girl who'd watched him.

She was looking up at him now, that eastern girl, with an expression of trepidation and longing on her pale face. She had freckles across her nose. He'd never realized that before. All his life he'd been a sucker for women with freckles.

She was wearing his clothes. Odd, it felt different to pull his moth-eaten sweater over her head instead of his, different to unfasten the pearl buttons on the faded flannel shirt. She stood utterly still as he stripped the clothes from her, neither helping nor hindering him as he pulled the T-shirt over her head, unfastened her jeans and shoved them down her hips. She had luscious hips, ripe and full. She smelled of the soap he kept in his shower, but somehow it had never smelled that good on him.

She'd leave him, and there was nothing he could do to make it different. Except make sure that this New Year's Eve was a night she would never forget.

She wore plain cotton underwear—a serviceable bra and panties that weren't supposed to be enticing. He was quickly discovering the amazingly erotic effect of white cotton, and she was watching him as if he were a cross between the white wolf and the buffalo. Half tamed, half dangerous.

He took a step back from her, taking a deep breath as he unsnapped his old denim shirt. She was the one who was dangerous, and she didn't even realize it. She was the one who could destroy him, destroy the tentative serenity he'd built up for himself.

He threw the shirt onto the growing pile of clothes on the floor, reaching for the snap of his jeans when he halted, a last ounce of common sense breaking through. At least she couldn't see the torment that was going through his head right now, fighting against the raging need of his body.

"Are you afraid of me?" she asked, and the simple truth of her question knocked him sideways.

He curled his mouth into a mocking grin, one he'd perfected long ago. "Why do you ask that?"

"Because I'm afraid of you," she said. She was less than a foot away, but she moved closer, putting her hand on his bare chest. She had strong hands, beautiful hands.

"I'm not Tommy Lee Gonyaw," he said. "I'm not going to hurt you. I told you you could leave if you have any objections."

"I'm not talking about that kind of hurt," she said, and her other hand came up to his chest as well. Her eyes were a wondrous brown color, and he could see himself in the reflection. "For some reason I'll never understand, I'm in love with you. It's probably just nostalgia—there's no logical reason I should care about you. But logic doesn't seem to enter into it. Any more than logic has anything to do with those two animals out in the barn. It's a lot easier to go to bed with someone you don't really care about."

"You make a habit of that, do you?" he drawled. If she'd slept with more than a couple of men in her life he'd be surprised—she still had an oddly unawakened sense about her.

She managed a wry smile. "That's the way it seems, looking back. I didn't even begin to feel for them what I feel for you."

"So what is this tender declaration of love all about?" He was trying to sound cynical, but he wasn't quite sure if it was working. "Were you expecting me to go down on one knee and propose?"

She shook her head. "No. I just thought..."

"Thought what?"

She said it all in a rush. "They told me you were afraid of caring about me."

"Who did?" he said blankly. Though he already knew the answer.

"The animals. Blanche and Pete. It's ridiculous, I know."

"Not as ridiculous as it seems," he muttered. "Listen, do you want to go to bed with me, or do you want to hash this out?"

She glanced over at the clock. It was after nine on New Year's Eve, and a light snow was falling. It was supposed to clear around midnight, but she wasn't going to count on it.

"How long do you think it will take?" she asked politely. Standing there in her underwear, her hands on his bare chest.

For a moment he just stared at her in disbelief. "Well, it can take as long or as short as you want. If you're in a hurry to get back to Edie's so you don't miss your plane..."

She moved closer, putting her hand over his mouth and silencing him, her nearly nude body pressed up against his. She was a tall woman, and her hips were up against the open front of his jeans, and he knew damned well there was no way he could convince her he wasn't interested.

"Don't be silly," she said. "I just want to make sure we can get out to the barn by midnight."

"Why?"

"Blanche is going to have her calf tonight."

"Listen, I've been around a lot of cattle being born, and let me tell you, Blanche is showing no signs at all of going into labor."

"No, she isn't, is she?" Kelly said calmly. "But she's going to have her white calf at midnight, and I think we're supposed to be out there."

"I'll humor you," he said dryly.

"You could do more than that," she said. And pressed her mouth up against his.

She tasted of toothpaste and coffee. She tasted of love and dreams he'd forgotten dreaming. He didn't even think, he deepened the kiss, opening his mouth to hers, and her fingers clutched his shoulders as a tremor danced over her skin and her hips rubbed up against his.

At this rate they were going to be done well ahead of midnight.

She pulled away from him, and he let her go, watching silently as she climbed up into his big bed and lay back against the pillows, her hair spread out around her. She belonged there. He knew it, and she knew it, whether or not it made any kind of sense at all. That bed had been in the family for generations: his father had been born in it, and his grandfather, too. She would lie in that bed and take his seed, and sooner or later his son would be born in that very bed. And his grandsons, as well.

The room was shadowed, but benevolently so. He yanked off the rest of his clothes and lay down beside her on the bed, pulling her into his arms. She went willingly enough, threading her arms around his neck, burying her face in his long hair as he finished stripping off her underwear, so that they were both naked on the rumpled white sheets, his darker body pressing against hers. She was frightened, she said. He was, too. Frightened of loving her. Knowing it was too late.

He kissed her mouth and her eyelids, the side of her neck and the base of her throat. Her breasts were full and rosy-tipped, and he tasted them as well, swirling his tongue around the taut nipples, sucking them as his child would, one day.

He bit her stomach, lightly, as his hands covered her breasts, kneading them. And then he put his mouth between her legs, shocking her.

She said something, but he wouldn't listen. She tried to push him away, but he ignored her, cradling her hips in his hands, holding her still as he loved her with his mouth. She was no longer fighting him, and the muffled sounds of protest sounded more and more like pleasure. Her heels were digging into the mattress, her fingers threaded through his hair, and he deliberately brought her right to the very edge of orgasm, letting the first tiny ones shimmer through her.

He pulled away, staring down at her, wiping his mouth on his shoulder. She looked dazed, lost, and she needed an anchor, a home. He slid into her, deep, hard, and she climaxed immediately, clenching around him so that it was all he could do to keep from following her over the edge.

But he wanted more. More from her, more from him. He waited until the shudders began to die down, and then he moved, pulling out almost completely, then sliding back in again.

It was better than anything he'd felt in his entire life. Her eyes were closed, her arms and legs wrapped around him as he pushed inside her, reveling in the sensations that had overtaken her. He wanted it to last forever, some crazy part of him sure that it would be the only time. He wanted to roll on his back and have her make love to him, he wanted to turn her over and take her from the back. He wanted her mouth on his body, all over it. A lifetime wouldn't be time enough to do all the things he wanted to do to her.

She was trembling again, and there were tears sliding down her cheeks from beneath her closed eyelids. He was trembling, too, and this time there was no place to hide. He put his mouth over hers, he put his hands between their bodies, touching her, and he thrust, hard and fast, in breathless succession, until she exploded, screaming against his mouth, and he came, too, filling her with his seed.

He didn't even remember climbing off her. All he knew was they were lying side by side, wrapped in each other's arms, and she was crying. He stroked her hair and smiled to himself. It was a good kind of crying, something she needed. If it were up to him they would be the only kind of tears she'd ever cry again.

Kelly didn't want to move. When she woke it was after eleven, the snow had stopped and the moon had risen onto a clear, cool New Year's Eve. She was lying on her stomach, naked, in Samuel Watson's bed. He was lying beside her, his beautiful body pressed up against her, his arm resting with casual possessiveness around her waist.

For the first time in her life it struck her that there could be a good kind of possessiveness. Not an owning, controlling kind of thing. But a sense of belonging, a mutual sense of being together. She wanted Sam's possession. She wanted to possess him, as well.

She heard the cry, and realized what had woken her from her deep, satisfied sleep. She slid out of bed as quietly as she could while Sam slept on, oblivious to the world. It took her a while to find her clothes amid the tangle at the foot of the bed, and in the end she settled for his denim shirt and no bra. She grabbed the clothing and tiptoed out, pausing to look down at him as he slept.

Would she have to leave him? Probably. He was a solitary man, distant, remote. He'd never shown any sign of caring about her, and if she was deluded enough to think he might, she'd have to face the truth soon enough. He probably couldn't wait to get her off his land.

And she'd go, if he sent her. But in the meantime, it was New Year's Eve, and there was a baby to be born.

She'd left him. Sam woke up, alone in the bed, colder than he'd ever been. He glanced over at the clock—five minutes to midnight. He wondered if Ramos had come back and given her a ride, or whether Edie had sent someone out to fetch her. It seemed unlikely, but there was no getting around the fact that she was gone.

He yanked on clean clothes, cursing beneath his breath. At least he could be thankful for one thing. He'd never told her he cared about her. Had any feelings at all about her. For all she knew, he'd taken the pleasure of a one-night stand and would be utterly delighted to see the last of her.

Utterly delighted? Where the hell had a phrase like that come from? From her. He'd been around her too damned long.

The house was deserted, but that was what he'd expected. She'd left him, like everyone else left him, sooner or later. It was his own damned fault—he drove people away. At least it meant he didn't need anyone.

Except that he needed Kelly. Needed her with his heart and soul, needed her with his body and mind. If he had any sense at all he'd check on the animals, make sure Blanche was all right, and then he'd go back to bed and forget about her. Congratulate himself on his lucky escape.

But he wasn't going to do that. The bed would smell of her, feel like her. Even if he stripped the sheets, changed the mattress, she'd haunt it.

He was going to go after her.

The door to the barn was open. The bright, full moon shone down on him as he stepped inside, and from the far end the light from a lantern illuminated Blanche's stall.

Kelly was there, kneeling in the straw, and he realized he knew she would be. She looked up at him, her eyes shining, her mouth curved in a wonderful smile. And she moved out of the way, so that he could see Blanche, curled peacefully next to a snowy white newborn calf.

"She was already born by the time I got out here," Kelly said in a hushed voice.

He knelt down in the straw next to her. "How do you know it's a she?"

"How did you know it was going to be white?" she countered simply. "The wolf's gone. He left when I came in. I don't think he's coming back."

"No," said Sam. "I don't think he is either."

Kelly managed a wry smile. "I guess you inherited the job of looking after Blanche and her baby."

"I guess I did. Pete must have figured I was up to the challenge."

"He trusts you," Kelly said.

Do you? he thought. "I wondered where you'd gone," he said. "I thought you might have headed back into town. You've got a plane to catch."

"That's tomorrow afternoon. And I'll get on that plane. If you take me to the airport and you tell me to leave."

"What if I ask you to stay?" he said. "Here, with me?"

"Then I'd marry you," she said, very calmly, "and give you a baby boy next New Year's Eve."

He didn't ask her how she knew, because he knew it as well. "I'm not used to loving someone," he warned her.

The smile on her face could have filled the whole stable with light. "That's all right," she said. "I'll help you practice."

And somewhere in the distance, a clock struck twelve. A white wolf howled at the moon in celebration.

And the New Year began.

* * * * *

Margot Dalton
LONNIE'S SECRET

Chapter One

"More lights?" Jared rummaged through a cardboard box packed with Christmas decorations. "You've already got about twelve strings of lights on that poor tree. It can hardly stand up."

Lonnie stepped back gloomily and surveyed the ragged little pine. "It looked so nice when I bought it. I thought it was the best tree on the lot. Now there's a big hole on this side."

"Every year there's a big hole on one side, and you always want to fill it up with lights."

Jared found a string of mini lights and carried it to the tree while Lonnie watched. He wore socks, jeans, a black T-shirt and a baseball cap pulled low on his head. Under the cap his hair was a mass of auburn curls, clipped short but still unruly. His body was tall and muscular, and he moved with athletic grace.

Jared had a square face, hazel eyes and, in Lonnie's opinion, the warmest, sexiest smile in all the world. He still retained a boyish air of humor and enthusiasm though he was almost a year older than Lonnie, who had just passed her thirtieth birthday.

Lonnie forced herself to stop looking at him. She took the string of lights and knelt to attach them to the dangling plug.

"How would you know what I do every year?" she asked, working busily behind the tree. "It's not like this is some kind of regular custom with us, you know."

"Sure it is. In fact, this is the third year I've helped you set up your tree."

Lonnie stood erect, frowning in surprise. "That can't be true. Three years?"

"Hey, Lon, where do you keep the little bird cages that turn around? I always like them."

"I think they're in one of those big cereal boxes." She gripped the string of lights in her hands. "I can't believe it's been three years. Stan and I were still married three years ago, weren't we?"

She connected the new string of lights and squinted at them to see how many were burned out.

"You kicked him out the day after Thanksgiving. When you found him in the upstairs bedroom with..."

"Oh, that's right." Lonnie's mouth twisted briefly. "I forgot. And a few weeks later you came over with your girlfriend and helped me put up a tree and decorate my house."

"Somebody had to. You were moping all over the place. We couldn't even get any work done at the station."

"Liar," she said calmly. "I never moped that much over Stan. In fact, I distinctly remember being kind of relieved when he left. What was that girl's name?" she added.

"What girl?"

"The one who helped you put up my Christmas tree."

"Tanya." Jared sighed and gazed into the distance. "What a fantastic body she had. And she dressed to show it off, too. She was a real head-turner, Tanya was."

Lonnie glanced down at her old jeans and baggy plaid shirt, both stained with green paint from last week's renovation of the rabbit hutch in the garage. Her blond hair was pulled carelessly into a ponytail, and she wore no makeup at all, not even lipstick.

"Why did you break up with Tanya?" she asked, searching for a package of unused bulbs. "As I recall, the woman was crazy about you. She kept coming over to the station and hanging around, hoping to get a glimpse of you."

Jared shrugged. "I couldn't talk to her."

"So what? When a girl's that gorgeous, you want to spend all your time having conversations?"

Jared glared at her over the pile of boxes. "For God's sake, Lonnie. You sound like one of the guys. Don't you know there's a whole lot more to a relationship than just sex?"

Lonnie thought about her ex-husband, whose embrace had once thrilled her so much. She and Stan never had a lot to talk about, either. In fact, she didn't even like the man very much, when all was said and done.

But, of course, she hadn't discovered that sad truth until it was much too late.

A ragged gray terrier trotted into the room, her toenails clicking briskly on the hardwood. She carried a blue plastic clown, worn and much chewed, about the size of a banana. The little dog placed her toy in a shoebox near the Christmas tree, then began to lick it with furious energy.

"Another false pregnancy?" Jared asked, watching in fascination.

Lonnie sighed and knelt to rub the dog's ears. "Poor little Puffy. I really wish she hadn't been fixed. I'd like her to have one litter of puppies just to satisfy these frustrated maternal instincts."

"Oh, great. That's all you need," Jared said with a grin. "More animals around here."

He lifted a hand and began to tick items off on his fingers.

"There's Puffy with her neurotic craving for a family. There's Harold the turtle, who only eats ribeye steak. Let me see . . . There's Shadow the tomcat, who spends all his time alienating the neighbors and stalking the sick crow that lives in the backyard, to say nothing of the two rabbits that were supposed to have found homes in the country already, and . . ."

"All right, all right," Lonnie muttered. "Here, sweetie," she added, stroking her dog and lifting the plastic clown out of the box. "Take your baby back into the kitchen."

Lonnie watched the terrier wander out of the room, trailing her surrogate puppy. Jared continued to dig through a large box.

"Are you having Christmas dinner with your parents at the ranch this year?" Lonnie asked.

"I guess so." He pulled some tissue from the bottom of the box and glanced at her. "Want to come along? They'd love to have you."

Lonnie shook her head. "I don't think so. Thanks anyway. Don't forget you promised to take the rabbits out there, Jared."

"Sure, I'll take them. But I want you to come, too." He was obviously warming to the idea. "My parents love you. Hey, you can bring your skates and we'll play some pickup hockey with the nieces and nephews. Dad says the lake's frozen solid this year.''

Wistfully, Lonnie pictured the scene he was describing. She and Jared Kilmer had been friends since childhood, when they'd attended elementary school together in West Reno. Their paths had met and diverged through the years until they took the same junior college course in television arts, then began to work at a local cable station.

Almost a decade later they were still working together, Jared as a senior photographer, Lonnie as a copywriter and set director. She'd been invited a number of times, usually as part of a group from the television station, to visit his parents' ranch in the mountains near Lake Tahoe.

Lonnie liked Seth and Betty Kilmer, as well as Jared's three married brothers and all the kids and animals out at the ranch. And the big cedar house would look so beautiful, nestled in the snow-covered pines and warmly decorated for Christmas....

''I'm busy this year,'' she said abruptly. ''In fact, I'm planning to cook Christmas dinner for a few friends.''

''Like who?''

''You know Pete, from film editing? He has no place to go for Christmas since his mother died.

And there's Mrs. Schwartz who lives in the unit next to mine, and my cousin Georgie, and Stan . . .''

"Stan?'' Jared echoed in disbelief. "You're inviting your ex-husband over for Christmas dinner, after the way he treated you?''

"Why not? He'll be all alone otherwise. Besides, I don't mind Stan so much, now that I don't have to be married to him anymore.''

Jared shook his head. "You're something else, James,'' he muttered. "I'll bet you don't even . . .'' His voice trailed off.

Lonnie glanced at her cheerful companion. He'd stopped rummaging in the boxes and appeared to be reading something. He sat on the floor with his back against the wall and his stocking feet resting comfortably on one of the boxes.

"Hey, this is neat,'' he said with a chuckle. "Did you really do all this?''

"What are you talking about?'' She craned her neck to see what he was holding.

He waved an old Christmas card. "This was packed away with all the other stuff. Apparently you used the back of the card to write down your New Year's resolutions last year.''

Lonnie felt a growing alarm.

" 'Try to be nicer to Gloria, even when she's acting like a jerk,' '' Jared read aloud.

"Give me that!" Lonnie dived at him, spilling a box of plastic holly garlands.

Jared held the card out of her reach and squinted at it. "God, your writing's so hard to... 'Wear a dress to work at least once a week.'" He lowered his head to smile at her. "Well, you sure haven't kept that resolution, kid. I'll bet we don't see you in a dress more than once a year."

"Jared, I'm warning, you, if you don't—"

"'Quit eating doughnuts for morning coffee break. Write to Aunt Emily once a month. Ask Mr. Allred for a raise before April.'"

Jared, please..."

"Hey, there's more. It looks like you wrote some really special resolutions here inside the—"

Lonnie's blood suddenly ran cold, and her heart began to pound. She launched herself on him in panic, drove him sprawling to the floor and leaped on top of him. Jared wrestled with her, laughing as he continued to hold the card just out of her reach.

Lonnie writhed against his muscular body and pummeled him with her fists, so terrified that she was on the verge of tears. Finally he drew away and glanced at her in surprise.

"Hey, look at you," he murmured. "You're really upset. What's the matter?"

She snatched the card from him and rolled away to sit up, dashing a hand across her eyes.

"Sorry, Lon. You know I was just kidding." He patted her shoulder awkwardly, got to his feet and reached for his leather jacket. "Well, I'd better shove off. I've got a date tonight."

Lonnie didn't ask about his date as she normally would. She followed him to the door, muttered a goodbye and waited in the doorway as he strolled down the front walk, got into his truck and drove away. For a while she lingered on her little veranda, watching the street while his taillights disappeared in the darkness.

Lonnie lived in a row-housing complex close to downtown Reno. The place was small, tidy and covered with liver-colored asphalt siding that was supposed to look like brick. Most of the tenants were elderly and liked the convenience of being close to shopping and bus routes. They tended their little yards, kept pot gardens on their verandas and gossiped happily over the sagging picket fences that divided their units.

Though she liked most of her neighbors, Lonnie hated the feeling of being crowded, surrounded by noise and people. She craved a place where there was sunshine and quiet, a world of open spaces, of lakes and trees and animals.

A place like that ranch in the mountains where Jared's family lived.

She wandered into the house and looked at the wrinkled card in her hand, on which she'd recorded all those brave intentions a year earlier. Slowly, her hands trembling, she opened the card and looked at the special resolution that was written all by itself on an inside page.

This was the one that really mattered, the one she'd sworn herself to keep no matter what other goals might fall by the wayside.

Random images crowded Lonnie's mind. She thought about Puffy with her sad, make-believe baby, about Jared's hazel eyes and endearing boyish grin, about the emptiness of her life and the thirtieth birthday she'd recently celebrated. And about her craving for a baby of her own, the fierce, secret yearning that seemed to grow more urgent all the time.

Lonnie stared at her messy handwriting, thinking about life and the swift passage of years, about resolutions made and abandoned.

She'd fully intended to do it.

Last year, Lonnie had even developed a foolproof plan whereby she would conceive and bear a baby, and the child's father would never know the truth. But her courage had deserted her at the crucial moment, and now another year had slipped by.

For a long time she stood irresolute in her cozy living room by the half-decorated Christmas tree.

She stared at the card again, then went into the kitchen to consult a small calendar hanging above the table. The timing was perfect. It was even better than last year. For a few minutes she continued to waver, battling a fear that was almost paralyzing.

Lonnie knew the man she wanted to sire a child for her. In fact, there was only man in the world who could possibly be acceptable. His name was written on the card she held, along with her firmest New Year's resolution.

"Get pregnant," it read. And on the next line, "Seduce Jared."

Chapter Two

"God, I'm exhausted. I probably didn't sleep more than three hours last night." Gloria leaned forward to examine her face in the mirror. "Do I look hideous?"

Lonnie sat on the counter, swinging her feet and watching her co-worker. Gloria Merrick was about Lonnie's age and had started working at the television station three years earlier, doing the daily weather. Everybody still called her the weather girl, although by now Gloria had insinuated herself into a lot of other things at the station, including commercials, broadcast commentary, even a weekly talk show.

She had turquoise eyes, a wide sultry mouth, a complexion like soft pearls and a luxuriant mane of hair that changed color regularly. At the moment it was dark red.

"You're still gorgeous," Lonnie said. "If I only slept for three hours, I'd look like death the next day."

"That's because you're not hardened to it." Gloria pulled one cheek down and twisted her mouth as she fitted a false eyelash in position. "You just stay home all the time, looking after your zoo."

"I was putting up my Christmas tree." Lonnie looked at the other woman curiously. "What were you doing last night?"

"An old friend stopped by. We went over to the Silver Legacy and played roulette until practically dawn, then had steaks and champagne."

"On a Tuesday night?"

"Why not?" Gloria attached the other eyelash, then took out a package of press-on nails and began to open it.

The two women were in the ladies' washroom, a large windowless room on the lower floor that also served as a dressing and storage area. Over the years Gloria had preempted more than half the washroom for her own use, making it into a fair imitation of a star's dressing room. A fluffy white rug graced one side of the linoleum floor, along with an upholstered gilt chair at the counter and a few bouquets of artificial flowers next to the crowded trays of makeup.

The far wall was covered with racks of clothes and bulletin boards displaying newspaper clippings of Gloria, along with photos of the weather girl posing with celebrities she'd met in the course of her job.

The other part of the room, consisting of a bare counter and sink, stacks of cardboard cartons and three toilet stalls, was used by Lonnie and all the other female employees.

Lonnie watched while Gloria began to fit the long red nails onto her fingertips. "I've never understood those things," she murmured.

"They're really not difficult." Gloria applied the adhesive with a deft touch. "Want to try a set?"

"That's not what I mean. What's the sense of them? Why bother?"

Gloria glanced at her in surprise. "Because they look terrific, you dummy."

"But why?" Lonnie studied the row of scarlet talons. "I mean, I can see why makeup is attractive, or high heels, even a fancy hairdo. But I honestly can't understand the appeal of bright red claws."

Gloria patted Lonnie's denim-clad knee. "Poor baby," she said, not unkindly. "That's why you crawl around backstage designing the sets while I get to be on camera."

"I have absolutely no desire to be on camera." Lonnie watched, fascinated in spite of herself, as Gloria began to fit a row of nails on her right hand.

After two decades of applying makeup, the woman was practically ambidextrous.

The door opened and Jared poked his curly head inside. "Four minutes, ladies. My crew's ready to go."

"Do you *mind?*" Gloria flounced in her chair and glared at him. "This is supposed to be a dressing room."

"No kidding." He lounged against the the door frame, grinning. "I thought it was supposed to be a toilet."

"Are the lights mounted where I wanted them?" Lonnie asked.

"All set. Those fake snowmen and little Christmas trees make a great backdrop, Lon. You're getting better all the time."

She smiled, warmed by his praise, and looked at her hands.

Gloria finished applying the nails and stood up to smooth her dress over her hips. She examined herself in the mirror, then turned and arched her back to study the line of her hips.

Lonnie saw the way Jared's eyes widened when he looked at Gloria's body in the clinging red dress. His face was suddenly hard, his body charged with attention. He stood erect in the doorway and clenched his hands.

Lonnie bit her lip, feeling miserable.

She and Jared had been friends for so long that she tended to look on him as a sort of personal buddy. Over the years when he talked about his girlfriends, even occasionally brought them to her house, Lonnie had schooled herself not to mind.

But she was increasingly troubled by her reaction when she saw him looking with active lust at a woman like Gloria. Lonnie didn't like to be reminded that Jared wasn't a boy anymore, but a grown man with powerful drives and a normal sexual life.

The truth was, she could hardly bear to think of him holding a woman like this, kissing her, stroking her naked body....

Lonnie shifted nervously on the counter and squeezed her hands together. Maybe Jared's reaction bothered her because she and Gloria were so utterly different.

The two women were about the same height and weight, but all similarities stopped at that point. Lonnie James and Gloria Merrick inhabited different worlds, opposing planets. And if Jared found Gloria attractive, there was no way in the world he would ever see Lonnie as anything but the girl next door, the casual playmate in jeans and T-shirts, the owner of sulky turtles, stray tomcats and neurotic terriers.

"Two minutes," Jared said curtly, his eyes still fixed on that lush body under the scarlet fabric. "Don't keep my crew waiting again, Gloria. We have to do a location shoot downtown in half an hour.''

He closed the door and vanished.

Gloria smiled at herself in the mirror. She stroked her breasts without self-consciousness, then lifted them to study the line of the dress.

''He's quite attractive in a rugged kind of way, isn't he?'' she asked idly.

''I wouldn't know.'' Lonnie slid from the counter and turned away to hide her flushed cheeks. ''I never think about him.''

''Really?'' Gloria raised her eyebrows. ''I thought you two were old friends.''

''Jared and I grew up together. We've known each other since we were practically babies. I think of him like a brother, that's all.''

''I see.'' Gloria leaned forward suddenly and examined her left eye. ''Damn, this mascara's smudged. Well, I'll just have to do it over.''

She settled herself in the gilt chair and reached for one of the makeup trays, scowling at herself in the mirror.

''One of these days,'' she said darkly, ''I'm going to have a network job at a *real* station and I won't need to do my own makeup anymore.''

''Don't even talk about it.'' Lonnie patted the woman's shoulder. ''You know we couldn't possibly get along without you. Come on," she added. "You look fine. Jared's crew is waiting."

"They'll have to wait a little longer, won't they?" Gloria extracted her mascara brush and twirled it carefully. "Don't be so anxious, sweetie," she added, meeting Lonnie's eyes in the mirror. "There's no reason in the world to let these men push us around, you know. It won't hurt them to cool their heels for a few more minutes."

Lonnie checked her watch. "If you don't start right now, we'll have to do the whole show in one take," she warned.

"No problem," Gloria said placidly. "Relax, honey. Sit here and talk with me some more."

Lonnie hoisted herself onto the counter again, knowing that Gloria's confidence was well-placed. The woman seldom required more than one take. In fact, she was so good that her job remained secure in spite of her outrageous antics.

There were murmurs amongst the staff that Gloria's job security also had something to do with her special relationship with Stephen Allred, the married station manager. But Lonnie didn't like being involved in that kind of gossip.

"Are you going to the New Year's party?" Gloria frowned as she plied the mascara brush.

Lonnie turned to examine her own face in the mirror, wondering how her eyes would look if she put all that stuff on them. They'd probably still be blue and childlike, she thought gloomily. No amount of skill or artifice would ever make her look like Gloria.

"Lonnie?"

"Pardon?" she asked with a guilty start.

"I asked if you were going to the New Year's party."

Lonnie shifted, feeling awkward. "I don't really like costume parties. Besides, it's so expensive."

"Oh, pooh. I can lend you something," Gloria said with the casual generosity that made it impossible to dislike her no matter how she behaved. "I've always loved the New Year's party. It's fun to dress up." She smiled at herself in the mirror. "And people are so much less inhibited when they're in disguise, don't you think?"

Lonnie didn't answer.

"So you're really not going?" Gloria asked.

"No, I'm not." Lonnie slid off the counter again, turning away from her reflection.

Two big lies in the space of five minutes, she thought. What a way to embark on the most exciting adventure of her life.

"That's a hundred and ten dollars, plus tax." The saleswoman pushed buttons on the cash register, giving Lonnie a bored smile.

"A hundred and ten?" Lonnie said in alarm. "But I thought the rental was only forty dollars. The sign says..."

"The rest is your deposit. It's refunded when you bring back the costume."

"I see." Lonnie shifted nervously and watched as the woman packed a mass of beads, shiny gold fabric and pale green silk into a box.

"You should see the condition some of these costumes are in when they come back to us." The woman shook her head and sighed. "Now, will that be on your credit card today?"

"No, I'll pay cash."

A good thing she'd cashed her paycheck the day before. Lonnie rummaged through her wallet, praying that she could find enough money for the rental.

"And I'll need a name for the deposit slip," the clerk said.

Lonnie hesitated, feeling panicky again. "This is for...could you just put down Gloria Merrick's name?" she said on impulse.

The saleswoman's eyes widened. "You mean the weather girl on Channel Seventeen? Oh, my goodness, I just *love* her. She's so glamorous."

"I know. I work with her, and we're about the same size, so she asked me to...to try the costume on for her because she's busy, and see if it fits."

Lonnie's cheeks turned scarlet. Why was she telling all these lies to a complete stranger? She didn't want her name associated with the costume she was renting, but what if Gloria happened to came into this same store later for her own New Year's outfit? What if she . . .

"What's it for?" the clerk asked.

"I beg your pardon?"

The woman tapped the costume box. "I heard the media are having some kind of party."

Lonnie gulped and nodded. "Every New Year's, five of the local television and radio stations get together and have a huge costume party in the ballroom at the Eldorado. It's . . . really fun."

Not that she attended very often. But other people were always eager to tell Lonnie how much fun the party had been.

"And this is the costume Gloria Merrick's going to be wearing?" The saleswoman leaned forward, breathless with interest.

"She's just going to try it on." Unhappily, Lonnie waded deeper into the swamp of lies. "But she has lots of costumes. She might still pick something else at the last minute."

"I wish I could see her wearing it." The woman gazed at her cash register with a dreamy expression. "She's going to be so gorgeous. That woman's a real star, you know. I'll bet she winds up in Hollywood someday.''

Lonnie muttered some kind of response, took the box and escaped into the decorated street, where plastic Santas and reindeer hung from the lampposts and store windows were festooned with pine boughs.

She stopped in a drugstore to purchase some eye shadow, false lashes and a pair of disposable contact lenses. After wavering a long time over the lens colors on display, she finally chose silky mink brown. Then she continued home, hurrying along the street with her packages while the twilight deepened and snow began to fall in big soft flakes.

All the animals were hungry when she arrived, even the beef-eating turtle. She shredded lettuce for the rabbits in the garage, put suet on a ledge for the injured crow and filled the matching yellow bowls in the kitchen for Shadow and Puffy.

Finally, tense with excitement, she went into her bedroom, stripped off her clothes and dressed herself in the rented harem-girl outfit.

The pants were transparent, a froth of pale green that displayed her legs all the way up to the brief silk-fringed panties. The whole effect was amazingly seductive. Especially the little gold jacket, designed to meet tightly under her breasts and force them into a cleavage so ample that it made her squirm with embarrassment.

The look was completed by tiny gold slippers, an ankle bracelet jiggling with bells and a silk head-dress that completely covered her braided hair and most of her face. Lonnie fitted the veil over her nose and mouth, then adjusted the rows of beaded fringe across her forehead.

A pair of blue eyes looked back from the mirror, wide and bewildered. But after she tipped her head back and inserted the dark contact lenses, the transformation was almost magical. A woman regarded her through the slit in the headdress, a sloe-eyed temptress, sultry and alluring.

All she needed was some heavy, Cleopatra-style makeup on her eyes to complete the look, and she'd already bought the supplies. There was a whole week to practice between Christmas and New Year's. She'd have the makeup perfected by then.

Lonnie pirouetted and examined herself from every angle with growing confidence. Nobody would ever recognize her in this outfit. Not even Jared.

It was perfect. Now, if she could only...

The telephone rang, shattering the hushed stillness of the winter evening. She rushed into the living room to answer, her ankle bells tinkling. From the kitchen, the animals gazed up at their mistress in blank surprise, then returned to their food.

"Hello?" Lonnie said, feeling ridiculous as she lifted the edge of the silk headdress to find a place for the telephone receiver.

"Hi, sweetie. What's up?"

"Hello, Mom." Lonnie relaxed and sank into the old armchair.

"You sound strange. Are you okay?"

"I'm fine." Lonnie looked at her bare leg under the gauzy fabric and her high-arched foot in its golden slipper. "Just fine. The same as usual. Nothing much going on."

"I called to say Merry Christmas."

"It's not Christmas for another two days, Mom."

"I know. But I'll be away, and you can't count on those ship-to-shore telephones."

"Oh, that's right," Lonnie said, feeling guilty.

In the excitement of her own project, she'd completely forgotten that her mother, who lived in a condo in southern Florida, was planning a romantic holiday cruise this year with Nels Ahlmeier, her longtime boyfriend.

"I feel so guilty," Rosemary went on. "Leaving you all alone at Christmas."

"Hey, I'm over thirty, Mom. You and Nels are certainly entitled to do whatever you want for the holidays without worrying about being around to fill my stocking.''

"I know, but still . . ." Her mother sighed. "You should have come with us, dear. You know how much Nels likes you."

Lonnie tried to picture herself celebrating Christmas on a cruise ship in the Caribbean, playing shuffleboard with Nels and his old cronies, waltzing stiffly around the deck under the stars.

"That's a really sweet thought, Mom," she said. "But I couldn't get the time off work. Christmas is such a busy time for us."

The silk headdress fell down, covering the receiver. Lonnie pulled it away and touched the swelling cleavage of her breasts, wondering nervously if the little jacket was entirely secure. Those breasts looked in danger of spilling out at any moment.

"So what are you doing right now?"

Lonnie swung her slippered foot, then stopped abruptly when the bells tinkled. "Nothing much. Just feeding the animals and doing some baking."

"Are you still having that big crowd over for Christmas dinner?"

"It's not a crowd, Mom. Just half a dozen people. We'll have fun."

"So how about the rest of the holiday? Have you got a nice date for New Year's Eve?"

Puffy wandered in, trailing her rubber clown, and stopped in alarm when she saw Lonnie. She sat on her haunches and growled in her throat.

"Shh," Lonnie whispered urgently, touching the dog with her slipper. "Look, it's just me."

Puffy growled again and edged forward, baring her sharp little teeth.

"Lonnie?" her mother said. "What's that noise?"

"Oh . . . it's nothing, Mom. It's just Puffy. She's growling at me."

"Really? Why?"

"She's . . . going though another of her little episodes."

"The false pregnancy thing?"

"She's all swollen and nervous, and she carries this plastic toy around and grooms it all day long. I think she's actually making milk this time."

"The poor darling," Rosemary said with feeling. "It must be terrible to want a baby that much and not have one."

"Yes." Lonnie kicked gently at her dog, who was attacking one of the golden slippers. "It must be awful. Go away, Puffy," she whispered over the tinkling of the ankle bells. "Go!"

"What's that funny sound, Lonnie? Is it bells or something?"

"Oh, just some...it's some Christmas stuff," Lonnie said vaguely, trying to still the jangling of her ankle bracelet.

She glared fiercely at the little dog, causing Puffy to gather her baby with an injured look and trot out of the room. The terrier stopped in the kitchen doorway to cast a bitter glance over her shoulder, then vanished.

"I was asking if you had a date for New Year's Eve," Rosemary said.

"Not really. I might go to the staff party at the Eldorado this year."

"All alone?"

"Hardly. There'll be five hundred people there, at least."

"But, honey..."

Lonnie didn't feel up to a lecture from her mother about the importance of maintaining an active social life. Especially not while she was dressed like a Mesopotamian strumpet.

"I have to go, Mom," she said quickly. "My butter tarts are burning."

"Oh, all right. Have a lovely holiday, darling. I'll be thinking of you."

"You too, Mom. Take lots of pictures and call me when you get home, all right?"

"Merry Christmas, Lonnie. Happy New Year. And have fun."

"I will, Mom." Lonnie stared at her lush cleavage again, feeling both terrified and elated. "I think I'll definitely have fun."

Chapter Three

Jared lay on the couch in his apartment, staring moodily at the ceiling. It was close to eleven o'clock on New Year's Eve, and he still hadn't decided whether to attend the media party at the Eldorado. Normally he enjoyed the annual costume ball, even though dressing up wasn't exactly his favorite entertainment. But lately, for some reason, life seemed to be losing a lot of its sparkle.

Jared drained his beer and set the can next to a couple of empties on the coffee table. He sighed and folded his hands under his head again.

Actually, he was reluctant to go to the party because he knew Lonnie wouldn't be there. It was embarrassing and distressing to him, this feeling he'd suddenly begun to develop for his longtime friend. She seemed to be on his mind all the time.

Whenever he closed his eyes he could see her grave blue eyes and shy smile, her womanly body under the casual jeans and shirts, the sunny warmth of her hair....

Jared moaned and rolled over, burying his face in his arms. He'd started dreaming about her at night, too. They were hot, sexual dreams that felt practically incestuous, considering the relationship he'd always had with her.

Jared had no idea what the dreams meant. He'd never felt this way when they were growing up together or during their adult friendship. Even when Lonnie met and married Stan Carlson, a handsome, amiable football player who painted houses in the off-season, Jared hadn't minded all that much.

Not until he found out that Stan was cheating on her. After that, he'd started hating the son of a bitch, and told him so.

There were times now when he yearned to go to Lonnie and open his heart, tell her the way he felt and see how she might respond. But she'd never shown any trace of romantic interest in him.

What if she was embarrassed by his disclosure? Or worse, even felt pity for him? Jared grimaced at the thought. In any case their friendship would be ruined, and then he'd lose her altogether.

But she was alone tonight. He could still call and go over to her place, in his comfortable old role as best friend. They could sit around and watch New Year's specials on television, play a few games of cribbage, maybe go for a walk in the snow after midnight and talk about their plans for the coming year. It was always so nice to talk with Lonnie.

Jared's spirits lifted.

He got up to dial her number and was crushed with disappointment when she didn't answer. He listened to her answering machine for a while, then hung up without leaving a message and glared at the darkened window.

Lonnie hadn't said anything about having a date tonight. She'd just told him that she wasn't going to the costume party.

So where was she?

At last, feeling lonely and dispirited, he dressed in his usual costume for the New Year's party. This consisted of pulling a pair of leather chaps over his jeans, slapping on a feather-banded Stetson and a pair of fake six-shooters and tying a red cotton bandanna around his neck.

Because he was still feeling the effect of the beers, Jared took a cab over to the Eldorado and strolled down the wide carpeted staircase to the lower ball-room where the party was in full swing. Hundreds of merrymakers swarmed through the opulent room, all of them in elaborate fancy dress.

Jared pulled the bandanna over his mouth and nose, bandit-style, then leaned in the doorway and watched as masked courtiers and pumpkins, mice and robots and vampires swirled noisily around him, eating and drinking.

He searched the melee for some trace of Lonnie, wondering what kind of costume she might have chosen if she'd decided to come to the party. His attention was suddenly distracted by a gorgeous apparition that appeared directly in front of him, dazzling in its loveliness.

A shapely harem girl stood there in transparent green silky pants and a little gold jacket that displayed her swelling breasts. She looked at him from behind her veil through exotic dark eyes, gravely offering a glass of golden liquid.

He took the glass, numb with astonishment, and lowered his bandanna to gulp the strong, sweet liquor. "Who are you?" Jared asked. "Do I know you?"

She shook her head and reached out to stroke his chest. Her hand brushed across the plaid of his shirt with a slow, lingering motion, and her fingertips crept past the top button to touch his bare skin.

Jared shivered, looking at the woman more closely. Her legs were long and shapely, more alluring under their frothy covering of pale green gauze than if they had been fully displayed. And her breasts were creamy, lush and perfect.

When he saw the sultry invitation in her dark eyes, there was no way in the world to stop himself from imagining reaching down to touch her breasts. He stroked one gently with his fingertips, then closed his hand around the sweet mound.

In his mind's eye, she trembled and edged closer, putting her hand over his, pressing his fingers tight against her breast. Jared's groin began to swell and throb. He felt an urgency that was all-consuming, a passionate need to be alone with this enchanting creature.

"Who are you?" he murmured again, leaning close to her.

She looked at him with her enigmatic dark eyes and gestured quickly.

"What?" he asked in confusion, then realized that she was motioning for him to finish his drink.

He drained it in one swallow, choking at the potency of the liquid. For a moment he wondered dizzily if the beautiful enchantress was trying to poison him. But then she was leading him into a very private darkened alcove behind a velvet drapery. Once they were alone, she ran her fingers across the top of his belt buckle, fluttering her thumb lightly against the front of his jeans until he was incapable of rational thought.

He pressed close to her, and in the shadows she allowed him to free her breast from the golden fabric and hold it in his hand. While she averted her eyes, Jared bent to kiss the firm pink nipple.

"My God," he groaned, burying his face in the scented skin of her cleavage. "Who are you? Why are you doing this to me?"

She didn't answer, just moved closer to him, her eyes dark and unfathomable under the beaded headdress. She reached out slowly, sensuously, and began to rub his crotch with the palm of her hand, caressing him with purposeful tenderness.

"Oh, no," he whispered, clutching her shoulders. "Oh, I can't...."

Silently she paused to adjust her breast within the confines of the golden jacket, then began to float away. She looked over her shoulder and moved on. Jared followed blindly, stumbling behind her as she drifted through the crowded ballroom and wove her way skillfully amongst the partygoers. At a table she paused to pick up another drink and hand it to him.

"More liquor?" He looked dubiously at the brimming glass. "I won't be able to..."

The woman gave him a flash of those smoldering eyes. He drank obediently, not pausing until he'd drained it all. His head felt like it was about to explode, and his vision blurred for a moment.

She watched him in silence, then took his hand and led him out of the room, through the lobby toward a row of brass-trimmed elevators. The lobby, too, was full of celebrants, shouting and stumbling around, waving noisemakers and streamers. Nobody noticed when they squeezed into one of the elevators with a crowd of other people and rode silently upward.

At the ninth floor the harem girl got off, pulling Jared by the hand, and hurried down the lighted corridor. He followed her like a man in a dream.

She produced a room key from somewhere in her skimpy costume, fiddled with the lock and drew him inside, closing the door on the hallway light.

Then she was in his arms in the dim stillness, kissing him fiercely. He could taste her lips, the inside of her sweet mouth, the probing sleekness of her tongue.

"You're so... Who are you?" he murmured, tugging at the veil that concealed her. "Let me take this thing off and..."

She twisted away with an abrupt gesture and turned her back.

"Okay," he said humbly. "I'm sorry. I promise I won't try anything like that again. Please, just let me touch you."

The mystery woman relented and allowed him to caress her again. She helped him to unfasten the little jacket so her breasts spilled free. They were magnificent, gleaming like soft pearls in the glow of the moonlight.

Jared kissed them reverently, sucking on the taut nipples, running his hands over her silken hips and pulling her against him.

She twisted out of the harem pants, kicked off the golden slippers and stood naked before him except for her heavy veil and her ankle bracelet. He'd never seen a woman so lovely, so perfectly formed and shapely, so utterly desirable. Slowly, hypnotically, she began to dance, swaying gracefully around the room in the moonlight, her ankle bells tinkling.

He stripped off his clothes as he watched, awed and silent. Finally he, too, was naked, his cowboy costume a jumbled heap on the floor. He moved toward the harem girl and danced with her in the silvery glow, so close that her nipples brushed his chest lightly, making him shiver with excitement.

"Now?" he whispered, drawing her toward the bed.

She shook her head and began to stroke his body, trailing her fingers down his chest, around his hips, across the hard, thrusting core of him. He groaned at her touch.

They stood close together and fondled each other's bodies, their hands warm in the silvered moonlight, until he could endure no more.

"Please," he whispered. "Please, whoever you are, I hope you're not just teasing me. Because I'm going to die if this goes on much longer."

At last, she went to the bed and drew him down with her. The woman's face was still hidden, her eyes remote behind the silky veil, strangely at odds with the lovely body displayed in such sultry abandon.

Jared leaned on one elbow and caressed her with long, gentle strokes of his hands, marveling at the perfection of her hips, her silken thighs, her abdomen and breasts.

"You're beautiful," he whispered. "So lovely. I've never seen anyone like you."

After all the liquor and the wild, unsettling stimulation of the whole encounter, he was afraid he wouldn't be able to last long enough to please her. But when she took him into her arms and pulled him close to her, then inside her, and he felt the deep, wet smoothness of her, he wanted their sex to go on forever. He thrust and stroked, thrust and stroked, gently, tenderly, loving the way she made him feel.

"What's your name?" he breathed in awe. "I need to know who you are."

She tensed and turned her head away. All he could see was the beaded fringe of the veil. He gave up and abandoned himself to the exquisite agony of prolonging his climax.

He could tell when she reached hers because her body arched wildly at the hips, then began to grip and release him with long, shuddering spasms that were unbearably pleasurable. Finally he lost control in a delicious surge of feeling unlike anything he'd ever known and collapsed in her arms.

"Whoever you are," he whispered, reaching to cradle her tenderly, "I think I'm in love with you."

She was silent, lying curled against him with her back turned. She hugged herself as if her body contained some kind of precious treasure that she was protecting from harm.

He wondered about that for a minute, the way she lay curled so tenderly around herself. But his senses were blurred with alcohol and fatigue. Soon he fell into a deep, sated sleep.

Jared didn't wake until a gritty dawn crept around the edges of the drapes. His clothes were folded neatly on a chair, and the mysterious harem girl had vanished as if she'd never existed.

Lonnie remembered hearing co-workers talking about a new home test so sophisticated that it could detect pregnancy a day or two after conception. She was tempted to go to the pharmacy and look for it, but the whole idea seemed too risky, like tempting fate.

Her future was in the hands of the gods. She had to wait.

Still, she did what she could. The first working day after New Year's, she called Mr. Allred and booked off two weeks of vacation time. The manager was startled by the suddenness of her request, but he could hardly refuse. After all, Lonnie had practically been running the station single-handed while everybody else took their holidays between Christmas and New Year's.

For the first few days at home she treated her body like some kind of fragile vessel. She slept late, took gentle walks around the neighborhood in the fresh winter air, ate small, nourishing meals. She called nobody, had no social contact and wanted none. It was satisfying to spend this time quietly with her animals, alone with the possibility of a miracle.

Even Jared didn't drop in to visit as was his usual custom, nor did he call. At first Lonnie was relieved by this, but toward the end of the week, his silence began to worry her. What if he'd discovered the truth and was so embarrassed and outraged by her behavior that he didn't want to see her again?

On Friday afternoon, coming in with Puffy from a walk in the melting snow, she found a message from him on her answering machine. She stood in the hallway, trembling, still clutching Puffy's leash in both hands. The sound of his voice brought back the whole episode with crushing vividness. Lonnie could feel his arms around her, his mouth against hers, his powerful body probing and thrusting.…

"Oh, God," she whispered aloud, then forced herself to listen.

"Hey, Lon, where are you? Pick up if you're home." There was a brief silence. "Okay," he went on, sounding a little harried and distracted, but otherwise normal. "I haven't heard from you in a while. I just wondered if you're okay, that's all. Give me a call if you need anything."

Then he was gone. Lonnie sagged against the wall, limp with relief. He didn't know. There was no way he could have sounded so casual if he knew.

She went outside to feed the lame crow in the backyard and dug under the snow to find some spears of damp grass for her turtle. At last she went into the house and began to organize the rest of her holiday.

Lonnie arranged for her neighbor, Mrs. Schwartz, to look after the animals for a few days. Then she drove south to spend most of the second week in the cool sunshine of Las Vegas, carrying her résumé from one small television station to another. She was called back for half a dozen interviews and offered a job after the fourth day.

"We'll be needing somebody starting around the first of May," the station manager said. She was a thin, clever-looking woman in a three-piece suit of gray pinstripes. "Would that suit you?"

Lonnie calculated rapidly.

If she had managed to conceive, she'd be four months pregnant by the first of May. Staying in Reno any longer would be risky, but four months should still be early enough to hide a pregnancy.

"Yes," she said at last. "The first of May will be fine."

"Good." The woman rose and extended her hand. "Keep in touch. We look forward to working with you, Ms. James."

Lonnie wandered onto the street, feeling dazed. This was all going so fast. She had a brief twinge of regret over what she'd just done, but suppressed it firmly.

Even if she hadn't conceived, it was time to move on. She couldn't bear to go on working with Jared every day, feeling the way she did about him. It was getting harder all the time to maintain an illusion of casual friendship. And now that she'd known the sweet joy of lying naked in his arms, the relationship was going to be impossible.

But she told nobody about her plans. At the end of the second week she went back to work, feeling as detached from all the station humor and gossip as if she'd just returned from the moon.

Steve, one of the junior copywriters, greeted her with a sheaf of new ads from a local department store. "I'm overworked—" He ran his hand through his hair. "I'm simply going out of my mind. Look at all this."

Steve was only twenty-six, but already balding. He wore baggy trousers, string ties and silk vests, and spent most of his spare time surfing the Internet. The man was also a terrible gossip. Lonnie was always careful what she told him.

She looked at the piles of yellow copy paper. "What are they?"

"Stills." He sighed heavily. "They need photographic stills for a whole year's supply of product commercials, everything from toothpaste to tires. I don't have time to set up all this crap. I have to do the theater copy, and we're going on a film shoot at the mall this afternoon."

"I'll set up the stills for you," Lonnie said. "Who's shooting them?"

"I think Jared's doing it. Amy and Joe will be going to the mall with me." Steve hugged her awkwardly. "You're a doll, Lonnie. A real doll. Jeez, I'm glad you're back." He scurried away, heading for the editing room.

Lonnie looked in dismay at the copy paper, wishing she hadn't offered. But that was ridiculous. She had to encounter Jared sooner or later. It might as well happen while they were both busy at their jobs.

Reluctantly she went into the small production studio and began to arrange a set for still photographs, concentrating on something dramatic enough to serve as an interesting backdrop, but sufficiently neutral to be used for a long time.

While she was working, Jared came into the studio with an armload of photographic equipment. He smiled warmly when he saw her.

"Hi, kiddo," he said. "I heard you were back. How was the holiday?"

Lonnie allowed herself one hungry look at his tanned face, his mouth and eyes and shoulders. Then she turned away to arrange folds of velvet around the base of a wooden pedestal. "It was okay."

"Where did you go? I left a couple of messages, but you didn't call back."

She sprinkled some artificial snow onto the velvet and stepped back to study the effect. "I went down to Vegas for a few days."

"Really?" He frowned at a box of lenses, then selected one. "I thought you hated Vegas."

"It's not so bad down there. Jared, this snow looks too seasonal, doesn't it?"

"Probably, but it makes a nice effect. Let's do a few shots including the snow and finish up with just the fabric, okay?"

He loaded his camera and she began to arrange products for filming. They worked together with the easy teamwork that came from long practice, but Lonnie knew he had something on his mind.

"Lon," he said at last, looking at his camera as he toyed with the shutter setting.

"Yes?"

"Something happened to me at the New Year's party."

Lonnie tensed, but his face was still hidden. All she could see was the curly auburn mass of his hair, and she yearned to reach out and touch it. Hastily she picked up a bottle of shampoo, holding it to the light.

"What happened?" she asked.

"I . . . met somebody."

"Who was it?"

"I don't know. She was wearing a costume. I wondered if maybe you knew who she was."

"How would I know?"

"I hoped you . . . maybe you heard who was wearing that costume, or something."

"What kind of costume was it?"

"A harem girl. Baggy green pants and a . . ." He paused and swallowed hard, clearly unsettled. "A little gold jacket. And an ankle bracelet with bells on it."

Lonnie frowned, pretending to search her memory. "No, it doesn't ring any bells." She gave him a brief smile. "Sorry, bad joke."

He didn't smile back. "I have to find her. I've been looking for her all over the city."

Lonnie felt a deep chill of fear. "Looking? What do you mean?"

"Well, for one thing, I checked with the hotel to see who booked the room we used. It was registered to Grace Michaels. She must have given a false name, because that doesn't match anybody in the local media."

It was my grandmother's maiden name, Lonnie thought. *But I've never told you that.*

"And I went to all the costume places and asked if anybody rented the harem outfit."

Anxiety stabbed her again. "So what did they tell you?"

"Four rental shops have the same costume, but only one of them kept the names of all the people who booked out costumes for New Year's."

She held her breath. "And who rented your harem girl outfit?"

"It was Gloria," he said with obvious reluctance.

Lonnie turned away to hide her relief.

Thank God I had the presence of mind to lie to that store clerk, she thought, remembering how excessive all her precautions had seemed at the time.

But then, she'd never suspected that Jared would go to such lengths to search out her identity.

"Our Gloria?" she asked with forced lightness. "Our very own weather girl?"

"Yes, but it wasn't her. This girl I met, she definitely wasn't Gloria."

"How do you know, if she was in disguise?"

"I just know," he said stubbornly. When he looked directly at Lonnie, she was surprised by the bleak pain in his eyes. "I have to find her, Lon. I'm going out of my mind."

"Why?"

He shook his head and reached for another camera. "Let's forget it, okay?"

Lonnie hurried to place the shampoo bottle on the pedestal, relieved that he'd chosen to drop the subject.

They began to work again, so close to each other within the small, brightly lit room that their bodies brushed together occasionally when they moved. She tried to stay calm and detached, to concentrate on her work, but it was almost impossible.

By now, Lonnie was four days late.

Chapter Four

The days slipped by, gradually turning into weeks. Lonnie knew that her disappointment would be unbearable if she hadn't conceived, so she tried hard not to think about what might be happening in her body. Instead she buried her speculations in work and the daily routines of life.

But she promised herself that if her cycle didn't resume its normal course, she'd see a doctor during the first week in February. In the meantime she began going through her belongings, sorting and choosing what to discard, getting ready to start packing for her move to Las Vegas.

Occasionally she went next door to have tea with Mrs. Schwartz and play a game of Scrabble. Stan dropped by one evening to complain about his problems with his new girlfriend. Pete, the film editor, asked her to go to a movie, but she declined.

Jared was apparently absorbed in his search for the mystery woman. He neither called nor visited.

Lonnie thought about him all the time, still unsettled by his grim determination to find the harem girl. The poor man must have been so befuddled by liquor and fatigue that he'd romanticized the whole incident.

Apparently Jared had deluded himself into thinking he was in love. If he ever found out the truth, he'd be upset and humiliated, utterly incensed with her. And he would have every right to be. For her part, Lonnie would simply die if her old friend managed to discover how shamelessly she'd exploited him.

At work she avoided him as much as she could, going out of her way to keep busy. She also began quietly to tidy up her files and organize her desk for the person who would be taking over the job, although she had no intention of giving notice until sometime in early April. At this point, it was safest to draw as little attention to herself as possible.

"Hey, Lonnie." Gloria stopped by her desk one morning at the beginning of February. "Can you help me for a minute?"

"Sure." Lonnie was busy blocking out a storyboard for a documentary film on teen violence. She looked up, vague and distracted. "What's the problem?"

"In my dressing room, okay?"

Gloria swept into the women's bathroom. Lonnie followed her, feeling both amused and a little annoyed, which was her usual reaction to Gloria.

Inside the room, though, she studied the other woman's face and felt a pang of sympathy. Despite a new turquoise suit that flattered her trim figure, the weather girl wasn't her usual gorgeous self. She looked pale and drawn, almost haggard.

"What's the matter? Are you feeling sick?" Lonnie asked.

"It's this flu that's been going around. Amy and Pete both had it last week, and now I understand that Mr. Allred is sick, too." Gloria leaned on the counter and studied herself in the mirror. "I'm not as young as I used to be," she muttered. "These things are starting to show in my face. God, isn't that a terrible sight?"

"You're just human," Lonnie said. "Don't be so hard on yourself."

"I'm thirty years old, and I'm doing the weather at a two-bit cable channel." Gloria continued to gaze at herself with brooding unhappiness. "I'm never going to make the big time, Lonnie. This is as far as I'll ever go."

Lonnie hoisted herself into her customary place on the counter. "Is that so bad?" she asked. "You're a local celebrity. Everybody loves you. You get recognized and applauded wherever you go in this city. You wear beautiful clothes, and the men fall all over you. What's so bad about your life?"

Gloria considered, nodding thoughtfully, then pulled out a tray of makeup and sat down at the counter. "You're a really nice person, Lonnie," she said casually. "Did you know that?"

"I'm not all that nice." Lonnie watched as Gloria applied blusher from a flat ebony case, working it skillfully into her pale cheeks. "I've done some pretty awful things in my life."

Gloria snorted, looking more like her old self. "Oh, I'm sure you have. Terrible, sinful things, like passing off outdated coupons at the grocery store. Or maybe sneaking ten minutes of parking without plugging the meter. Capital crimes, almost."

Lonnie felt vaguely annoyed by this appraisal of herself. She watched as Gloria searched through a basket for the right shade of lipstick.

"So, what did you want?" she asked.

Gloria held up a tube. "Luscious Mango, do you think? Or would an earth tone be better with the turquoise?"

"You asked me to come in here and help you," Lonnie said impatiently. "What's the problem?"

"Oh, that." Gloria decided on the first tube and applied it carefully, stretching her mouth into a mock smile as she worked. "I'm supposed to do a spot with Jared this afternoon over at one of the high schools. They're having a fasting day for world hunger. I wondered if you'd do it for me because

I'm feeling so rotten. It's just a voice-over," she added. "You shouldn't have any problem. I mean, you won't have to change your clothes or anything."

All of Lonnie's sympathy disappeared in a wave of exasperation. Gloria would never willingly give up a camera spot to anybody, but voice-overs were different. If she wasn't going to be seen, she wasn't all that interested.

"Sorry." Lonnie slid off the counter. "I can't do it. I'm busy this afternoon."

Gloria looked at her piteously. "Please, Lonnie. You don't know how awful I'm feeling. I can't drag myself over there. Honestly, I just can't."

"Then you'll have to find somebody else." Lonnie paused in the doorway. "I'm afraid I can't help you."

"Why not?"

"Because I have a doctor's appointment at three o'clock."

Lonnie smiled sweetly, then closed the door and hurried back to her storyboards.

"So, Lonnie." Dr. Barret closed the file and folded her hands on her desk. She was a plump, sweet-faced woman in her fifties with a cloud of gray hair and a gentle smile.

"So," Lonnie said nervously.

The physical examination was over and she was dressed again, but she still felt clammy and uncomfortable, tense with anxiety. She looked over the doctor's head at a chart on the wall showing fetal development.

"You came to see me because your period was a couple of weeks late, right?"

"Almost three," Lonnie murmured.

"And I assume the thought of pregnancy had crossed your mind?"

"It . . . crossed my mind," Lonnie admitted.

"What did you think about the possibility? Were you dismayed?"

"Not really." Lonnie gazed at her hands. "In fact, I was hoping it might be true."

"You were hoping to be pregnant?" The doctor sounded mildly surprised.

Lonnie's heart sank. "Sort of. Yes." She looked at the doctor. "As a matter of fact, I'd give anything to have a baby. I knew there wasn't much chance because I've only had intercourse one time in the recent past, but it was right during my fertile period and I thought maybe . . ."

The words trailed off, leaving her so miserable that she could hardly hold back the tears. She blinked rapidly, looking at her hands again.

"Well," the doctor said in a matter-of-fact tone, "you thought correctly."

"I don't . . . What do you mean?"

"I mean, dear, that you're pregnant. Probably about five weeks, by my calculation. I'd estimate that you conceived somewhere around the end of December."

"New Year's Eve," Lonnie whispered, feeling numb. "That's when it was."

The doctor smiled. "I see."

"Five weeks," Lonnie said in wonder.

She looked at the chart. In the baby's spinal column she could see the tiny vertebrae, as smooth and graceful as a string of pearls. And the rounded skull enclosing the marvelous brain, and the big eyes and developing limbs with buds for fingers and toes . . .

"Oh, my," she whispered, beginning to cry. "Oh, what a miracle."

The doctor was talking, telling her about vitamin supplements and dietary rules, offering pamphlets and charts. Lonnie responded with dazed happiness.

"So try to read all this and come back in for the lab tests sometime next week, all right? I'll want to see you again in a month," Dr. Barret said.

"Thank you so much." Lonnie brushed at her eyes, gathered the documents and left the office, walking on air.

The snows of early January had vanished, and the weather in Reno was now seasonably mild. The sun beamed down from a cloudless blue sky, and the mountainsides were green except for a bright frosting of snow at their peaks.

Lonnie stood near a park bordering the Truckee River, taking deep breaths of fresh air that was as intoxicating as wine.

Gently, she touched her abdomen under the woolen coat.

"Hello," she whispered, oblivious to a couple of children who watched her curiously, then ran off through the park. "Hello, darling. I can't believe you're really there."

A baby, she thought, still astounded by the miracle of it all. A baby of her own, growing and developing at the secret core of her body, nestled safely under her heart.

Jared's baby.

Lonnie was almost overcome by the desire to tell somebody. She wanted to run through the streets, shouting her news to all the world.

But that was impossible. She couldn't breathe a word of this until she was ready to move to Las Vegas. Then she could tell her mother, at least. For now, she and this tiny new life inside her would stay wrapped together in their silent world of tenderness.

"I love you," she whispered, overcome with feeling. "And you know what? I love your daddy, too. I love him more than anything."

Tears began to flow down her cheeks again. Lonnie forgot to brush them away. She stood gazing at the bare tree branches, etched like delicate lace against the blue winter sky. When the season was full and those trees were cloaked in a blaze of autumn colors, her baby would be born.

Valentine's Day was soon upon them. Lonnie and Jared were busy with the spring campaign launched by local auto dealerships to sell massive amounts of their inventory.

Lonnie's job was to come up with creative, interesting ways to advertise new and used cars, and Jared's task was to turn her concepts on paper into images on film. They were both very good at what they did.

On a windy Thursday afternoon in mid-February, they worked on the lot behind one of Reno's downtown car emporiums, making vehicles disappear. Jared's camera was mounted on a tripod, set up for time-lapse photography and aimed at a long row of cars. Lonnie had a crew organized to polish each car before its filming, then drive it away while the camera was turned off. Another assistant hurried to scatter a handful of dust in the empty parking spot while Jared turned the camera on. When the film was edited, it would look as if the cars were vanishing one by one in a mysterious puff of smoke.

"You'd better hurry. Come and get yours," Gloria would whisper alluringly in the voice-over, "before they all . . . *disappear.*"

The work was slow and tedious. The assistants, including Steve, were sullen and increasingly irritable. Lonnie felt an intermittent nausea that tugged at her like a nagging cough. She chewed handfuls of dry crackers from her coat pocket and tried to ignore her stomach.

Jared strolled across the lot to examine her in concern. "Are you okay, honey? You're looking a little pale."

"I'm fine," Lonnie said curtly.

She could hardly stand to look at him. He wore jeans, a denim jacket lined with sheepskin and his old baseball cap. His face was ruddy with the cold, and so handsome that it was all she could do not to throw herself into his arms.

Ever since she'd learned about the baby, a strange thing was happening between her and Jared. It was as if the baby created a sort of magnetic force field at the center of her body, pulling her toward this man. The attraction was so strong that she could hardly control the feelings emanating, it seemed, directly from the child she carried.

Lonnie was immensely relieved that she'd found the job in Las Vegas and would be moving soon. Otherwise, there was no telling what kind of disaster might happen.

"The peasants are revolting," Steve announced, bustling toward them with a self-important air.

The balding copywriter indicated their ragtag crew from the television station. Three young people clustered in a doorway at the dealership office, looking rebellious.

Jared surveyed the crew in disgust. "They certainly are. If they'd work a little faster, we could probably have this thing done by lunch."

"They demand a coffee break. Otherwise they're going to quit."

Lonnie and Jared exchanged a glance.

"Okay," Lonnie said to Steve. "Tell the kids they can go to the doughnut shop across the street for fifteen minutes. Not a second more."

"Where are you guys going?" Steve asked.

"Into the dealership," Jared told him. "We need to block out the final scene and decide where we'll do the close-ups."

Steve loped away toward the crew. "Wait for me, okay? I'll be right back," he called over his shoulder.

When they were alone on the dusty lot, Jared grinned and put a casual hand on Lonnie's shoulder. "How did we manage to inherit this guy? Are we just lucky, or what?"

"Steve has career aspirations. He's hoping I'll leave so he can take over my job."

Jared groaned and hugged her. "Don't ever leave, kid. I couldn't stand it."

She quivered under his touch but said nothing.

Steve dispatched the crew and went inside the dealership with Jared and Lonnie. The three of them sat around a desk in one of the empty sales cubicles, sipping drinks from the vending machine while they studied Lonnie's storyboard and discussed camera angles.

Jared leaned over to peer into Lonnie's cup. "What are you drinking? Is that *milk?*"

"My stomach's a little queasy today. I don't think I could stand coffee."

He brushed her hair away to touch her forehead. "You're not catching anything, are you? I can take you home if you're feeling sick, Lon. We can finish up here without you."

She ducked away from his hand. "I'm fine. Quit fussing over me."

"Hey, did you hear the news?" Steve perched on the corner of one of the desks, swinging his legs and looking pleased with himself. "I mean, the *real* scoop." The copywriter wore black tweed pants with huge pleats, a striped orange-and-yellow sweater and an incongruous red bow tie.

"What news?" Lonnie asked.

"If we pan across the front of the dealership," Jared was saying, "we can get all the cars in the showroom, then zoom in on—"

"I'm not supposed to tell anybody. But it's *so* exciting."

"Well, don't tell if you're not supposed to." Lonnie turned to the scene Jared was sketching.

"Gloria's up the stump," Steve announced.

Lonnie's mouth dropped open. "What did you say?"

"Knocked up," Steve told her. "In a delicate condition. With child."

"Gloria?" Lonnie stared at him. Jared, too, was listening now, his eyes narrowed with disbelief.

Steve beamed and settled back on the desk, clearly enjoying the sensation he was causing.

"I have it on the very best authority," he said smugly. "She told Mr. Allred's secretary yesterday after she went to the doctor. Gloria and Sonya are quite good friends, you know."

"And Sonya's already passed it on?" Lonnie shook her head. "I thought she was supposed to be a *confidential* secretary."

Steve giggled. "Oh, come on, sweetheart. There are no secrets in a place as tiny as our little station."

Lonnie thought about her own precious secret and her resolve strengthened.

"So, who's the father?" Jared asked, munching on a granola bar as he studied his box of lenses.

"Nobody knows." Steve got up to buy himself a cup of coffee at the vending machine.

"Somebody must know," Lonnie said. "It takes . . . it takes two people to make a baby," she added, looking at the storyboard.

"But that's the most delicious part of the whole story." Steve returned to the cubicle with his cup. "Gloria told Sonya that it must have happened at the New Year's Eve party but she was too drunk to remember a thing about it."

"So how can she be sure that's when it happened?" Lonnie asked.

"Because Gloria had an adventure." Steve giggled. "Apparently she has a vague memory of arriving at the party and dancing for a while, drinking quite a lot. She met somebody and they went upstairs to one of the hotel rooms, using a key she borrowed from a friend whose name she can't remember. After that it's all rather a blur, I gather. Next thing she knew, the lovely Gloria was riding home in a cab, feeling very sick." His face brightened with spiteful amusement. "As it turns out, she was also very pregnant."

Lonnie could sense Jared's shock and tension. His jaw knotted, and his hazel eyes were dark with intensity under the peak of his cap. "Does she remember anything about this guy she went upstairs with? Is it somebody she works with?"

"She has a vague feeling that the man was familiar, but she can't recall him. Sonya says she doesn't remember much at all, poor girl, until the part about finding herself in the cab on the way home."

Jarred slumped in his chair and buried his face in his hands.

Steve looked at the photographer, startled. "What's wrong with him?" he asked Lonnie.

Lonnie touched her friend's arm, feeling dazed and confused. "He's just... He's got a headache today. It's this flu that's going around. We've all got a touch of it." She gave another troubled look at Jared's drooping shoulders, the tense, callused fingers that concealed his face.

"Steve," she said to the copywriter.

"Yes, my angel?"

"Did Sonya say anything.... Do you happen to know what Gloria's planning to... do about this baby?"

"That's another fun part of the story. Our little mother is all excited. She's already begun shopping for designer maternity clothes and brass-plated Jolly Jumpers.''

Lonnie's mouth dropped open. ''Gloria plans to *keep* the baby?''

''Oh, my, yes. Apparently she believes the whole thing is quite amusing. Gloria thinks it's going to be marvelous to have a tiny little clone of herself. She's hoping for a girl, of course.''

Jared raised his head and looked at Lonnie with bleak, helpless misery. ''My God,'' he muttered.

''Hey, guys,'' Steve said brightly, looking from one face to the other. ''What's up?''

''Go get the crew,'' Jared said curtly. ''Tell them to be back here in five minutes.''

Steve began to protest, then looked at the photographer's hard face and thought better of it. He scurried across the car lot, baggy pants flapping in the wind.

''It's mine,'' Jared said to Lonnie when they were alone. ''Gloria's pregnant with my baby.''

''Maybe not,'' she said, feeling appalled and helpless. ''I mean, it could be a... It could have been...''

''Look at the facts, Lon. I slept with somebody on New Year's Eve in a hotel room at the Eldorado. She was gorgeous and sexy, even though I didn't see her face. She was about Gloria's size. She was wearing one of the costumes that Gloria rented.

Now Gloria's pregnant, and she says it happened with a guy at the party that night. This is no coincidence.''

"But, Jared—"

"Oh, hell," he muttered in agony. "Not *Gloria!*"

Lonnie couldn't think of anything to say. When he got up and strode from the room, she hurried miserably along behind him, clutching her armful of storyboards and her ragged script.

Chapter Five

When Jared was a boy, he'd discovered that he had a rare knack for whittling small objects out of wood. Through the years his hobby had developed into a genuine art form.

Now he spent a lot of his free time carving birds, exquisitely accurate little replicas about four inches high. His work was so precise that every feather showed distinctly, along with the dainty talons and the detailed beaks and eyes. He painted the finished birds, using a field guide to get the colors right, and sold them to a gallery in downtown Reno where well-heeled tourists came from all over the world to admire and to buy.

Nobody knew about his pastime except for a few close friends like Lonnie. Sometimes when Jared stopped in at the gallery, he was embarrassed to see the prices that his little birds commanded. His job at the television station paid for all his daily needs and expenses, but the proceeds from his hobby would soon be enough to buy the place in the country that he longed for.

Later on the day of the conversation in the car dealership, Jared sat at his kitchen table working on a cedar waxwing, laboring over the smooth, velvety texture of the feathers as he brooded about love and responsibility.

Gloria was carrying his baby. He didn't have any doubt in his mind that she was the woman he'd slept with that night.

It was a painful disappointment to learn the truth, after the romance of his long search for the mystery girl. But Jared admitted to himself that the passionate memory had begun to fade lately. In its place he'd found himself once again thinking embarrassing things about Lonnie.

He recalled the way she'd looked at work, so pale and troubled. It was all he could do not to call her, just to see if she was feeling all right.

Grimly, he restrained himself. He lifted a small file and began to brush the surface of the wooden bird.

He was certainly going to have to forget all his fantasies about Lonnie after this. If there had ever been a chance of getting close to her and making her look at him as more than a friend, that was all gone now.

Gloria was pregnant. It was Jared's baby she carried, and the reality had to be dealt with. In spite of his dismay, Jared couldn't stop thinking about the baby.

His baby. His own child.

He thought about the harem girl in the moonlit bed and the wondrous mystery of an act that could merge their two bodies to create a whole new person.

Jared was surprised by the depth of his feeling for this unborn child. He'd only learned of its existence a few hours ago, and yet already he loved the baby he'd fathered.

A father. He repeated the word softly to himself, enjoying the sound it made.

Through the years, Jared had behaved much like other men his age. He'd tried to avoid commitment, kept himself free of permanent entanglements. But he was over thirty now and ready to settle down. He liked the idea of being a father.

He studied the little bird, then began to carve the top of its head, working carefully on the dainty crest.

He wanted to be involved right from the beginning, to change diapers and give feedings, to push the kid in her stroller and take her out for walks. He wanted somebody to call him Daddy.

But Gloria . . . Could he stand to be that closely involved with Gloria?

There was no option. The woman was going to be the mother of his child. If he wanted to be close to the baby, he had to learn to get along with Gloria. At the very least, he had to acknowledge his paternity and express a willingness to share expenses and responsibilities.

Finally he got up from the table, went to the telephone and consulted a list of staff phone numbers pinned to the wall.

"Gloria?" he said when she answered. "It's Jared Kilmer."

"Jared? Have I forgotten something I was supposed to do at work? Or were you just dying to hear the sound of my voice?"

She seemed the same as always, both languid and flirtatious. Jared gripped the phone tensely.

"I wanted to talk with you about something."

"Talk away, honey. But hurry it up, okay, because I have to hang up when the alarm clock goes off."

"The alarm clock?" He looked at his watch in confusion. "It's eight o'clock in the evening, Gloria."

"When the alarm clock rings, it's time to take the sea-kelp treatment off my face and apply the cucumber astringent."

"Oh." He hesitated, feeling increasingly awkward.

"What did you want, sweetie?"

"I wanted to ask if you'd like to go out for dinner some night this week."

"Is there some kind of staff function? I can never keep track of these things."

Jared swallowed hard. "No, just...you and me."

There was a brief silence. "I see," Gloria said at last, sounding thoughtful. "Just you and me. That could be fun."

"Friday night?"

"Terrific. Pick me up at six."

Jared agreed, then hung up and wandered to the table where the waxwing perched, regarding him with bright, mocking eyes.

On Friday night, Jared and his date sat at a linen-covered table in one of the posh dining rooms at the Silver Legacy, which was Gloria's favorite casino. She wore a fitted white dress with emerald earrings and necklace and looked beautiful.

Every man in the room probably envies me, Jared thought.

He tugged miserably at his tie, wishing he could be at a burger joint with Lonnie, wearing jeans and his old leather jacket and talking about the upcoming baseball season.

Gloria frowned at the menu. "Nothing seems all that appetizing these days," she said. "I think I'll just have a bit of pasta."

"Would you like to order a bottle of wine?"

"Not for me, thanks. I'm firmly on the wagon."

Jared cleared his throat. "I heard that you..." He fell silent abruptly, remembering at the last moment that Gloria had told her story in confidence to Allred's secretary.

But the weather girl merely glanced at him with wry amusement. "What did you hear, darling?"

"That you... weren't feeling well."

Gloria laughed. "That I'm pregnant, you mean?"

"Yes. I guess that's what I heard."

Gloria seemed unperturbed. She sipped a glass of milk and nibbled on a bread stick. "Well, I'm afraid it's true."

"That's what I wanted to talk with you about tonight, Gloria."

"My pregnancy?" She looked at him in surprise. "Whatever for?"

Jared folded his napkin into a little square, then unfolded it to look at the pattern. "I think," he said in a low voice, "that it's my baby."

"Yours?" her mouth dropped open. "You mean it was *you* that I slept with on New Year's Eve?"

He nodded and took a hasty gulp of water. "I don't remember much about the party, either, except that you were wearing a transparent green outfit. It was really sexy."

"Of course it was. Why else would I choose it?"

"And you were..." He paused awkwardly.

"Great in bed," Gloria said with a placid smile. "I always am, my boy. Even when I'm drunk."

He gave her a cautious glance. "How much do you actually recall about that night? Try to remember, Gloria. It's really important to me."

Gloria sobered and frowned with concentration. "I remember getting to the party late and having quite a lot to drink. They had some kind of punch that must have been spiked. It was really potent."

"In crystal glasses on a side table, close to the desserts?"

"That's the stuff. You remember it, too?"

Jared nodded gloomily. "You gave me two glasses of it."

Gloria laughed. "How naughty of me. No wonder things got out of hand. What happened after I gave you the drinks?"

Jared remembered standing in the shadowed alcove, fondling her breast. His throat tightened. "We...sort of danced a bit, then went upstairs. You had a key."

"I don't remember a thing about it. My very last detailed memory is dancing with one of the disk jockeys and listening to him singing in my ear. After that it's a blur until I found myself in the taxicab, heading for home at about four o'clock in the morning."

"I didn't wake up until about eight. You were long gone by then."

"You wore your cowboy outfit, right? The same as last year."

Jared nodded. Gloria narrowed her eyes, gazing at the velvet draperies.

"I think I remember that. You had a plaid shirt and chaps, and a bandanna on your face."

"And a holster with fake six-guns."

She chuckled ruefully. "But you weren't shooting blanks, were you, sweetheart? My goodness, you've certainly gone and complicated my life."

Jared was a little puzzled by her casualness. The whole thing seemed utterly momentous to him, but she treated it like some kind of joke.

"I understand that you're...planning to keep the baby."

Her eyes widened. "Of course I am. What else would I do?"

"But your career... Aren't you worried about the effect this is going to have?"

Gloria shrugged. "What effect? I'll simply get to buy a whole new wardrobe of designer maternity clothes and then take a few months off from my job. Life will continue."

"You'll go back to work?"

"Everybody goes back to work. The days of the little mother at home in her apron are pretty much dead, don't you think?"

"But what will you do with the baby?"

"I'll hire a nanny." Gloria paused, toying with her glass. "It's not exactly common knowledge, but I have lots of money, Jared. My daddy owned a silver mine as big as the one this place is built on, and I was his only child."

Jared hadn't known this, but he was relieved to hear it. At least she wouldn't suffer financially over her decision to bear and keep the baby.

"I expect to contribute," he said. "I want to be responsible about this."

Gloria gave a peal of laughter. "Well, you're certainly responsible *for* it, but I just told you, I don't need any help."

"I'm not necessarily talking about money." Jared took a sip of water and looked at her directly. "This is my child, too, Gloria. I want to be involved."

"In what way, sweetie?"

"In every way. I want to be a father."

She nodded thoughtfully, still gazing at the window. "I see. So how will we go about this?"

"The best thing," Jared said after a moment's thought, "would be for us to get to know each other first, don't you think?"

"Yes, that's probably an excellent idea. Where shall we start? I understand we're already pretty terrific in bed."

Jared flushed. "I know, but I don't want to... I think we should postpone any kind of sexual relationship for a while."

She raised her eyebrows. "That's pretty much locking the barn door after the horse is gone, don't you think?"

"Maybe, but having sex can interfere with getting to know somebody. People make it a substitute for communication."

"So what do you propose?"

"I think we should start having regular dates, get acquainted and try to be friends. Then maybe we can...grow closer." He stumbled a bit while Gloria gave him a bright, amused glance. "And if we don't, well, it's still better for the baby if we're good friends. Right?"

"That sounds like an excellent plan, my dear. So when should we have our next date?" she asked.

"How about Sunday? We can go for a drive up to Tahoe."

Gloria brightened. "Oh, good! I love Tahoe."

"My parents have a ranch up there," Jared said. "I'd like you to meet them."

Her look of anticipation faded somewhat, but she made no protest. "Is it a big ranch?" she asked after a moment.

"Not very big. Sort of a mom-and-pop kind of operation."

Gloria sighed and nibbled at her bread stick.

St. Patrick's Day came and went. Gloria wore a kelly green sequined sheath to do the weather for two nights in row, and everybody said she'd never looked more radiantly beautiful.

Lonnie spent the next weekend in Las Vegas, shopping for an apartment. She booked a third-floor suite in a pleasant treed area near the university and was told she could move in any time after April fifteenth. But pets weren't allowed, except for small dogs.

She drove to Reno and glumly surveyed her little menagerie. Puffy could go with her, so she'd be no problem. The crow was almost recovered and could soon fly away. Nobody was going to object to the turtle. But Shadow, the tomcat . . . he was another matter.

Lonnie stood in the backyard on a Sunday afternoon, scattering cracked wheat for the crow while Shadow watched with greedy attention.

Jared strolled around the corner, startling her. "Hi, Lon," he said, giving her a hug and dropping a casual kiss on her cheek. "How's my favorite girl?"

Lonnie pulled away from him. "I need to find a home for Shadow," she said abruptly. "Do you think your family would let him stay at the ranch, Jared?"

"Why can't he live here?"

"The landlord is upset with him. He scratches the walls and baseboards." Lonnie exchanged a private, apologetic glance with her cat, who never caused any damage in the house.

"If he goes to the ranch, he'll have to live in the barn," Jared warned.

"That's all right. He'd like that. And he could catch mice, too. Shadow's a great mouser."

"Okay," Jared said idly. "I'll take him. Hey, that crow's almost better, isn't he?"

They watched as the big bird pecked lustily at the grain.

"You should do a model of him," Lonnie said. "He's so beautiful."

Jared grinned. "Most people don't look on crows as collector's items."

"But look how smooth and glossy he is. When the sun strikes his feathers just right, you can see all the colors of the rainbow."

Jared hugged her again. "I really love you, Lon," he said, his voice husky.

"Do you want a cup of hot chocolate?" she asked, heading inside.

"Sure." Jared looked at a stack of boxes on the porch. "What's all this?"

"Spring-cleaning. I'm clearing out a bunch of stuff to give away."

Jared sat at the table, booted feet extended, and sipped coffee while Lonnie looked at him with guilty hunger. The man had never looked so handsome, so utterly desirable.

And to make it worse, she was almost three months pregnant with his child.

"So," she asked, busying herself with the wrapper on a package of oatmeal cookies, "how are you and Gloria getting along these days?"

"She's not as bad as people think, you know. She's really quite a nice person."

"I know she has lots of good qualities," Lonnie said. "I've always liked her, even when she annoys me."

She sat opposite him at the table, studying the place mat. Again she wrestled with the same weary problem that kept her awake every night.

As Jared drew closer and closer to Gloria, apparently excited by the prospect of being a father, Lonnie became less certain what her own responsibilities were in this whole messy business.

Wasn't she obligated to tell him the truth? After all, the child Gloria was carrying had nothing to do with Jared. It was probably sired by one of the local disk jockeys or a gaffer from another station, somebody who clearly wasn't turning up to claim responsibility.

Meanwhile, Jared's child was safe in Lonnie's womb. Didn't the man have a right to know?

She wanted so desperately to keep it all a secret, to slip away from Reno and have nobody be the wiser. Sometime in the future when Jared came to visit her in Las Vegas and saw that she was pregnant, she planned to tell him that it had been the result of a casual affair, certainly none of his business.

But now, everything was changed. No matter how much he might despise her for her actions, Lonnie felt morally obligated to tell him the truth. And she should do it now, immediately, while she still had a bit of courage. . . .

Jared glanced at his watch. "Gloria and I are driving out to the ranch again for the evening," he said. "Do you want me to take the cat now?"

"Today?" she asked in alarm.

"Why not?"

Why not, indeed. She had to move within a month or so. Any loose ends that could be tied up early were that much less to worry about.

Aching with sadness, Lonnie went outside to lift the tomcat in her arms. He nestled, purring, and rubbed his head under her chin.

Lonnie held him a moment, looking at the springtime freshness of the yard where crocuses and tulips grew around the old stone foundation and the trees were starting to bud.

She knew it was at least a month too early, but she fancied she already could feel the baby growing within her, swimming happily around in his safe, watery world.

Jared needed to be told. He had a right to know that his real baby was here, inside her body. She dreaded the revelation and its messy aftermath, but it was the only fair thing to do.

Still holding the cat, she marched inside, stiff with resolve.

"Hey, Shadow," Jared said cheerfully, taking the big tomcat onto his knee and stroking him. "You want to go for a nice ride in the country and make some new friends?"

Shadow arched and purred, rubbing against his shoulder.

"He'll be fine at the ranch, honey," Jared said to Lonnie, obviously misreading her unhappy expression. "You should see how much fun your rabbits are having."

Lonnie sat down opposite him. "Jared . . ."

He frowned into the depths of his hot chocolate. "I've got something to tell you, Lon."

"What?"

"I think Gloria and I are going to get married."

Her jaw dropped. *"Married?"*

Jared stirred uneasily in the chair. "I know it's pretty sudden, but we've been talking a lot about it, and we think it's best for the baby. Both of us want to be good parents."

"But, Jared," Lonnie whispered in despair. "Do you . . . do you love her?"

"What's love?" he asked with a touch of bitterness. "A guy can be in love with a girl and never get the chance to tell her. People don't usually get together with the ones they want, anyway, and it's probably best that way. The trick is just to make the best of the hand you've been dealt."

"But if you don't—"

"I really, really like her," he said firmly. "And I want to do this. It's not just about the baby, either. Gloria and I have been spending a lot of time together over the past month, and we care about each other. We're going ahead with it, so don't try to talk me out of it, Lonnie. I've even discussed it with my parents already. In fact, I'm telling you now because we both want you to be one of our attendants at the wedding, along with Tony."

"Tony Newell?"

Jared nodded. "I called him last night. Tony said he'd be happy to come down from L.A. for the wedding."

"I've only seen him a couple of times since college."

"I know. By the way, Lon, he said hello to you, too."

Lonnie gripped her hands tightly in her lap, still appalled by what he'd said.

"So, will you?" he asked.

"What?"

"Stand up at our wedding?"

"I...don't think I can," Lonnie whispered. "When is it?"

"Probably Easter. About the third weekend in April. I'll let you know more details as they develop."

As they develop.

Lonnie thought about the baby in her womb and felt herself drowning in sadness.

"Lon? Was there something you wanted to tell me? I think I interrupted you a minute ago."

Lonnie remembered her decision to tell him the truth. But how could she possibly do that now? If he and Gloria really cared about each other, then telling Jared the truth would just be a shoddy, destructive thing to do. It was better to let him go on thinking he was the father of Gloria's child, since he seemed bent on marrying the woman.

In the meantime, Lonnie would soon be escaping from all of them. She would drive away, head south into the shimmering heat of the desert and leave the whole mess behind.

"Why are you crying, honey?" Jared leaned forward tenderly to stroke her cheek.

"I'm just . . . so sad to see . . . Shadow leaving." Lonnie jumped from her chair and ran into the bathroom. "Please, Jared, take him now. Go, before I change my mind."

When she came back, both Jared and the cat were gone, and her house was quiet in the afternoon sunlight.

Chapter Six

The days ticked on to mid-April. Lonnie gave her notice privately to the station manager and asked him to keep her plans quiet. She also made arrangements to move out of her apartment on Saturday, the day of Jared's wedding.

It was Monday morning, five days before the fateful day, and Lonnie was working with an artist on a new weatherboard. Gloria had already announced her intention to switch from her usual pastels and wear black and navy exclusively during the later months of her pregnancy, so they would soon be needing a lighter board as a backdrop.

Gloria came into the art studio while they were working. She looked slim and radiant in a yellow silk jumpsuit. Like Lonnie, she still showed no outward signs of pregnancy. Over one shoulder she carried a plastic garment bag containing a suit made of ivory silk, crusted with seed pearls and lace.

"My wedding outfit," she said, displaying the suit for Lonnie who sat cross-legged on the floor next to the artist, helping him sketch an overlay for a cold front. "I ordered it from Neiman-Marcus, and it just arrived."

"It's beautiful," Lonnie said automatically.

"Jared's wearing a tux with black tie. I've tried for weeks to talk him into white tie, but apparently there are limits to what the man will tolerate."

Gloria rolled her eyes in exasperation, then looked more closely at the big weatherboard leaning against the wall.

"See how good it looks?" Lonnie turned to the artist, a shy little man with steel-rimmed glasses and a knitted vest. "Helmut and I have got this almost finished. We plan to use gray for storms, beige for warm fronts and pink for the jet stream."

"How about temperature ranges?" Gloria asked.

"We're considering shades of green." Lonnie displayed a sheaf of color chips.

"Okay." Gloria cleared a space on the worktable, hoisted herself into a sitting position and watched, swinging her feet in their high-heeled sandals. Occasionally she leaned forward to display an ample cleavage that almost spilled over the front of the jumpsuit.

Helmut began to look nervous. His big ears turned pink, a sure sign of agitation. At last he scuttled away, muttering something about coffee.

"That poor little man is terrified of me," Gloria said with a chuckle. "He seems to think I'll gobble him alive if I get close to him."

"Why not? You'd gobble anybody if you had the chance," Lonnie muttered.

The weather girl looked unperturbed, but Lonnie immediately regretted her sharp words.

None of this, after all, was Gloria's fault. In fact, Gloria and Jared were both honestly trying to make the best of an awkward situation. Lonnie was the one deliberately lying and misleading people.

On her knees, she worked her away across the bottom of the weatherboard to study the Hawaiian Islands, wondering if they should be darkened a bit.

"Are you sure you can't come to the wedding?" Gloria watched as Lonnie shaded color into the islands. "Poor Jared is simply crushed. He says you're his best friend and he wants you to be there."

"I know. I'm really sorry to miss it," Lonnie said, keeping her face averted. "But I have a date I can't possibly break."

"No kidding. Anybody I know?"

A turtle, a terrier and a U-Haul trailer, Lonnie thought grimly. *That's my date.*

She looked at the other woman. "Are you happy, Gloria? Are you glad to be getting married?"

Gloria shrugged. "Happy enough, I guess, though it certainly wasn't my original plan to be doing this right now. Still, Jared's a nice man, and he's so excited about being a father. I can hardly deny him the right to be with his child."

"But is that the only reason you're marrying him? Because of the baby?"

"Goodness, no!" Gloria said with a fond chuckle. "I mean, face it, the man's a complete stud. Have you ever seen him with his shirt off?"

Lonnie shook her head, concentrating on the weatherboard.

"He's funny, bright and hardworking, and very considerate. Besides, the poor thing absolutely adores me. A girl could hardly do better. I never really thought I was capable of falling in love, but I'm starting to change my mind."

"I see." Lonnie's heart ached. She fought to hold back the tears.

"Do you happen to know Jared's best man?" Gloria asked idly.

"Tony Newell?"

"That's the name. Jared introduced us last night when we were having our rehearsal dinner over at John Ascuaga's."

"That's where you're getting married?" Lonnie asked. "At the Nugget?"

She tried to picture Jared saying his wedding vows in a casino with his family looking on. But of course, none of this was her business.

"The casino manager is a good friend of mine." Gloria smiled. "He's letting us use one of the private rooms and he'll lay on a terrific spread for the guests. You really should come, honey. It's going to be one hell of a party."

"It sounds very nice," Lonnie said.

"Getting back to Tony Newell . . ."

"We all went to college together." Lonnie frowned at a collection of yellow smiley faces representing sunshine. "Jared and Tony and I were inseparable, like the Three Musketeers. But Tony's the one who went on to bigger things."

"Jared tells me he's a director now, actually working in Hollywood."

"He's had three big movies in the past two years," Lonnie said proudly. "Last year he was nominated for a Golden Globe."

"I know. Did you ever have a romantic interest in him?"

"Tony?" Lonnie asked, surprised. "No, he was always a little too ambitious for my tastes. But he and Jared are great friends."

Gloria frowned, suddenly restless. "I hate those ridiculous smiley faces. Couldn't Helmut come up with something different? Daisies or chrysanthemums, something like that?"

"Flowers?" Lonnie looked dubiously at the board. "I guess I could talk to him about it, but I don't know if—"

"Chalk it up to the whims of pregnancy," Gloria said cheerfully. "I never know what mood I'm going to be in from one minute to the next."

Lonnie took a deep breath. This was a moment she'd dreaded for weeks, but it couldn't safely be put off any longer, and today was as good an opportunity as any.

"Guess what, Gloria?" She cleared her throat awkwardly. "I'm pregnant, too."

Gloria's eyes widened. "You *are?* Really?"

"Really." Lonnie got to her feet and crossed the room to sprawl in one of the shabby armchairs. "In fact, I'm about as far along as you. I got pregnant sometime around Christmas."

"Well, isn't this exciting! Lonnie, you little dickens, you haven't said a word to *anybody.*"

"I didn't want to talk about it at first," Lonnie said. "In fact, I only told my mother last night. She was thrilled."

"So?" Gloria asked brightly.

"So what?"

"Who's the lucky guy?"

"He's..." Lonnie nibbled cautiously on her thumbnail. "He's somebody I've been involved with for a long time."

"How perfectly delicious. Will you be getting married, too?"

"We're talking about it," Lonnie said, reluctant to tell any more lies. "In fact, he and I have been talking quite a bit lately about the idea of getting married."

"But why didn't you *tell* us?"

"You were so happy and excited about your own situation." Lonnie looked at her sneakers. "I didn't want to distract anybody."

"Well, for heaven's sake. Look, why don't we have a double wedding?" Gloria's eyes brightened. "Hey, this is a great idea! It would be such fun, Lonnie. And we'd get all kinds of coverage," she went on with growing excitement. "Maybe we could even pull a national spot if we promoted it right. Old friends from local television station exchange vows in glamorous double ceremony. Wouldn't it be marvelous?"

"I don't think so," Lonnie murmured. "We're . . . my friend and I aren't quite at that stage, Gloria."

"Oh, all right." The weather girl subsided, pouting, then looked at Lonnie with new interest. "Have you had morning sickness, sweetie?"

"A little, but it's not really confined to the morning at all. The nausea seems to happen mostly when I get hungry."

"Me, too," Gloria said. "I keep soda crackers in my desk and nibble them all day long. I find that herbal tea helps, too."

"Really? I've given up coffee and everything else with caffeine, but I never thought about using herbal teas."

"They're soothing on the tummy and they help you sleep better. I can loan you a whole package. Look, do you find yourself running to the bathroom every ten minutes?"

"Ten minutes?" Lonnie said with a rueful smile. "I can't even make it for that long. I've been interrupting copy meetings, leaving the set in the middle of every shoot, excusing myself from phone conversations . . ."

Gloria chuckled. "Isn't it awful? And this blotchy stuff all over my face. What's that all about? I can't even cover it with makeup anymore."

"My doctor says the blotches disappear toward the end of the second trimester."

"Who's your doctor?" Gloria hoisted herself lightly from the desk. "Come on, I'm going to write down the name. My doctor never tells me anything."

They left the art studio, deep in conversation. As they headed for Gloria's office, Lonnie was struck by the sad irony of the situation.

For the first time in their lives, she and Gloria were talking together like friends. And their new warmth was occurring at a moment when Gloria was about to steal away the love of Lonnie's life, the father of her unborn child.

"So guess what I learned yesterday?" Gloria gave Jared a bright glance across the table.

"What did you learn yesterday?"

"Guess."

He sighed. These little games were cute, but tiring after a hard day at work. Besides, Jared had other problems on his mind. He was getting married in a few days and he wasn't at all sure that he wanted to.

But there was no way out. The room was booked, invitations were sent, his tux was ordered.

And Gloria was pregnant with his child.

Jared sighed again and looked at his plate. Lately he had to fight an almost overpowering urge to go to Lonnie's house, put his head on her shoulder and pour out his heart. While Gloria continued to chatter, he concentrated on his steak in brooding silence.

This situation was like those times when you couldn't decide between two options, so you flipped a coin. While the coin was dropping, you tended to realize which side you wanted to turn up.

For years he'd been reluctant about committing to marriage and responsibility, but now that it had happened, Jared knew with absolute certainty which woman he wanted. The trouble was, his revelation had come too late.

For the thousandth time, he cursed himself for that moment of lustful recklessness at the New Year's party. A man of thirty, and he'd gotten himself caught in a snare like some hotheaded adolescent.

But the thing was done. Gloria carried his baby, and he had strong feelings of responsibility toward the unborn child.

Wearily, Jared's mind circled in the same old track. Was he really behaving responsibly by marrying this woman when he didn't love her? After all, he could be a father without marrying.

He was concerned about the child's welfare, but Gloria might turn out to be a loving, stable parent all on her own. She certainly seemed committed to having a healthy pregnancy. Perhaps it wasn't necessary for Jared to live with her. He could give her money regularly and arrange some kind of visiting rights with his child, just like fathers who were divorced.

It wouldn't be the ideal situation, of course, and certainly not the kind of family life he craved. But it would leave him free to...

"What did you say?" he asked suddenly, jerking his head up.

Gloria looked at him with wry amusement. "You haven't been listening to a word, have you, sweetie?"

"You wanted me to guess something. After that you started talking about Lonnie."

Gloria sulked briefly, then relented and leaned forward, lowering her voice to a dramatic pitch. "Have you noticed anything different about her lately?"

"Not really. She seems kind of quiet, I guess. After Christmas I thought she was looking a little pale and sick, but she seems better now." Jared sighed. "I hardly ever get to talk to her anymore. She's busy all the time."

"She certainly is." Gloria leaned back in her chair and took a sip of milk.

"What do you mean?"

"I mean, darling, that your little friend is pregnant."

Jared's mouth dropped open. *"Lonnie?"*

Gloria smiled, obviously pleased by the effect of her news. "Absolutely. She told me she got pregnant around Christmastime."

Jared tried to remember what Lonnie had been doing throughout the holidays. He'd invited her to the ranch for Christmas dinner, but she said she was planning to cook for a few people.

Who were they?

He frowned, struggling to recall the conversation.

Mrs. Schwartz, Pete from film editing, her cousin, her ex-husband.

Jared felt a sudden chill of fear. "Did she say who the guy is?"

"An old friend, apparently. She says they're talking about getting married."

It had to be Stan. Lonnie didn't know anybody else well enough to be discussing marriage.

Jared thought about Lonnie's charming, faithless ex-husband. It had been hard enough to believe that a woman like her would ever marry Stan, let alone fall into the same trap a second time after all the misery he'd caused her.

But if she was pregnant . . .

Jared clenched his hands in anguish, picturing how it could have happened.

Stan had probably lingered after all the other guests left. He and Lonnie sipped some wine and relaxed in the romantic glow of the Christmas tree. They started to reminisce about old times, and then . . .

"I knew she was lonely," he muttered. "I should have spent more time with her. She was too vulnerable."

Gloria watched him with a look of thoughtful appraisal. "But that's not all I learned," she said at last.

"What else?"

"I had coffee with Stephen Allred yesterday afternoon. He confided something to me in strictest confidence, so don't breathe a word about it to anybody, okay?"

Jared's alarm deepened. "What are you talking about, Gloria?"

"Lonnie's leaving the station. In fact, Friday is her last day of work. She asked Stephen not to say anything until she was gone."

Jared stared at the woman's beautiful face. "You're crazy," he said flatly. "Lonnie would never do all this without telling me."

"Apparently her feelings for you aren't as warm as you thought. Every word of this is true, Jared. She's pregnant, she's got a job at a station in Vegas, and she's leaving on the weekend. I assume that's where the boyfriend lives, too."

"I can't believe she'd go away without saying goodbye."

"We're getting married on the weekend, remember?" Gloria gave him a teasing smile. "I guess

Lonnie didn't want to cast a shadow on our day, so she's just going to slip away without any big fuss, then contact everybody later.''

Jared shook his head, still feeling stunned and miserable.

Gloria reached out to squeeze his hand. ''Don't look so tragic, darling,'' she said with genuine sympathy. ''Lonnie will be happy in Las Vegas. I'm sure she will.''

Chapter Seven

Jared's wedding day dawned bright and clear, a glorious spring morning in the mountain city.

Lonnie woke from a troubled sleep and lay in her bed in the cool stillness of dawn, surrounded by packing boxes, dismantled furniture and stacks of clothes.

She covered her face with her hands to block out the light that filtered through the faded curtains. At last she groaned, climbed out of bed and wandered into the kitchen in her pajamas.

The dishes and utensils were all packed, but she'd left a mug on the counter along with a box of crackers and a few packets of Gloria's herbal tea. Lonnie put a tea bag into the mug and covered it with hot water from the faucet. She searched in vain for a spoon, then used one of her car keys to prod the bag.

Munching crackers, she carried her tea to the window and looked out in brooding silence. Puffy trotted into the room carrying her blue plastic clown, which she dropped hopefully at Lonnie's feet.

Lonnie bent to pat the little dog. "Today's the day, honey. We'll finish packing this stuff and load the trailer, and then we'll head off to our brand-new life. It's going to be so much fun."

And while they were driving south, Jared would be saying his wedding vows.

She went outside and sat on the step in the thin morning sunlight. As if sensing her misery, Puffy scrambled along behind her and crawled into her lap, whimpering softly. Lonnie stroked the little dog's silky coat as she stared at the sky.

She carried Jared's child in her womb, and the baby was worth anything she had to suffer. In just a few months, Lonnie would hold a newborn child in her arms. This part of Jared was hers forever, even if she never saw the man again.

She choked back a sob. Puffy licked her hand and gazed at her, dark eyes liquid with sympathy.

Lonnie set the mug down and cuddled her dog close to her, drowning in sorrow. She buried her face against Puffy's side for a moment, then released the dog and got up.

This wasn't accomplishing anything. There was a ton of work to do before she could close the door and drive away. And the harder she worked, the less she'd be able to think about what was going to happen today, across town in that glamorous casino.

With luck, Lonnie could be heading out early in the afternoon. By the time darkness came she'd be far away, ready to begin settling into her new place. The job of unpacking would keep her busy for hours.

Far too busy to think about Jared's wedding night and his smiling tenderness as he held the beautiful woman who was his wife.

Lonnie sobbed and rushed into the house, hurrying to change into jeans and a T-shirt, pull on socks and sneakers. After a few minutes she became aware of a plaintive, distant crying, and realized that Puffy was still locked outside in the yard.

She let the little dog into the house, then settled down to work with grim determination, packing and lugging boxes outside to the rented trailer parked by the curb.

The wedding was scheduled for two o'clock. Jared and Tony, his best man, arrived at the casino shortly after lunch, both resplendent in black tie and tux, and were ushered upstairs to the private room Gloria's friend John had provided.

Tony Newell was a powerfully built man with a rugged face, a nose that had been broken twice during his boxing days in college and a dusting of gray in his curly dark hair. He carried himself with smiling arrogance and wore heavy gold rings on both hands.

"Wow," he muttered, standing next to Jared. "Look at this spread. You'd think the woman planned it for years."

The place was indeed awesome. A windowless room in the bowels of the huge casino had been magically transformed into a spring garden chapel, complete with flower-covered trellis, rockery and fountain. Small gilt chairs were threaded with ribbons and arranged to face the bower. Each chair held a complimentary basket filled with dainty bits of candied fruit and nuts and a wrapped piece of wedding cake.

Gloria had even unearthed an organ somewhere and installed it at one side of the room behind a bank of spring lilies and daffodils, manned by a little dark-haired man in a white tuxedo. Soft strains of Debussy filled the room, soothing and beautiful.

"Somebody's getting married here today, all right," Tony said with chuckle, punching Jared on the arm. "You lucky dog."

"Lucky," Jared echoed, feeling ghastly. "Is that what you think?"

"She's a beautiful woman." Tony gave him a curious glance. "And you're in love, aren't you?"

Jared avoided his friend's eyes. "She's pregnant with my baby."

Tony watched him a moment longer, then looked around restlessly. "I wish Lonnie was coming. It's been years since I've seen her. I can't believe she didn't want to come to your wedding."

"I think Lonnie's getting back together with Stan and she's afraid to let us know about it. She's pregnant, too, and she's moving to Vegas. I told you all that, didn't I?"

"Stan!" Tony muttered in contempt. "What a jerk. I never could figure out what Lon saw in him."

"Me, neither," Jared said gloomily. "Women are a mystery, I guess. But I thought Lonnie would have learned her lesson."

His family stared to drift in, parents and brothers with their wives and children. The Kilmer clan stood gazing around in startled admiration at the lavish decorations.

Jared's mother was tanned and attractive in a pale blue dress. She came over to hug her son. "Are you really happy, dear?" she whispered, drawing back to look up at him with a troubled, searching expression.

"Sure I am, Mom." Jared forced a smile. "It's my wedding day."

"I know. But I always thought..."

Seth Kilmer, Jared's father, approached to put his hand on his wife's shoulder. "Come on, Betty," he whispered. "Let's find a place to sit down. Jared and Tony have things to look after."

"Hi, Dad," Jared said.

The two men shook hands, and Jared looked into his father's weathered face with a desperate, seeking glance.

"We love you, son." Seth clapped a big hand on his shoulder. "Your mother and I, we're always behind you, whatever you do."

Jared's eyes burned with tears, and he turned away hastily.

Gloria's family and friends had begun to arrive. Most of them were people Jared had never met, but Tony was clearly impressed. "There must be enough diamonds in here to carpet the floor of a Rolls-Royce," he said, looking around. "This is a very classy group you're marrying into."

"Yeah, well, I'm a very classy guy," Jared muttered.

A little girl edged close to them, wearing a long white lace dress and a circlet of spring flowers on her head. She carried a straw basket filled with rose petals and was looking shyly at her patent slippers.

Jared recognized the little girl as Gloria's niece, though he'd last seen her in denim overalls and a sweatshirt printed with dinosaurs.

"Hi, Emily," he said when she paused at his knee. "You look like a princess."

The child murmured something inaudible.

Jared bent closer.

"What did you say, honey? I couldn't hear."

"Gloria wants you," the little girl whispered in his ear. "She says you're supposed to come right now."

Jared stood erect and looked at his groomsman. "I'm not supposed to see the bride before the wedding, am I? Isn't it bad luck or something?"

Tony grinned. "I doubt that your lady cares much about all those little traditions. Where is she, honey? Let's go find her."

The flower girl turned with obvious relief and led them out of the makeshift chapel, down the hall to a room where there was a bustle of staff and guests carrying wrapped gifts, cases of champagne, flowers and other supplies.

Emily paused on the threshold and looked gravely at the two men. "I'll tell Gloria you're here," she whispered.

The child vanished and emerged soon afterward, accompanied by a flurry of people. Apparently Gloria was clearing out the room.

"You can come in now," Emily whispered, then bolted down the hall with the others, trailing her basket.

Jared and Tony entered to find Gloria sitting alone at an ornate golden dressing table, examining herself in the mirror. She looked radiant, so lovely that Jared felt a lump in his throat.

"You're beautiful, Gloria," he said quietly, standing behind her and meeting her eyes in the mirror.

She wore a creamy silk suit trimmed with lace, fitted to show off her figure and her spectacular legs. On her piled hair, a circlet of pearls held a modish veil that barely covered her face.

Jared dropped a hand on her shoulder and patted the silk awkwardly, hardly able to believe that this ravishing creature would be his wife in just a few minutes.

Gloria reached up to touch his hand, still meeting his eyes steadily in the mirror. "I need to know if you're having any second thoughts, Jared."

Tony shifted on his feet and looked uncomfortable. "Look, if you two want me to leave—"

"Don't you dare," Gloria told him. "I want you here. You're Jared's best friend, and you've known him a long time. Does the man really want to marry me?"

"Sure, he does." Tony looked at his friend in surprise. "Don't you?"

"Of course I do. You're a beautiful woman, and you're going to have my baby." Jared took a deep breath. "I wouldn't change any of this. I'm doing exactly what I want to do, Gloria."

She turned in the chair to look at him. "But do you really think we're compatible? We have such different tastes, you and I. There's almost nothing we can share."

"We'll share the baby." After all his reluctance, Jared was surprised to find himself defending the opposite position, almost pleading. "Hey," he added with a smile, "we're terrific in bed, too. That's something we'll definitely share."

"I don't remember what we're like in bed." Gloria looked at a sheaf of rosebuds lying on the dressing table. She reached out to touch the delicate petals. "I have no memory of that particular occasion, and we haven't slept together since."

"Well, it was great," Jared assured her. "Believe me, Gloria," he added huskily, "I'm looking forward to being with my harem girl again."

Gloria's face turned pale beneath the makeup. She gripped one of the flowers and pulled it slowly from the wrappings, shredding the petals. "What did you say?"

Again Tony began to edge nearer to the door. "Well," he said heartily, "if you two don't mind, I think I'll just—"

Gloria got up and strode across the room to grasp Tony's hand. She hauled him back to sit next to her at the dressing table, while Jared stood looking at them.

They made a nice couple, he thought. The two of them really looked like they belonged together. Then he realized in confusion that he was thinking about his best friend and the woman he was about to marry. He shook his head, feeling dazed.

"What did you say about a harem girl?" Gloria repeated, leaning forward tensely. She was clutching Tony's hand with such a firm grip that Jared could see his friend wincing.

"It was... Come on, Gloria." Jared laughed awkwardly. "It was the costume you wore to the New Year's party. You were a harem girl in transparent green pants and a heavy veil, little gold jacket and slippers, bells on your ankles..."

Gloria leaned back in the chair, shaking her head. "I certainly wasn't. I was a nymph of spring."

"But you said— We've talked about your sexy green costume."

"Oh, it was green and transparent, all right." Gloria turned to stare at herself in the mirror. "But it was a long dress and sandals, with a silk mask covering my face and a circlet of flowers on my hair like Emily's. I don't remember much about the rest of that party, but I definitely know what I was wearing."

Jared's head swam. "I don't remember anything like that. I remember a little gold jacket and green pants, and a beaded green headdress with just your eyes showing. And bells on your ankle."

"There were no bells on my costume, Jared." Gloria looked at him with sympathy.

"Then why do I remember them so clearly?"

"Because it wasn't me you went to bed with that night. And you're certainly not the man who fathered my baby."

Tears began to trickle down her cheeks, along with dark smears of mascara. Tony took a tissue from the dressing table, lifted her veil and dabbed at her face with surprising tenderness. Gloria leaned against the other man and gave him a wan, grateful smile.

Jared gripped the back of a chair, his head spinning. "But... Why are you telling me all this now?"

Gloria shrugged. "A girl's got to be fair. As sweet as you are, darling, I still don't want to acquire you under false pretenses. If you're really just marrying me because of this baby—and I suspect you are—well, I'm afraid you're making a big mistake."

"But all those people out there—"

"They can have a nice party even if there's no wedding." Gloria began to display some of her old briskness. "In fact, they'll hardly miss the ceremony. This way, they can head straight for the buffet without any distractions.''

Tony patted her arm and smiled, his face warm with admiration.

''But I— That night...'' Jared was floundering helplessly. ''I mean, there's no doubt that it happened. I wasn't *that* drunk.''

''Of course it happened, you idiot,'' Gloria said with a touch of impatience, though she was still sniffling. ''It just didn't happen with me, that's all. Your harem girl was a different woman altogether.''

''Who?'' Jared leaned forward, suddenly intent. ''Do you have any idea who she was?''

Gloria frowned at herself in the mirror. She reached for a brush and some tissues and began to repair the ravages of her tears.

''Well, now, I might,'' she said with annoying languor. ''I think I just might know who your mystery girl was, sweetie.''

Chapter Eight

Jared grasped her shoulder. "Who was it?" he asked. "Who wore the harem costume?"

Gloria rolled her eyes at Tony. "We have this big media costume party every year on New Year's Eve," she told him. "It's so much fun. We all dress up and lose our inhibitions."

"For God's sake, Gloria!"

She ignored Jared and continued to address the groomsman. "I like to spend a lot of time choosing my costume. In fact, I usually rent half a dozen outfits at different places and try them on at home before I make my decision."

Tony nodded gravely while Jared shifted from one foot to the other, resisting the urge to shake her.

"When I took my costumes back to one of the stores after the party, the girl at the desk asked me if I'd worn the harem outfit. I was surprised, to say the least, because I hadn't rented anything like that. I asked her to check the books, and there it was, a green harem girl costume, booked out to Gloria Merrick."

"I know all about that," Jared muttered. "I checked the same place."

"Well, knowing that I wasn't the one who rented that costume," Gloria went on, "I asked the clerk if she could remember who picked it up and gave my name."

She faced the mirror and pulled her cheek down to dab at the smeared mascara. Solicitously, Tony handed her another box of tissues.

"And?" Jared said.

"And she told me it was a pretty woman in blue jeans, with long blond hair in a French braid."

Gloria swiveled on her chair and cast a significant glance at Jared, who watched her in stunned silence.

"Does that ring any bells, sweetie?" she asked.

Jared's head began to whirl again. *"Lonnie?"* he breathed. "You think it was Lonnie who wore that costume?"

"It could well have been." Gloria tapped a bottle of nail polish on the surface of the dressing table. "I had no idea until just now that your mystery date was a harem girl. I thought it was me, the Nymph of Springtime. In fact, I didn't really give the whole matter much thought at all. But, you know," she reminded him with deliberate casualness, "Lonnie happens to be pregnant, too."

His mouth dropped open, and he grasped the back of the chair. "My God," he whispered. "You think . . ."

"It's a distinct possibility." Gloria continued to examine the bottle of nail polish. "After all, I don't think the poor woman exactly has an active sex life, do you?"

"But that means…" Jared looked from one face to the other.

"It means you should probably get on over there," Gloria said calmly, raising a silk sleeve to look at her watch. "And you really should hurry, dear, before she leaves the city."

Tony reached out to give the bride a hug. "Gloria, you're one hell of a woman," he said warmly.

She smiled at the handsome groomsman. "Tell me, Mr. Newell, do you have any plans for the evening? I think I might just happen to be free, after all."

Overcome with emotion, Jared bent to kiss her cheek. Then he left the room, striding down the hall and into the chapel where the guests waited in their chairs, caressed by the soft music of the organ.

Gloria followed him, with Tony keeping a protective arm around her shoulder.

Jared was so dazed with relief and excitement that he could hardly contain himself. He walked up to the bower at the front of the room, cleared his throat and turned to face the startled guests.

"I'm sorry, folks, but Gloria's decided she doesn't want to marry me after all," he said. "I know I'm losing a wonderful woman, but I hope we can all still be friends."

He looked at Gloria, who stood near the back of the room. She gave him an encouraging grin and blew him a kiss.

The crowd gaped at him, then craned their necks toward Gloria, who nodded and smiled in queenly fashion.

"I have to leave now," Jared went on, "but you're all welcome to stay and enjoy the buffet and the music. Gloria and Tony will be here to look after all of you. I hope you have a great time."

In the hushed silence that followed his announcement, he left the front of the chapel and walked over to hug his mother.

"Jared," she whispered, "what on earth is happening?"

"It's okay, Mom. I'm going across town to see Lonnie," he told her softly. Then he clapped his hand on his father's shoulder and turned away.

The last thing Jared saw before he left the chapel was the sudden blaze of happiness on his mother's face.

One of the neighbors helped Lonnie haul the bigger pieces of furniture into the trailer, then left her alone to finish the job. She was hot, tired and dirty by the time she loaded the last of the boxes. Her back ached, too, probably because of her developing pregnancy. The thought of driving for eight hours and then unpacking all that stuff made her feel desperately weary, but it had to be done. There was no choice but to keep plodding ahead.

She wandered into the house to wash her face at the kitchen sink and dry it on the sleeve of her jacket. With Puffy trotting at her heels, she went through the empty house room by room, checking for anything she might have missed.

The place looked so sad and shabby, echoing in the silence. Lonnie could hardly believe that she'd lived here for years and had so many happy times.

Friends had lounged around the table, talking and laughing, and enjoyed barbecues on the patio. Jared had sat by that window in the kitchen, chatting with her while he worked on his little carved birds.

She remembered his strong, tanned hands, the way he gripped the knife while curls of wood fell neatly onto the table....

Tears burned in her eyes. She bent to scoop Puffy into her arms, grabbed her handbag and left the house, running down the walk to her car.

Inside, she settled the dog on a nest of blankets in the back seat and gave her the little plastic clown.

Puffy nosed her baby lovingly, then tucked it under the edge of the blanket and rested her chin on her paws.

Harold the turtle watched her balefully from the terrarium on the front set. His little eyes were dark with suspicion.

"You'll like Las Vegas," Lonnie told him. "It's a fun place for turtles, Harold. It really is."

Somewhat cheered by the sound of her own voice, she put the car in gear and pulled away from the curb, looking over her shoulder to make sure the trailer was following properly.

Lonnie made her way onto Virginia, then drove along the Strip on the road that ran through Sparks, heading for the Fallon junction.

She had a bad moment when she passed the Nugget and saw its lofty bulk against the blue skyline.

It was almost two o'clock. Jared and Gloria would be saying their wedding vows in a few minutes. Tears blurred her eyes, and she sobbed aloud, then set her jaw with grim determination and headed onto the freeway.

Lonnie was almost half an hour out of Reno, ready to pull off the freeway and turn toward Fallon, when she gripped the wheel in sudden alarm and braked to a stop on the shoulder of the road.

Puffy woke up and blinked at her as the soothing movement of the car paused abruptly.

"The keys," Lonnie told her dog. "I forgot to leave the damn house keys. They're still in my purse."

Puffy sighed and nestled deeper into the blankets.

"I guess I could mail them." Lonnie rummaged in her handbag, frowning. "But I promised I'd leave them on the counter. If the landlord gets upset, he might not give me the full damage deposit, and I can't afford to..."

Harold eyed her bitterly from the depths of his terrarium.

"I know," Lonnie told him. "It's going to set us back a whole hour if I turn around now. But I don't really have a choice, Harold. We'll just have to stay at a motel in Vegas tonight and wait until tomorrow to unpack this stuff. Oh, *damn.*"

Almost sick with frustration, she pulled onto the first exit ramp, turned the car around and headed back to the city, trying not to look at the Nugget as she drove past.

They'd be married by now. Gloria would be Mrs. Jared Kilmer, and the wedding guests would all be celebrating.

Lonnie went along Virginia and onto her street. After a moment's thought she headed down the alley and parked at the back to save time. Leaving Puffy in the car, she ran up the walk to the house, letting herself into the kitchen.

The place seemed so quiet and deserted in the quiet of the spring afternoon. Lonnie dropped the keys on a counter next to the sink.

Something caught her eye, and she leaned over the sink to look out the window. A man in a dark suit was sitting on the veranda steps with his face buried in his hands.

She went through the living room and opened the door, stepped hesitantly onto the veranda and paused in astonishment.

"Jared?" she asked.

He leaped to his feet and stood looking at her, wearing a black tuxedo with a silk cummerbund and a bow tie that hung loose at his neck. He looked incredibly handsome, even though his hair was rumpled and his face taut with strain.

"Lonnie," he said at last. "God, I thought I'd missed you. I thought you were already gone."

"I was. I got all the way out to Wadsworth, then realized that I'd forgotten to leave the house keys and had to turn around."

He moved toward her, reached for her. Lonnie evaded his grasp and watched him with growing bewilderment.

"Why are you here, Jared? Why aren't you at the wedding?"

"There was no wedding."

Her jaw dropped. "No wedding? What are you talking about?"

"Did you wear that harem costume to the New Year's party?"

He stared at her, his face hard and intent.

"Tell me the truth," he said, gripping her arm when she didn't reply. "I know you're pregnant. Is it my baby you're having?"

Lonnie tried to pull away. "I have no idea what you're talking about."

"We've been friends for a long time, Lonnie." He moved closer and grasped her shoulders, pulling her toward him. "You've never lied to me before. Did you sleep with me that night?"

Lonnie tried to resist, but his arms were around her now, and they felt so good. She hid her face against his white shirtfront.

"We shouldn't be doing this," she muttered. "My clothes are all dusty. I'll ruin your tux."

"To hell with the tux. It was you, wasn't it?"

Lonnie nodded, her face hidden. "I'm sorry," she whispered at last. "I wanted to get pregnant, Jared. I wanted to have your baby. In fact, it's been my New Year's resolution for the last two years, and I finally did it. I know it was awful of me to trick you like that, but I couldn't think of any other way."

"Why?" he asked. "Why did you want it to be me?"

Lonnie gulped back a sob. "Because I—" Her voice broke, and all her brave resolve melted away. "Because I love you. I guess I've loved you all my life, but I didn't realize it until—"

His arms tightened around her. "Oh, Lonnie," he whispered huskily. "My God, Lonnie."

"It doesn't mean you have to do anything about it." She studied the row of black studs in his shirtfront. "Like you said, we've always been friends, Jared, and nothing's going to change. I don't expect anything from you. I'm moving away to have my baby and I can look after myself. Really."

He ignored her and reached out to touch her abdomen. "My baby," he said, looking dazed. "You're pregnant and it's my baby."

"How did you find out?" she asked.

"Gloria told me."

Lonnie stared at him blankly. "But... I told Gloria I was pregnant, that's all. How did she ever figure out that it was your baby?"

"She talked to the clerk at the store where you rented that costume. The clerk remembered you." He made an impatient gesture. "I'll explain it all later. God, Lonnie—"

She went to stand by the railing and looked at the street. "What about the wedding? Are you still getting married?"

"Not to Gloria." Jared leaned against one of the veranda columns, studying her intently. "I can't believe you'd actually have let me marry the woman when you knew it wasn't my baby she was carrying."

Lonnie hugged her arms and refused to meet his eyes. "I thought you loved her, and she seemed to be crazy about you. After you two announced your engagement, I knew it would be really destructive of me to tell the truth and come between you like that. The whole thing was like a nightmare, Jared. I just wanted to get away from here."

"When Gloria told me you were pregnant, I figured it must be Stan's baby. I thought the two of you were getting back together."

"Stan?" she asked in disbelief. "That's crazy. What would I be doing with *Stan?* I suffered through that relationship once before. I'm certainly never going to try it again."

He moved closer and put an arm around her shoulder. "I love you, Lonnie."

"You . . ." She couldn't believe her ears. "What did you say?"

"I told you that I love you. I've loved you since we were little kids."

She pulled away, feeling a rising anger. "Oh, come on! Don't start this all over again, Jared."

"Start what?"

Lonnie glared at him. "Just because you've found out about the baby, there's no need to start pretending you have feelings for me. I can look after myself and my baby, too. I don't need your help."

His face hardened. "I'm telling you the truth, dammit. This has nothing to do with the baby. It's *you* I'm in love with."

"I don't believe you. If it's true, why didn't you ever say anything before?"

"Why didn't you?" he asked.

Lonnie was silent, watching him.

"Look, we both had the same problem," Jared told her earnestly. "It's not easy to start being romantic with your best friend. In fact, it's really embarrassing to make the first move after all those years of kidding around and being comfortable together."

Lonnie knew, all too well, how true this was. Gradually the wonder of what he was saying began to dawn on her.

"You really mean it?" she asked. "You're in love with me? No kidding?"

"No kidding." He put his arms around her and bent to kiss her.

The sweetness of his mouth was almost more than Lonnie could bear. After all the heartsick months of loneliness, she found herself drowning in happiness, faint and dizzy with the sheer pleasure of holding him.

"Oh, my," she whispered at last, her mouth moving against his. "That feels so good."

"Talk about feeling good." She could feel his lips curving into a smile. "Do you remember anything about that night at that party, Lon?"

"Of course I do. After all, I planned the whole thing. I knew exactly what I was doing."

He pulled away to give her a teasing glance. "So you remember how it felt to..."

Lonnie's cheeks turned warm with embarrassment. "I remember," she murmured.

He laughed and hugged her fiercely. "God," he whispered. "I can't believe it. What a woman this is."

Lonnie pulled herself back to reality with an effort. "Where's Gloria?" she asked. "Did you jilt her at the altar?"

He chuckled. "Not really. Gloria's playing hostess at a big party and having a wonderful time. Besides, she's already found somebody to comfort her."

"Who?"

"Tony." Jared bent to kiss her again. "She and Tony are getting along just fine. I think there's romance in the air."

"My goodness." Lonnie considered this, startled. "She and Tony would make a great couple, wouldn't they? He'll probably take her to Hollywood and make her into a big star."

"I hope so." Jared sobered. "Gloria's a nice person under all the nonsense, and so is Tony. They might just be really good for each other."

Lonnie smiled and nestled in his arms, delighted to hear this news about Gloria and their old school friend. She was so much in love that she wanted the whole world to be happy.

But suddenly she stiffened again and looked up at him in horror.

"Jared!" she wailed.

"What?" he asked, clearly alarmed. "What's the matter?"

"I have to start my new job next week! I've got all my stuff packed in a trailer right now, and I still have to move it down to Las Vegas today."

He relaxed and smiled. "No problem," he said calmly. "Give me another kiss."

"But what are we going to—"

"I'll drive down there with you this afternoon and help you unpack, then catch a flight back and get my own stuff organized so I can move. It's nothing to worry about, honey."

"But what about your job?"

"I can get a job in Vegas any time I want. Besides, I've got enough money saved that I don't need to work for a while. I might just open my own gallery and start carving full-time."

Lonnie trembled in his arms, trying to comprehend the wonder of what he was saying.

She didn't have to drive into that sprawling desert city and live there all alone. She didn't have to spend her nights longing for Jared, knowing he was married to another woman. She didn't have to carry and bear a child all by herself and raise it without its father.

Jared was going to be with her.

Lonnie sighed in bliss and nestled against him.

Suddenly, from the depths of her body, she felt the stirring of a gentle touch, a breath of unfamiliar movement as soft and mysterious as the distant fluttering of angel wings.

She held her breath, waiting, and it happened again.

"Jared," she whispered.

"What, honey?"

"It moved. I just felt it. The baby moved."

He tightened his arms around her, holding her tenderly.

Lonnie knew that she was going to remember this forever, the moment when she stood with Jared in a glow of warm spring sunlight while her heart sang with happiness and his baby moved and stirred within her for the very first time.

*   *   *   *   *

Heartbreak RANCH

Four generations of independent women…
Four heartwarming, romantic stories of the West…
Four incredible authors…

Fern Michaels
Jill Marie Landis
Dorsey Kelley
Chelley Kitzmiller

Saddle up with Heartbreak Ranch, an outstanding
Western collection that will take you on a whirlwind
trip through four generations and the exciting,
romantic adventures of four strong women who
have inherited the ranch from Bella Duprey,
famed Barbary Coast madam.

Available in March,
wherever Harlequin books are sold.

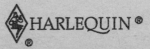

HARLEQUIN ®
®

HTBK

Harlequin and Silhouette celebrate
Black History Month with seven terrific titles,
featuring the all-new *Fever Rising*
by Maggie Ferguson
(Harlequin Intrigue #408) and
A Family Wedding by Angela Benson
(Silhouette Special Edition #1085)!

Also available are:
Looks Are Deceiving by Maggie Ferguson
Crime of Passion by Maggie Ferguson
Adam and Eva by Sandra Kitt
Unforgivable by Joyce McGill
Blood Sympathy by Reginald Hill

On sale in January at your favorite
Harlequin and Silhouette retail outlet.

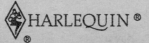

LOOK FOR OUR FOUR FABULOUS MEN!

Each month some of today's bestselling authors bring
four new fabulous men to Harlequin American Romance.
Whether they're rebel ranchers, millionaire power brokers
or sexy single dads, they're all gallant princes—and
they're all ready to sweep you into lighthearted fantasies
and contemporary fairy tales where anything is possible
and where all your dreams come true!

You don't even have to make a wish...Harlequin American
Romance will grant your every desire!

Look for Harlequin American Romance wherever Harlequin
books are sold!

"You sure ~~~~ **Sunday school teacher I know.**

"I probably would have gone to church more often as a kid if I'd had a teacher as pretty as you." Dustin winked at her.

Isobel blushed a bright, becoming pink, though Dustin had only been voicing an opinion he'd had since the moment he'd first seen her.

Dustin was perplexed. She obviously wasn't used to compliments, yet Isobel was a beautiful woman, inside and out. It made him wonder what her past had been like.

At length, she smiled at him. "And here I am standing here staring at you like a constant reminder of your troubles with your brother. Like a porcupine rubbing against you."

"A porcupine?" he repeated, sounding stunned.

He looked her over with an amused grin, his eyes twinkling with merriment. "I don't *think* so. Not in a million years."

"But it bothers you to have me here," she hinted.

"No," Dustin answered definitively. "You, my dear Isobel, are the best thing that has happened to me in a long time. Maybe ever."

Books by Deb Kastner

Love Inspired

A Holiday Prayer #46
Daddy's Home #55
Black Hills Bride #90
The Forgiving Heart #113
A Daddy At Heart #140
A Perfect Match #164
The Christmas Groom #195
Hart's Harbor #210
Undercover Blessings #284
The Heart of a Man #345

DEB KASTNER

is the wife of a Reformed Episcopal minister, so it was natural for her to find her niche in the Christian romance market. She enjoys tackling the issues of faith and trust within the context of a romance. Her characters range from upbeat and humorous to (her favorite) dark and brooding heroes. Her plots range widely from a playful romp to the deeply emotional.

When she's not writing, she enjoys spending time with her husband and three girls and, whenever she can manage, attending regional dinner theater and touring Broadway musicals.

The
Heart
of a Man

DEB KASTNER

**Steeple
Hill**®

Published by Steeple Hill Books™

STEEPLE HILL BOOKS

**Steeple
Hill**®

ISBN-13: 978-0-373-87382-1
ISBN-10:   0-373-87382-4

THE HEART OF A MAN

www.SteepleHill.com

Printed in U.S.A.

Then Moses said to the Lord, "O my Lord, I am not eloquent, neither before nor since You have spoken to Your servant; but I am slow of speech and slow of tongue." So the Lord said to him, "Who has made man's mouth? Or who makes the mute, the deaf, the seeing, or the blind? Have not I, the Lord? Now therefore, go, and I will be with your mouth and teach you what you shall say."

—*Exodus* 4:10–12.

To my sweet middle girl, Kimmie, who is the absolute last word on fashion in our house. This incredibly talented girl can make anything with a piece of fabric and some thread. My own personal image consultant, she continues to remind me fashion can be comfortable, just as I continue to break that rule by wearing sweats when I write.

Much thanks and gratitude to my oldest daughter, Annie, who transcribed much of this book for me onto the computer, as I am one of those dinosaurs who still prefer to create in longhand.

Chapter One

"How do you do that?"

The question came from her best friend since childhood, Camille O'Shay. They had grown up together in a tiny rural Texas town, attended the same college and now were sharing living quarters in the heart of downtown Denver.

"Do what, Millie?" she asked absently, her eyes carefully scrutinizing the gentleman under her authority, her eyes taking in every seam and pleat as she tucked and pinned.

"Completely change people's appearances, Izzy, like someone's fairy godmother or something," Camille said with a laugh. "I'm completely astounded by your ability to wave your wand and work wonders."

Isobel Buckley shrugged. "It's my job to dress and press these gorgeous gals and pretty boys and get them looking their best for the boardroom. The final product depends on me. It's hard work, not waving wands, that yields a final product I can be satisfied with."

She wasn't telling her friend any new information—Camille was well familiar that Isabel was a personal shopper and image consultant for a select, high-end clientele. And Camille likewise knew Isobel was every bit the perfectionist she sounded.

"You know, when you think about it, it doesn't really take much to make high-quality fashion look good on those pinup model hunks you work with," Camille observed wryly. "Although, of course, dear heart, you do it better than most."

"What's that supposed to mean?" Isobel was busy straightening a silk tie on one of those so-called pinup model hunks who wanted to look his best for a national conference, and was only half paying attention to her friend's happy chatter.

"Turn around for me," she told the man, who willingly complied.

"Oh, nothing," Camille replied, not sounding the least bit convinced as Isobel turned her attention back to her friend for a moment. "I was just wondering if you could do the same kind of work with an *average* man, someone who hasn't ever read a men's fashion magazine."

"What are you talking about?" Isobel said, throwing a quick glance in Camille's direction. "You're babbling nonsense."

"Am I?" she shot back, her grin reminding Isobel of a cat crouched to pounce on a helpless mouse.

"What do you think about adding a run-of-the-mill variety guy to your clientele? The kind of guy *I* usually date, as opposed to the kind of guy you *could* date if you weren't so caught up in your career?"

Isobel rolled her eyes. "I'm going to pretend you didn't say that."

"So are you up for it?" Camille actually sounded excited, as if she were taking the idea for real.

"I beg your pardon?"

"Making a normal slob of a guy into *Mr. Right.* Blue-collar material, ya know? It would be fun."

Camille was definitely warming up to the idea, while Isobel was beginning to cringe. Her friend was sounding all too serious about this fanatical, half-baked scheme.

"Here's what we'll do. I'll pick the guy, and you'll have six weeks to make him into a real man. The man of every girl's dreams."

"You're kidding, right?" Isobel took a deep breath and held it. She could only hope.

Camille shrugged, a noncommittal gesture. "Maybe. Maybe not. But don't be surprised if I come knocking on your door with a fellow who desperately needs your help for a makeover."

Isobel pinched her lips, deciding to ignore her friend's obviously off-the-top-of-her-head twaddle. It would come to nothing in the long run.

She hoped.

Not more than two days later, her dear childhood confidant made good on her threat. Bursting into

Isobel's office, Camille announced in a loud, triumphant voice, "I've found him!"

"I'm sorry," Isobel said, distracted by the pile of paperwork she was muddling through, piece by agonizingly slow piece. "You found whom?"

"The guy, of course. The one you're going to wave your magic wand over." She looked disappointed for a moment. "Our average guy, remember?"

Isobel smoothed her thick, long brown hair with her palm and sighed, desperately wishing she *didn't* remember. "I would ask if you were joking, but I know you better than that. What possessed you to go through with this crazy scheme? This isn't even remotely close to real life, Camille."

"I wasn't even looking! I'm telling you the truth. No one could have been more shocked or amazed than I. All I was doing was talking with a regular patron at my hotel—a *rich,* quite handsome, very well-connected patron, I might add."

"All the people who spend time at your hotel are rich," Isobel reminded her friend blithely. "And well-connected. Handsome, though. Since when is that a requirement for hotel patronage?" she teased.

"Oh, Isobel. You have no idea. This guy is out of this world!" She stopped suddenly and clapped a hand over her heart, sighing loudly and dramatically, even as a dark blush stole up her cheeks. "Addison Fairfax."

"But that's not the point." She faltered for a moment, and Isobel found a bit of humor in the fact that her dear friend was actually flustered over this

Addison Fairfax. It took a lot for Camille to show interest in a particular man, preferring in general the whole of mankind.

"Go ahead, Camille," Isobel encouraged with a smile and a sly wink that let her friend know she was on to her. "Handsome and…?"

Camille placed a hand on her reddened cheek and continued. "We were making our usual small talk, you know, and I was telling him about my brilliant idea for you to make over some regular guy—not anything like Addison, of course. He dresses divinely."

She followed her high-speed discourse with another long, drawn-out sigh.

Isobel chuckled.

"Well, the next thing you know, he's telling me all about his problems. You are the answer to his prayers, Isobel, I kid you not. Neither of us could believe it!"

"I might as well hear it," Isobel said with a groan. "Go on."

"Okay, I'll tell you," she agreed, casually stringing it on with a laugh. "But Izzy, you have to promise to listen all the way through before you jump to any conclusions."

Isobel smiled. She was certain she'd be *jumping to conclusions* long before her friend was finished telling what was sure to be a wildly fantastical story—but she *could* promise to keep her thoughts to herself, at least until she'd sorted the whole wild, bizarre idea out in her mind.

"So, it's like this," Camille began with a flourish of her hand.

"Once upon a time," Isobel teased.

Camille threw her a mock glare. "If you're going to keep interrupting every time I speak, I'm never going to get through this."

Isobel chuckled. "Sorry. It won't happen again." She made the motion of zipping her lips closed with her thumb and index finger.

"So there's this man I was telling you about, Addison Fairfax, who often uses our hotel for his meetings and conventions," Camille said, her voice growing with excitement at every word. "He's the CEO of Security, Inc. You know it?"

"I've heard of it," Isobel replied. Of course she knew the name. It was only one of the most prestigious financial firms in Denver, probably on the continent.

Everyone had *heard* of Security, Inc.

"You can only imagine how successful Addison is, not to mention how wonderfully handsome he looks. He's always polished, precise and dressed meticulously."

"So, what's the problem?" Isobel asked, wondering how she could help such a high-and-mighty being, and why on earth he would think to pay her for it. Sounded to her as if he had it made.

Unless, like many of her clientele, he was simply too busy to worry about fashion. But then, where would be the challenge in that? He was the type of man Isobel worked with on a regular basis in her business, not something out of her league.

"Oh, it's not Addison," Camille said, holding her hands up, palms out. "You can trust me on this. That man is perfect just the way he is."

Isobel laughed. "It sounds as if you have a genuine, fully loaded crush on the man."

"A *crush?*" Her friend sounded mortified. "I would never stoop so low. I haven't had a crush on a man since ninth grade." She sniffed, her nose in the air like a cat who'd been offended.

"Tenth grade. Mr. Monahue, our history teacher," Isobel reminded her with a smile.

Camille chuckled. "Oh, he was cute, wasn't he? If I recall, I wasn't the only one who thought he floated over the ground."

Isobel shook her head, smiling at the memory. *Every* tenth-grade girl in Mr. Monahue's class had had a crush on the charming teacher.

She shook her head again, her mind returning to the present dilemma. "Okay, so Addison Fairfax is *interesting,*" she said, rephrasing for her friend's sake and to keep the conversation on line. "But I still don't understand what that has to do with me."

"It's his younger brother, Dustin. Now, Dustin is a mess—a regular slob, in Addison's words. And Addison actually wants to *pay* you to whip him into shape. Six short weeks of work and an enormous salary tacked on as a bonus. Think of it, Isobel! You don't even have to stop your own work to help him."

"Why would I want to do this, again?" Isobel asked, crossing her arms and tipping her executive-style black leather chair as far back as it would go, wishing for a short moment it would crash backward, sending her down through the twenty-two floors below and away from her glassy-eyed friend and the half-cocked ideas spouting from her lips.

"Remember our conversation from the other day?" Camille reminded her, dangling the thought out before her like a carrot to a rabbit.

"I remember *you* saying a bunch of stuff. I don't remember *me* saying anything at all. Most particularly that I wanted to participate in such nonsense."

"Oh, but you do, Isobel, whether you want to admit it now or not. Think of the tremendous challenge involved. I know you love the idea, deep down. Admit it!"

Isobel crossed her arms and shook her head. Vehemently.

"Don't you see? Dustin Fairfax would be a test of your true strength as an image consultant." Camille raised her hands to emphasize the mental marquee board. "I mean, they make gorgeous hunks into ugly bums all the time in the movies. Don't you think you could do the opposite for one poor man who needs what only your special brand of fashion sense can bring to him? He'll be a new man!"

Isobel admitted—in her heart, anyway—that she was intrigued, despite every bone of sense in her body screaming to the contrary. Something about the whole setup just didn't seem right, though she wasn't sure what was bothering her.

It sounded innocent enough on the outside, but something…

"How old is this man?" she asked after a slight but pregnant pause.

"Dustin?" Camille asked, her eyes gleaming with the victory she sensed was coming.

Isobel was quite aware Camille knew her better than anyone. They'd spent their whole lives together, been best friends forever. Camille would know that once Isobel capitulated in the least, she had her bagged and roasted for sure.

Camille certainly looked like a tiger hunter in full triumph, stripes sighted down her scope.

"Well, I know Addison is thirty-three," her friend supplied thoughtfully. "And since Dustin is his younger brother, I would guess he'd be about thirty, give or take a year."

"And what, exactly, is wrong with him?" she asked, feeling as if she ought to be taking notes. "I have to know the truth, here, if you want me to help."

"Oh, nothing's wrong with him, really," Camille exclaimed with a high laugh. "Addison said he's just—flighty. That's the word he used."

Isobel raised one eyebrow. Here, she suspected, was where the roof caved in.

"At least by Addison's standards, Dustin doesn't dress very well. He's not sophisticated. That shouldn't be a huge challenge for you."

"He's not a homeless man or something like that?" Isobel was still cautious. Too much about this story still didn't mesh. Something was off just a little, though she couldn't put her finger on just what it was.

She gave Camille a hard, serious stare. "Dustin is aware this is going to happen to him? He has agreed to work with me?"

"He happens to own a small flower store on the 16th Street Mall. Retail, you know? He's successful, in his own way, I guess, though he's a long way from the clientele you're used to working with."

Camille paused, running her tongue along her bottom lip. "And as for your other question, he hasn't exactly been told. Yet."

Isobel opened her mouth to argue but Camille held her hands up to cut her off.

"As soon as you agree, Addison will make sure Dustin knows to expect you. It's all been arranged, but Addison didn't want to speak to his brother about it until I'd finalized things with you."

"What if Dustin says no?"

"He won't," Camille said with a firm nod. "He might want to, but he won't. You see, there's money riding on this venture. Apparently quite a lot of money."

"He will get a lot of money if he learns to dress well?" Isobel asked, stymied. "But deep down he really wouldn't want to do this. Is that what you're really telling me?"

"It's complicated," Camille explained with a

patient sigh. "Addison was left to execute his father's will, and Izzy, the poor man is beside himself, with the situation being what it is. I feel so sorry for him. What a predicament!"

"Go on," Isobel urged, not at all certain she wanted to hear more.

"Apparently their father was afraid Dustin would squander his inheritance away instead of doing something useful with it. Addison is terribly worried about his brother. I guess he's kind of stubborn, and he's definitely his own man. Marches to the beat of his own drummer, so to speak."

She paused, clasping her hand over her heart in the melodramatic way that was uniquely Camille's. "Can you imagine the tremendously heavy burden their father left on poor Addison?"

"How so?"

"Addison was named Dustin's trustee in the will, even though Dustin is a full-grown man. You can imagine how *Dustin* felt. And Addison certainly didn't ask for the formidable task of bringing Dustin into line. According to the terms of the will, Dustin has certain obligations to meet—delineated by his father—in order for Addison to release the funds to his brother."

"He has to learn to dress well?" Isobel asked again, befuddled. "In order to get his hands on his rightful inheritance?"

None of this made the least bit of sense, and Isobel was beginning to feel very much as if she'd stepped into another dimension.

What kind of a man was Dustin, that his father would put such insane demands on him?

One thing she knew for certain—*she* would balk at such radical and unusual demands being placed upon her. If Dustin were *half* the independent spirit Camille had described him to be…

Camille laughed. "No, of course not, silly. He has to make a splash in society or something outrageous like that, and of course clothes make the man, right?

"It's a good start," Isobel said with a laugh and a shrug. *I'd be looking for a little more than that in a man.*

Camille giggled. "After I told Addison about you, he thought you'd be the perfect person to bring Dustin around. You, of all people, can guide him in making a true contribution to society. Those are the exact terms of the will. Can you believe it?"

"I see," Isobel said under her breath, though she wasn't sure she did. The idea was intriguing, of course; definitely intriguing. The thought of transforming a scalawag of a man into a prince would be a challenge, but it also sounded kind of fun.

"Okay," she said after only a brief pause to consider the short- and long-term ramifications of her decision. She didn't want to examine her own motives too closely. "I'll do it."

She didn't ask how much money she would make. She was taking on this *project* for the challenge, and she trusted Camille that the time she spent would be worth her weight in gold. Literally.

And she was surprised by how excited she was at the prospect of making over the erstwhile Dustin. It had been a long time since she'd done something truly stimulating, and her heart was pounding with anticipation.

"I knew this was something you'd want to do," Camille squealed, throwing her arms around Isobel's neck and dancing her around in dizzying circles. "Oh, how wonderful for you!"

"Wonderful for *me?*" she asked, laughing at her friend's excited antics. "I thought Dustin was the one to benefit from this deal."

"Oh, he will," her friend agreed immediately. "He most definitely will. But won't it be such fun for you, as well? Admit it. You love the idea. *Pygmalion* at its best."

"I suppose the idea has merit," she agreed. "I do have one condition, however, and I refuse to take on this *project* unless it is met unconditionally."

"What's that?"

"This Dustin guy—he has to go into this experiment with his eyes wide open. If he doesn't agree to the makeover, if he is not comfortable with the idea of working with me or if he expresses doubts or disinterest, I do not want to move forward with this." Isobel listed items on her fingers. "The project must all be conducted on the up-and-up, with everything laid out up front for Dustin and for me. No surprises and no reluctant subjects. Do you understand what I'm getting at here?"

"I'll speak to Addison immediately," Camille assured her, obviously trying to rein in her high, excited tone and appear more businesslike and reserved. It didn't fool Isobel for a moment.

Her friend continued, gulping in air to remain calm. "He said he would be the one to speak to Dustin about it and firm up the final details. After that I'll be able to let you know when and where you two can meet and get the ball rolling toward Dustin's new look. He's got to agree. He just has to." She winked. "Especially when he meets *you*."

"What's that supposed to mean?" Isobel squawked, feigning offense and pressing her lips together to keep her smile hidden.

"Why, you're so pretty you'll knock his socks off. And then, my dear friend, you can replace them with preppie argyles."

"Oh, I just love it when I get to play fairy godmother," Isobel teased, waving an invisible magic wand through the air. "But this sounds just a little too weird to be real."

Camille laughed and whirled about on her toes like a ballerina. So much for her businesslike demeanor, Isobel thought, smothering her grin. She didn't know where her friend got all her energy, but she wished just a little of it would rub off on her.

"There's a first time for everything, Izzy," Camille said, clapping her hands in anticipation. "And you, my dearest friend in all the world, are going to be the best thing that ever happened to Dustin Fairfax. He won't even know what hit him."

Chapter Two

Dustin lifted the drumsticks into the air, adjusting his grip on the wood so he could play the drum set that curved around the stool on which he sat. He closed his eyes and with a flick of one drumstick, adjusted his backward black-and-purple Colorado Rockies cap to keep his curly black hair out of his face.

His music of choice, at the moment, anyway, was a trumpet-licking jazz CD he'd picked up over the weekend. Eclectic was the only way to describe his taste—in music, or in anything else he had a strong opinion about.

The drum set was new—or at least, new to him. A friend who had been a drummer in a high-school band was getting rid of it to make room for a baby crib.

Dustin had grabbed the opportunity and bought the set for a song. He'd never played a percussion instrument in his life, but he figured now was as good a time as any to learn.

It wasn't the first instrument he would have taught himself to play in his life.

How hard could it be?

He made a couple of tentative taps on the snare drum with his sticks, and then pounded the bass a few times with the foot pedal.

Smiling with satisfaction, he began pounding in earnest, perfect rhythm with the beat of the jazz CD. He didn't care at the moment whether or not he sounded good. He was only trying to have a good time. Technique would come later, with many strenuous hours of practice, he knew.

He sent a timely prayer to God that the insulation in his house would be sufficient to keep his neighbors from knocking his door down with their complaints about the horrible din.

Suddenly, out of nowhere, someone clamped his hand tightly on Dustin's shoulder.

Dustin made an instinctive move, standing in a flash, turning and knocking the man's hand away in one swift motion of his elbow and then crouching to pounce on the unknown intruder.

"Hey, take it easy," Addison said with a deep, dry laugh Dustin immediately recognized. "I didn't mean to startle you. I tried knocking, but you couldn't hear me over all that racket. Sounded like the roof was caving in or something."

Dustin chuckled.

Addison shook his head and laughed in tune with

his brother. "The door was open, so I just let myself in. I hope you don't mind."

Dustin wiped his arm against his forehead, as his hands were still tightly gripping the drumsticks. "Naw. Guess I was pretty distracted, messing with this thing." He popped a quick beat on the snare drum for emphasis, then clasped both sticks together and jammed them in the back pocket of his jeans.

He crossed his arms over his chest and stared at his suit-clad big brother. "What are you doing here, Addy boy?" he asked in genuine surprise.

Addison rarely visited Dustin's small house, which was located in Wheatridge, one of the many sprawling suburbs of Denver. In fact, he'd never been there without a direct invitation first.

He had shown little interest in Dustin's hobbies, or anything else for that matter. They had never been close, even as children. Addison was the jock, and Dustin the artist. It had always been that way.

Addison wasn't fond of anything artistic, from drama to Monet. Football, baseball, soccer—these had made up Addison's teenage world.

And Addison had always been the brains in the family, in Dustin's estimation. As the CEO for a major financial corporation, and an important person in the Denver social scene, Addison didn't have time to dabble with anything beyond the walls of his chic, downtown penthouse condo and lush corner office. His only interest in the arts as a successful adult was as his business required, and nothing more.

"I've come about Dad's will, Dustin—specifically, the terms of the trust fund," Addison said tersely and abruptly in the crisp business tone he always used. Dustin sometimes thought Addison hid behind that tone in order to keep his emotions on a back burner. The two brothers certainly weren't as close as Dustin would have liked, though he put the blame for that more on his father than on Addison.

Dustin clasped his hands behind his back. His father's will was not something he really wished to discuss, though he knew it was inevitable. It had to be done, and sooner rather than later. Addison was right on that one point, anyway.

Their mother had died when Dustin was fourteen and Addison was sixteen. He remembered her as a sweet, delicate woman who always smiled and always had an eye and an open hand for the poor and needy. She had kept the house full of laughter and singing, and always had a prayer or a song of praise on her lips.

His father, on the other hand, was as cold as stone, a strict disciplinarian who practiced what he preached—that God helped those who helped themselves.

Never mind that *that* particular "verse" wasn't really in the Bible.

Addison Fairfax, Sr., had worked long hours establishing the firm Addison Jr. now led and held a majority interest in.

Dustin knew his father had wanted him in the

company, as well. Addison Sr. had been bitterly disappointed when, as a young man following his own strong, surging creative impulses, Dustin took a different career path.

To Dustin, being boxed up in an office all day would be like caging a wild beast; and the thought of spending all day crunching numbers—especially anything to do with money—made him shiver.

It was enough just to balance his checkbook every month. That was not the kind of life for him, caged behind a desk with nothing but figures on paper for company.

He wanted to help people, but in another, more creative fashion. One on one, where he could reach out and touch his customers, smile and encourage them to smile back at him.

He pinched his lips together to keep his smile hidden from his brother's observant gaze. It was an understatement to say that math had never been one of Dustin's better subjects.

And so now it came down to his father's last wishes, laid out plainly, literally in black and white. Dustin had been at the formal reading of the will. He knew what it contained, especially in regard to what he was expected to accomplish in order to win the coveted trust fund, which Dustin desperately wanted, but for reasons he would disclose to no one.

At least not yet.

And that was no doubt why Addison was visiting him today. It was up to his big brother, as trustee of the fund in Dustin's name, to see that Dustin cleaned up, became a pillar of society and made a *real* contribution to the world in some way not explicitly drawn out in the will, but legal nonetheless.

Dustin knew Addison wasn't thrilled with the job. He had enough responsibility with his own work without burdening himself with his younger brother's supposed faults. But there was one thing Dustin knew about his older brother—he would follow his father's dictates to the letter without question.

Even if Addison didn't necessarily agree with the terms. Besides, it was legal, drawn up and finalized by their father, who'd known exactly what he was doing.

"You want the money, don't you?" Addison asked crisply, his golden-blond eyebrows creasing low in concern over his blue eyes, all traits of his father.

Dustin had his mother's curly black hair and green eyes. It was a startling contrast between the two brothers, and just one more way they were different from one another.

Dustin took a deep, steadying breath. "Yes, I do," he said solemnly. "You know I do."

That was as much information as he was willing to offer, which no doubt perplexed his older brother.

"Hey, Addy boy," he said, cheerfully changing the subject, "you want a soda or something?"

"I've asked you repeatedly not to call me that," his brother responded through gritted teeth, shaking his head in warning.

"Why do you think I do it?" Dustin responded with a laugh.

"You little punk," Addison said affectionately. He grabbed Dustin around the neck and scrubbed his knuckles across Dustin's scalp, just the sort of roughhousing they'd done as kids. "Don't forget I'm bigger than you. I can still knock your block off anytime I want."

"I'd like to see you try," Dustin challenged, grabbing his brother by the waist in what amounted to a wrestler's hold.

Addison sighed and abruptly released his hold on Dustin. "As much as I'd like to monkey around with you, bro, I just don't have time today. I'm behind on my schedule already just by being here. Can we just get this painful business settled as quickly as possible so I can return to work?"

This business. Was that all it was to Addison? Another piece of business to settle and then move on? It was only Dustin's life they were talking about.

And so much more. If only Addison knew. But Dustin wasn't ready to trust his brother with more information than he'd already given.

Dustin felt like no more than a thorn in Addison's side at times, a trial to be borne through and just as quickly forgotten.

Addison was staring at him. "I'm sorry to say this, little brother, but you need a makeover," he said soberly, though his eyes were gleaming with amusement at the prospect.

Dustin grinned and crossed his arms over his chest in an instinctively protective gesture. "Oh, like a facial and a mud bath, right? You want me to get a manicure and a massage?"

Addison cleared his throat and looked out the nearest window, gazing for some time before speaking. "This is a very serious matter. You joke about everything," he said softly.

Dustin shrugged. "Of course. In my book, it's better to go through life with a smile than to be grouchy all the time."

"Grouchy? Is that how you see me?" He sounded genuinely surprised.

Dustin shook his head. "I was speaking in relative terms."

"Yes, well, I'm not sure I believe you, but let us get back to the subject at hand. As it happens, per the will, I've hired a girl—"

"No way." Dustin cut him off with his voice, and concurrently made a severe chopping gesture with the flat of his hand. "My personal life is mine. I won't be set up, even by you."

"I'm not talking about your personal life, Dustin," Addison said, sounding as if he were straining to be patient, and yet with the hint of laughter to his voice. "I'm talking about your image. Who you know, where you go and especially how you dress. A change you and I both know would make our father happy."

Dustin looked down at his old tennis shoes, faded

blue jeans and worn gray T-shirt. "What's wrong with the way I dress?"

"That's exactly the point, my man. This woman I hired, Isobel Buckley, knows what's in fashion and helps people change their image. She does it for a living, and I'm sure she could advise you better than I. Honestly, baby brother, you don't have a clue. Admit it. You're a world-class chump."

Dustin felt pressure building up in his chest. Addison was forcing his hand, and they both knew it.

And they both knew he would cave, eventually, before it was all said and done.

He *had* to cave. For the sake of the money. There was no other way.

For a moment, he considered tackling his older brother and wrestling him to the ground, as they had often done as youngsters. It would serve his big brother right to give him the good pounding he had threatened and that he was now certain Addison deserved.

With deep restraint he denied the urge, knowing it would do nothing more than prove Addison's point. Bad clothes and bad manners.

A chump.

"Frankly—" Addison continued in his best, solid business voice "—and you know I'm right in saying this, Father was concerned about the way you would spend your inheritance."

Addison paused, leaning one hand against a nearby table and pulling his brown tweed jacket back to put his hand in his slacks pocket.

To Dustin, it was like seeing his father all over again.

"You have no vision, Dustin. You own a small flower shop, you bang like an Aborigine on this drum of yours in the name of *fun,* and that's all you have to show for yourself. For your time. For your life."

"Is that you or Dad talking?" Dustin goaded through clenched teeth.

It wasn't a fair question, and Dustin immediately regretted his hasty query. It was clearly his father's intention to make Dustin into a different man. Addison was merely the messenger.

The urge to pounce on his burly brother and mess up his fancy suit was growing by the moment, but he knew better than to shoot the messenger, no matter how tempting it might be. It wouldn't solve anything in the long run, and he needed access to that trust fund.

"It's *my* life," he complained, sounding as surly as a little boy. "What's wrong with my flower store?"

"Nothing is wrong with your little shop. But have you ever thought about opening up a chain of stores? What about making a real name for yourself in the Denver social scene? Why not cater to a higher-level clientele, boost your own income?

"You spend as much time gallivanting around town, and who knows what else, as you do putting your strength and effort into your business." Addison took an extended breath. "What you need is to go to the right parties and rub elbows with the right people. Build up relationships that mean something. Really make something important of yourself."

Addison rubbed his palms together like sandpaper on wood. "I'll help you. I have the connections, Dustin. But you can't meet the right kind of people in jeans and a T-shirt."

Dustin shook his head and grunted in disdain. "Relationships that mean something? Mean what, exactly? More money? More prestige? A nicer car? I'm never going to be like you, Addison. That's not what I want out of life."

"Perhaps not," Addison agreed with a curt nod. "You and I have traveled different roads. Nevertheless, I do think Ms. Buckley can help you with this trust-fund issue, and I insist you meet with her."

Dustin balked inside, but he didn't let it show. He didn't like being ordered around, especially by members of his family. "How long?"

"Six weeks. That shouldn't be too much of a strain, even for you." Addison began to pace, a sure sign he was losing his patience. Dustin knew his brother didn't like this any better than he did.

And why should he? Dustin knew Addison wasn't a bully at heart, childhood pranks notwithstanding. He was as pinched by their father's will as anyone.

Better to wrap things up and let Addison get on his way. Back to work in his posh office, where he was more in his element.

"At the end of the six weeks, then, I get my inheritance money?"

Addison met his gaze straight on, staring as if trying to read his soul. Dustin let him look, knowing his own expression was unreadable. It was something he'd practiced.

"You know I'm taking a calculated risk here." Addison cleared his throat and continued pacing back and forth in front of Dustin, his arms clasped behind his back. "And I expect a full return on my investment."

"Meaning?"

"I want you to cooperate with Ms. Buckley fully. If she gives me a bad report, I will put your trust fund on hold and you won't be able to touch it."

Dustin opened his mouth to protest against these rules, but Addison held one hand up, palm out. He clearly didn't want to be interrupted.

"If, however, you make a genuine effort toward your reform, the money is yours, with no limitations from me or anyone. I know that's what you want. You just have to make an effort."

He gave Dustin a genuine smile, but Dustin just winced at his brother's stilted effort.

"This will work, Dustin, if you just give it half a chance."

Dustin clenched his jaw tightly, still hardly believing his brother had set up such a scheme. Addison wasn't married—he was as careful in dating as Dustin himself was. And for good reason.

Every woman in the world wanted to change a man; it was in their very nature to meddle that way. Every man alive knew that, and ran from it with his whole being until he inevitably got caught in some woman's snare.

It was the extraordinary, seesaw-like balance between men and women that Dustin didn't even try to comprehend, and generally attempted to steer away from.

That was at least partly the reason Dustin remained single at age thirty. His experience with relationships with the opposite sex had, frankly, made him more than a little world-wise when it came to women.

He liked being on his own, being his own man and answerable to no one but himself and God.

And for some strange woman to get paid for meddling in his private affairs, pushing her ideals on him—what kind of woman would take such a job?

This Isobel Buckley must be on a real power trip. He could only guess at what kinds of torture she would concoct for him.

Still, it was only six weeks.

What could happen in six weeks?

Chapter Three

Isobel was more than a little anxious about meeting the man she'd heard so much about. With all she'd been told, she had absolutely no idea what to expect when she actually met the real person.

Dustin Fairfax.

She had thoughtfully recommended a public venue for their first meeting, knowing both of them would feel a bit more comfortable with other people around, especially at this first encounter.

She admitted being nervous herself, at least inwardly, which was silly, really. She did this for a living, after all.

But this was different. The nuances weren't lost on her, and she was certain they weren't lost on *him*, either. Dustin wasn't coming to her for her expertise and help—or at least it was not his idea to do so—and she wasn't even certain he was coming willingly.

Camille and Addison had made the arrangements,

and here she sat, in a quiet deli on 16th Street, waiting for Dustin to show up.

If he actually materialized.

She still wasn't convinced he was a willing guinea pig in this experiment, and that fact was something she meant to establish before this day was over. She wouldn't blame him if he found somewhere else to be and didn't make their meeting at all.

He was already twelve minutes late to their appointment, not that she was counting. She tried to distract herself by watching the people around her, the usual eclectic hodgepodge of faces and accents that made Denver so interesting. Coffee shops were the best for finding interesting people to view.

But no matter how hard she tried, her gaze kept straying back to the front door, her adrenaline rushing every time the bell indicated a new customer was entering or exiting.

She had purposefully taken a seat at a corner table where she could easily see the entrance. She wanted to have a moment to watch Dustin before they were formally introduced.

She wiped her palms against her conservative navy blue, calf-length-split rayon skirt, ostensibly to straighten it—for at least the tenth time. She straightened her back and adjusted her posture, an incidental habit she was hardly aware of but often performed.

Suddenly a man burst through the door like a Tasmanian devil, lifting his hat and scrubbing his hands through his thick black hair. He looked around, his eyes sweeping across the tables with a glazed, harried look.

He was obviously searching for someone, and he definitely fit the profile she'd been given for Mr. Fairfax—six feet tall, medium build, black hair, green eyes.

Isobel froze, not giving any indication she saw him at all. She lowered her eyes to the table and pinched her lips.

She was afraid this was how it would be.

Her first impression wasn't good.

Dustin's black hair, what she could see of it from under a backward-faced, navy newsboy cap, was long—nearly shoulder length—and thick and curly. She wondered if anyone had ever told him his hairstyle had gone out in the eighties.

Way out.

The thought made her laugh, and she politely covered her mouth with her hand.

His big green eyes were friendly, though, and he was smiling. Those were immediate pluses, in her book. Not many people faced life with a grin these days. It was a rare blessing to see.

Polishing up the outside of a man would be a piece of cake for her, but how could she ever hope to turn some weirdo into a socialite?

Apparently, that was one worry she could cross off her list. Kindness showed in every line of his face. Somehow, after seeing him in person, she felt in her heart she could work with him.

His clothes were another matter.

He was attired in faded, holey blue jeans and a navy blue T-shirt that had seen better days. She couldn't even decipher the writing on the front. And his old tennis shoes—once white, as far as she could guess, but now a scuffed gray—were abominable.

She bit her bottom lip thoughtfully. Part of her screamed to duck under the table, however ungracefully, and hide from the man. Back out of the plan. Get away from it all.

But then she remembered her purpose here, and with this thought came resolution. This was a job like any other job, however different in form it—*he*—presented itself.

It was time to buck up and do what she was hired to do.

Of course, Dustin was an unconventional scalawag who was continually late to his appointments. Hadn't she discussed this very thing with Addison and Camille? Why else would Addison feel compelled to hire an image consultant to clean him up and generally organize his life for him?

And how hard could it be, really?

Her mind was already envisioning a sharp pair of scissors in her hand, lopping off great handfuls of his thick black hair. Her smile widened.

"Mr. Fairfax," she called, waving her hand. "Over here."

The man turned at her voice and smiled as he approached. "Please, call me Dustin," he said, his voice deep and resonant. "All my friends do. And you must be *Iz-a-belle*," he said, pronouncing her name with a crisp Italian accent. His emphasis was strongly on the last syllable. "Belle. It has a nice ring to it." He laughed at his own joke, but Isobel just shook her head.

She stared at him for a moment, trying to get her bearings. No one had ever, in the whole course of her life, called her Belle before.

Everyone, even her mother, called her Isobel. Camille called her Izzy sometimes, but they had known each other forever.

"Isobel Buckley," she corrected subtly, hoping he'd take the hint.

"Dustin Fairfax," he said, turning his chair around and straddling it. "But of course, you already know my name."

"Yes," she agreed mildly, linking her fingers on the tabletop to keep from fidgeting. It was important that Dustin have confidence in her dignity and refinement if he was going to take any advice from her. It wasn't his problem she was feeling as if she were walking on shaky ground at the moment.

"Don't feel awkward on my account," he said with a wink.

Despite herself, her heart fluttered. The man was certainly a charmer, if a badly dressed one. And how had he known she was feeling off-kilter? Had he seen it in her expression? She determined then and there to take better control of herself and the situation.

She cleared her throat and looped a lock of her deep brown hair around her index finger, twirling it in lazy circles. "Let's start at the beginning," she suggested.

"Sounds reasonable," he agreed. That he was genuinely amicable was clearly apparent to Isobel and worked immediately in his favor. He appeared unusually relaxed and free of the usual stark brassiness most men his age wore about themselves like a cloak.

Dustin was simply himself, and he offered that openness willingly to her; and, she suspected, to all those he encountered in the—what was it?

Oh, yes. *Flower shop*.

If she was successful in her endeavor, she very well could be about to change all that. It was one of the things his brother had mentioned—in the negative category of Dustin's life.

One small shop was all he owned. He didn't even have a second one located across town at one of the many available malls and outlets.

She felt a shiver she couldn't identify as anticipation or warning.

"You were late," she said without preamble. She had to start somewhere.

"I had the worst time finding a place to park," he explained with a shrug and an easy grin. "You know how Denver parking can be."

"You drove your *car?*" Isobel asked, surprise seeping into her voice.

"Doesn't everybody?"

She knew he was teasing her, but she couldn't resist answering him. "I assumed—well—that you could walk here from your shop. Or take the mall bus, although I admit that doesn't appeal to me, either."

His grin widened. "I did walk. My shop is only a few blocks down from here. But what would have been the fun in telling you that?" He chuckled. "I drove my car to work, though, since I live in the suburbs. I'm telling you this in case you want to tool around in it later." He gave her a wide, cheesy grin.

Dustin was clearly on the far side of sense. What had she gotten herself into?

"As I'm sure you'll quickly learn," he clarified, "I'm not everybody. Run-of-the-mill does not apply to me. I often walk, but I have a nifty little sports car and I like to drive it."

"Oh," she said lamely.

"And you came in…?"

The question dangled before her, taunting her silently for an answer.

She blushed. "A Towncar."

"Yeah? Huh. Well, what do you know? That doesn't surprise me in the least. You look the type. You wouldn't catch me dead in a Towncar, though."

"Why is that?" she asked, intrigued despite wondering if his attitude might be condescending to her. It didn't show in his tone or facial expression. His smile was genuine and kind. He had a strong, masculine smile that made her heart beat faster in response.

He was pulling her under his spell and she knew it, but she was helpless to stop herself. Maybe that was exactly what he wanted, and she was playing right into his hand, but she'd never been as cynical as she oftentimes thought she should be.

She immediately decided to take Dustin at face value unless he proved her wrong. It was only fair, and he seemed nice enough.

She cupped her chin in one palm and leaned forward to better hear his answer.

"Well, I can't afford it, for one thing," he said. "At least, not until I get my inheritance." He laughed at his own joke. "And for another, I think fancy cars give off kind of a hoity-toity attitude to the general public, don't you?"

Isobel nearly choked. Towncars were a regular, accepted part of her existence as an image consultant, and something she'd taken for granted. She had been raised in a small Texas town and had not grown up with such luxuries, yet she admitted now she'd never given a single thought to how a person on the streets of Denver, perhaps someone less fortunate than herself, would consider the mode of transportation she chose.

"But you said you drive a sports car," she countered tightly as it occurred to her. It was an accusation, and she knew it sounded like one.

"That's true. I do," he said, smiling. He didn't look the least bit offended, but he offered no further explanation.

"And that's okay with you."

His grin widened. Then he lifted his dark eyebrows and shrugged.

"Are you hungry?" Dustin asked, meeting her gaze squarely. She had the feeling he knew exactly what she was thinking and was playing rescuer to her own guilty conscience.

It was an unnerving feeling. She shook her mind from the thought and said, "No, thank you. I try not to eat much after noon."

He glanced at his watch, as if he weren't already aware it was well after the noon hour. "You're kidding. That can't be good for your health."

Isobel chuckled. Ten minutes into their first conversation and *he* was already trying to change *her*. What an amusing paradox.

"A drink, at least?" he coaxed in a warm, rich voice. "You aren't going to sit across from me with nothing while I stuff my face, are you? I missed lunch and I'm starving."

"All right," she said, giving in gracefully to this one small concession. "I guess I might enjoy a good cup of hot tea. Herbal. And make sure it has no caffeine or sugar."

He stood and saluted. "Yes, ma'am. I'll bring you just what you ordered."

"Thank you, Dustin," she said with a sigh as she watched him approach the counter. She wasn't sure if he'd heard her or not, for he didn't turn or acknowledge the comment.

"Dearest Lord, what have I gotten myself into?" she prayed under her breath as she stared at Dustin's broad back. "I'm feeling a little overwhelmed here. This is a new one for me. A little help? Please."

Actually, she could use a *lot* of help. She felt she was way out of her league where Dustin Fairfax was concerned.

He quickly returned to the table with a loaded tray, placing it on the table before turning his chair around properly and seating himself.

"One cool-mint hot tea for you, and two large, completely indigestible pastrami sandwiches with extra jalapenos and onions, extra-large French fries and a large cola for me."

With a cheeky smile he leaned on his elbows and began unwrapping his first sandwich.

"Are you *trying* to give yourself a heart attack?" she quipped.

He burst into laughter and had to cover his mouth to keep from spitting food. Putting his index finger in the air in a gesture for her to hold on for a moment, he chewed and swallowed his large bite of sandwich, then chased it down with a big drink of cola.

"This stuff doesn't bother me," he assured her. "I'm as healthy as a horse."

She eyed his meal in disbelief, then twisted her lips and met his sparkling gaze. "Right. Tell me those same words again in ten years."

"I had my cholesterol checked when I turned thirty. Honest."

She shrugged. "Eat whatever you want. They're your arteries."

With a grin, he picked up his jumbo-sized sandwich and took another big bite, right out of the middle of the bread.

Etiquette was evidently going to have to be added to Isobel's list of things to go over with Dustin in their six weeks together.

She was amazed at how fast the sandwiches and fries disappeared, especially since Dustin was doing most of the talking during the meal.

He cheerfully talked about his childhood—about growing up in the Fairfax household, how he had felt having a controlling father and a competitive older brother like Addison around.

He glossed over the death of his mother, though Isobel thought it must have made a huge alteration in the life of a considerate, impressionable young man, both then and now. Certainly such a tragic event would have had a great deal of influence on the man Dustin had become.

Addison was Dustin's only sibling, and according to Dustin's many laughter-filled stories, they had done their share of fighting and wrestling when they were young. Addison had always been bigger, but Dustin was slick, smooth and, he told Isobel with a smile that could spark up a lighthouse, he could run faster. So the disputes had remained fairly even, and Dustin spoke of his brother with affection.

He asked Isobel about her family, but she said as little as possible, other than that she was an only child and grew up in a small town in Texas.

Since Dustin's parents had been together forty-five years until his mother's death, Isobel felt awkward discussing her own parents' divorce when she was an infant, and the many ways that had affected her.

Besides, everyone's parents got divorced these days. Why should she have been any different?

She didn't remember her father, and though she'd made peace with that, it rose up to haunt her now. She felt overly emotional trying to discuss her childhood, though Dustin had been open about his.

Not that she'd had a bad life—her mother had become a Christian soon after her father had left, and Isobel had been raised healthy, happy and loved, with plenty of hard work to bind them together in strength and lots of support from their home church.

Still, she didn't like talking about it, especially to a man she hardly knew. She didn't even want to think about it.

When she said as much, Dustin seemed to take it in stride, though he tried time and again to engage her in talking about herself; if not her childhood, at least what she was doing now.

"I have a small condo in the city that I share with my best friend, Camille. Have you met her?" she asked inquisitively.

He shook his head vigorously. "No, but I've heard she's a great girl."

"Camille would have a fit if she heard you calling her *girl*," Isobel replied. "We're both twenty-eight, you know."

"Oh," he said, frowning as he strung out the syllable. "*Old* ladies, then."

She couldn't help it. She kicked him under the table, and thought she made good contact with his shin.

He didn't even acknowledge that he'd been kicked at all, except perhaps in the tiniest widening of his all-male grin.

"I have the rest of the afternoon off," he said with his usual casual bluntness. "If you want to take advantage of me, that is."

Isobel choked on her tea. She knew her face was flaming, and it didn't help that Dustin only chuckled mildly when he realized what he'd said, or rather, how it had sounded.

He shook his head and cuffed the side of his head to indicate he hadn't been thinking. "What I was really trying to say was—"

"I know what you were trying to say," she said, surprised she could speak. "And I'm going to surprise you by taking you up on that invitation, however awkwardly it may have been worded," she teased, enjoying the way his attractive smile widened when their eyes met.

She fought a grin as she considered her plan. Oh, she would take advantage of Dustin, all right—or rather, of his easygoing nature.

Isobel was certain she could make him a changed man in a single afternoon. She thought even Addison would be impressed, not to mention pleased, with such a feat.

Maybe Dustin would get his inheritance after all, if she had anything to do with it.

And she did.

Chapter Four

"Do you want to take a ride in my sports car?" Dustin offered, jingling the keys in his pocket as he held the deli door open for her and gestured her through ahead of him.

She glanced up at the dim sunlight. At least it didn't look as if it was going to rain, or worse, snow. Colorado winters were unpredictable. "Tempting as the offer sounds, a ride won't be necessary. We can walk where we're going."

As soon as they stepped out onto the sidewalk, he automatically repositioned himself so he was walking closer to the curb. The sign of a true gentleman, Isobel thought. Maybe this wouldn't be so hard after all.

Dustin kept his hands in his pockets and whistled as he walked, glancing at her from time to time and genuinely smiling, although a bit as if he had a secret he wasn't yet ready to share with her. He seemed in no hurry, but rather content just to walk slowly and casually, as if they were old friends.

And he was certainly taking this well, having to make sudden changes in his life dictated by another person he had only just met and had no reason yet to trust.

If she were in his position, she knew she would be balking and pulling at the reins at such outrageous and uncomfortable demands.

Then again, maybe he didn't really know what he was getting himself into.

Yet.

She stopped and gestured at a shop door. "We're here."

Dustin glanced up at the sign and froze.

"No way," he said, his voice low and guttural. "No possible way."

"Now, Dustin, be reasonable," she pleaded, reaching up to place a hand on his shoulder, hoping he would take the hint and look at her.

He did.

And when their eyes met, Isobel felt exactly what he was feeling—the shock, the panic, the desire to run.

Truth told, she felt like running, herself, and pulling him along. But that wasn't what she was here to do, and Dustin had to start somewhere. Here was as good a spot as any.

She would not back down, no matter how his bright green puppy-dog eyes implored her to do so.

"It's not as bad as all that," she assured him, not certain how committed she sounded.

He shook his head. "Says you."

"Trust me?" she urged.

His gaze asked, *Why should I?* His jaw was clenched, but he stepped forward and opened the door for her. "After you."

She grinned in triumph, her heart pumping at the battle of wills she had just fought and won. This was a big victory for her—her first—and would no doubt be one of her best. It would pave the way for other small successes and triumphs.

The end result, of course, would be a final product of which she could be proud—and more importantly, of which *Dustin* could be proud.

"Ricardo, please meet my friend, Dustin," Isobel said as her regular hairdresser rushed forward and kissed both her hands.

Ricardo was unique and not a little odd with his spiked purple hair and dozens of gold necklaces that encompassed his broad, hairy chest, not to mention his bombastic personality and shrill voice.

His personality and flashy looks took some getting used to, but when it came to hair, Ricardo was the best in the industry.

Dustin, his eyebrows raised and his expression one of pure panic, was halfway out the door before Isobel caught him by the elbow.

"No way," he whispered in her ear. "Look at that guy's hair. I'm not letting him anywhere near me

with a pair of scissors. He obviously has no clue
what he's doing."

She laughed. "Hairdressers don't do their own
hair," she said, nudging him back into the room.
"Haven't you ever heard the elementary-school logic
problem about the small town with only two barbers?"

He looked at her as if she'd gone mad. She smoth-
ered a smile.

"Obviously not." She burst into laughter at the
horrified, stubborn look on his face. He was adorable
when he was being mulish.

With a flourish of her arms, she continued with her
story. "So, then. There were only two barbers in this
small town. One of the barbers had a neat trim, and
the other's hair was chopped at odd edges. Now think
about it, Dustin. Which of these two barbers would
you rather go to?"

Delighted, she was aware of how his eyes immediately began to sparkle with understanding and his
amused gaze turned on her.

He chuckled and shook his head. "I've never heard
that one before, and I'll admit you have a valid point.
But then again, I have no reason to trust Ricardo,
despite your clever stories." He winked at her. "I
haven't seen the other barber, so to speak," he reminded
her, his voice grave but his eyes alight with humor.

"Oh, yes, you have," she countered, grinning back
at him. She ran her fingers through the thick lengths
of her long, chocolate-brown hair, circling the ends
with her fingers. "You're looking at her."

"*That* man does your hair?" he said in an incredulous whisper. "Surely not."

"Oh, but he does. Ricardo is a genius. He not only cuts my hair, but he has a clientele list that would blow your mind. The best haircuts in Denver are provided by this man, I assure you."

Dustin yanked off his newsboy cap and scratched the top of his head, still looking as if he might bolt. "I can't believe I'm doing this," he muttered.

Isobel wordlessly took his arm and led him farther into the hair studio. Ricardo, who had no doubt heard most of their conversation, elegantly gestured to a barber chair and indicated Dustin should sit. Isobel was surprised the hairstylist's expression didn't betray a thing.

He drew a smock around Dustin and directed his gaze to Isobel. "What would you like done with the young man, my dear?"

"His hair," Isobel joked.

"Really?" Ricardo made a gesture of surprise, his hands over his mouth. "And here I was all ready to give him a pedicure."

Dustin's eyes widened and his jaw dropped at what he no doubt considered a threat. Pinching his mouth closed with a frustrated twist to his lips, he quickly tucked his feet under the smock, making Ricardo howl with unabashed laughter.

"Cut it short," said Isobel decisively, and Dustin cringed, shirking his shoulders and glaring first at her and then at Ricardo.

She paused a minute to let him stew before continuing her direction to Ricardo, not allowing herself the satisfied smile she was feeling inside.

"Not too short, though. A business cut. Something to keep his curls in order. And he's still young—keep the front long enough to comb back."

"I'm going to look like a toddler," Dustin grumbled good-naturedly.

"Not with Ricardo's help, you won't," she assured him, moving forward to place a hand on his shoulder. "He is perfection itself."

She turned halfway away from him and muttered, "Not like you *could* look like a toddler."

"What was that?" Dustin asked immediately, sounding suspicious.

She turned back to him and grinned. "Oh, nothing. I was just thinking aloud."

Dustin's gaze met hers in the large mirror in front of them. He still didn't look convinced.

"Trust me," she pleaded. "I really do know what I'm doing."

He gave her a clipped nod.

Knowing no amount of verbal persuasion would help, she stepped back then and let the master hairdresser go to his work.

The first thing Ricardo did, after giving Dustin a thorough shampoo and returning him to his chair, was to turn Dustin away from the mirror, which Isobel immediately understood and thought was an excellent idea. The worst thing that could happen would be for Dustin to run out before his haircut was finished.

Half a haircut would definitely not be an improvement on no haircut at all. She curled her fingers around in front of her mouth to hide her amusement, but Dustin caught her motion and glared at her anyway.

Dustin closed his eyes as Ricardo trimmed the back of his hair flush with his neckline. The more the hairdresser snipped, the curlier Dustin's hair became, but they were soft, natural curls instead of the long, frizzier style he'd worn before.

Finally, Ricardo dropped a bottle of hair gel into Dustin's lap without a word.

"What am I supposed to do with this?" Dustin growled, picking up the bottle and eyeing it suspiciously. "I'm a wash-and-wear kind of guy."

"Allow me to demonstrate," Ricardo said, not taking no for an answer. "You put a nickel-sized amount of the product on your palm and then work it through the tips of your hair with your fingers. Work the hair up and out. There is no need to work it into your scalp."

The hairdresser took the bottle from Dustin and held out his palm. He squirted a dollop of orange gel in the exact shape and size of a nickel, dropped the bottle back in Dustin's lap, then rubbed his hands together and began stroking his fingers expertly through Dustin's hair.

Dustin was still staring at his lap, hardly watching what Ricardo was doing. "I've never in my life…" he said, sounding stunned, or at least stubbornly uncomfortable.

"There's a first time for everything, right, Dustin?" Isobel asked quietly, totally amazed at his transformation. "Take a look at yourself."

Holding her breath for his response, Isobel turned Dustin's chair back toward the mirror.

Dustin stared at his reflection, hardly recognizing the man staring back at him. Who was this slick-haired man?

Perhaps he *had* worn his hair in the same style for a few years longer than he should have. Isobel may have had a point.

Of course, that was her job, wasn't it? To find the best places to make changes in order to make him a better man?

He still wasn't completely sold on the idea, but this was one point in her favor.

That said, he wasn't at all convinced about putting sticky orange gel in his hair every morning. But he had to admit the guy staring back at him in the mirror had his own charm.

Between the haircut and the gel Ricardo had meticulously applied, the hairdresser had done an outstanding job taming the wild curls Dustin had battled all his life. Ricardo had parted his hair just off to the right side of center and combed every strand of hair neatly back into place. Only a few stray curls escaped.

As Isobel had instructed, the hair on his forehead was combed back in the current style. He had to admit it looked good, though he wasn't at all sure he could duplicate the process when he was alone in his own home.

But in the end, the score was: Isobel one, and Dustin zero.

He stared in the mirror one more second, memorizing every detail.

He looked, well, contemporary.

And though there was no way he would admit it to anyone—especially Isobel, who would no doubt report such findings straight to Addison—Dustin found he rather liked his new look.

Especially with a hat.

"Double or nothing," he mumbled under his breath with a quick shake of his head.

"What was that?" she queried back, looking wary and more than a little suspicious.

He adjusted his newsboy cap backward on top of his new haircut, winked at Isobel and walked out the door without a word.

Chapter Five

Dustin didn't wait for Isobel to call him. Part of him—probably the sensible part—wanted to hide from her and tenaciously avoid her for as much of the prescribed six weeks as possible, but something about Isobel intrigued him. Completely apart from the stupid agreement he'd made with Addison, perhaps even in spite of it, he wanted to get to know her better.

Besides, in the long run it *was* the only way to get to his trust fund. He wouldn't examine his motives any deeper than that.

Isobel was certainly a beautiful woman, with her deep brown hair filled with red highlights and her warm brown eyes. She was tall and lithe. Maybe she could stand to gain a pound or two, in his opinion, but she still had the hint of womanly curves that would turn any man's head.

What caught him most, though, were her gorgeous

bee-stung lips and knockout smile, especially when it was directed at him.

Perhaps it was this thought that made him hold his breath as he dialed her number.

"Dustin," she said when he greeted her. She sounded surprised, but did he hear a bit of excitement in her voice, as well, or was it his imagination and a healthy dose of wishful thinking? "I certainly didn't expect to hear from you so s-soon," she stammered.

"Well, I figured you owe me one." He waited for her response, a grin pulling at his lips.

Dead silence.

He listened to the telephone line crackling and the praise music in the background, obviously coming from Isobel's stereo.

"Look at it this way. I put up with your torture yesterday, so today you're on my terms. And that's why I'm calling." He chuckled.

"That's not how this scheme is supposed to work," she protested immediately in a high, strained voice that only made Dustin's smile widen. "We're not supposed to be having a social relationship. I'm working on you, remember?"

"How are you going to help me become an honest, hard-working citizen if you don't know anything about me?" he countered. "Granted, you chopped off my hair without even knowing my middle name, but I don't think you can turn me into the best I can become without knowing a little bit more about the *real* me."

"What *is* your middle name?" she asked, sounding distinctly uncomfortable.

"So, you want to know now, do you? *After* you whack my hair off?" he teased. "How fair is that?"

"Dustin," she pleaded.

"James."

"Dustin James Fairfax. That's very nice. Now I will know that crucial bit of information for future whacking and/or cutting."

"Is that a threat?"

"Oh, no," she said with a laugh. "Consider it a promise."

"That doesn't sound good," he said. "Even more reason for us to get together today, though, if you ask me. Which you didn't," he pointed out wryly.

She sighed extravagantly. Pointedly.

"What did you have in mind?" She sounded as if he were about to ask her to walk the plank.

The horrible pirate captain. That was him, all right. Fit him like an old pair of sneakers. He held in the callous chuckle that would befit his pirate status, but he was tempted.

Instead, he told her why he'd really called. "I thought you could join me at my flower shop. To see what I do all day, you know? The regular nine-to-five thing my brother doesn't really think I have going on."

She breathed an audible sigh of relief, and this time it sounded genuine. "That actually sounds reasonable."

"And you sound surprised."

She laughed. "Perhaps I shouldn't be. I have an

active imagination. You'll learn that about me as we work together. I'm more tempted to believe the moon is made of green cheese than that astronauts have landed."

"I thought so—something like me holding you at sword point as you walk the plank?"

"Mmm. Something like that," she murmured thoughtfully.

"Aaargh," he said playfully in his best gravelly pirate's voice.

Dustin gave her directions to his shop on the 16th Street Mall, and they planned to meet at ten o'clock, a half hour away.

In the meantime, Dustin set out to fix his hair, which he had been ignoring until this point, since no one had been going to see him. At least no one who would care.

His old style had been easy—shower, comb it and leave it alone. But this hairstyling business—this was new to him.

And yet he had to make the effort. For the acquisition of his trust fund. He would do well to remember his true purpose in this six-week make-a-new-man-out-of-him process—getting his money.

Why then, as he combed through his hair, did he think his primping and preening might have just a little to do with Isobel, the woman?

He used the gel, but that only made his hair worse.

Every single hair on his head was sticking up, and from Dustin's viewpoint, each and every strand was going in a different direction from all the others.

He looked like a startled porcupine.

Dustin was befuddled. Ricardo had made it look so easy.

With a frustrated growl, he picked up the gel bottle and squirted another large dollop of gel into his palm, then slathered it through his hair.

Now his hair was not only prickly, but stiff as a needle. He took his bristle brush, the one he'd used for years, and slicked his hair back.

Oh, boy.

He gave his reflection a sinister look with shaded eyes and a whacky half smile.

This was better, if he were going for the crazy-man look.

He sighed aloud and began to part his hair on the side. Curls immediately began popping up, but he thought he looked better than he had before, if only marginally.

Less than a half hour later, Dustin he was in the back room of his shop, designing a floral arrange-ment for an upcoming wedding, when Isobel showed up, making her way slowly through his shop and appearing to take in everything. She stopped several times to admire one bouquet or another, even leaning forward to inhale the fragrance of the sweet-smelling blooms.

When she reached his work table in the back of the shop, she stood silently, watching him as he selected various flowers and placed them in an eye-catching manner within the arrangement.

"You're very talented," she said softly, stepping forward.

"Thanks," he responded, grinning at her. "It's a great way to express my creativity. Arranging flowers is something I particularly enjoy."

"I would hope so, considering you own this place," she teased. "If you hated flowers, I would have a real problem trying to reform you, now wouldn't I?"

"I meant it's one of many things that bring joy to my life," he corrected with a laugh.

"Oh," she said softly. Then, obviously trying to change the subject, she gestured at the vase he was working on. "That looks complicated."

"It's not just putting flowers together," he explained, handing her five yellow carnations and gesturing to the arrangement. "It's so much more. If you let it be, flower arranging can be a real work of art, like painting or sculpting."

Isobel clutched the flower stems, wondering what he meant for her to do with them. She'd come here today, as he had put it, to see him in his natural environment, so to speak, and to assess what needed to be done in the remaining six weeks.

She'd certainly not come to arrange flowers, and she had not the least idea what she was doing. Her artistic tendencies, such as they were, leaned toward fashion, not flora.

She eyed Dustin, who merely gestured toward the arrangement and grinned. "It's for a wedding," he informed her, adjusting a bloom here and there as he spoke. "The bridesmaids will be in yellow."

"Hence the yellow carnations," she said, winking back at him. "But please don't expect me to place these flowers in the arrangement. I'm sure I'll do it wrong, and then you'll just have to start it all over again."

"How will you know unless you try?" he asked quietly, but with emphasis. "Give it a go, Belle. It will tell me a lot about you."

He gestured at the unfinished bouquet. "The worst that can happen is that I'll have to help you, and I really don't mind doing that. It's a risk I'm willing to take," he said with a chuckle.

She flashed him a surprised look at the nickname, but didn't comment on it.

Dustin was trying to figure *her* out. Why would he do that? Everything felt all backward, and Isobel's stomach was filled with psychopathic butterflies.

She was supposed to be analyzing *him*.

It suddenly occurred to her that perhaps an attempt at working a flower bouquet would do just that. Give her a chance to see him interact with her as she destroyed his beautiful floral arrangement with her incompetence.

Would he become angry, or was he more of a patient man? Isobel would bet on the latter, but there was no time like the present to see for sure.

She stepped forward and tentatively began placing carnations carefully within the arrangement, gently and one at a time.

Dustin whistled low and clapped his hands slowly and in rhythm, each touch of his palms echoing in the large, colorful room and reverberating through Isobel's heart. "I knew it."

She looked up from her work, surprised, and met his gaze. "Knew what?" she asked, her mind half-distracted with her work.

"That you're a natural artist."

"You're kidding," she said honestly, feeling somehow elevated by his heartfelt praise. "I've never done this before. The closest I've come to flower arranging has been jamming a bouquet of flowers I bought at the grocery store into a vase."

Dustin laughed and then winked at her as the bell rang over the door, indicating customers were entering the store.

Isobel stood quietly by as Dustin assisted several of his obviously well-appreciated clientele, some of whom looked to be affluent, and many of whom had just walked in off the street amidst their 16th Street shopping.

This was what Isobel had been waiting for. It was an excellent opportunity to observe Dustin in his natural surroundings, when he was dealing with his everyday life and not her chaotic uprooting of his life, and she took advantage of the moment.

Oddly enough, she found herself enjoying her perusal of the man in his natural environment.

The first thing she noticed about Dustin was that his smile never left his face. Nothing seemed to ruffle him—not an irate customer being, in Isobel's opinion, absolutely ridiculous in her demands and refusing to calm down despite his best efforts. Not even this forced intrusion of Isobel into his life disrupted his careful attitude as she attempted to turn a frog into a prince.

Part of her problem, she thought—glad she was watching him from a distance and he would not be able to see her expression—was that Dustin was one very cute frog.

Even in faded blue jeans and a plain black T-shirt, Dustin was a man that women would naturally notice—*and* find attractive.

He wasn't handsome, at least not in the classic sense of the word, but something about him drew Isobel to him, and she knew she couldn't possibly be the only woman who felt that way.

Dustin was irresistible in the way of a tough, self-reliant stray tomcat. Not necessarily in the mood for a cuddle, but ready to jump in and stir things up.

And though he was big and independent, his green eyes emanated warmth and kindness, and that attracted Isobel more than any of his physical features could.

And then there was his hair.

She thought he looked infinitely more approachable with this new cut. He had obviously tried to emulate Ricardo in recreating the style, but he'd used too much gel and his hair looked stiff and stubbornly unmovable.

Even so, a few curls slipped out, the most noticeable of which was the curl across his forehead. She had the *most* indescribable urge to brush that lock of hair back where it belonged.

Suddenly, she realized the store was empty and she was still staring at Dustin.

Only, now he was staring back, and his green-eyed gaze was full of amusement.

He approached her slowly. "What do you think?" he asked, standing so close to her she could smell the cinnamon gum he was chewing.

She didn't want Dustin guessing what she was really thinking, so she glazed him with her most cheerful smile and said, "Oh, I don't know."

He lifted an eyebrow, silently challenging her off-the-cuff explanation.

She paused, searching for the right words. "Charming. Absolutely charming."

That she was talking about *him* and not the shop would be left unsaid. She could hardly be expected to think straight when his gleaming eyes so cheerfully held her gaze. She barely remembered to breathe.

He smiled. "Why, thank you, ma'am," he said with a put-on western drawl as he tipped an imaginary cowboy hat to her. "Glad you like it. I'm rather fond of the place myself."

Isobel chuckled. Addison had indicated that Dustin didn't put enough time and effort into his work, but Isobel saw he was wrong.

Dustin cared a great deal.

"The shop looks very successful," she said

thoughtfully, hoping her astonishment didn't register on her face or in her voice.

From everything she'd been told about Dustin, she admitted—at least to herself—that she had pegged him for a flighty man who couldn't settle down or make a commitment to anything.

So it was no surprise that she expected his flower shop to be somewhere between thoroughly disorganized and completely run-down.

She wouldn't make that mistake again.

From now on, the only opinions she would form would be from her own factual observations, and not what she had been told secondhand. As it was, she had a lot of backpedaling to do in order to get to a place she could really start with Dustin.

"I'm here seven days a week," he qualified, as if in answer to her unspoken question, "though I don't always work regular hours. In that sense Addison is right, I guess."

She could stand it no longer. His close proximity was getting to her. He was leaning into her space, so close she could smell his gum.

Taking a deep breath, she clenched her hands together at her sides and pinched her fingernails into her palms, but to no avail. Try as she might, she could not stand it a moment longer.

With one trembling hand, she braced herself against his shoulder. Reaching on tiptoe, she ran her fingers back through his sticky-soft hair and put that stubborn lock of hair back into its rightful position.

"There," she said, stepping back and placing her fists on her hips, happily surveying her handiwork. "Much better."

"I can't promise it will stay that way." As soon as he laughed, the willful curl dropped right back down on his forehead.

"I don't believe it!" she exclaimed. "I just don't believe it."

"Told ya so."

He shrugged, grinning at her stunned expression, and then slowly made his way around the store, straightening items and locking up, whistling a song Isobel recognized but couldn't identify as he worked.

Her heart was in her throat, beating an irregular tattoo as she watched him clear the cash register and prepare his daily deposit. Isobel wondered if this would be the end of Dustin's *planned day* together.

Oddly, though it was past her normal working hours, and though Isobel had gathered more than the amount of information Dustin had meant for her to have, she found herself hoping it wasn't.

Of course, she had a lot of work to do with Dustin's transformation. But really, she admitted privately, she just liked spending time in Dustin's company, and she didn't want the day to end for personal reasons.

He cleared his throat, his back to her as he covered up a display of roses with soft, silky netting. "I, uh—that is—I hope you don't have anywhere you need to be just yet."

Isobel let out the breath she hadn't known she'd

been holding. "No, I don't have anything special planned tonight. Why?"

He shrugged and looked away from her, though she caught his secretive smile first. "I thought maybe you could go out with me."

There was a brief, brightly flashing moment when her heart caught in her throat at the words *go out with me* before reality set in.

With a start, she reminded herself of the true relationship between the two of them. She was only here because Dustin's brother had ordered it to be so.

Dustin probably hadn't given any thought to what he was saying. He had simply misphrased his question.

She tried to speak but found her mouth too dry to form words. Clearing her throat, she tried again. She could not—would not allow herself to—make a big deal of nothing. "Where?"

Dustin turned and leaned his back against a wall, one foot flush against the surface.

Isobel's gaze was immediately drawn to his face. His smile was the genuine article. His eyes glowed in the half-light of the security lamps.

Again she considered how attractive he was to her, though not in the conventional way.

Cute.

That's what Dustin Fairfax was. It wasn't a new or currently fashionable term, she was sure, but it *was* Dustin. She'd picked up the word from her youth, when boys would walk by and her girlfriends would exclaim, "Oh, he's so cute!"

And that's what Dustin was, not that Isobel was going to share her newfound insight with him. She had no doubt he'd be appalled by her conclusion.

Men wanted to be thought of as handsome and dashing and strong and mysterious.

Definitely not *cute*.

"I just want to take you for a walk," Dustin answered vaguely, startling Isobel from her reverie.

For a moment she couldn't figure out what he was saying, and then she abruptly remembered she had asked him where he planned to take her this evening.

"It's a nice night for a stroll in downtown Denver. Would you like that?"

She nodded, wondering if he could have presented a scenario which she would have refused. She couldn't think of anything at the moment.

He reached around the cash register and picked up a bouquet of red roses he had prepared, and then escorted her out the back door, locking it securely and turning on the security alarm.

She wondered about the flowers. Did he mean to give them as a gift to her?

She was pleased by the thought.

But if he did plan to give her roses, why had he not done so at the shop?

Maybe he had a special hand-delivery to make, and planned to drop the bouquet off during their stroll.

He was being mysterious again, with that half grin hovering on his face. What was he up to this time?

She wasn't sure she wanted to know.

And yet she did.

"How did you come to be in Denver?" he asked as they walked along the crowded sidewalk. "I know you said you grew up in a small town in Texas. What made you move to a big city?"

"Fashion," she said thoughtfully, but said no more than that.

He chuckled. "Care to elaborate? I'm picturing you following this trail of translucent pink-scarf material until you reached your destination."

"Hmm?" she asked, glancing at him. "Oh, right. Texas." She cringed inside, but quickly determined to give him the short, happy version of her childhood, and leave it at that.

"As I mentioned before, my best friend, Camille, and I grew up in a rural Texas town. I remember summers riding horses from sunup until sunset."

"You learned fashion from riding horses?" he teased lightly.

"No. My mother didn't— Well, my father wasn't around, and so Mom had to work extra hours to keep us afloat. I had a lot of time alone, so I taught myself to sew on my own when I was eight."

"What, uh—" He hesitated. "What happened to your father, if you don't mind my asking?"

She did. But his voice was lined with such sympathy and compassion she knew what he was thinking.

That her father had died.

She should just leave him believing what he liked. She hadn't told any lies.

Exactly.

And if it were anyone else she'd known for less than a week, in any other circumstances but these, she *would* have left well enough alone.

Instead, she found herself blurting out the truth. The whole truth, for once.

"My father left my mother for another woman when I was three years old. They're divorced."

Dustin's tone didn't change. Neither did his expression. "I'm sorry to hear that. Are you close to your father?"

Isobel bit back the retort that sprung to her lips. "I never saw him or heard from him again. Even the government couldn't find him to get him to pay child support."

"I'm sorry," he said simply, and then wrapped her in a warm, tender hug.

Isobel took refuge for a moment in the sheer masculine strength of his embrace. Slowly the bitterness eating at her heart began to crumble.

Dustin was so strong, like a fortress against her painful thoughts. She felt safe in his arms.

But she wouldn't cry. Not for her father. She'd decided that long ago.

He wasn't worth it.

At length she straightened her shoulders and broke the embrace. Dustin immediately stepped back, his face awash with pity and compassion.

Isobel did not want to be pitied, not even by Dustin. Especially not by Dustin.

But his next words put her back at ease. "So, you said you taught yourself to sew. You must really have a gift for it—from God. I'd love it if you would tell me more about it."

It took her a moment to compose herself.

"Mom had a sewing machine she'd kept packed up away in the attic. One day Camille and I decided to be explorers. High adventurers, you know?"

Dustin chuckled.

"So, we visited the attic and found the sewing machine. I was instantly in love. I instinctively knew how to use it. I can't explain it to you, except perhaps that it was trial and error. And I did instinctively know a lot of things, as if it were already placed in my mind for me to use."

Dustin grinned. "God," he said firmly.

"God," she agreed. "Anyway, the work kept me busy. And happy. I always had a knack for knowing what was in fashion. As you said more than once, I believe it is, for me, a gift from God. And I thank Him for it every day of my life."

"Amen," Dustin said softly and fervently under his breath, though not so low that Isobel was unable to hear it.

Suddenly he stopped and tugged on her elbow to get her to stop, as well. "We're here. This will be perfect for what I have in mind."

What he had in mind? What in the world was that supposed to mean?

Isobel looked around her, puzzled. People buzzed

in and out of shops and up and down the sidewalks, reminding Isobel of a swarm of bees. None of the shops looked like somewhere Dustin would deliver flowers, but she shrugged. What did she know about the business?

Everyone everywhere had a sweetheart, it seemed. Why not someone in one of these quirky shops?

"All right, so now what?" she queried, flashing him a confused smile. At least he'd gotten her thinking about something other than her father's cruel betrayal.

He grinned back, his eyes gleaming with mystery. "Now," he said, "we go down there."

Isobel's eyes widened as Dustin indicated a long, dark alley she hadn't noticed was there until he pointed to it. It was dark and dank, definitely the sort of place she usually avoided at all costs.

"C'mon, Belle. Bring back some of that adventuresome spirit into your life and let's see the world." Again, he gestured down the alley.

She hung back. The alleyway was so long she couldn't see its end, and the bright light from the streetlamps didn't reach into its darkness.

She was frightened.

She knew she was being ridiculous. She'd taken care of herself all her life. And if that wasn't enough, she had a big, strong man with her. In a real pinch, she trusted Dustin enough to know he would protect her.

But an irrational sense of fear flushed through her nonetheless. Her heart leapt into her throat and lodged there, beating double time.

"No, thank you," she said, her throat tight. "I think I'd rather not accompany you at the moment. I'll just wait out here for you."

Dustin scowled. "Oh, no, you won't, Belle," he said in a low, crackly voice that wouldn't be denied.

And with that, he put his arm around her and gently but firmly, and without giving her the opportunity to protest, led her step by step deeper into the darkness of the bleak, damp alley.

Chapter Six

Dustin gently urged Isobel to follow him around the corner. He kept his grip tight to reassure her and to remind her he was there by her side.

Though she remained silent and walked with her chin high, he sensed he was taking her well out of her comfort zone; although, to be fair, dark alleys were out of *most* people's comfort zones.

Suddenly she clasped a hand on his sleeve, her grip tight. "What are you doing?" she whispered quickly in a low, stiff voice.

"*We* are visiting an old friend," he said with a low chuckle. "Or at least, she'll be a friend once you've met her. Trust me?"

She shrugged and marginally loosened her grip on his sleeve. He knew he had her on that one—it was the same question she'd posed to him just before she'd had all his hair lopped off.

She gave a clipped nod.

Dustin spotted old Rosalinda huddling against an aged brick building, using the side of a large steel trash bin to ward off the nip in the air. The alley was damp, and without the benefit of cleansing sunshine, snow still lingered here and there.

The one wool blanket she apparently owned was wrapped tightly about her shoulders. It was ragged and full of holes. Dustin made a mental note to bring her a new blanket the next time he saw her. Or maybe a sleeping bag.

"Rosalinda," he called, loudly enough for his voice to echo in the alleyway. His intention when he'd yelled was to keep from startling her with his approach, but the old woman jumped to her feet with amazing dexterity for her age and immediately reached for her shopping cart, which Dustin knew contained all her worldly possessions.

For what they were worth.

Not much. Not by anyone's standards. It made his heart ache just to watch her.

He glanced down at Isobel, unsure of her reaction to a situation that was heart-wrenching at best, and wondering not for the first time if he'd made a grave miscalculation in showing her this hidden facet of his life.

He was surprised to see that her eyes were alight with the emotions he imagined were raging through her as she took in every aspect of the situation.

Fear still glittered in their deep brown depths, but

there was another, more prevalent emotion shining through above the fear.

Compassion.

Dustin grinned, his heart pounding as he looked at the beautiful woman at his side. He knew he'd been right about Isobel.

She was as attractive on the inside as she was on the outside.

"It's Dustin." He waved his hand at the old woman and she lifted a hand in response. "I've brought a friend with me."

Isobel raised her hand and waved, offering a quivering smile as she did. She squeezed his hand and stepped close into his shadow. It wasn't, he sensed, that she was afraid of Rosalinda, but rather that she had never been put in this position before.

Perhaps she needed his guidance.

He chuckled and stepped forward. "How are you doing, Rosalinda, sweetheart?" he asked heartily. "You look absolutely stunning."

As he spoke, he plucked a single rose from his bouquet and grinned widely as he presented it to the old woman with a bow and a flourish. "A rose for my Rosalinda."

Isobel hoped her mouth wasn't gaping open. After the initial shock of seeing the poor, tragic state of Rosalinda's circumstances, she had recovered enough to realize Dustin was obviously trying to help in his own adorable, quirky way.

But when he gave her a rose, Isobel's head had

gone into a whirl. The gift of a simple flower seemed so completely incongruent with the situation, and yet was such a tender gesture, made so simply and honestly, that it brought tears to her eyes.

And she was not the only one affected by Dustin's gift. Rosalinda's face crinkled into a thousand wrinkles as she flashed her nearly toothless grin.

She reached over and patted Dustin on the back with one gnarled hand. "What would I do without you, Dustin? You always make me smile."

After a moment, Rosalinda turned her attention to Isobel, smiling her gap-toothed smile. "Your young man here never fails to brighten my day."

The first thing to register was that this wasn't Dustin's first visit to the old woman, but rather one of many.

And then the old woman's words hit her with their full impact.

Isobel opened her mouth to speak, to clear Rosalinda of the grievous misunderstanding that Dustin was *her* young man.

It was odd enough for her to be looked upon as a youngster in the old woman's eyes—she hadn't been called *young* for years—without Rosalinda somehow assuming she had a thing for Dustin.

But just as she was about to clear the air on the inaccuracy, Dustin squeezed her hand and gave an infinitesimal shake of his head.

The message was clear.

Leave it be.

Isobel ruffled as if she were a cat with its hair being brushed the wrong way, but she quickly realized Dustin was probably right.

The old woman almost certainly wouldn't remember the connection between her and Dustin, anyway, though she certainly remembered Dustin from his previous visits to her.

"Here, darling Rosalinda. This'll do you for a spell." Dustin discreetly handed the old woman a folded piece of blue paper.

Rosalinda wrapped one knobby hand around his fist and brought it to her cheek, unabashed at the tears flowing from her eyes.

"Thank you, Dustin," she said with quiet dignity.

"Now, Rosalinda, I've told you before and I'll tell you again, all the thanks belongs to God." He grinned charismatically. "I'll spare you the sermon if you promise to eat. Jesus is the reason, and all that."

"Isn't that a Christmas saying?" Isobel broke in, brushing her hair away from her face with the tips of her fingers. "Jesus is the reason for the season or something like that, right?"

"As far as I'm concerned, it's good all year round," said a laughing Rosalinda. "At least the part he quoted is."

"I second that motion," Dustin added.

"I suppose you're right," Isobel agreed thoughtfully.

Dustin patted Rosalinda on the back and smiled down at her. "Keep the faith."

Isobel could see the faith shining from both her

companions, gleaming in their eyes as, one at a time, their gazes met hers.

Every sweet morsel of the scene amazed her— Dustin for having the courage to share his faith in this way and Rosalinda for the courage to recognize her real treasure was in heaven.

Impulsively, she leaned down and patted the woman's hand, an act that was new and foreign to her.

She wasn't the touchy type.

"Thank you," Rosalinda said in her old, crackly voice. She turned her radiant smile upon Isobel.

"But I didn't do anything," Isobel protested, her voice a high, tight squeak. Her heart was pounding a mile a minute.

"Rosalinda, we'll be seeing you again soon," Dustin said, his tone friendly and respectful. "God bless and keep you."

"And you," Rosalinda replied shakily.

Dustin took Isobel's hand and tucked it into the crook of his arm, then turned them both around toward the light of the street.

"You told Rosalinda you didn't do anything for her," he whispered close to her ear. "You're dead wrong about that, you know."

Dustin glanced down at the woman next to him as they stepped into the muted brightness of the street-lamps, stopping her with the touch of his hand as the streamlined mall bus drove past.

Cars weren't allowed on 16th Street, only pedes-trian shoppers and the free mall buses, which ran both ways along the street for the convenience of the patrons who didn't wish to walk from end to end of the mall.

Right now, Isobel looked as if she might have run right into that bus if Dustin hadn't stopped her when he did. Her expression gave a brand-new meaning to *dazed and confused*.

He laughed.

She started as if suddenly awakened.

"What's so funny?" she asked warily, pulling away from him. "Are you laughing at me?"

Dustin's expression instantly sobered. She wouldn't look at him, so he used his finger to turn her chin so his gaze could meet hers. "I would never do that."

"No? What, then?" She didn't sound as if she believed him, and she was pulling away from him again, looking anywhere but at his face.

"You're just so sweet," he admitted after a long pause, and trying to choose his words with care. "What can I say?"

"Sweet?"

To Dustin's surprise, she looked genuinely offended, cocking her hands on her hips and glaring back at him as if he'd just called her a bad name.

What had he said?

At least she was looking at him again, he supposed, approaching the issue with his usual humor.

"Sweet?" she repeated, her voice an octave higher than usual. "Dustin James Fairfax, I may be many things, but *sweet* is definitely not one of them."

Dustin shoved his hands in his pockets and pulled his shoulders in tight. When she used his middle name like that she sounded like his mother.

"Sorry," he said, not quite contrite but refusing to admit it. He wondered how he was going to manage six weeks with this woman.

And they called *him* flighty.

"Well?" She stood frozen in the same intimidating position, staring him down.

If she was trying to make him feel smaller, it wasn't working. She wasn't going to intimidate him, no matter what she did.

He wouldn't let her. A lifetime of intimidation had made him strong against those kinds of tactics.

She was still staring at him.

"*Well* what?" he snapped, getting tired of all her wily female games. He'd given her a compliment, after all. What was the big deal?

She remained silent, continuing to stare at him as if he'd grown an extra nose.

"Are you waiting for me to take it back?" he asked, his voice gruff. "Because if you are, you'll be waiting for eternity."

And even then he wasn't sure he was going to be ready to concede, he thought mulishly, crossing his arms over his chest.

She sighed loudly and rolled her eyes. "What I *want* is an explanation."

"Oh, that," he said as if he'd moved long past the scene she'd just witnessed, though now that he was really looking at her he could see her head was still spinning from the encounter.

"Yes," she said blithely, imitating his tone, which he now realized sounded faintly temperamental. "*That*. I take it you do *that* often?"

He shrugged noncommittally. He hadn't really given his actions much thought, other than that they helped another human being. Wasn't that what everyone did? "I get out when I can."

"Well, I think that's spectacular." Her expression told him more than her words could have done. She looked at him as if he were truly someone special.

He turned to her and grasped her gently by the elbows. Her eyes were shining in the soft twilight and his heart was beating double time. No one had ever looked at him that way before. "Do you really think so?"

"Dustin, that was incredible. Remarkable. *You* were remarkable."

"No, Isobel, I'm not. I'm just a man. I do what I can," he repeated again. He felt like squirming under her intense scrutiny and had the feeling she was looking at him like some kind of superhero or something.

"Why did you give her that piece of paper?" she asked quietly. "I don't mean to pry, so feel free not to answer if you don't feel comfortable in doing so. I thought it might be for food or something. Dinner."

"A French dinner," he corrected with a laugh, shaking his head at her expression.

"Even more intriguing."

"Well, I'd have bought her a bag of groceries, but what would she do with it?" His hands slid up her arms to her shoulders. "She doesn't have a microwave or a refrigerator."

Isobel's expression was so melancholy he wanted to hug her, but he didn't know her well enough to fold her in his arms. His words would have to do, though that didn't seem like nearly enough.

The harsh reality was that he couldn't save Rosalinda, he could only be her friend.

"I can't just give her money, Isobel. She'll buy a bottle of liquor with it. That's a fact."

Isobel shivered despite the fact the evening was warm for winter in Colorado. The old woman had been so sweet, so fragile. And yet the reality was she was a homeless alcoholic.

"She's made her own choices," Dustin said firmly, taking Isobel by the shoulders and gently brushing his palms down her upper arms. He felt her shiver, and knew it wasn't the brisk night air.

"We can help, but we can't change her ways unless she wants to change. Right now, Rosalinda isn't ready for that kind of commitment. All we can do is give her what she's willing to take, and maybe in some subtle way keep tabs on her to make sure she's okay.

"A friend of mine owns a restaurant and has a heart for the homeless. It's a fancy, high-class French joint. I'll have to take you there sometime for dinner. The food is delicious. I think you'd like it."

Isobel brushed over what almost sounded like an invitation. A date. But, of course, that was ridiculous. She was working for him—or rather, his brother.

A date with Dustin was out of the question. So why did it sound so appealing?

"And he seats the homeless people right in the middle of the dining area? Wouldn't they feel uncomfortable in such a setting?" she asked in disbelief. "Not to mention the guests."

"Not he. She. Linda."

Isobel didn't outwardly react to the news that Dustin's friend was a woman, but she couldn't deny the internal tug of disappointment—or was that jealousy?—she experienced upon hearing the information.

He paused, his fingers playing with the curl on his forehead. "And she already had in mind what you were saying. In fact, she built a special room for the comfort of the homeless."

He was impressed that Isobel had thought of Rosalinda's comfort first, rather than the rich patrons who usually frequented the restaurant.

As if suddenly realizing his grip on Isobel had tightened, Dustin suddenly dropped his arms and stepped back, clasping his hands behind his back and clearing his throat. With a light smile, he began walking down the street, nodding his head for her to follow.

He didn't look back to see if she was behind him or not, but assumed she would keep pace with him, as she had all evening.

He was wrong.

Isobel narrowed her gaze on his back, her hands on her hips. "You haven't told Addison about this little hobby of yours, have you?"

He froze midstep, his back and shoulders turning rigid.

"That's what I thought," she said, taking his posture as an answer.

"Don't even think about it," he said, his tone low and tense. "I didn't bring you with me today to show off to you, Belle. I don't want Addison knowing a thing about what just happened."

Isobel smiled softly at Dustin's pet name for her. She had no idea where he'd dreamed it up, but for some reason she liked it—though, if the moniker were to come from someone's lips other than Dustin's, she was sure she'd be mortified.

Stepping forward to catch up with him, she laid a reassuring hand on his arm. He had to know she respected his motives. How could she not? He had the gallantry of a medieval knight.

But if his brother knew of his compassion for the homeless, wouldn't that be a big plus in his favor of getting the trust fund? Dustin might not have to endure these six weeks with her if he only came clean with what he did in his spare time.

It just didn't make sense to her.

"Dustin, I would never do anything without your permission, but I really think Addison's opinion of your *contribution to society* would change if he could see you with Rosalinda—and all those other homeless people I suspect have been touched by your good heart. Don't you think it would be worth a try?"

"That would ruin everything," he snapped tersely. "Stay out of it."

Isobel knew the stress Dustin's older brother was putting on him was starting to wear thin. She could see the strain in his expression. And yet for a long moment, he didn't speak.

She stayed quiet, patiently waiting for the explanation she sensed was forthcoming. She'd not known him long, but she knew him enough already to know he had his own reasons for doing things; he wasn't exactly conventional in his methods.

Eventually, Dustin sighed and she sensed the tension slowly easing from his body. He clenched his fists for a moment, and then gradually released them.

Finally, he turned to look at her, his gaze warm and tender, his arms stretched toward her, almost pleading as he approached her.

"Sorry, Isobel, I don't mean to take it out on you. I shouldn't have been so irritable." He shrugged his shoulders. "This whole money thing is a bit much sometimes, but I shouldn't take it out on you. Sometimes I just want to punch something, you know? Like a brick wall?"

"I can't even begin to imagine," she said earnestly, placing a hand over her heart as a gesture of sincerity.

"I mean, I know you're right in one sense," he said

thoughtfully. "That if I told Addison about Rosalinda, he might be more inclined to release the funds to me."

He took a deep, steadying breath and shook his head. "I would have all this money to use to build a homeless shelter or something."

He paused a moment, jamming both hands into his already untidy hair. "There's just something that feels *wrong* about telling Addison."

Isobel nodded. "But when you do a charitable deed, do not let your left hand know what your right hand is doing, that your charitable deed may be in secret; and your Father who sees in secret will Himself reward you openly."

"Matthew 6:3-4," Dustin choked out. "So you're a Christian, then. I thought you might be."

She nodded. "I taught my fifth- and sixth-grade Sunday school class that verse last year." She smiled at the memory.

"A Sunday school teacher, huh?" He winked at her. "You sure don't look like any Sunday school teacher I know. I probably would have gone to church more often as a kid if I'd had a teacher as pretty as you."

She blushed a bright, becoming pink, though Dustin had only been voicing an opinion he'd had since the moment he'd first seen her in the deli.

"Well," he said, deciding to have mercy on poor Isobel, who was hemming and hawing and squirming. "At least you get what I'm trying to do here."

He watched as she slowly calmed down, and he

was perplexed. She obviously wasn't used to compliments, yet she was a beautiful woman, inside and out.

It gave him pause to wonder what her past had been like.

At length, she smiled at him. "And here I am, standing here staring at you like a constant reminder of your trouble. Like a porcupine rubbing against you."

"A porcupine?" he repeated, in a high, stilted voice, sounding stunned.

He turned and looked her over with an amused grin, his eyes twinkling with merriment. "I don't *think* so. Not in a million years."

"But it bothers you to have me here," she hinted without the least bit of subtlety. She wasn't about to mince words now.

"No," he answered definitively. "You, my dear Isobel, are the best thing that has happened to me in a long time. Maybe ever," he added in a quiet undertone.

He looked away from her, suddenly studying the still busy activity of the street.

Isobel felt a choking sensation at his words, and became even more emotional when his gaze suddenly turned back to her and she stared into the sincere brightness of his eyes.

Eyes that pleaded with her to understand, to walk with him in this one thing.

And how could she do less?

He was so real, so in the moment, that it almost frightened her, more now than at any other time since she'd been with him.

"But you won't tell," he said softly, again looking away from her, stuffing his hands in the pockets of his jeans in a gesture she now recognized as a subtle form of anxiety in the most carefree man she'd ever known.

It was just another incongruity in Dustin Fairfax, another puzzle Isobel meant to solve before her six weeks were over.

She heard the catch in his voice and knew his words were a question, though he'd artfully phrased it as a statement.

"No," she assured him, her voice suddenly unable to go above a whisper. "I won't tell."

Chapter Seven

Dustin arrived at the Regency Oak Towers in the Denver Technical Center shortly after 5:00 p.m. Dressed in his usual jeans, T-shirt and a bomber jacket, he felt a little uncomfortable entering the flashy hotel lobby.

He cringed at the very thought of the time, because five *sharp* was when Isobel was expecting him, and he knew exactly what that fact meant for him.

He was gonna get chewed.

It was her job, after all. Miss Perfectionist, with her intimidating habit of constantly looking at her watch, a habit he doubted she even noticed.

With Isobel, Dustin knew, even a minute late was *late,* and he was at least ten minutes behind—maybe more, with the way his life tended to run.

He didn't know the exact time because he forgot to wear a watch.

Okay, so he didn't *own* a watch. But what was a little semantics between friends?

Isobel would consider it showing his true colors, and it would no doubt make the *image consultant* part of her wish to give him the tongue-lashing he so richly deserved by his actions.

Dustin found it amusing to think of Isobel this way, on a high horse and full of righteous indignation…as long as it wasn't aimed right at him.

He chuckled under his breath. Whether or not she followed through on her career-focused instincts remained to be seen.

Would she take him to task on a few measly lost minutes?

The Tech Center, the major business hub in Denver, was surrounded by huge international firms and was the centerpiece for out-of-town business. Thus, a number of high-end hotels with excellent service and gigantic conference rooms to service their affluent and prestigious clientele were at virtually every corner of the complex, each vying for the upscale business.

Wishing not for the first time he'd picked up one of those five-dollar, big-faced watches at a discount store as he had considered doing for Isobel's sake, he pushed through the highly polished revolving glass doors and made his way into the hotel.

He really did hate watches—they made him too aware of time. They made him tense and stressed when he didn't want to be—and especially when he needed to be at his best.

Like now. And he was *late*.

At least he could have brought Isobel a bouquet of flowers to ease the way into her good graces. He owned a flower shop, after all. He hadn't even considered the obvious.

How dumb was that?

He was still pondering his error when he was hailed by a bouncy, lively Camille, who looked like—by her hair and the way she flittered around—she'd had a few too many double-shot espressos. Dustin had never met her in person but Isobel had described her with remarkably accurate detail, right down to the Irish red hair.

She was waiting for him behind the concierge desk. Her palm drummed out a nervous rhythm on the desk and she sang softly with the beat she had created, all the time waving to him with her other hand.

"Dustin," she called sharply as he wandered aimlessly through the lobby. She continued her energetic arm movements, waving over her head so there was no way he could possibly have missed her.

He removed his ball cap and scratched the top of his head. His gaze remained on Camille as he smiled a bemused hello.

"Dustin Fairfax. You're just the way I pictured you." Her voice was a rich, vibrant alto, bouncy and full of life. Quite a contrast to Isobel's soft, high voice, Dustin mused.

He nodded.

"She filled me in on every detail of what has happened to you so far. For what it's worth, your hair looks great. I heard all about it—Ricardo is really something, isn't he? He does my hair—but I'm not afraid to tell you I was scared out of my wits when Isobel first recommended him. As long as the guy does his job well, though, don't you know what I mean?"

Dustin didn't have an opinion on the issue—he only wondered if he would be allowed to get a word in edgewise if he did. Camille was like a machine gun; her words shooting out so quickly he couldn't make heads or tails of any of them.

This was something Isobel hadn't mentioned when she'd told him all about her best friend. She'd obviously told Camille more about him than she'd told him about her closest friend and roommate.

Camille continued to prattle on, waving her hands enthusiastically as she spoke. "Isobel wasn't fibbing when she called you the next major hunk to take Denver by storm."

The woman didn't seem the least bit embarrassed or shy about her statements. It wasn't that she appeared a ditz, not aware of what she was saying, and blathering on and on about everything. Rather, her soliloquy appeared to be a clear-cut judgment of how she saw things in the world. No blushing or pandering with Camille, just an honest assessment, straight up.

He kind of liked it, and immediately saw how Camille complemented Isobel. It gave him insight into why they had become fast friends.

He already liked this happy, carefree woman who

was Isobel's best friend from childhood, and thought he understood why Isobel shared such a close-knit bond with such a happy, outgoing person.

"Did Isobel really say that about me?" he queried, his grin widening.

Camille barked out a laugh. "Ha! You know Izzy better than that by now—or at least I hope you do!" she said, waving her hands in denial.

"She'd never say anything like that—not in so many words, anyway. But Izzy is the best image consultant in the industry, if I do say so myself—and I do. You can bet by the time she's through with you, you'll be just exactly what I said you will be—the next major hunk to hit the Denver area."

Dustin replaced his cap. "I don't know about that," he replied, honestly but not warily. "Isobel's been good for me, that's for sure."

Camille eyed him with intelligent, amused, interested green eyes. "Do you think?" She laughed heartily at her rhetorical question.

He answered it anyway, nodding vigorously. "Yeah. I sure do."

"I'm Camille, by the way. Isobel's best friend. She told you about me?"

Dustin laughed. "She told you about me, didn't she?" he queried.

"Well, yes. She tells me everything, of course. You're just—"

Dustin cut her off. "A hopelessly backward male who needs some refinement?" he offered.

Camille laughed with delight. "I like you. I really like you."

"I like you, too," Dustin said honestly.

His mind brushed quickly over the details he knew about Isobel's friend.

Camille had joined Isobel in pursuing their higher education in Denver from some kind of Texas backwoods childhood, choosing a career in the hospitality arts, whereas Isobel had pursued the fashion industry. With Camille's bubbly, open personality it was no wonder she was a successful businesswoman, having risen to assistant concierge of one of the most prestigious hotels in the metro area.

"I think you'd better get up there," Camille said. "Isobel is anxiously waiting for your arrival."

"*Anxious* being the key word," Dustin said, groaning. He lifted an eyebrow. "Up where, exactly?"

"Fifth floor. It's the second conference room to the left."

"Got it. Thanks for the help. And it was nice meeting you, Camille." He fingered the rim of his cap and tipped his head.

"Oh, no," Camille protested with a friendly wink. "The pleasure is all mine. I hope we see each other again soon."

"I'm sure we will," he responded politely, his mind already half on what was to come.

Actually, he wasn't exactly sure what *was* to come. But he had more pressing matters at the moment.

He wasn't too fond of the glass elevator that skimmed its way up and down the exterior of the hotel, but the view of brightly lit downtown Denver in the dusky twilight was almost worth the way his stomach turned upside down as he rose floor by floor.

Almost. He didn't especially like heights—particularly in see-through elevators.

He was most heartily relieved to reach the fifth floor, and he quickly stepped out onto the firmness of the hotel floor, letting out a deep breath as his feet touched the solid, unmoving floor.

Staring at the beckoning door to the conference room, he ran his tongue across his dry lips and sighed deeply, then removed his ball cap and stuffed it into the back pocket of his jeans.

The things he was willing to do for a trust fund.

Dustin thought the convention room he entered must be the hotel's largest, for it had effectively been transformed into a fashion runway.

Isobel had said the hotel would be the location of a prestigious spring fashion show, but he had never expected an actual *runway*. Not in the middle of a conference room more suited for, well, *conferences*.

There was a small, gold-curtained stage near the back, obviously constructed just for the event. The chairs for the guests had been assembled in straight rows around the runway and were draped in shimmering strips of gold.

The only thing missing from the sparkling picture was Isobel.

Dustin shoved his hands into his bomber jacket pockets and just stared at the spectacle for a moment, taking it all in and feeling a tight, cold fist in the bottom of his gut.

This was where Isobel belonged, amongst all this glitz and glamour. For a moment, he thought he might have caught a glimpse of her heart.

But shimmering and gold was all that Dustin was not. If she was thinking to change him into this, she would have to think again.

"What's wrong?" Isobel asked, having come up from behind him and noticing his low brow and the stubborn set of his chin. "You look like your dog just ate your ice-cream cone."

He jumped back like a kid caught with both hands in the cookie jar.

"What's wrong?" she asked again, patiently looking up at him.

Dustin's features evened out, settling into his usual cheerful countenance. "Nothing's wrong. You just startled me."

"I don't believe you," she said frankly as she met his guilty-eyed gaze, and felt a little hurt at his reticence to confide. "But I'm not going to push you into telling me what you were really thinking."

He gave a dry laugh. "I thought that was your job—pushing me around."

She felt heat rush to her cheeks and knew Dustin would be able to see the result of his teasing on her reddened face, if teasing was indeed what he had meant by his remark. He had sounded quite serious, and his expression gave nothing away. She didn't know whether to laugh or cry.

Deciding to ignore his unsettling comment, she changed the topic. "Well, I'm glad you're here," she said in as light a tone as she was able. "We have a lot to do this evening, and we need to get started right away if we're going to accomplish anything."

"Do?" Dustin stiffened. "I was hoping you were going to say you just wanted to give me a tour of this place. You know, show me the ropes of what you do around here."

She lifted an eyebrow.

"I'm interested in what you do for a living," he insisted, giving her his best cheeky grin. "This is all new to me."

"Trust me," Isobel purred. "I'm going to *show you the ropes.*"

Dustin narrowed his gaze on her, his green eyes gleaming with amusement. "I've heard that tune before," he reminded her in a dry, suspicious tone.

Isobel laughed gaily, curving her arm through his. "Come on. I promise this won't hurt nearly as much as your haircut did. It's nothing permanent or irreversible. Who knows—you might even like it."

He snorted. "Famous last words. I notice you didn't say it wasn't going to hurt, only *not as much.* What am I supposed to take from that?"

She frantically pulled in the smile that threatened to crease her face from ear to ear. Dustin needn't know how funny and boyish his expression looked as she purposefully goaded him.

She leaned into his arm, running a delicate hand across his biceps. "Never tell me a big, strong man like you will let something as harmless as a new set of clothes scare him."

"Clothes?" he choked out, pulling down on the rim of his ball cap. "That definitely has the same ring to it as *haircut*."

Isobel laughed again and continued to pull him forward toward the stage. "C'mon, big boy, and let me introduce you to a couple of my good friends, Jon and Robert. I'm sure you'll like them."

Dustin threw her another suspicious look. "Who are Jon and Robert?"

"They work in the industry. You should feel honored. These guys are giving us their time for free as a favor to me."

"Oh, joy," he said, with just a touch of sarcasm lining his voice.

Isobel sniffed, letting him know she was offended by his candid remark. "They happen to be top-of-the-line experts—the very talented and creative assistants of Wanda Warner."

He shook his head, his gaze letting her know the name didn't ring a bell. "And she would be…?"

"Oh, *please* don't tell me you've never heard of the most popular western clothing designer on two continents. I'll be mortally offended if you do."

He shrugged. "Sorry. No."

He didn't sound sorry.

He sounded amused.

She wanted to shake him. What planet was the man living on that he had never heard of Wanda? She was always appearing on the news and specialty television shows, and her face regularly turned up in local and national newspapers.

She even had her own television shopping network that was shown worldwide.

It was almost as if Dustin purposefully kept himself distanced from the world—a virtual hermit if not a literal one. Did he not even read the daily paper?

"Well, you're about to be introduced," she said firmly, earning a groan from Dustin. "And, please, Dustin, try to be nice to them," she added, remembering their encounter with Ricardo the hairdresser. "It will go easier on you in the end."

It was a veiled threat, and he groaned again, rubbing his forehead with his palm.

She set her face in a businesslike expression, unwilling to let Dustin take the enjoyment out of what was most certainly—at least for her—going to be a fun and extraordinary evening.

Grabbing him by the hand, she tugged him toward the stage, up three steps onto the platform and eventually through the sparkling gold curtain to the back, where her colleagues were waiting.

She was totally aware Dustin was literally dragging his feet, scuffing along like a boy on his way to the dentist's office, but for the moment she chose to ignore his antics and stall tactics. "Jon, Robert, come meet your designated project for this evening."

She felt him pull back again, slamming on the mental brakes, so to speak; but she didn't feel entirely guilty at provoking him.

Jon and Robert were obviously twins, aged somewhere in their mid-twenties. They had polished good looks, but were not the least conservative in their dress. Their clothes were colorful and loud, if carefully coordinated, and definitely western, right down to polished snakeskin cowboy boots.

Isobel knew Dustin wasn't used to working with highflyers like these.

Still, he could be just a little more of a willing participant, in her opinion. He had, after all, agreed to this arrangement between the two of them in the first place. He was the one who would benefit from it in the long run, if he would just give her half a chance, instead of fighting with her every step of the way.

It wasn't exactly as if she were going to be drawing blood.

Dustin surprised her by releasing her hand and offering a firm handshake to each of the two young men in turn.

"Glad to meet you fellows," he said with none of the reticence or patronization she expected. "I hear you've got plans in store for me."

The two men looked at each other and then back at Dustin, breaking into friendly grins.

She wasn't sure if it was a blessing or a curse that

Dustin appeared to have decided to trust her and had capitulated in his attitude.

Finally, he was submitting to her plans with the good grace he usually showed. The night-and-day difference astonished Isobel.

"What's going on here tonight? A fashion show?" Dustin asked, smiling down at her in that quirky way of his that at once conveyed his unspoken apology for his earlier behavior and sent Isobel's heart leaping into her throat, beating a quick, sharp, patent rhythm that she was beginning to recognize as uniquely pursuant to Dustin's warm smile.

It was Dustin's signature on her heart.

He could really be charming when he wanted to be, and right now, he was laying it on full force.

"The fashion show isn't until later this week," Jon said, leaning casually against the nearest wall and crossing his feet at the ankles. "You oughtta ask Isobel to get you a ticket. Five-star event, but our Isobel has that kind of clout, you know."

Dustin cocked an eyebrow and looked down at her, his expression unreadable. "No, I didn't know that about Belle. Not that it surprises me," he continued softly, chuckling under his breath.

Isobel shrugged, feeling uncomfortable with the attention the three men were paying her. To the last man they were staring at her with pride, the younger guys with a touch of envy, and it made her uncomfortable.

"I'm sure you'd really enjoy it, Dustin," Jon said, kindly taking the focus off of her, and not a moment too soon. She'd been on the verge of turning and running. She grinned at him, silently thanking him for rescuing her.

Dustin stiffened, his face screwed into a ball of lines. Isobel realized he was holding back a laugh.

"I'm sure I would," he said in a blithe tone Isobel hoped Jon and Robert wouldn't recognize. "Our Isobel is full to bursting with ideas on how to spruce me up, make me another man."

She knew exactly what he was implying with every word he spoke, so she not so gently laid her heel down on his toes in silent warning, leaning back until she was certain he felt it.

He'd *better* feel it. The cad!

Next time she would stomp.

"What we're doing tonight is kind of like a fashion show," Robert offered, brushing a hand through his curly mop of hay-colored hair.

Isobel gave a small, startled shake of her head to warn the young man off, but the damage had already been done.

"And by that you mean?" Dustin asked warily, looking around at the three of them.

"You'll see," Isobel said, just the littlest bit too brightly.

To her assistants, she merely said, "Guys, why don't we get started?"

Chapter Eight

"Jon and Robert, as I briefed you earlier, and as you can now obviously see for yourself, my client needs a fashion makeover in a mean way."

She cringed inside. She had almost said *friend*, and deep down she knew it was true. Dustin was very much becoming a friend.

But she had to keep her professional boundaries, not get her priorities mixed up. She had a job to do. He was her client—and that was only for what was left of the six weeks they would spend together.

"I'm *mean?*" Dustin queried, raising both his eyebrows. Isobel had opened herself up for it, and he just couldn't resist teasing her about it.

"I hope that's not meant to be literal, Belle." He grinned at Isobel and winked.

She held a straight face, but he could see the sides of her lips twitching. "Wait and see, Fairfax."

She clapped her hands twice. "Jon and Robert, let's get started."

Started, Dustin soon discovered, was trying on an inordinate number of outfits—slacks, dress shirts, jeans, casual shirts—even shoes! More clothes than he'd ever seen—or *wanted* to see—in his whole life. Where did they get all these things?

But the three fashion moguls in his company were undaunted, and continued to send him back and forth from the dressing room with new sets of outfits. They commented amongst themselves at each new combination of garments, but didn't let him hear a word until Isobel was ready to proclaim her final opinion.

And the tuxedos, sports coats, and hats.

So many different kinds of hats! There was an entire rack of them!

He was given baseball caps—which he didn't mind too much; felt fedoras that, in his opinion, made him look like a gangster out of the 1920s; and even one top hat which, he had to admit, looked pretty classy.

Even on him.

There were so many clothes, and he quickly found he would have the unfortunate experience of putting on and taking off every single item.

It wasn't exactly his first choice for a night out. Not even in the ballpark.

And his feet were beginning to hurt from some *very* uncomfortable oxfords squeezing his toes together.

"Oh, now *that* is a nice look," Isobel commented on one particular outfit, making her opinion known as she had on every other. "It's casual, yet it lends the distinction of class."

Dustin stared in the three-way mirror, shaking his head in astonishment. For once, he couldn't formulate the words to tell her how he felt.

Maybe it was because his brain had turned into a speeding highway, one thought after the next threatening to collide with one another. He couldn't find room in his mind to make audible speech.

The tight indigo-blue designer jeans they'd given him were all right, he supposed, though in truth he much preferred his jeans loose and well-worn.

But a pink shirt?

It was a nice, snap-down dress shirt, made of extra-soft material Dustin couldn't identify. It fit his broad shoulders perfectly and tapered to his waist, where he tucked it into his pants.

In other circumstances—or more precisely, other colors—Dustin would have been impressed by the shirt, maybe even have worn it, despite the western look to it he wasn't real keen on.

But pink?

No way.

Not on this man.

"It's gorgeous," Isobel proclaimed, clapping her hands together in sheer delight.

"It's awful," Dustin replied instantly, cutting her off before she could rant and rave some more.

"And I'm taking it off. Now."

He made good on his threat and began unsnapping

the shirt, not even bothering to go back into his dressing room to do so.

"But Dustin!" she protested, slapping her palms over her cheeks as he peeled off the shirt right in front of her.

"I draw the line at *pink,* Isobel," he said, trying to keep his voice sober, though he knew a gleam of amusement must have shown from his eyes. He wasn't really angry as much as annoyed.

How could she think he would be the kind of man who would wear pink? He wasn't *that* comfortable with his masculinity.

Deep down, he wondered how much she really knew about him, when she couldn't even pick out appropriate colors for him to wear, colors that matched his lifestyle and personality.

It seemed to be the sort of thing an image consultant ought to know instinctively, and especially after spending some time together with him.

"But it looks good on you," she protested again in a gravelly tone, moving her hands to her hips. "Spectacular, even."

"You have got to be kidding." He wasn't going to argue about this.

"You are so closed-minded," she retorted, angrily stepping forward to face him.

"Mebbe," he growled low in his throat. "But I," he informed her through gritted teeth, "will never, ever wear anything *pink.*"

He paused for effect.

"Not a pink shirt, not pink pants, not pink shoes and not a pink hat," he said, feeling as if he were quoting something from Dr. Seuss. "I won't even wear pink pajamas, thank you very much. So can we please move on to another subject? Like *blue?*"

Isobel let out a loud huff of breath as Jon and Robert, whom Dustin had mentally tagged *Riff* and *Raff,* chuckled under their breath.

"Some people's children," Isobel muttered irritably as she turned to find something new on the wardrobe rack. She pushed the clothes hangers around loud enough to make sure every one of the men in her presence knew she *meant* to stir up a ruckus.

"What was that?" Dustin queried, chuckling and raising an eyebrow.

"Nothing," she snapped, keeping her back to him and continuing to riffle through the clothes.

"You mean nothing I'd want to know about," he corrected casually.

She whirled around and glared at him, her eyes spitting fire. "Whatever."

Dustin knew then that he'd really offended her, and he took the offensive to make it right with her again, submitting to the ministrations of Riff and Raff and cracking jokes that made the men, at least, loosen up and laugh a little bit.

But it took another long, excruciating hour before Isobel finally settled on an outfit that both pleased her and that Dustin didn't whine about.

"You are so lucky," she informed him, her tone

still a little sharp and exasperated. "Do you know
how many men can get away with pleated slacks
with cuffs, and actually look good in them?"

He rolled his eyes but then grinned in her direction, trying to ease the tension between the two of
them but still not ready to give in to her demands.
"No, Belle. Tell me."

Either she didn't hear the irony in his voice or she
was ignoring it. Or maybe her answer would have
been the same either way.

"Close to none," she said crisply, brushing her
palms together as if brushing off any rebuttals he
might have made.

"Honestly," she continued before he could speak,
"so many men wear pleats and shouldn't. You need
broad shoulders to balance the look, and of course a
trim, tight torso."

Dustin grinned and patted his stomach. "Three
hundred sit-ups each and every morning, first thing.
Guess it's done the trick."

"Evidently," she said wryly, looking anywhere
but at him.

He chuckled.

"Besides you, Dustin, I can only think of one man
who really does those pants justice, and he's a television hunk."

Both of Dustin's eyebrows hit his hairline at her
words and his mouth dropped open.

"Hunk?" he teased.

She brushed his comment off and kept her eyes

carefully averted. Isobel didn't want to be thinking about his nice physique right now, unless it was related to the clothes she wanted him to wear.

"Whatever."

Truth be told, the real hunk was standing before her, and despite their differences in opinion over fashion styles and what he should wear, she knew she was succumbing to his innate charm.

He was one of those men who didn't have the slightest idea what they had going for them—which was just as well. He'd be a dangerous, and no doubt arrogant, man if he knew the effect he had on women.

On her.

She mentally shook herself out of her emotional relapse. She still had work to do, and she wouldn't let her latent feelings for Dustin keep her from getting the job done.

Without a single word to him, she held out her hand to him.

He took it without comment and allowed himself to be pulled through the golden stage curtain and on to the runway.

"This is very important, Dustin, so please try to follow my instructions to the letter." Her voice was low and crisp.

"Yes, ma'am," he replied with a playful salute. "Whatever you say."

"Spotlights, Jon," she called loudly. Immediately a hot, bright spotlight put Dustin and Isobel at the center of the action.

"Spotlights?" Dustin queried warily, dropping her hand. Something was up, and he wanted to know what it was. "What's with the spotlights?"

"You'll understand in a minute, hon," Isobel said with a short laugh.

"Why do I think I'm not going to like this?" he asked wryly, lifting his left eyebrow. His muscles tensed as if in preparation for the worst.

"Oh, it won't hurt. I promise."

Dustin just shook his head.

"It's that simple, really. All I want you to do is put on some attitude. Be your usual confident self, only with a little punch."

"And?" he asked. It sounded as if he might be gritting his teeth, and Isobel well knew she was gritting hers.

He wasn't going to like this.

"And," Isobel continued, half holding her breath, "I want you to walk down to the end of the runway, turn around as if there were big crowds of fashion-conscious magazine editors out there in those chairs watching you, and then walk back to the curtain."

She paused. This was an important moment. If she couldn't get him to comply in this one area, to show off the confidence she believed he possessed, then it would be all uphill from here.

How else would she ever begin to get him up to snuff for the really important moments, when people would be present?

Watching him. Judging him.

"Nothing could be simpler, Dustin. It might be fun, even." Her voice cracked, and she wondered if he noticed the slight lapse.

"Not a chance," Dustin informed her in a deep, slow, firm monotone voice that indicated he would brook no argument.

"I'm not asking you to do anything illegal," Isobel retorted, mild anger showing in her tone despite her best efforts. She'd known this wasn't going to be easy, but she'd hoped for the best, despite it all.

He grunted.

"What could be easier that walking the runway? No one is here to see you but me."

"Don't forget Riff and Raff," he pointed out, crossing his arms and sounding just a bit like a pouting child, at least to Isobel. "And as for the runway, I can tell you right now I would look like an idiot strutting around like that, showing off some dumb clothes."

He looked at her then, his gaze pleading in a way his words could never do. He looked as if he were in pain, and it struck right at her heart.

After a moment, he groaned. "Don't ask me to do this, Isobel. It isn't me."

She wanted to let him off the hook. Her heart was screaming to give the poor man a break.

But this was for his own good, she reminded herself. He needed to do this, needed to see what it felt like under the spotlight.

"Please?" She was begging now, and they both knew it. "For me?"

He shook his head, but at the same time stepped forward and onto the runway, glowering down at her from his new height. "Very well," he said, his voice tight. "For you."

With a frown, he started down the runway. It wasn't long before Isobel detected his intentions weren't entirely honest. Fire and ice fought inside her as she watched him make a mockery of her life, and his chances of getting the trust-fund money.

It began subtly, with a turn of his hips and an occasional hand flipping in the air in an unusually cocked manner. Then he started strutting and jerking all the way down the aisle.

The only sound was the click and thump of the boots he was wearing with the outfit Isobel had devised. It didn't take a neurosurgeon to figure out he was doing a man's imitation of a female runway model.

Poorly.

For Isobel, it was the last straw.

She threw down the clipboard she was holding and let it clatter to the floor.

The noise stopped Dustin in his tracks, though he didn't turn and look at her.

"That's it," she said, unable to keep the anger and frustration she was feeling from her voice. Rage surged through her in hot waves.

And the worst part was she didn't care. "You want to change, Dustin Fairfax, do it yourself. At this moment, I couldn't care less about you, your brother's crazy ideas or the money in your stupid trust fund."

She drew in a large, loud breath and glared at his back. "I quit."

It was the first sensible thing she had said all day—maybe for weeks, she thought to herself. It was as if a weight was lifted from her shoulders, now that the stress of the situation was gone.

And the sooner she got away from Dustin Fairfax, the better.

She turned and hiked toward the door, not daring to look back to see what Dustin was doing.

"Isobel," he roared, and she froze solid in the spot despite her best efforts to keep moving.

Every bone in her body screamed for her to run, but there seemed to be a short between her brain and her limbs. She couldn't move a muscle.

"Turn around." His hard voice was a command, and she knew she should be offended, but she didn't move.

She couldn't.

"Isobel, please."

The tender, genuine ache in his voice as he spoke moved her heart as no cold command could have.

She didn't stride off in indignation.

She turned.

If his genuine honesty had compelled her to stop and turn around, it was the hopeful pleading in his wide green eyes that made her stay.

"Belle, look at me," he said, his voice low and hypnotic. "Just stand there a moment more and watch me. Please."

How could she not?

She was mesmerized by him. His every move was slow and calculated, and graceful in the way of a large wildcat in its mountain home.

Slowly, sweat dripping unheeded from his forehead, step by excruciating step, he walked down the runway, putting every effort into transforming himself into the poised and well-postured man Belle wanted him to be.

He exceeded every aspect of a true runway model. His male ego would settle for nothing less. His boots made no sound this time as he glided along; all she could hear was his labored breathing.

No swaying hips or obnoxious comments in a falsetto voice followed these movements, and she was overwhelmed by the pull of his will alone.

He was sleek, smooth and oh, so masculine, in a way none of the male models of her acquaintance could even remotely simulate. His face was a study in strong lines and smooth planes as the lights teased his shadowed expression and his concentrated steps.

After what seemed an excruciatingly long time, Dustin reached the end of the runway and paused. Electricity crackled in the air.

Isobel held her breath in unconscious anticipation, thinking he might do something boyish and silly and totally Dustin to ruin the moment—something like taking a running leap off the constructed platform and screaming like a banshee all the way down.

And yet...

He broke for only one moment in order to flash

her a cheeky grin that made her heart skip a beat. Then he was absolute model material again, as he carefully removed his sports coat and, with a beautifully executed turn that reminded her more of a dancer than a model, turned back toward the stage, flipping the jacket with casual ease onto his shoulder.

With another smooth turn he stepped confidently to the end of the runway and pulled at the silk tie, then unbuttoned the top button of the rose-pink shirt he vowed he'd never wear in public.

Pink or no pink, the man oozed masculinity.

When he was finished with his spotless routine, he gave a subtle, after-work casualness to his overall appearance, like he'd finished his workday and was just beginning to relax and kick back.

Isobel had never seen anything like the performance Dustin Fairfax was giving her right now.

Everything from his confident male swagger to the stray lock of hair that fell over his forehead was as professional as it was endearing. She swallowed hard, forcing herself to keep breathing, to keep watching this magnificent sight. She was certain she'd never see anything quite like this again.

Dustin pivoted once more and walked back up the runway until he disappeared behind the sparkling gold curtain.

Isobel didn't move, not at all sure what to expect next. She thought perhaps she ought to follow him backstage, but her legs felt like jelly and she wasn't sure she could walk even if she wanted to.

A few moments later, Dustin slid back through the curtain, and Isobel released the breath she hadn't even realized she'd been holding.

The coat was gone, his pink sleeves were rolled up over his elbows, he'd unhitched the second button on his shirt and his baseball cap was back—or more accurately, *backward*—on his head.

He cocked his chin and raised his hands in question, turning around once for her inspection, laughing at his own performance.

Isobel just stared at him, thinking he looked every bit as handsome the way he was now as he did dressed up out of his measure.

Maybe more.

"Well?" he asked when she didn't speak. "Am I forgiven?"

Chapter Nine

Isobel supposed she was giving a bit of a peace offering when she showed up at Dustin's door Saturday morning, with a dozen or so new outfits for him in the trunk of her car.

This time she'd included a few casual outfits she hoped he might actually wear, for she now knew Dustin's personality well enough to know he would never really convert to wearing business suits and ties.

That just wasn't Dustin.

That being said, there would be times when he could not avoid wearing a suit, and at the moment, both of them knew this six weeks was in that category. The grand finale was a posh dinner hosted by his brother. Dustin would *have* to dress up for that.

Feeling oddly nervous, she took a deep, cleansing breath and glanced at her watch.

9:00 a.m.

Isobel was a morning person by nature, and it

hadn't occurred to her until this moment, when she was literally standing here on his doorstep, that Dustin might not be.

She wished she'd thought of it earlier.

If Dustin was a night owl and liked to sleep in late, he was not going to appreciate her gesture of good-will when the sun was still low in the east and bright in the sky.

She hesitated a moment before raising her hand to knock. For a moment, she thought of turning around, leaving and returning later in the day.

But, after all, she was already here, she reasoned, so she might as well go ahead and knock. If he was rumpled and grumpy and growled at her to come back later, she would.

She knocked several times, pounding harder with each effort. She called Dustin's name, thinking he might be deeply involved in some project and, in typical Dustin fashion, had become entirely unaware of the world around him as he worked at whatever it was he was doing.

His ability to lose himself completely in whatever he was doing, working at everything he did with his whole heart, was actually a quality she much admired in him, as she herself was always ultra-aware of her surroundings and what was going on about her, often to the point of distraction.

At this particular moment, however, his tendency to get lost in things was annoying her. She had hand-picked the outfits she had with her to give him as a present, and she was going to be very disappointed if he wasn't home or wouldn't answer his door.

She realized in hindsight she probably should have called first as a common courtesy, but she had wanted to make her appearance at his door a complete surprise—hopefully a good one.

Well! She had done that, all right. He was so surprised he wasn't even home.

Crestfallen, she shifted her attention to her surroundings. There were two cars in his driveway. The first was a practical compact car, appropriate for a single man to get around with, she supposed, though in truth a little boring for her perception of Dustin.

The second was a beat-up piece of junk Isobel barely recognized but supposed she would classify as some sort of old-time sports car.

His *sports car!*

Could it be?

She laughed aloud as she looked the car over. She would doubt if the thing even ran, were it not that he'd said he'd had it with him when they first met— offered her a ride, in fact.

Maybe she should have taken him up on it.

She stifled another laugh, but couldn't help the grin that continued to line her face.

So much for first impressions.

With Dustin, nothing was ever what it seemed on the surface. Everything about him was a mystery, and what he offered openly was completely incomprehensible to the normal female mind.

At least hers. But then, she thought wryly, not too many people she knew would classify her as *normal*.

Her curiosity piqued, she stepped around the side of the house and found a Kawasaki motorcycle, every piece of chrome polished to a bright shine, parked against the redbrick wall.

Isobel chuckled. Dustin definitely wasn't a Harley man, but it didn't entirely surprise her to find he tooled around on a motorcycle.

He marched to the beat of his own drummer, that was for certain.

She examined the motorcycle, as she had never actually been this close to one before. It looked a little dangerous, with all those pipes and rods. Her heart beat a little faster.

Suddenly and quite abruptly, she became aware of music.

She froze in place, her ear tuned to discovering the location of the pleasant sound, which she had quickly identified as some form of classical music being played on a piano.

But where was the delightful music coming from?

She couldn't quite place it, and suddenly had an incorrigible need to know. Maybe it was that incomprehensible connection she felt with Dustin. She hadn't known him that long, yet for some reason she thought it might be him, despite the fact that he had never mentioned music, much less played the piano in front of her before.

Was she right? Was it Dustin?

She walked slowly around to the back of Dustin's house, letting herself in through the unlocked picket gate and feeling a little like an intruder prowling about where she didn't belong.

She wasn't sure what Dustin would think of her letting herself into his backyard that way, but once struck, she could not help but continue until her curiosity was met as to where the sound originated.

The music led her on.

She turned the corner of the brick house. Dustin's backyard was overgrown with weeds from end to end, hadn't been mowed in ages and, most surprising of all, hadn't been landscaped.

Not a single flower bloomed. No color budded from the ground.

And him owning a flower shop.

Dustin was a paradox. An enigma.

And she was more determined than ever to figure him out.

After she had found out where the music was coming from. The longer she listened, the more intrigued she became.

There were sliding glass double doors at the back of Dustin's modest home, and one was open a crack, though the long white drapes were still pulled against the blazing sunlight.

She crept forward, every moment half expecting Dustin to jump out from behind a bush or shrub, shouting "Gotcha" at the top of his lungs and frightening her half out of her wits.

It would be just like Dustin to do that.

But then, who would be playing the piano?

Every nerve on end, she pulled the glass door open mere inches more, only because, she told herself, she now had no doubt whatsoever that the music was coming from within Dustin's house.

Someone was in there playing, and she had to know for certain who it was.

And it was not, she assured herself, any sort of jealousy that led her on, like the unwanted thought that some beautiful woman was in Dustin's house playing on his piano and to his delight.

It was the music and nothing more.

In moments she had confirmed her theory. The piano melody was definitely coming from his house, and she closed her eyes for a moment to savor the warm, familiar classical refrain.

Whoever was playing, he—or she—was good. No, not good.

Gifted.

Hardly knowing she did so, she slid the door half-open so she could slip inside the house. She followed the sound of the music like a tiny mouse at the mercy of the Pied Piper.

Not thinking. Feeling.

She crossed through an empty room that looked as if it served a variety of purposes. There was a computer, a wide workbench with a variety of wood products on it and a table spread with flower cuttings.

Not, she thought with a small smile, flowers fresh from his own garden.

The room had a wood floor that looked as if it had seen better days. It needed a mop and a good dose of wax, not to mention some elbow grease.

As soon as she hesitantly stepped through the open double doors onto the white shag carpet that covered the next room, she finally located the source of the wonderful music.

Dustin sat straight-backed at a highly polished baby grand, his eyes closed as his fingers flowed effortlessly over the keys.

This room was full of light from the many windows and, unlike the room she'd come from, was fully furnished with what looked like expensive, high-end wood furniture and a posh set of black leather sofas and chairs that looked fabulous against the plush white carpet.

Nicely framed black-and-white art posters lined every wall, placed with a remarkable sense of balance that finished off the room with class and distinction.

Isobel couldn't help the smile that tugged at the corners of her lips. Apparently he hadn't completely lost a sense of his upbringing.

Suddenly she realized the music had ceased and she froze in place, almost afraid to turn her head in Dustin's direction.

After all, she was, technically, an intruder. Whether that was a good thing or not was still to be decided.

As much as she would have liked to avoid it, her gaze turned almost of its own consent toward the piano, holding her breath at what she might find there.

Dustin's eyes were open, one eyebrow arched. His arms were crossed over his chest, and his inquiring gaze was upon her.

And that was all.

He didn't even look particularly surprised she had suddenly appeared in his house without being invited. He looked as if he might be wondering *why* she was there, and was only mildly and amusedly curious at discovering the answer to that.

Isobel's face flamed as she realized she *had* no explanation, no rational excuse at all.

She cleared her throat and looked at the floor, stalling for time, though she knew he wouldn't wait forever. She would have to think of some excuse at some point.

Preferably sooner than later.

"Well?" he encouraged, unabashed laughter lining his voice.

"I followed the sound of the music," she blurted at last, then felt her face flame at the weakness of her poor explanation.

He laughed aloud then. "You followed the music. From your condo in downtown Denver?"

She scowled at him, though in truth she was put out with herself. What kind of fool walked into someone's house uninvited, especially a man she'd only known a short time?

"From your front porch," she answered in a clipped tone. "I dropped by as a surprise to, uh—to give you a present," she stammered.

Dustin's grin disappeared as soon as he heard the word *present.*

A *present?*

Up until this time their acquaintance had been casual, even businesslike, although admittedly he considered her a friend at this point.

He intended to get to know her over these six weeks. He hoped to stay friends with her after his brother's crazy experiment was over.

But still…

What had he missed?

Some sort of three week anniversary or such?

It wasn't his birthday.

His male mind scoured the details of their acquaintance for a clue to his oversight and he felt sweat beading on his forehead.

The crux of the matter was that *he* didn't have a present to give to *her.*

He didn't know why it mattered.

She was the one who'd wandered into his house without an invitation, and somehow she'd already turned it around so he was the one pulling at his collar and fidgeting on his piano stool.

Women.

No wonder he was single at thirty.

He'd never understand the female mind, not if he lived to be a hundred.

"Don't look so shocked, Dustin. It's not personal," she said with a chuckle. "It's a professional gift, and your brother paid for it. So you can take a deep breath and relax, cowboy."

Dustin scrunched his face and cringed dramatically. And it wasn't all for show. For one thing, he didn't want anything to do with his brother's handouts, even in the form of beautiful Isobel Buckley.

"Oh, now, stop that fidgeting and take it like a man. I know you can handle it."

She paused long enough to make him fidget again. "Anyway, I picked everything out myself."

"Everything?" he asked warily.

"Every last piece."

He gazed at her warily. "Piece of what? Dutch apple pie, I hope."

She chuckled. "You wish. You men and your stomachs. I'm sorry to disappoint you, but I'm speaking of clothes, as I think you already know."

He cringed again. "I was hoping you wouldn't say that. And yet, somehow I knew deep down in my heart, despite my growling stomach, that was what you were going to say. I wonder why?"

She propped her hands on her hips, and he knew she wasn't buying his propaganda. "If I didn't know better I'd think you were afraid of new clothes."

He chuckled, placing a fist on his hip, mimicking her moves and her voice. "If I didn't know you better, I'd think you were obsessed by them."

She tossed him a catty grin. "What an astute observation. How long did it take you to come up with that one?"

They stared at each other. A silent moment passed between them.

"So?" Dustin asked, amused, though maybe still a little uncomfortable. He was not in a big hurry to get to the *clothes* part, but resigned himself to the inevitable.

"So?" Isobel repeated, obviously pulling back from her thoughts and looking a little dazed.

"So are you going to get those new clothes out of your car so I can see them, or what?"

"I…uh…" Isobel stammered. "I wasn't thinking about the clothes," she admitted, her words muddled together as they tumbled from her mouth.

Dustin threw both hands up to his unshaven cheeks and drew in a sharp, dramatic breath. "You've astonished me."

She narrowed her eyes on him.

"It's a compliment." He nodded his head vigorously when she raised her eyebrow.

"Hmm…I wonder."

"Well," he prompted with a grin, "if you weren't thinking about what an incredibly changed man I'll be in your new clothes, just what exactly were you thinking about?"

She cleared her throat and looked out the window. "Your music," she mumbled under her breath.

"My what?"

"The piano. I followed the sound into your house.

Although in my defense I did try knocking on the front door first."

Her face was a delightful shade of pink, growing red, and Dustin's grin widened.

"And of course I didn't hear you. I pound around so voraciously on these old ivories it makes the dogs howl clear down the street."

She lifted an eyebrow.

"And just wait until I start wailing along with the music," he added, laughing with her. "I'll have the whole neighborhood up in arms in a matter of minutes."

"I'm sure that isn't true," she replied instantly. "From what I heard of your piano playing, you're pretty good." She paused. "Actually, that's an understatement. If you sing half as well as you play, you'll have no trouble impressing me."

"Is that what I'm doing?" he queried lightly, his gaze brushing over her.

She swallowed hard and straightened her hair with her palm. "You tell me."

Not in a million years, he thought as his heart raced as fast as his thoughts. He wasn't about to admit to anything but his name, rank and serial number. And that was if he could speak at all.

He ran his fingers across the ivories, so swiftly that they didn't make a sound. It was one of the nicest feelings in the world, his fingers on the keyboard.

"I do love playing," he admitted softly.

"Play something now, then. For me?" Her voice

was soft and so compelling he didn't even think about toying with her.

With a clipped nod and pinched lips holding back any expression of emotion that might betray him, he brought both hands to the keyboard, brushed his fingers lightly across the ivories and began playing a familiar hymn. It was slow and emotional, and Dustin closed his eyes to capture every nuance.

Isobel also closed her eyes, savoring the beauty of one of her most beloved hymns. How had he known "The Old Rugged Cross" was one of her particular favorites?

Suddenly, Dustin switched gears and started playing an upbeat praise song Isobel recognized from one of the CDs in her car. He was hitting so many notes one after the other Isobel was certain his fingers must be flying over the keys.

Her eyes popped open in surprise and Dustin smiled at her without missing a beat.

"Sing with me," he said, and looked out toward the sunshine-jammed window before breaking into an upbeat tune with his deep baritone.

"Oh, no, I don't think—"

"Isobel." Dustin cut her off with a warning look. "Remember, I know how to be every bit as stubborn as you do."

"Yes, but I—"

"Is-o-bel." He drew out her name, pleading this time instead of ordering.

She couldn't resist the soulful look he gave her

with his big green eyes. For some reason this appeared to be very important to him, and she immediately capitulated to his endearing puppy-dog look.

"Okay, but don't say I didn't warn you," she said with a laugh.

"I will take full responsibility for your actions," he assured her, joining her laughter as their gazes met and held.

"Now, let's see," he said, flipping through a stack of books on the top of the piano. "What do you think we should sing?"

"'Mary Had a Little Lamb'?" Isobel suggested, placing a hand over her mouth to suppress the laughter surging from her.

"Come now, Belle," he said fondly. "Surely you can do better than that!"

"You choose, then," Isobel said, suddenly tense. She was not at all comfortable with her own voice, though she hesitated to mention her fears to Dustin. "Just make it something easy."

Once again massaging the keys with his fingers before he started playing, Dustin broke into a simple praise melody Isobel was completely familiar with, one with a straightforward melody and without much range.

It figured.

He couldn't choose a song she'd never heard before, so she could honestly beg off. It had to be the most likely song in the world she *might* be able to sing.

Oh, well. It was his problem. He'd asked for it, and had more or less told her to sing.

He might just come to rue it.

She joined in, tentatively at first and then, as Dustin smiled his encouragement, slowly and steadily with more gusto.

She couldn't have been more surprised if he had pinched her.

It was *fun* singing with Dustin.

Her voice might not be anything to write home about, but his certainly was, and for some odd reason she almost felt as if they sounded good together, as if their voices somehow blended.

But of course that was ridiculous. Water and oil didn't mix, no matter how hard a person might shake them.

She was relieved when the song ended.

Dustin sat straight-backed on his piano stool, staring at her, his hands folded in his lap.

When she finally had the nerve to look at him, he merely raised an eyebrow.

"What?" she finally asked when he continued to sit stone-faced and unspeaking.

"Well?" he prompted in return, looking and sounding as if he expected something from her.

"Well, what?" she asked, exasperated. She couldn't stand to play games, especially right now when she was feeling self-conscious. She was embarrassed enough as it was, without him rubbing it in.

"What was the big shock I was supposed to experience when you sang?" he asked her bluntly, looking her right in the eyes.

"What do you mean?"

He shrugged, as if the answer were obvious. "From the way you talked, I expected—well, I don't know—something awful."

"Wasn't it?" Shock rippled through her body at his intimation.

"No. Not at all." His voice was warm and reassuring.

"But I thought…my voice…I mean I really can't…" she stammered, but he cut her off with a shake of his head.

"What?" he asked, his voice gentle and firm. "You can't *what?*"

She didn't answer. She couldn't. She just stared at him, knowing he would force the issue anyway, but unable to say the word.

"Sing?" he suggested in a whisper, his gaze full of compassion.

She let out a relieved breath she hadn't realized she'd been holding. "Exactly."

Somehow, it was easier when he put it into words for her.

"Isobel, you have a nice voice. Trust me."

He sounded so genuine Isobel's heart did a flip-flop into her throat.

"I don't sing off-key?" she asked, her voice squeaking with surprise.

"Who told you that?" He sounded more surprised than she felt.

She blushed, trying to think where she'd first received that impression and what had led her to feel that way. "Why, no one, I guess. I used to sing all the time when I was a toddler and in preschool," she remembered with a sudden fondness. "I always liked music, especially Sunday school songs."

Her mind drifted to less happy times. "I remember," she said, choking on the words, "that my mother used to yell at me when I would sing."

"Aw, Belle," Dustin said, empathy dripping from every syllable. "Everyone's parents holler at their kids when they get too loud."

"Yes," Isobel replied quietly. "I know. I probably am making a big deal out of nothing." Her heart ached, screaming to the contrary.

In a moment he was by her side, grasping her hands gently in his, stroking her fingertips in a calm, rhythmic manner. "Of course, it's not nothing," he said in a gravelly tone.

He paused a moment and continued fervently, "Talk to me."

He led her to the couch and seated them both, never letting go of her hands.

"I remember a specific time," Isobel said slowly, looking over his shoulder so she wouldn't have to meet his eyes.

He nodded. "Go on."

"I was about five, I think. My mother was on the

phone. I was singing with the television—one of those old children's programs. I didn't know who Mom was talking to, or that it was important. But suddenly she slammed the phone down and turned on me. Her face was as white as paper, and I remember noticing how bad she was shaking."

Dustin continued stroking her fingers with light reassurance.

"She yelled and yelled, until her face was bright red. She said my voice was annoying, and she wished for once I would just shut up. She kept yelling the words 'shut up' over and over again."

"She was in a really bad way," Dustin said. "Did you ever find out what was going on?"

Isobel shook her head. "I never did find out what that phone call was about. I always thought it must have been my father, but I don't know. I do know I never sang again."

"So you assumed that you must sing off-key?" he asked seriously.

She could feel her face growing warmer by the moment. "I don't know. I thought perhaps I was tone deaf. I always stand quietly in church and let others do the singing, though I praise God in my heart."

"You should sing," he admonished promptly, wagging a finger at her.

She shrugged, asking with her gaze for him to tell her what he was thinking.

"In the first place, Belle, today you hit every single

note right on key, with a beautiful tone of voice I'm sure many people would love to hear."

"Oh," she said mildly.

"And second of all, you broke through today, Isobel. You sang with me. Don't go backward from here.

"Third," he said, his voice turning a little gruff, "that's not the point of music in the first place."

"I'm not following you," she said, honestly confused by his words.

"What is music really for, Isobel?" he queried seriously. He stood and returned to his piano stool, leaning his elbows on his knees and staring right into her eyes.

When she was silent, he answered his own question. "To worship God."

"Of course," she whispered reverently. It was something she'd always known, yet Dustin was showing it to her in a new way.

"And do you think God cares if a person sings a bit off-key? If he sings from the heart, I expect that song comes off as beautiful to God's ears as the entire heavenly host put together."

Isobel just stared at him.

His smile wavered and he pinched his lips together. "And I'm preaching, aren't I?"

She shook her head. "No. Not at all. I've never heard it put that way. You're absolutely right. And it's a lovely thought."

She looked away from his bright gaze, seeking refuge in one of the posters lining his walls.

"What?" he asked.

She laughed at herself for her own folly. "I'm somewhat hesitant to admit this, but I wasn't thinking of God's ears so much as yours."

Dustin broke into laughter.

She was cute, that one. Cute, truly intelligent and completely fun to be around. He loved the way she spoke her mind no matter what, even if it got her into trouble or was potentially embarrassing.

He could respect a woman like that.

But that was more than he wanted her to know. He felt vulnerable enough around her as it was.

In fact, he couldn't ever remember a time in his life when a woman had touched his soul as she had in three short weeks. She was truly unique, and he silently thanked God for the opportunity to get to know her better.

What had started as an unmitigated disaster of a plan concocted by his brother was now time Dustin found himself looking forward to, more and more as the days went by.

He only had three weeks left.

Chapter Ten

Isobel was still staring at him, a peculiar look on her face, when Dustin started from his reverie and realized he'd been woolgathering.

"Why did you stop singing completely? After a while, didn't you wonder?"

"Well I never…I mean, other people were so…and I…" She paused from her stammering and took a deep breath. "You can't really know if you're good or not," she finished lamely. "After a while, it just seemed easier that way. Besides, my voice sounds different to my ears than it does everyone else's."

He decided to interrupt her soliloquy and spare her further agony.

"Isobel, sweetheart, let me put you out of your misery. You have a sweet, pleasant alto and you hit every note right on key."

"No squeaking?"

"Nothing remotely reminiscent of any kind of animal," he assured her, shaking his head and chuckling at his own joke.

"Oh," she said, still sounding surprised and a little stunned. "Thank you."

"And remember, I'm a musician, so I know what I'm talking about."

"You are that," she agreed readily. "Who was your teacher? Where in the world did you learn to play the piano like that?"

It was an obvious attempt to change the subject, but Dustin let it go.

He coughed and brushed his fingers across the ivories, trying unsuccessfully to hide a bittersweet smile. "I didn't."

"You didn't what?"

"Have lessons," he admitted painfully. "Although in my defense, I did practice several hours every day when I was a kid."

"No one taught you," she repeated, sounding stunned.

He could tell she didn't believe him.

"My parents didn't believe in the extracurricular—except maybe for competitive sports, and that was my brother's department, not mine. Anything in the arts was definitely out of the question."

"But your dad was a multimillionaire!" she exclaimed. "Surely he could afford something as simple as piano lessons."

Dustin ground his teeth against the first reaction

that stabbed through his chest and threatened to exit his mouth. He would not say aloud how much it hurt him, no matter how soulfully her eyes looked at him and begged for him to share.

It took him a good moment to regain his composure, and the fact that Isobel was scowling—presumably on his behalf at his mistreatment by his parents—made the task of pulling himself together even more arduous.

It would be easier if he didn't know she cared. But for some reason, she did. It showed in her glistening brown eyes and in her hurt expression.

"My father was a strict businessman," Dustin explained hoarsely. "He worked his way up from a poor family to a multimillionaire by sheer effort and will-power. Frankly, he didn't see the point of studying fine arts, so we didn't."

"But there was a piano in your home," she said, stating the obvious.

"Oh, yes," he said, drowning out her last word. He had lived in a house, but despite his mother's best efforts, he realized now it had never really been *home* to him.

He squeezed his eyes shut and cleared his throat again. This was more difficult than he would ever have imagined. "It was the most expensive grand piano they could find. It was purely for aesthetic purposes, to make the room nice. It didn't mean anything significant to anyone. No one ever played it."

"Except you."

"Except me." He felt hollow inside as he made the admission, yet he felt compelled to go on, to tell her the whole story before he lost his nerve.

"My father was almost always away from home, building his business, so I rarely saw him. Every time my mother left the house to shop or meet with her friends, I practiced on the piano."

Isobel's eyes were bright with unshed tears, as she moved to stand behind Dustin, and he swallowed hard.

"That must have been hard for you," she whispered, placing her small, soft hand on his arm.

He nodded. "It was. I didn't have any music books or anything to work with at first. I had to wing it completely on my own."

"You succeeded admirably."

He nodded to acknowledge her compliment, and then continued with his story, his voice coarse with emotion. "When my mother died, music was my only solace. I bought music books and put what I learned on my own to use, learning notes and staffs and keys and stuff."

"All on your own?" she asked softly. "Without any help from anyone?"

"Not a soul even knew I played the piano until long after I'd reached adulthood."

"I can't believe your father," Isobel said angrily, squeezing his arm in protest. "I'm surprised you aren't permanently emotionally scarred by what that man did—or rather, didn't do."

"Who says I'm not?" he joked, forcing a chuckle through his dry throat.

"Dustin," she retorted, moving to sit on the soft leather sofa opposite the piano. Leaning forward, she ran her fingers casually over the coffee table, as if examining its planes and ridges.

"Play me a song," she urged him. "Something sweet and classical."

"Whatever the lady wants," he said with a wink, glad to have something positive to do, something to take the sad expression from Isobel's face.

He ran his fingers across the keys as was his unconscious habit, and then was instantly lost in the beautiful music of Bach. It happened all at once, as it had in childhood, his forgetting all his problems and cares as music swept him away.

He closed his eyes, savoring every note and measure, wanting the music to be especially pleasing to Isobel's ear.

He wanted her to hear what he heard, feel what he felt with music.

As he finished the piece, he took a deep, cleansing breath and turned to see how Isobel liked it, hoping the music had brought some manner of peace to her, as it had done with him.

To his surprise, she didn't appear to have been listening at all.

But when she turned to him, her eyes were glowing. "Bach was wonderful, and despite what it may look like, I really was listening to you."

"Glad to hear it. It sure didn't look to me like you were listening," he groused under his breath, trying not to look like a pouting child.

"All I can say is that you continue to impress and astound me. Your piano, your singing, your work at the flower shop—you are truly gifted by God in so many ways."

"Hobbies," he corrected. "Believe me, I'm no kind of genius or anything."

"You know, I don't think I even *have* a hobby. I spend all my time working. At night I get takeout and then fall into bed completely exhausted."

Dustin laughed, genuinely this time. "That's not good for you, you know."

"I know, I know. It's a bad habit of mine that I just can't seem to break."

Isobel was suddenly aware that she had intruded on his privacy. She had quite literally walked in on him when she hadn't even been invited into his house. And then she had continued to push and prod him around his house as if she owned it.

"I'm sorry," she blurted, feeling her face flush with heat. "I came here to give you clothes, not to take up your whole day with my prattling. Let me go get them for you."

She rushed out of the room and out of the house, gulping fresh air as she exited the door, and feeling just a little bit faint.

What was it about Dustin that made her long to

linger? She would have to watch herself around him. She seemed to lose brain cells when he was near.

She pulled out a folding clothing rack and set it up with one hand, a trick she'd learned in college. She then carefully placed each outfit on it in what she would consider a reasonable order.

She smiled as she surveyed the colorful variety of materials and fabrics. Dustin would definitely be overwhelmed by the quantity and magnitude of her gift. She'd have to try to go easy on him so he didn't have a heart attack on her.

Carefully, she wheeled the rack up the driveway and bounced it up the single cement step to the porch, using both hands to stabilize the shaky rack.

Dustin came to help her, propping open the screen door for her, opening the main door wide, then holding the screen with one foot so he could assist her as they yanked and pulled till they had the rack in the carpeted foyer.

It was frustrating but not impossible to trek toward the den on the thick plush carpet, with both of them working at it. The wheels squeaked and groaned, complaining all the way.

Isobel sighed in relief when she reached the den. "That was quite a challenge," she said. "I have a tuxedo for you for the Elway benefit," she teased. "It's black, with a black-and-white-striped ascot. You'll look great in it."

When he didn't reply, Isobel thought he was being

stubborn. She turned, expecting to see Dustin by her side, frowning and throwing a boyish, if adorable, fit.

"Thanks for coming today," Dustin said gruffly, not looking at her.

"I was glad to. I—I'm glad you weren't angry with me for intruding."

"Never," he said, opening his arms to her.

Isobel stepped into his embrace without a word. With her head resting against his chest where she could hear the rapid beat of his heart, there seemed to be nothing left to say.

Chapter Eleven

Dustin was in his flower shop completing an arrangement for a wedding, but his heart wasn't really in it. Try as he might, he just couldn't keep his mind on his work.

He had discovered a soft side to Isobel, a woman he'd first thought was made of steel and who might not possess a heart at all.

Shows how much he knew.

She was a woman who followed classical music to its source without considering the consequences.

This Isobel followed her heart before her head. She was willing to take a chance even when she thought she'd fail, like singing when she thought she couldn't carry a tune.

He laughed at that now. How sweet she was, tentatively singing the praise song despite her fear, not realizing that not only was she right on key, but that she had a sweet, pleasing voice.

Why hadn't anyone ever told her what a lovely singing voice she had? Of course, if she never sang, that would pretty much explain it.

Well, he decided, jamming flowers into the arrangement with both fists, *he* was going to tell her. And he'd tell her over and over again until she believed him.

Until she believed in herself.

Suddenly, he knew what he had to do, and it couldn't wait, not one more second. He stopped arranging the bouquet and told the two employees hard at work he was leaving.

He couldn't remember being this excited about anything in a long, long time.

Maybe ever.

Making one quick stop at a local music store, he hurried home, anxious to begin this new project he'd concocted on a whim but knew in his heart might be one of the best ideas he'd ever had.

Once home, he shed his coat and went straight to the piano. With gentle reverence, he opened his new package and carefully placed the lined, blank staff sheets before him.

For a moment he felt overwhelmed, about to dive in far over his head with nothing but one quick gulp of air. The lines and blank spaces were intimidating, challenging him to fill in the notes.

Could he really do this?

He'd never composed music before, only played it. He hadn't the remotest notion of whether he could create a piece of his own, compose his own melody and write his own words.

Yet he had to try.

For her.

Besides, to his surprise, music was already beginning to form in his head. He realized it was already there, fully formed in his mind. All *he* had to do was get it down on paper.

Soon he was completely involved in the project, a pencil behind his ear and that stubborn lock of hair falling down on his forehead.

It was more complicated than he thought it would be, but he was certainly improving as he went along.

He was writing music!

He realized now it would take quite some time to finish the piece, far longer than he'd originally thought. But he was determined to complete it before the six weeks were up, so he could give a gift back to Belle for all she'd done for him.

Dustin didn't raise his head for several hours. He was so fascinated by the process of putting the music in his head onto paper that he threw himself wholeheartedly into the work.

When he looked at the clock, it was ten after seven at night. At first he thought he might go back and work some more, but there was something else niggling at his brain, something he was supposed to remember.

What was it?

He was growling under his breath about how he needed to start writing things down so he could remember his appointments, when it hit him.

He was supposed to be at the John Elway Foundation benefit. It was a high-class event and Dustin knew Isobel had had to pull strings and call in some favors to get invited.

And, he realized with a sharp spike in his adrenaline, he was supposed to be there at seven o'clock sharp.

He was late.

Really late, since he still had to put on the tuxedo Isobel had left him. And then it was at least a thirty-minute drive downtown, and that was if the traffic was good.

He looked in the mirror, critically surveying his appearance. His hair was a bit mussed, but that could be easily remedied with a comb and some gel. His black T-shirt was brand-new, and his jeans were still discernibly black, through a bit faded in spots.

He shuffled though the clothes rack Isobel had brought him and immediately came upon a nice black-and-gray sports coat. He chuckled and pulled it down from the rack even as his plan formed.

Isobel would have to be pleased by his ingenuity in the heat of tardiness.

Besides, he didn't like tuxedos anyway.

Isobel stood in the corner of the large, highly decorated conference room and watched the entrance door like a hawk. Occasionally she would tap her foot in an impatient rhythm.

Where in the world was Dustin?

He'd *promised* to be her escort tonight, and though she was generally quite comfortable mingling with the crowds on her own in such situations, for some reason tonight she felt as if a part of her was missing.

It was an unsettling notion, and Isobel didn't really like it. Certainly she wouldn't mention her awkward feelings to anyone, especially Dustin.

If he showed up.

She would not look at her watch again, knowing it would only be one or two minutes since the last time she'd looked.

Instead, she looked again at the door, thinking he might be planning to make a grand entrance just to surprise her and throw her off guard, as Dustin was so very fond of doing.

For a moment she dwelled on that unlikely fantasy, most especially the first glance of Dustin in a tuxedo. She had no doubt he would be breathtakingly gorgeous. Tuxedos always made men look dashing and elegant, but she suspected Dustin would look especially charming.

But he wasn't there.

At least she thought he wasn't until she made a casual sweep of the room and her gaze stopped on Dustin. He was at the opposite end of the crowd, already in an animated conversation with the mayor of Denver.

No wonder she hadn't recognized him. She'd been looking for a man in black.

What was he wearing?

Though he was obviously unaware of it, Dustin looked as if he'd crawled out from under a rock, and Isobel wanted nothing more at that moment than to crawl right underneath the very rock Dustin had come out of—after she'd had a chance to wring his neck.

Steam rose from the tips of her toes to the tops of her ears.

He had *promised!*

On time, and dressed in a tuxedo.

Zero for two, by her count.

How could he do this to her?

As if sensing her stare, Dustin turned around and looked straight at her. His smile brightened noticeably as he saluted her with his hand. He then turned to the mayor, said something that made the mayor chuckle and made a beeline for Isobel.

"Hey, Belle, I've been talking to the mayor. Did you know he goes to—"

"You're late," she said flatly, cutting him off. She was in no mood for his cheerful chatter. She had so many things she wanted to say to him that her words were all mixed up in her head. "You—you—"

"Wrascally Wrabbit?" he suggested, chuckling at his own jest.

"How can you joke at a time like this?" she demanded in a huff of hot air.

He made a sweeping gesture that encompassed the

whole room. "Is this a party, or what?" he asked in a bright voice, obviously ignoring the female warning signs she was inwardly wrestling with and which she was sure showed in her posture and on her face, not to mention in her voice.

"Yes, Dustin. It's a party. An *upscale* party," she emphasized.

He merely shrugged.

"Look how everyone is dressed—in tuxedos and cocktail dresses. This was supposed to be a test drive of the new you, remember? All I see is the same old Dustin Fairfax."

He looked down at his own clothing and frowned. "Well, yes," he admitted with a groan. "I had noticed I'm a bit underdressed, but then, I usually am."

"And your excuse is?"

He looked at her blankly for a moment. "My excuse," he repeated halfheartedly. "Am I supposed to have an explanation?"

He looked a bit rattled by the simple request, which surprised Isobel for a moment. She'd expected him to be blurting wild excuses a mile a minute.

But he wasn't.

Isobel took that moment to push him.

"I'm sure it's fascinating, how you were on your way to the benefit and some homeless person needed to borrow your tuxedo for a night out on the town."

"Hey," he protested. "Lay off, already. I have a good reason."

"I'm sure you do," she said wryly. "I'm just surprised you haven't divulged it yet. You always seem to surprise me."

"I…it's just that I was…" His eyes lit up even as he struggled for words.

He stopped suddenly, set his jaw and met her eyes squarely. "I was busy with a project at the house, and I lost track of time. It's as simple as that."

"And the clothes?" she prompted.

"I thought you would want me to be here as soon as possible, so I improvised and rushed to get here as quickly as I could. I've been to these events before, Belle. I knew the choice I was making."

His excuse sounded lame to both of them, but Isobel found her heart softening to him. Why did he always have that effect on her?

"Did I mention I'm more comfortable than any other man here?"

She glared at him.

"Please, Isobel," he begged softly. He touched her arm and implored her with his soft green eyes.

Suddenly he was serious, his tone grave. "*Please* don't ask me to explain more than I have. I can't." He frowned. "I won't. Can you find it in your heart to forgive me?"

She couldn't help it. Her heart capitulated.

She reached up and touched the hard line of his chin, running her finger along the rough-whiskered edge. "You missed a spot."

"Did I?" he asked, chuckling. "Guess that's what

happens when you try to shave and tie your sneakers at the same time."

Her eyes dropped to his well-worn sneakers, her gaze once again full of surprise.

Dustin inwardly cringed. As soon as he had said the words, he realized he had just brought the subject back to his clothes, which was the last thing he wanted to talk about and certainly the very last thing he wanted Isobel to be thinking about.

Holding his breath and expecting a firm reprimand, he was saved by the announcement of dinner being served.

He breathed a sigh of relief as people immediately began milling around them, looking for their place cards among the many tables and making far too much noise for anyone to have a real conversation.

"Where are we?" he asked, moving closer to her. After a moment, he placed an arm around her shoulders to keep them from being separated by the hungry crowd.

She reached into her bag and drew out a carefully folded piece of paper. "Table eight," she said, glancing across the room. "Although I admit I'm not sure where that is. I should have checked earlier."

He slid his hand down across her waist and then slid his hand into hers, linking her fingers with his. Isobel suddenly forgot what she was doing as the pad of his thumb stroked over hers.

She shook her head in confusion.

"Don't worry. I know where it is," he said, winking down at her and squeezing her hand. "I saw it when I came in. Just stick with me."

Dustin was glad he had taken the time to look, so this time, anyway, he could come off as the hero.

Gallantly offering his arm, he escorted her to the table and held a chair for her. She was glowing with pleasure, and he suddenly realized that she was completely in her element here—the fine dining, fancy clothes and fancy talk.

He, on the other hand, felt completely overwhelmed. Too many people, too much noise and definitely too much silverware.

It wasn't that he'd never seen such a layout, but he hadn't used one since he was a kid under the instruction of his nanny and the cook before a big dinner at their home. And even then he'd been relegated to the kids table with only one fork and no knife at all.

"I—er—" He paused and cleared his throat. Leaning in close to her ear, he whispered, "Why doesn't everyone just use one fork and scrap the rest of the silver? Less for the dishwashing folks, you know?"

She chuckled and tapped his nose playfully with her finger. "You can be really adorable sometimes, do you know that?"

Her words created a funny, fluttering feeling in his gut. He cocked an eyebrow and flashed her a cheeky smile. "I hope so."

Using her index finger under his chin to pull him closer to her, she whispered, "The small, sharp fork is for appetizers. Next to that is the one for salad. Then you have your main-dish fork."

He turned his head just slightly, putting them eye-to-eye and nearly touching foreheads. "Whose idea was it to make it so complicated?" he asked in a stage whisper that he knew didn't mask his alarm. "My father's, probably."

"Let's keep it simple," she said with a small nod that closed the gap between their foreheads until they were touching. Her brown eyes beamed with fondness and amusement. "There's a trick to it. Start on the outside and work in."

"Perfect," he said, his voice softening even as his gaze warmed on the beautiful woman beside him. "And I mean you, not the silverware. Although now that you mention it, I do recall Nanny saying something to that effect."

Without conscious thought, he leaned in slowly, crossing the small gap between his lips and hers.

His heart racing in his chest, he gave her plenty of time to figure out what he was doing, to be the one who, in the end, made the choice.

Though her arm stiffened under his hand, she didn't move a muscle to pull away from him. Only her eyes, her breathlessly warm brown eyes that felt as if they were staring right into his soul, widened slightly.

He didn't need more confirmation than that. He took her gaze as a yes and closed his eyes as he brushed his lips over the bee-stung softness of hers.

At the touch of his lips on hers, Isobel slammed

back in her chair so intensely she thought she might tip herself over. She quickly tucked her elbows into her side to keep from flapping around in what she supposed would be a most inelegant manner.

If she fell, she fell; but she wouldn't make a scene doing so.

Dustin, too, pulled back, but his movement was only to straighten his spine and turn his gaze straight forward, away from her. He looked every bit as stunned as she felt, as if he hadn't initiated the contact.

"Sorry," he said gruffly. "I forgot you work for my brother."

Isobel felt the impact of his words like a dart in her heart. She hadn't meant to have it look as if she were turning *away* from his kiss—it was the sweetest moment she had ever known.

In that moment, she had finally come to the realization that Dustin wasn't just some sort of challenging makeover project.

And she was attracted to that man, as a woman was drawn to a man. He was no longer a challenging project.

He was a man.

But that wasn't the reason she had jerked away. It was a sudden sense of guilt that had caused the fatal movement.

He was her client—at least in a sense. And although there were no set doctor/patient types of rules in the fashion industry, she was struck by her own sense of responsibility to the work she'd been hired to do, and to those she was accountable to.

It was a silly thing, really. She considered herself rational and down-to-earth, and here she was being flighty and nonsensical.

She attempted to smile at him, but he would have none of it. He was pretending she wasn't even there. She had never seen Dustin look so grim, not even when faced with a table full of silverware.

He was punching into his salad—with the correct fork—as if he had to spear and kill the lettuce in order to eat it.

And he wouldn't look at her, or even in her direction. Not for one second.

He was polite and cheerful with the other guests at the table, keeping the conversation moving right along, but Isobel could tell something was wrong and she knew she was the cause of it.

Oh, why had she pulled away from him? He was taking it all wrong.

Try as she might, she could not engage Dustin's attention. Throughout the meal, she attempted to add to the conversation, especially when Dustin was voicing his own opinions.

But he wouldn't speak to her, wouldn't even look at her.

Not a glance.

It appeared the only way she was *really* contributing to the evening was in making the most easygoing, laid-back man she had ever known become stiff and tense.

Frustrated, she got up and began milling around

the room, unsuccessfully attempting to put Dustin and his ill humor out of her mind.

As if that were possible.

What was she supposed to do?

Apologize?

Ask for another kiss so she could do it right and not offend him this time?

In the end, she decided it would have to be his move. She'd just have to wait and see.

Chapter Twelve

Isobel waited.

She waited. And waited. And waited.

For a whole week she waited.

By the following Saturday, she had decided Dustin wasn't planning to contact her at all.

Ever.

Why she should be surprised by that was beyond her, she decided. After all, she was the one hired to make over Dustin, and not the other way around. She should be contacting him.

Not to mention the fact she was certain she had offended him when she'd pulled away from his kiss at the charity banquet.

No wonder he wasn't calling her. Who wanted to be rejected?

She should have followed up the next day, she realized, mentally kicking herself for her tactical error. She'd been acting as if she were in an emotional relationship with Dustin, not as his image consultant, which was the truth of the matter.

He owed her nothing.

She owed him a job well done.

What had she been thinking?

She could have—*should have*—called him Sunday afternoon and professionally reviewed what he *should* have worn to the banquet. She should have been calm, cool, collected and proficient.

The truth was that he had pulled it off. And in all honesty, it hadn't bothered her as much as it should have, especially given her profession.

Maybe it was just that the look was completely, uniquely Dustin.

Of course, critiquing his clothing would no doubt have led to an argument, but at the very least they would have been talking. And they'd always worked out their differences before.

Now, too much time had passed for her to call and nag him about his clothing selections. In fact, try as she might, she couldn't think of one single viable reason to call him now at all.

Short of the money—and she refused to be that shallow ever again.

She had dropped the ball.

She was still mulling over her dilemma when the phone rang, intruding on her thoughts like rapid gunfire. She jumped and put a hand to her chest to still her banging heart.

"Isobel?"

"Dustin!" she exclaimed. She hoped she didn't sound as relieved as she felt, but knew he could probably hear the excitement in her voice. "It's good to hear from you."

"Yeah," he said with a chuckle. She could imagine him shaking his head in mirth. "I kind of thought you would call me on Sunday and chew me out for my jeans and T-shirt combination."

She laughed, relived at his usual warmth and candor. "Your jeans, your T-shirt and a few other choice items." His tennis shoes came to mind.

"Why didn't you?" he asked, sounding suddenly serious, his voice low and gruff. "Call me, I mean. Surely my tennis shoes alone are worth a few good words, if nothing else. I was really surprised when you didn't contact me at all. Not even a phone call."

"I…" Isobel started, and then stopped again. She was about to say she had been afraid to make contact with him after the way she had acted, which was the truth of the matter.

But she couldn't tell the truth. She felt vulnerable enough simply thinking the thoughts. To dare to speak them aloud was unimaginable.

"I was busy," she said, amazed at how calm and sure her voice sounded to her own ears. She didn't sound shaky at all.

She wasn't accustomed to lying, and as she said the words the remorse she felt in her heart made itself into a prayer for God's ears. Later, she would have to apologize to Dustin.

"Busy?" Dustin repeated, laughing loudly. It sounded forced to Isobel's ears. Guilt gushed over her like an ice-cold waterfall.

"Too busy for me? But I'm supposed to be first on your schedule," he complained, his lips tight. "I'm sure my brother made that clear to you, and I'm pretty sure he's paying you a load of cash to see that I'm first on your *busy* agenda."

"Why, yes," she said, not able to hide her surprise at his vehemence. He sounded almost as if he were chastising her, like a parent with a child, and her hackles rose. "You *are* my highest priority, of course. I had a matter which I could not put off. It was—unavoidable."

"I see," Dustin's voice softened though he still sounded strongly suspicious.

She knew he didn't believe her, yet his next words were, "I'm not going to press you, Isobel."

Her throat tightened until she felt she was choking. She couldn't have spoken if she'd been given a million dollars to do so.

How did he understand her so well when she didn't even understand herself?

"Well then, Belle," Dustin said, his pure baritone caressing each syllable. "Can you come out with me *today?*"

"Yes, but, wh-where are we going?" she stammered, suddenly unable to keep her nervousness in check any longer.

Dustin could hear the hesitance in her voice. "Did

you already have other plans made? Because we can always postpone if you'd rather. It does have a direct correlation with fashion, however."

He really wanted to spend the day with her, but couldn't help himself in giving her an out if she didn't want to go.

"Then how could I possibly refuse?" she immediately reassured him, though Dustin thought her tone was rather forced and affected.

Dustin restrained a laugh. "Perfect. I'll pick you up in a half hour. That is, if you tell me how to get to your house."

"It's a condo," she corrected halfheartedly. "I'll give you directions. But where are we going? I don't recall you saying."

"I didn't say," he replied cheerfully. "It's a surprise."

"Surprise?" she repeated, her interest clearly piqued, judging by the high, squeaky tone to her voice.

He laughed with his whole heart. What woman didn't like surprises?

A little more than a half hour later, Dustin arrived at Isobel's house. The moment he rang the doorbell, she opened her front door. He wondered if she'd been waiting for him. She was dressed in a pretty pink number and even had a sweater tucked around her shoulders.

"Shall we go?" he asked, cordially offering his arm. She tucked her hand though the crook and smiled.

"Lead on, good gentleman."

He was happy to do so, and she was a willing participant, at least until she spied his means of transportation.

She stopped and stood as stiff as a brick wall, staring with her mouth pinched tightly shut and her eyes wide. Her hands were clenched into fists at her side.

He just grinned, having known this particular idea was going to take some selling on his part. "I take it you've never ridden on a motorcycle before."

She continued staring for a moment. "You could safely say that."

He struggled not to continue laughing, knowing Isobel would not appreciate his good humor. "Then this will be an adventure."

"Or a nightmare," she countered.

He surveyed her outfit again, a short skirt and a blouse made of some soft, silky pink material. And high heels.

"Go back in and change," he ordered lightly. "Jeans and a T-shirt. I won't take no for an answer, so you may as well just go."

"You're kidding, right?" Her expression clearly let him know she hoped he was jesting with her, and would pull a comfortable Towncar out of his pocket.

"Didn't I say this was a fashion expedition?" he prodded cheerfully, flashing her a cheeky grin.

She planted her hands on her hips and glared at him. "A T-shirt?"

"And tennis shoes," he continued as if she hadn't spoken at all. "You just can't ride a motorcycle in heels, Isobel, no matter how much you'd like to."

"But I—"

"Go!" He cut her off in a brisk, no-nonsense tone, chuckling as she dashed back up the walk.

Isobel appeared five minutes later in navy blue designer jeans, a red T-shirt that read Shopping Is my Therapy and a worn pair of white tennis shoes.

"Wow," Dustin said, whistling softly and running his hand along his jaw.

"Wow, what?" she said, flashing her gaze at him. "Are you making fun of me?"

His amused gaze met hers. "Well, to tell you the truth, Belle, I really didn't think you *owned* a pair of tennis shoes. And those even look well-used." He pointed to her feet. "I am impressed."

"Knock it off with the sarcasm, Dustin," she said, pushing his shoulder playfully. "I wear tennis shoes all the time."

He lifted his eyebrows in disbelief.

"I do," she said, pulling herself to her full height of five foot seven. "Inside my house. When I work *out*."

He laughed heartily. "Today you're going to be wearing them out."

She hesitated. "I have a nice pair of black boots that—"

"Have a two-inch heel on them," Dustin finished for her.

She made a face at him.

"So I'm right."

"Don't gloat," she said, shaking her head but smothering a laugh.

"Who's gloating?" he asked with a criminal grin. "I just like getting my way."

"I've noticed that."

This time he was the one to make the face. He then moved to his bike and removed the leather jacket and helmet he had stored at the rear of the seat and fastened down with bungee cords.

Isobel put the jacket on without comment, but when he held up the helmet, she threw her hands up and shrieked in earnest.

"Oh, must we?" she asked, shaking away from the helmet and putting both hands out in unconscious defense. "I have a lovely pair of sunglasses I can wear. That's the law, isn't it?"

Dustin rolled his eyes. "Isobel. Don't be stubborn. I don't give two hoots about the law. Your health might have crossed my mind, though."

"But my hair—"

"Will be all tangled and frizzy by the end of the ride with your sunglasses," Dustin cut in. "Unless, of course, you wear this."

He dangled the helmet in front of her by one finger.

"Helmet head," she muttered, but she took the offending headpiece and awkwardly placed it on her head nonetheless.

Grinning, Dustin adjusted the straps under her chin and made sure it was a secure fit.

"You'll live," he teased.

"That," she said with a pouting twist of the lips, "remains to be seen."

Isobel had never in her life even remotely considered riding on a motorcycle. The only risks she took were calculated.

She left the death-defying feats like motorbikes to men like Dustin.

So she was surprised at the pleasant surge of adrenaline that shot through her as she clutched her arms around Dustin's waist and he put the cycle in gear, quickly accelerating so the wind rushed around them and the cycle purred into life.

"Woo-hoo!" she shouted as they zipped through suburban back roads and Dustin showed off the capacity of his motorcycle.

"Fun, huh?" he yelled back at her.

"Can this thing go any faster?"

Dustin roared with laughter and cranked his bike up.

He never would have thought Isobel would actually *like* riding a motorcycle. He'd only brought it out to prove a point, and maybe because he was still a little angry at her shallow behavior at the benefit.

But all of that seemed inconsequential now.

It was a beautiful, sunshiny winter morning, so typical of Colorado weather and yet always an enjoyable surprise. He had a powerful vehicle beneath him, the wind whipping around him and a beautiful woman clutched to his back.

What more could a man ask for?

Impulsively, he popped a wheelie and buzzed down the street on one wheel. Isobel held him more tightly but seemed to make the move with grace.

She made some sort of sound he couldn't quite discern. He thought she might be laughing.

At the end of the street he pulled his bike to the side of the road and pulled his helmet off, scratching his fingers through his thick, ruffled black hair.

"How was that?" he asked, out of breath but with a smile on his face.

Isobel flipped her faceplate up. Her complexion was rosy and her brown eyes were sparkling with delight as she smiled back at him.

"Incredible," she answered, sounding out of breath. "I feel so…"

She hesitated at length, so he completed her sentence for her.

Several times.

"Free?" he suggested. "Alive? Impressed? All shook up?"

She laughed and waved her hand at him. "All of the above."

"You need some spontaneity in your life, Belle," he said sincerely. "Too much of your life is planned exactly by the book."

"Dustin," she said, pulling in a loud breath and placing her hand flat over her rapidly beating heart, "you are definitely all the spontaneity I can handle in one day."

He grinned widely.

"But no more pop-a-wheelies, okay? I thought I was going to slide right off the end of the motorbike. It's a good thing I had you to hold on to."

Now why did he not feel chagrined?

Instead, he threw back his head and laughed heartily. "Quite a jazz, isn't it?"

She nodded, the motion amplified by her over-sized helmet. "It is that, yes." She paused, then poked him in the chest with her finger. "Don't do it again."

He laughed and grabbed her hand, giving it a gentle squeeze. "I promise. But we have to use the freeway to get where we're going today. Are you going to be okay with that?"

"Oh, sure," she agreed with a smile of anticipation that made her look childlike and vulnerable, and made Dustin's protective instinct surge to the surface. "Just no more—"

"Yeah, right," he agreed, knocking her helmet lightly with his fist. "I promise. No more pop-a-wheelies. At least for today."

Then he turned back in the seat and revved the motor, smiling to himself when she scooted in close to his back and clutched tightly to his waist.

Chapter Thirteen

Twenty minutes later he pulled up at their first stop of the day, a deep brown, stone-hewn church with stained glass windows and its front double doors painted a bright cherry-red, though the paint was peeling to show the wood beneath.

Isobel craned her neck up to see a pointed steeple complete with a belfry.

"A church?" she asked as she pulled her helmet off and brushed her hair back around her face. She didn't bother to state the obvious, that they weren't exactly in the best part of town.

Dustin swallowed hard. It was hard to concentrate on her words when the sunshine played off the highlights in her hair in such a beautiful way. "Where were you expecting to go?"

She placed her helmet on the cycle and fumbled with the bungee cords meant to tie it down. "I don't know. The only thing I can say for sure about you is that I can't say anything for sure about you."

"Hmm. And here I thought women were attracted to men of mystery," he said, swishing an imaginary cape across his shoulders.

Her face turned a delicate shade of pink and it took her a moment to answer. When she did, it was in a tight, squeaky voice. "I—uh—*they* do."

He opened his mouth to tease her some more, but she cut him off.

"In theory." She stared into his eyes. "But you know, in real life it can be—frustrating. Sometimes I feel like I don't know you at all."

"And sometimes I feel I know you better than anyone else on earth," he countered, crossing his arms over his chest.

They stared at each other for a long moment, each either unable or unwilling to break the tense moment by speaking.

Finally, Isobel broke eye contact and looked back up toward the steeple, gesturing at the big bell. "This is a really pretty church."

It was lame, but it was a start.

"Yeah," he agreed, his voice deep. "Too bad it's off the main way where no one can see it. Hardly anyone knows it's here."

He paused and ran his fingers though his hair. "It's almost a hundred years old. But believe it or not, the bell still rings."

"How cool," she said. "But you still haven't told me why we are here."

"Tell you?" he asked with a wink. "How about I show you?"

He took her hand and pulled her toward the red doors. "I can't wait for you to see this."

With great aplomb, he opened one of the doors and gestured her in.

"I'm breathless with anticipation," she teased as she walked by him.

He yanked gently on the back of her silky dark hair as he followed up behind her.

"Belle," he whispered in her ear, causing a shiver to run all the way up her spine.

To Isobel's surprise, the small sanctuary was buzzing and alive with a veritable hive of teenagers. Though the room looked as if it would hold no more than one hundred and twenty parishioners, there were at least forty youths hanging about.

From Isobel's perspective, they ranged from junior high to nearing high-school graduation. It was a beautiful sight, seeing all these kids together inside a church, with nearly every conceivable shade of skin represented—not to mention *hair*—and everyone smiling and mixing about.

But what was this about?

She turned to Dustin, questioning him about what she was seeing without saying a word.

"Watch and learn," he said with a clipped nod and a mysterious grin.

Nodding back at him, she slid into the last pew at the back of the sanctuary and leaned in to see what would happen.

As Dustin moved into the middle of activity, he experienced a moment of pure nerves that nearly made him freeze to the spot.

What would Isobel think about what was about to happen?

Would she understand the passion of his heart?

A moment later, he forgot to be nervous as the youths began gathering around him. He knew and loved each and every one of these kids.

"It's the music man," one of the older boys crowed loudly.

"Hey, Dugan," Dustin responded. The boy approached and they popped fists, then hands, and then wrapped their arms around each others' shoulders and gobbled like turkeys.

It was an old and traditional male sort of rite of passage, and Dustin didn't think anything of his usual decorum until he heard Isobel roaring with laughter in the background.

He turned to her and gave an elaborate mock bow before calling for the kids to get organized.

It took a few minutes and a lot of noise to get forty teenagers moving in the right direction, but eventually the kids were seated by section, and were relatively quiet and ready for his direction.

Moving to the piano, he said, "Let's start with

some warm-ups, and then we'll go ahead and tackle the anthem for next Sunday."

As he ran scales for the teenagers to follow, he surreptitiously glanced back at Isobel to see how she was taking what was happening.

She was sitting straight-backed in the pew, her hands clasped in her lap and her face unreadable. Her gaze was glued to the teens, so he couldn't see her eyes to discern whether or not this meant something to her.

Well, maybe this would surprise her.

He ran his fingers over the ivories, as was his habit before playing, then cranked into a modern, upbeat version of "Amazing Grace."

The piece featured one girl soloist and one guy, who then came together in a touching duet in the middle of the last verse. The young voices had a purity to them he knew he would never find in adult voices, and he coveted every moment, feeling blessed to be their director.

He loved both the music and the words, and closed his eyes as the song ended, his heart reaching out to God in worship.

Praise God.

When he opened his eyes, his first act was to peer back at Isobel.

She had her eyes closed, too. He hoped that was a good thing.

The hour's practice flew by as Dustin led the choir in a variety of sacred tunes, some modern and some classic.

He was proud of his kids, proud to bursting. They had come far in the short time he had been teaching them, and not just vocally, either.

Spiritually, they had grown closer to each other and to God. Gone were the gang-type references and fist-fighting Dustin had dealt with in the beginning.

And as bad as the boys had been, the girls had been even worse, with their petty rivalries often blowing up into catfighting that easily put the boys' fistfights to shame.

Boys fought fair. Dustin knew what to expect from the male gender.

But girls?

Man, when their fur was flying, it was no holds barred. Girls used *all* their resources—scratching, pulling hair, biting, poking at eyes, using knees and elbows… Well, he was glad he'd worked past that stage with them for the most part.

Once again he glanced back at Isobel. She continued to sit straight-backed and unmoving, and her face gave nothing away.

Disappointment washed through Dustin.

He had trusted her, opened his heart to her and shown her a part of his life he'd kept secret from the world until now.

He thought she'd understand.

And she couldn't care less.

He set his jaw, gathered himself together and called for prayer time.

The kids gathered around, taking hands and speaking softly amongst themselves.

When he called for prayer requests, several of them jumped right in with their problems. One young lady's grandmother was in a hospital dying from cancer. A young man named Jay asked for prayer for his older brother, who he thought might be using drugs.

Suddenly he heard a soft, sweet voice behind him, as Isobel took his hand and joined the circle. A tingle spread down Dustin's back.

"This isn't anywhere near as serious as some of the things I've heard from you," she said, making eye contact around the circle. "But I'd appreciate prayers for my mother. She's thinking of moving to Denver from a small town in Texas where she's lived all her life. It's a big move, and frightening."

She shrugged. "I guess she wants to be near her grandchildren. That is, if I ever get married. And if I ever have children."

The teens' reaction was half laughter, half hooting calls to Dustin to help out his girlfriend's mother and marry Isobel. They were especially interested in the *kids* part.

In response to their interest, Dustin couldn't help but give Isobel a smacking kiss on the cheek, which caused her to turn bright red, though she was laughing.

She flashed him a look that told him he had most definitely committed a major felony and ought to be ashamed of himself.

He absolutely wasn't feeling any sort of remorse, especially since he was enjoying the amusement of the teenagers immensely.

The kiss had been nice, too, though he'd never admit that to Isobel.

After the noise had died down to a bearable level, Dustin called for prayer.

The teens prayed openly and spontaneously for the needs that had been mentioned and some that hadn't. Isobel was squeezing his hand tightly, and he found himself rubbing the pad of his thumb against hers.

He wasn't sure why she was shaking with emotion until he peeked though one half-closed eye and saw there were tears on her face.

He wondered if *he* had somehow inadvertently made her cry, and then realized with a metaphorical thump in the head that he was thinking like a guy.

Isobel's tears were clearly tears of joy.

He closed his eyes, smiled and gripped her hand back tightly. Funny how the moment was suddenly causing a scratch in his own throat.

Probably just the start of a cold.

But whatever he told himself to explain away his own emotions, he couldn't deny the way his heart raced to life when he heard Isobel pray.

"Father, thank You for this blessed and talented group of youth, and for giving me the opportunity to enjoy their lovely voices today. These young people offer their voices as the purest form of worship, and their faith puts my own to shame. Shower them with Your love and blessing, Father, and I pray You'll address all their individual needs, both those spoken and those left unsaid."

The church was so quiet after Isobel's prayer that even the tiniest sound echoed. Dustin thought those around him must have been able to hear the frantic thump of his heart.

After a few more minutes, Dustin ended the prayer. "Thank You for hearing our needs, Father. All this we pray in Jesus' name. Amen."

The kids immediately broke into a buzz of activity, grabbing coats and purses and personal CD players. Many spoke to Isobel as they left, and her smile was genuine as she made compliment after compliment to each of the young people.

As the last of the youths left, the church once again became quiet. Dustin closed the red wooden doors and turned back, leaning against the old, solid wood. Isobel stood just where he'd left her, at the front of the sanctuary.

She had her arms clasped about herself as if she were feeling a chill, and her gaze arched up to the large cross at the front of the church.

"Thank you," she said quietly as he approached, her voice scratchy with emotion. "I know you risked a lot in bringing me here. Again, you've shown me a side of you that I *know* your brother doesn't know about, in allowing me to participate in what transpired today."

Participate. Not watch.

Dustin grinned. "They are a pretty awesome crew, aren't they?" he asked promptly. "I'm really proud of them."

"As you should be," she agreed in a heartbeat. "They are almost every bit as awesome as their wonderful director."

Before he could see it coming, she reached on tiptoe and kissed his cheek.

"Scratchy as usual," she complained in a teasing voice.

He ran a hand across his jaw, his mind still swimming. "Mmm. Yeah, uh, sorry."

"Don't be," she said, waving off the comment. "I find I'm getting used to the unshaved look. Who would have known?"

He laughed and ran a hand across her silky hair. "Should we call that progress?"

"Oh, no," she said, shaking her head. "I'm not the one on trial here. Besides, if anything, I'm moving backward."

He groaned. "Don't remind me."

"While we're on the subject…" Isobel began, and then stopped with a pregnant pause.

"Oh, what now?"

"This isn't about clothing," she assured him. "For now, anyway."

He blew out a breath and grinned at her. "That's a relief."

"However," she continued, automatically switching to her business voice as she faced him, "I do have a few questions."

"Shoot," he said, looking as if he meant it in the literal sense of the word.

"Am I correct in interpreting that you do this on a permanent basis?"

Dustin nodded. "This, and three different choirs at other churches in the area. Each group sings once a month."

"You have *four* youth choirs?" she clarified with a cough.

"My home church completely approves of my ministry," he said, sounding just a bit defensive. "I went through the vestry to get my marching orders."

"And I know you haven't told Addison about this," she repeated, a statement rather than a question.

"No," he said emphatically, his eyes widening as he realized where she was going with this. "And I'm not going to tell him now."

Two minutes ago she seemed to understand. Now she was pushing him again.

He bristled.

She touched his sleeve. "Why not?" she queried softly. "Surely if Addison knew of your work here, he would gladly release the trust fund to you. He would surely see this as I do. Dustin, this is not like your work with the homeless people. This is a legitimate ministry. You should at least consider the idea."

"No," Dustin snapped, his jaw tight.

He made eye contact with her and held the gaze,

his green eyes flaming. "This ministry isn't about a trust fund. It's about me, the kids and God, and I plan to keep it that way."

He clenched his fists at his side. "Promise me, Isobel. Say you won't give me away."

Isobel couldn't move for a moment, couldn't breathe as she looked upon this strong, handsome, godly man who had so much to offer the world.

Finally, she broke the silence. "I promise, Dustin. Your secret is safe with me."

Isobel saw his shoulders and jaw relax at her words, and she relaxed a little bit herself.

"I knew you would understand," he said in a low, husky voice.

"And yet," Isobel said with sudden insight, narrowing her eyes warily on him, "this *is* about the trust fund, isn't it?"

He cleared his throat and pulled at his collar, even though he was only wearing a T-shirt. He shifted uncomfortably. "How do you mean?"

"I mean," she said firmly, taking his other hand and turning him toward her so she could look him right in the eye, "that you do not want the trust-fund money for yourself at all. Do you?"

He looked away from her gaze and shrugged noncommittally.

"Come clean, Dustin Fairfax," she ordered, using her hand to turn his chin back to her. "Admit the money is for the kids."

"So what if it is?" he growled, turning and walking away from her.

Isobel ground her teeth. Why was it so difficult to get any real information from him? He was like a mule when it came to his feelings. Sometimes she felt as if she were talking to a brick wall.

Stubborn man.

"For college," he said suddenly, turning back to her with a half smile on his face.

Isobel didn't say a word, waiting in anticipation for Dustin to continue.

His gaze showed the love and compassion he felt for the teenagers, as he clearly considered the words to explain what was in his heart.

"Some of the youth feel a call to ministry. Others just want an education in a Christian environment. But private colleges are ridiculously expensive— way out of the reach of the most well-to-do student to whom I teach piano lessons. These kids are from this neighborhood. They would never get there on their own."

"I'm beginning to see where you're going with this," Isobel said, her excitement growing as love expanded in her chest.

"Scholarships," he finished. "I want to provide a way to help the kids get a much-needed lift in an otherwise menacing world."

"I still say you should tell your brother," she urged. "Surely if he knew—"

"No!" The subject was clearly and adamantly

closed by the sheer tone of Dustin's voice. He stood taller, hovering over her. "You promised."

"I did. And I will keep that promise, Dustin," she vowed.

Suddenly he grinned at her, the light, buoyant smile that was classic Dustin. His smile alone was a tremendous relief.

"I haven't shown you everything yet," he said mysteriously.

When she smiled, he winked.

"Close your eyes," he said, taking her hand in both of his.

"Lead on," she said, closing her eyes as he'd requested, relaxed and entirely trusting him to keep her safe.

Slowly, gently, he led her around several twists and turns until she had no idea in what part of the church she was. It smelled musty, like old wood.

"'Kay, open," he said, sounding as excited as a little boy on Christmas morning. "See what you've been missing, Belle."

He emphasized his special nickname for her, chuckling with happiness.

They were in the belfry, the long thick ropes that led up to the big bell dangling directly in front of both of them.

"Are you ready?" he asked, leaning in toward her and stretching his arms until his hands met and clenched the ropes.

Isobel also clasped her hands around the ropes, but

she could hardly concentrate on anything but being in the cradle of Dustin's arms. His musky western aftershave wafted around her and made her feel dizzy. His strong arms were tight around her; his warm breath tickled her neck when she turned.

She couldn't breathe and she couldn't move.

And suddenly she realized she didn't want to do either. She had no desire to move out of the comfort of his arms.

Ever.

"Ready?" he whispered close to her ear, and suddenly bells were ringing in Isobel's heart.

Chapter Fourteen

Isobel would never understand why people made such a fuss about Valentine's Day. Why make a special day to celebrate love? It only caused the majority of people to feel bad about themselves, and realize how alone they were in this world.

Not Isobel, of course.

She didn't buy into the commercials.

Well, okay, she usually splurged on a box of chocolates for herself. But chocolate was chocolate—a female ritual, right? So what if it happened to come in a heart-shaped box?

Only, this year Valentine's Day wasn't about a box of chocolate.

She had a date. Even though it technically wasn't a *real* date, she couldn't stop her mind from thinking about it.

Or rather, *him.*

The last six weeks had been a genuine eye-opener for her. She was sure she'd learned more from Dustin, her supposed student, than he could ever have learned from her in twice the time.

He had shown her the world, taught her to really look at people and not just their clothing. He had made her care.

Care about the homeless. Isobel had been to see Rosalinda twice on her own since that first day, and the old woman was beginning to trust her.

Care about low-income youth. The choir had stunned her and opened her eyes to issues she'd never before considered.

Care about *him.*

Oh, but she was in trouble.

Because even though her own feelings were beginning to manifest in her heart and crystallize in her mind, she was terrified even to consider if Dustin might feel the same way about her.

There was no use pretending any different.

Talk about heartbreak.

From the beginning, Dustin had been the epitome of a gentleman in every way. She'd never met a man like him. He even opened doors for her.

But that was Dustin.

A true gentleman.

Yet there was nothing personal about that. He would, she was sure, be just as polite to any woman of his acquaintance.

Her thoughts drifted back to the kiss they'd

shared, but she didn't dare put stock in it. She'd been wrong before, associating physical affection with emotional strings.

Worse, at least in the long run, was that he hadn't made many changes in their six weeks together.

In fact, she wasn't positive he had taken to change at all, she thought, her mind sweeping over the events that had taken place at the John Elway Foundation benefit—and before and since, for that matter.

The Elway benefit had been sort of a midterm test for him, and he had blown it big-time. They had talked about it afterward—or rather, she had lectured. But what difference did it really make?

This was one of the major reasons she was standing on Dustin's doorstep at noon, when Addison's fundraising function wasn't until eight at night.

Or at least that's what she told herself as an excuse for the truth.

The fact that she knew this was their last day together, and she wanted to spend as much time as possible with Dustin, might have something to do with it.

But she wasn't about to admit it.

Her throat tightened. She was a professional, and Dustin was a business transaction.

She would not let herself cry.

At least not until she was back in the safety of her own condo.

Dustin opened the door on the first knock, surprising her. It was almost as if he'd been waiting for her arrival, which was impossible since she'd indicated she would show up closer to five o'clock.

"Hey, there, Belle," he greeted heartily and affectionately.

Isobel smiled at him, but her heart dropped like a stone tossed in the ocean. She was going to miss him so much the pain was indescribable.

For a moment she considered, as she stepped into the foyer and shed her jacket into Dustin's ready hands, that perhaps this didn't have to be the last time she saw Dustin.

She'd had a job to do, and she'd done it. She would make certain Addison was impressed with her work no matter how much she had to torture Dustin into a tux.

She would corner Addison and remind him what a gifted brother he really had. Steer the trust-fund issue by emphasizing Dustin's stellar personality and gentle heart.

Surely Addison would hear—and had to know, deep down, anyway—the truth about his brother.

Dustin *would* get his trust-fund money. That objective had become all-important to her, now that she knew what the man was really like.

"You don't look surprised," she accused, putting her hands on her hips and staring up at him. "At my being early, I mean."

"I'm not," he stated, mimicking her movements. "As a matter of fact, I guessed you would make an appearance right about now. Actually, I wouldn't have been that surprised had you shown up at dawn."

Isobel was mortified and shot back, "Is that why you were standing at the door?"

He laughed. "What, you mean peeking though the peephole in anticipation of your arrival? I don't think so."

He closed the door and leaned his back on it.

"I'll go, then," she said, very aware of the way he casually blocked the door.

"Oh, no you don't. You're here, so now you have to wait and see the real reason I was so close to the door when you knocked."

"Oh, really," she said wryly, crossing her arms in defense of who knew what. "And what is this big mystery I should be aware of?"

Dustin's gaze swept across the floor and into the different rooms visible from the foyer. He appeared to be looking for something.

"What are you looking for?" Isobel asked at last.

"It's a she, not a what," he said vaguely, still looking around.

Isobel felt like she'd been shot in the heart, and not by Cupid's arrow, either.

Thick, green slimy jealousy oozed through her bloodstream as every nerve in her body quivered with this new information.

She?

He was chasing some woman around his house.

And he expected her to stand here and watch!

Who in the world was she, and more to the point, *where* was she?

Isobel had the sinking feeling Dustin was going to tell her something she really didn't want to know. She wanted to clap her hands over her ears like a child and wail, "La, la, la—I can't hear you!" at the top of her lungs.

Only her dignity saved her, and then just barely. She straightened her spine, tipped her chin and prepared for the worst.

For meeting the woman Dustin had apparently given his heart to, if the sweet, gentle sound of his voice when he talked about her was anything to go by.

"She's around here somewhere," he assured her, stepping away from the door and drawing her into the house with his hand at the small of her back.

Isobel allowed herself to be led, even when she felt like turning and running away.

"I can't wait for you to meet her," he continued, apparently, if the tender tone of his words was anything to go by, completely unaware of her stiff gait.

He led her to the living room and seated her on the couch. She couldn't help but feel a little jealous.

"She's pretty temperamental," he warned congenially, flashing Isobel a bright smile. "Hang on a minute and I'll see if I can find her."

Isobel sat straight-backed on the edge of the sofa, her hands brought up and clasped—not clenched—in her lap.

Composure, she coached herself.

She would maintain her dignity and refinement no

matter who Dustin brought through that door. No matter how beautiful or poised that *woman* was.

She could be poised, too.

Please, God, let her maintain her poise.

And then Dustin appeared in the doorway and she screamed as if the house had caught fire.

Dustin nearly lost his footing, not to mention his surprise, as he scrambled to cover at least one ear against her racket.

She'd never been so surprised in her life, and she couldn't contain the joy flowing through her.

So much for dignity and refinement.

The fluffy little white kitten Dustin was holding in his arms stole her heart with its first tiny mew and one look into its luminescent blue eyes.

"I know you own your condo, Belle, but I didn't have time to check into your covenants before I got her. She was sort of an impulse purchase, but I couldn't seem to help myself."

He reached forward, offering the tiny, adorable fur ball out to her, and she instantly clasped it to her. "One of these *homeless* things, was it?" she teased.

He laughed.

"Is a kitty okay where you live?" His expression was an adorable mixture of excitement and anxiety.

He was almost as cute as the cat.

"Dustin," Isobel said, her throat tight.

She was half in shock as the kitten purred and pushed at her with its tiny paws, trying to find the most suitable position for a nap.

She'd never in her life taken to an animal as she did that little kitten. Her heart was swirling around in her chest—and not just because of the cat. Dustin's worried look was enough to make any sane woman forget to breathe.

She didn't say anything, enjoying the kitten and the small, innocent thrill of torturing Dustin a moment or two longer.

At length, he groaned. "I did the wrong thing again. I'm sorry."

"Dustin," she murmured, fairly at a loss for words but suddenly needing to comfort him.

"I was at the Humane Society yesterday," he explained in a gravelly voice. "I saw this little kitty and it reminded me so much of you, Belle. She's fancy, but she's also a real cutie."

Stroking the soft fur of the now comfortable cat, Isobel laughed and said, "Don't tell me. Let me guess. You volunteer at the shelter in your *spare* time."

She was pleased to see a little color darken his face. He shrugged and chuckled. "You caught me."

"Is there anything you don't do?" she teased, smiling and winking at him.

"Shoulder massages," he quipped merrily. "But I could work on that. In fact, I really think I should."

So saying, he moved behind the sofa and began working the knots out of Isobel's shoulders. His strong hands were soft and tender, a real paradox, but one she didn't wish to ponder at the moment.

She hadn't realized how tense she'd been until

Dustin's gentle touch unwound her tight, tired muscles and she started to relax.

"The weight of the world shouldn't be on these delicate shoulders of yours," he said huskily, his warm voice close to her ear.

She sighed. "I know what you mean. It feels like it sometimes, though. I think I take life too seriously most of the time."

She'd never admitted that to anyone, but Dustin's kind ministrations were having a funny effect on her brain—and her tongue.

She found herself telling Dustin things she'd never told another living soul, not even Camille. She quietly admitted what it was really like living with a bitter mother and no father at all.

She told him how she always wondered if she was the reason her father had left, and not for another woman, as her mother had said. Isobel always wondered if her mother resented her, though of course she'd never shown it in any way.

But she would always wonder why her father had never come back.

She told him how badly she wanted to get away from Texas—to do more, *be* more, than most of the people in the small high-school class she'd graduated with, the majority of whom were still working on the family farm.

Just like the movies, right? Farm girl makes good in the big city.

Except it wasn't good—or at least not as good as

she'd thought it would be. The same hollowness in her heart followed her everywhere.

Dustin just focused on her, asking quiet questions once in a while and letting her know with verbal assents that he was listening.

All the while he kneaded her shoulders and neck, thinking he might at least be able to help with some of the physical tension, even if he was not able to reach the emotional pain she carried.

A deep, gut-wrenching pain chewed at him all the while.

He didn't just want to commiserate.

He wanted to fix her problems.

Suddenly Isobel glanced at the digital clock on the end table next to the sofa and clapped her hand over her mouth. Her face flamed with embarrassment as she realized just what she'd done.

"I've been talking nonstop for over thirty minutes, Dustin," she exclaimed. "Why didn't you tell me to shut up?"

He chuckled. "Because I like listening to you," he replied gently, slowly brushing his hand down the length of her sleek brown hair. "And I think you needed to talk about some of that stuff. It's not healthy to keep things like that inside."

She shifted away from him, standing with the kitten still curled in her arms. She stroked the purring fur ball slowly, petting all the way down her back and smoothing any ruffles in her soft coat.

"What shall I name her?" she asked quietly, for

some reason suddenly shy to look at Dustin after all she had revealed. She kept her eyes on the cat.

She felt, rather than saw, him smile as he came around the couch and up behind her, gently placing his hands around her waist. This time, his touch didn't make her immediately stiffen, though the longer they stood there, the harder it became.

"You're going to keep her, then?" he asked softly, close to her ear.

She fought the urge to tense at his nearness, wondering why he affected her so.

Her heart knew the answer without question, but she pushed the epiphany aside just as quickly as it arose in her mind.

"Snowball?" he suggested, reaching around to stroke underneath the kitten's small chin. "She's as white as new snow."

"She is," she agreed, holding the fluff ball in the air so she could see its bright, curious blue eyes. "But somehow I think she has another name, if only I can figure out what it is."

"Take your time," he said, giving her waist a squeeze. "There's no hurry to name her. You can keep her for a week or so and get to know her own little special personality."

And as soon as he had said the words, Isobel knew her cat's name.

"Epiphany."

Dustin turned her around, took the cat in one arm

and brought his other hand up to her cheek, stroking it gently as he petted the cat.

"That's a good name. I like it. Unusual, but I agree it fits her."

She gazed up at him and nodded.

"You're shaking," he said.

"Am I?" Her breath increased as she tried to still whatever physical symptoms were giving away the uneasiness of her heart. "It's a little cold in here, I think. Maybe that's it."

He lifted an eyebrow.

"Well, maybe I'm nervous about tonight. I mean, it's a really big night for both of us. A lot is riding on our presentation, right?"

"Right," he parroted, sounding not the least bit convinced. But then, under his breath, he continued, "I hate tests."

He brushed the pad of his thumb across her cheekbone, his gaze warm and tender. Isobel never wanted the moment to end.

Her *moment* would end all too soon as it was. Tonight was it, and then *it* was over. She wanted to savor every second with him.

She looked up at him—more charming than she'd ever imagined possible with that kitten cradled in his arm.

Dustin stared back, transfixed. He brushed his hand gently through Isobel's hair, using the tips of his fingers to feel the softness.

"Your hair is so beautiful," he said huskily. "It picks up all the highlights of the sun."

Emotion washed fiercely through her and she knew she was shaking.

But as his hand returned to her face, she realized he was shaking, too.

She plucked the kitten from his grasp, knowing subconsciously they were both using the poor cat as a pawn, and moved to the safety of the opposite side of the room from Dustin.

She couldn't be next to him right now. She couldn't control the emotion—the *love*—flowing through her.

When had this happened?

She was going to do or say something really stupid and ruin the event for him—more than the evening, but the opportunity to win his trust fund.

Panic surged through her in nauseating waves. What was she to do?

Dustin stood across the room from her, his arms relaxed at his sides, his gaze on her.

He looked calm.

Handsome.

Perfect, in his faded jeans and plain black T-shirt.

She wouldn't change a thing.

What on earth was happening to her?

"Can I keep Epiphany here at your house until after the banquet?" she asked, surprised that her voice worked at all.

He looked down at the kitten, and then grinned up at her. "Absolutely."

She couldn't help thinking that tonight, when she picked up Epiphany, Dustin probably wouldn't be around much longer.

And she wondered if he was thinking the same thing. His gaze was suddenly pensive, his lips tight as their gazes met.

She wondered if they could part as friends. She hoped as much with all her heart.

Yet she had been hired to do one specific job, and that task would come to total fruition this evening at the banquet.

Dustin was ready.

They had been practicing every spare second, had discussed scenarios to make him appear more of what Addison was looking for.

He was going to wow more than his brother with his newly refined looks and manners. He would confidently present himself to his brother and receive the trust fund that was his due.

Dustin would be everything his brother hoped for, and more. She knew in her heart he wasn't going to blow it this time.

And then…

And then he would be nothing but a memory, out of her life forever.

Chapter Fifteen

Dustin fidgeted for the umpteenth time in as many minutes. He hated having a shirt buttoned clear up to his neck. He felt like he was choking, but resisted the urge to pull at his collar, an effort that was sure to be superfluous.

His red cummerbund was tight around his waist and made his back itch.

His whole outfit was bothering him. But right now, his mind was mostly on Isobel.

His heart pounded in anticipation of seeing Isobel—in a gown, jeans or otherwise. As far as he was concerned, she looked great in jeans and a T-shirt.

She looked great in every kind of clothing. How could a man ask for more than that?

In his book, clothes didn't make the woman.

Her *heart* did.

He'd never met a woman like Isobel, and he

wasn't foolish enough to think he ever would again. She was one of a kind.

A keeper.

Somehow, he had to find a way to keep her in his life.

A quick rap on the door pulled him abruptly from his thoughts.

Scooping Epiphany into his arms—and wondering briefly why Isobel had named the fur ball Epiphany in the first place—he opened the door.

The vision standing on the other side of the door was beyond words.

His breath swooshed out of his lungs in a rush. He dropped his arms slack to his sides, his mouth gaping—he hoped not too wide. The kitten made a mew of protest and gingerly hopped to the carpet.

He barely noticed her scurry away, tail held high in exasperation.

Dustin's gaze was riveted on Isobel, whose flowing red cocktail dress was gently blowing in the breeze, making the ruffles at the edges of the dress, just over her knees, stir and rustle like leaves in autumn. The red material made the brown in her eyes look like rich, dark chocolate, and she was gleaming with happiness.

He couldn't take his eyes off her.

"Dustin?" she asked, her light, twinkling voice sounding hesitant.

"Mmm," he answered, not exactly a question. It was more that he couldn't form coherent words at the moment.

She shifted uncomfortably, losing her smile to a shaky, pinched mouth. She stayed on the porch even after he opened the screen and gestured her in.

"Say something," she pleaded, her voice now noticeably high and squeaky.

"Stunning," he said hoarsely. "Radiant. Electrifying. Stupefying."

Well, he'd got the last part right, anyway.

Stupid, stupid, stupid.

Now that he'd finally gotten his voice back he couldn't seem to shut up.

She brushed past him. "Thank you. I think."

He grinned inanely and turned as she walked by, his gaze still glued to her beautiful dress.

And smile.

And hair.

She looked him over, from the tip of his spit-shined black patent leather shoes to the top of his carefully groomed hair. Then she grabbed his arms and turned him around.

Once.

Twice.

Finally, she turned him back toward her and reached up to adjust his bow tie.

"There," she said with a satisfied grin. "Now you, also, look stupefying."

She flashed him a cheeky grin just like the one he was so fond of giving her. "And all those other things."

He roared with laughter and wrapped his arms around her small waist, lifting her up as if she were a feather and spinning her round and round until she begged for him to put her down.

When he set her back on her feet, he couldn't help but brush a kiss across her soft cheek.

She blanched and looked panicked for a moment, then pushed away from him with her palms against his chest and moved well into the room, away from him.

His throat closed until he thought he would choke.

Was his touch so repulsive to her? Had he misread the signals of all the time they'd spent together, that she would be so uncomfortable in his arms, or being kissed by him?

This wasn't at all how he wanted this evening to start, and his own panic drove him back to her side, determined not to let that one action set the course for their evening together.

He wouldn't let this night be the end for them. Somehow, some way, he had to convince her of his love, and that they were meant to be together for the rest of their lives.

Isobel had regained some of her color, but she still looked wary around him. It made him want to scream at the top of his lungs, he was so frustrated.

"So I pass muster?" he asked instead, giving her as playful a wink as he could manage.

She swallowed hard enough for him to notice. "Yes, sir, you do."

"May I suggest, then," he said in the smooth tone of a complete gentleman, "that we depart for the party immediately? I'm sure we're expected as soon as humanly possible."

"You *are* the guest of honor."

He offered his arm, but he didn't expect her to take it. "Shall we?"

"Thank you," she said with quiet dignity, and then looped her hand through his arm.

He led her to the door and opened it for her. He felt as if he was sweating like a pig, and hoped it didn't show. He did hope, however, that his first surprise of the evening would show, and quick.

"Oh, Dustin!" Isobel exclaimed as they stepped out onto the porch. "I can't believe you did this. It's so—not you."

"Yes, Isobel," he agreed wryly, "but it is very much you. Do you like it?"

"Like it?" she parroted. "Dustin, I'm absolutely thrilled to be taking a limousine to the party. We'll make such a splash! It's brilliant. Whatever made you think of it?" Her glistening wide-eyed gaze met his.

He laughed. "You did, of course. Do you want the truth? I was thinking back to our first conversation. Do you remember?"

She hovered one white-gloved hand over her mouth and chuckled. "Oh, I do. There was something about a sports car, as I recall. You wanted to give me a zippy ride around downtown Denver."

He lifted his chin and sniffed his offense at her remark. "It *is* a sports car, thank you very much. I've worked hard on it."

"Maybe, but it's still an old piece of junk," she teased merrily, apparently having forgotten her earlier problems. "I'm surprised it works at all. I'd be *afraid* to ride in it."

"Then I'll be sure to make you take a ride sometime, just out of spite." He grinned. "Do you remember how we talked about how snooty limousines could be? And here I am splurging on one."

She met his warm gaze and held it. "Thank you for this special, once-in-a-lifetime treat. Snooty or not, you're making me feel like royalty."

"Then follow me, my dear, beautiful princess. Your coach is waiting."

"Will it turn into a pumpkin at midnight?" she queried mischievously.

"Eleven o'clock. I couldn't rent the thing all night, you know. What do you think I am, a millionaire with money hanging out his pockets?"

"I certainly hope you don't have anything hanging out your pockets," she replied. "It's very unfashionable—unless it's a handkerchief."

Dustin patted his chest. "I've got that, and it even matches my bow tie."

"Impressive. Very impressive," she said with a chuckle.

The driver of the limousine parked at the curb, got out and opened the door for them. He was snappy and well-dressed in his uniform, and he gave them both a friendly smile.

Dustin helped Isobel inside, sliding close onto the

seat next to her, though there was a lot of extra seat space in the vehicle.

Holding his breath, he reached his arm up and around her shoulders, where he settled with nonchalant ease, almost like a teenager on his first date at a movie theater.

He thought she might object to the close quarters, but she beamed up at him, her eyes glazed over with pleasure.

It made his heart turn over.

He cleared his throat. How could one look make his head spin until he wasn't sure he could think at all, much less speak?

"I special-ordered drinks for us for the trip over to the hotel." Somehow he got the words through his tight throat and dry mouth.

She looked at him as if he'd grown horns.

"What?" she chirped.

He raised an eyebrow, perplexed.

She likewise raised an eyebrow at him, and suddenly he laughed.

"I didn't mean *drinks,* Belle, I meant *drinks.*"

He smiled and tipped the end of her nose with his finger. "I meant *real* drinks. You know—iced tea. Orange juice. Soda."

"Water?" she asked, her gaze again gleaming.

"Ice-cold, refreshing water. Only the best for you."

She smiled. "Please."

He opened the minifridge and twisted the top on a

cold bottle of mountain spring water from Colorado, then opened a bottle of orange juice for himself.

With a big smile, he held up his bottle and indicated a toast. She grinned back at him and held her bottle aloft as well.

"To my princess. May every day be a fairy tale for you," he said in a husky voice.

"To my adventurer," she replied. "May tonight be the beginning of your dreams."

They tapped bottles and then both took a sip, their gazes locked on each other. Slowly they put their bottles down, but for a long while neither of them said a word.

It was a comfortable silence, but the electricity in the air felt sizzling, at least to Dustin. He wondered if she noticed the static buzz.

Finally, Isobel broke the silence, coughing softly before she spoke.

"Are you nervous?" she asked, taking a sip of her water.

"Me?" he responded, doing his best at sounding surprised by her question, though in truth what he was really trying to do was hide the nervous tension he felt sitting so close to her.

"Nah. I don't get nervous." He waved her question away with his hand.

She stared at him a moment, looking pensive. He didn't know whether she believed him or not until she shook her head and spoke. "No, you really wouldn't be, would you?"

"You sound jealous," he teased. "Don't tell me the phenomenal image consultant Isobel Buckley is afraid her greatest work won't pan out."

"Of course not," she said, sounding at once mortally offended and yet unsure of herself. It was a charming combination.

"I won't let you down," he vowed, his voice low and serious. His gaze met hers, pleading with her to believe in his strength—in *God's* strength. "You've done too much work on me for me to fail you now."

"Dustin," she said, turning every bit as serious as he was, and making him feel immediately uneasy, "I want to tell you something. It's really important to me that you hear me out on this."

She reached out and pulled his chin toward her so their eyes would meet. "Oh, what a nice, smooth shave," she said in surprise, rubbing her hand along his cheek and jaw.

"Huh? Oh, yeah. I went out of the way for you this time. I shaved twice today. It gives a new meaning to clean-shaven." He chuckled.

"You look nice," she said softly, sweetly and almost hesitantly.

He looked her straight in the eye as he spoke. "Thank you."

"Be that as it may," she continued as if he hadn't spoken at all, "I want you to know something about tonight."

She sounded incredibly earnest and resolute, so he didn't throw a wisecrack at her this time.

"Go ahead," he urged.

"I think you look absolutely perfect. I think the things you do—known and unknown—more than account for making a contribution to society.

"In short, I think you've made progress in every area I was hired to work with you on."

"Thank you."

"Maybe you aren't taking my meaning," she prodded, though in truth Dustin thought he knew exactly what she was getting at. He supposed he didn't want her to go there, though it looked as if he had no choice in the matter, as she was pursuing it anyway.

He nodded and stared into her chocolate-brown eyes, feeling as if he could get lost in them. His arm around her shoulder tightened territorially.

"It may be," she said slowly, obviously carefully selecting her words, "that your brother will not agree with my assessment of your progress up to this point."

She took a deep breath. "I cannot fathom how that could happen, Dustin, but nevertheless, it is an eventuality we should think about and prepare for, in case the worst-case scenario becomes a reality."

"Believe me," he said gruffly, "that's almost all I ever think about anymore. That stupid trust fund. I hate it." He knew his annoyance showed in his voice, but he couldn't help it.

He didn't want to obsess over money, even if it was for a good cause. He hated that his father had done this to him, and yet here he was, on his way to *the* banquet.

"In short," she continued, interrupting his

thoughts, "you might not get that money, Dustin. Addison may deny you your trust fund. You may have gone through all this agony for nothing."

"Agony?" he repeated dumbly, wondering what she was talking about.

He didn't remember any pain at all.

He remembered the way Isobel swished her long brown hair when she was irritated.

He remembered how her eyes glowed when she was happy.

He remembered the sweet, high tone of her laughter.

Was that agony?

Maybe, in a way, it was. It sure produced turmoil in the general area of his heart.

"It's okay," he said gruffly, squeezing her shoulder to show his support. "I'm fully prepared for the contingency you mentioned." He laughed, but it was an empty sound. "This is my family we're talking about, and I, better than anyone, know what they're capable of."

He paused, thrust his fingers several times through his once carefully combed curls, and said, "I love my brother, and I know he loves me. Whatever happens, happens."

"I think you do." She reached up to stroke the backs of her fingers across his cheek. The soothing movement calmed him a little.

He paused, embracing the emotion that was enveloping him completely. He struggled to gain control.

"Addison is the only family I have. No matter what the outcome of the trust fund, he is my brother—and my brother in Christ." His throat grew tighter at every word he spoke.

Isobel cuddled into his arm and laid her head upon his shoulder. His head swirled with emotion as he tightened his embrace around her.

He wanted to feel this way for his entire life. He wanted to take care of Isobel, to hold her and protect her in his arms.

And most of all, to love her forever.

"I wish I had a brother or a sister," she said wistfully, squeezing his arm. "All I have left is my mother."

"But she's moving out here to Denver, right?" he asked, stroking her arm. "To be with you? See her grandkids?" he teased.

Isobel laughed. "Well, maybe someday. About the grandkids, I mean."

She took a deep breath. "Mom will be moving up next month, if the weather permits and she can close on her house. I've found a nice apartment for her here in one of the retirement centers.

"She likes the idea, and it will be nice to have her around. Sometimes a girl just needs her mother's advice—even if that girl happens to be approaching thirty."

She curled into him, as if seeking his warmth. It felt wonderful to him, and he pulled her in closer next to him.

Isobel sighed quietly. "You know, Dustin, I'm still working through my issues with my father. I don't think he was a good man. Not at all.

"And of course I will never be able to rid myself of the guilt, always wondering if it was me."

He groaned softly in agreement. "I know what you mean."

Oh, how he wanted to be a shield around Isobel, protecting her from the kind of pain she had experienced with her father. It made him angry that anyone could treat her with anything but respect and love.

"I'm getting through it, though," Isobel continued. "With God's help, I am."

She paused, catching and holding his gaze, though he wanted to look elsewhere.

"Forgiveness is a powerful thing, Dustin. I long for the day when that tremendous weight will be lifted from me for good. When I can finally forgive my father for all he has done—and not done—for me."

Dustin stiffened. "You've only told me a little bit about what your life was like as a child, but I can imagine the rest. What he did to you is unforgivable. It won't be easy to let go of." His voice was low and fierce.

"No. It won't be easy, Dustin. Not at all. In fact, I think it will be the hardest thing I will ever do," she said sincerely.

"And yet…" Dustin said, his voice laced with anger and frustration.

Already an idea was forming in his mind. What had really happened to Isobel's father? Something just didn't add up.

Isobel continued, breaking into his thoughts.

"What my father did was unforgettable, but not un-forgivable. God is not the author of *forgive and forget,* though I think we often get confused by that."

She paused until Dustin looked her way. "God only asks us to forgive."

He frowned and creased his forehead, thinking of his own father, of the situation he was now in because of that man. "I don't know. I just don't think I'm up to that sort of thing. You have more grace than I."

"Oh, Dustin," she implored.

"I could never forgive my father," he said vehemently. "Not ever."

Chapter Sixteen

He would have said more, but the limousine came to a stop at the hotel, and the driver opened the door to allow their departure.

Dustin stepped from the car and offered a hand to Isobel, thinking that as bad as his tuxedo was, it must be that much more difficult to wear a gown.

He was glad he was a man. Especially with Isobel on his arm.

Isobel took his hand as they approached the hotel, unconsciously lacing her fingers with his. She didn't even notice until he smiled softly and squeezed her hand.

Apparently he didn't mind.

She was quite disturbed by their conversation in the car. Dustin was carrying around as huge a burden as she, and her heart yearned to help free him from it, to help his pain go away, even if she could not relieve her own.

If only he could believe her words.

What her father had done still hurt her, and it still came to mind from time to time. That was only human nature.

Anger and distress had lessened from those memories as the years had gone on. God had relieved her of some of that pain, made her realize that no matter what had happened, it was still within the realm of God's reach, and though she hadn't known it at the time, He had taken care of her, carried her through the difficulties and on to a newer, better life in Christ.

If only Dustin could see what she saw, could know what she knew.

It would be a start.

She was shaken from her thoughts the moment they entered the hotel. Camille hailed her in a loud and boisterous voice.

"Isobel! Dustin! I've been watching for you for like—forever!"

Isobel laughed. "I imagine you have. Have the festivities started?"

Camille smiled at her friend. "Only just. And of course it won't really get off the ground until the guests of honor arrive."

"Oh, don't call us that," Dustin said with a loud groan. "I'd really rather be a wallflower than the life of the party. Or at least this once I would."

Isobel raised her eyebrow at him. The man who could and did talk to everyone without the least discomfort now wanted to be invisible?

"I do," he insisted.

Isobel squeezed his hand. "I'm afraid that's just not possible this one time, Dustin. No matter how much you wish it."

Camille's gaze dropped to their linked hands, and she smiled widely and winked at Isobel, then made a funny face indicating that she was aware that they were entering as a couple.

Isobel flushed with embarrassment, and then realized she didn't care what Camille thought. She was proud to be with Dustin, and it wasn't something she wanted to be embarrassed about.

Dustin pulled at his collar with his free hand, yanking it around as if trying to find a comfortable place to breathe.

"So then, Camille, can you point us in the right direction?" he said in a scratchy voice.

"Certainly," she said, using all her charm on Dustin, who didn't appear to notice Camille at all. He only had eyes for Isobel, and for tonight, she was going to enjoy it.

"I think you'll find the surroundings familiar," Camille continued, "although admittedly the atmosphere has changed substantially."

"I beg your pardon?" Dustin asked, looking adorably confused.

Camille grinned at both of them, her smile like that of a cat. "Oh, surely you remember. Fifth floor? Ring any bells?"

Isobel and Dustin looked at each other and broke into laughter.

"You know," Dustin said as they entered the glass elevator, "I really dislike heights. Especially glass elevators."

Isobel laughed, shaking her head at his obvious distress. "Why didn't you tell me? We could have taken the stairs."

He pointed at her two-inch heels. "In these outfits? We wouldn't make it up one flight of stairs, much less five. Can you imagine what Addison would say if we didn't show up because we were stuck in a stairwell?"

By then the elevator had reached the fifth floor. Isobel chuckled as Dustin stepped out and planted his feet firmly on the floor.

"It's good being on dry land again," he said, theatrically wiping his brow. "I'm so incredibly relieved. I can't even begin to tell you, Belle."

"Ha!" Isobel replied. "You think you're sweating now. Just wait until we walk in there."

She pointed to the open double doors, behind which was Dustin's one opportunity to make or break his chance at his trust fund.

Dustin scowled for a moment, sizing up the open doors, which to Isobel looked very much like a mouth—a whale's mouth, perhaps, or a tiger's.

Suddenly Dustin shrugged and grinned. "No time like the present," he said, offering his arm. "Would the lady care to accompany me to my doom?"

She curtsied playfully before taking his arm. "I'm

absolutely honored to be with you under any set of circumstances."

Oh, how true her words were.

If Dustin only knew the truth.

As soon as they walked into the ballroom, they were met by Addison, along with many friends and acquaintances they both knew.

Isobel recognized many prominent faces in the room, people who would gladly give generously to a cause such as the Children's Hospital cancer ward, which Addison had picked as his charity of choice for the evening. This would be a good night for the hospital.

She was glad for that.

"Welcome, Isobel," Addison said, politely shaking her hand and giving her a friendly smile, which she returned in spades.

Then he turned to Dustin, his expression giving nothing away as he looked his brother over from head to foot.

Isobel realized suddenly that Dustin had never fixed his hair from when he'd run his fingers through it. His curls were showing.

She held her breath.

"Hello there, Addy boy," Dustin said at last, shifting from foot to foot.

Addison hesitated a minute, just staring at his brother. Then he suddenly stepped forward, smiled broadly and threw his arms around Dustin. "It's good to see you, bro."

Isobel's eyes moistened with tears, and as she met Dustin's gaze, she thought she saw a telltale gleam there, as well.

She smiled and stepped aside as Dustin animatedly returned the bear hug, giving back what his big brother had offered.

"You two look great," Addison said huskily as he moved back and dropped his arms. "Feel free to mingle around the ballroom and enjoy the food."

Addison turned to her. "Isobel, your friend Camille picked the caterer, and let me tell you, the hors d'oeuvres are spectacular, and that says nothing of the meal she has planned."

"Camille has a gift for these things," Isobel said with a laugh.

Addison waved his hand at Dustin. "From what I can see, Isobel, you have a gift, too. I've never seen my baby brother look so spiffy."

Isobel's heart raced. Did this mean Addison approved of what had been done and saw beyond the obvious—that Dustin would get the money in his trust fund?

She could only hope.

But she was also aware that this might not be the last test of the evening. Dustin would have to continue to be on his best behavior, and he might be called upon to disclose a little more than he was comfortable with.

Dustin once again offered her his arm, and they moved deeper into the room, talking to various friends and colleagues, and making general conversation with those they did not know.

Dustin leaned down close to her ear. "This place looks so familiar," he teased. "Although I have to say it does look a lot different tonight." He laughed. "I don't see a model's runway anywhere, thank goodness. Or any racks of clothes. Whew."

"It's more like the ballroom of a prince's castle," Isobel whispered, her head swirling as she looked at the red and gold decorations that had transformed the room so completely.

"I can assure you, Addison is no Prince Charming," Dustin said with a laugh.

Isobel looked up at him, her eyes wide and her heart in her throat. She thought if her heart swelled with any more love than she felt at that moment that she might simply burst.

"I wasn't thinking of Addison," she said quietly and tenderly.

Dustin's eyebrows immediately pinched together, as did his lips.

Isobel felt an urgent sense of panic.

She had said the wrong thing.

She was making an issue out of something that simply did not exist, at least on Dustin's part. When would she get that through her thick skull?

She immediately promised herself she would be more careful about what she said and how she acted around Dustin for the rest of the night.

She could not give her feelings away.

That would not be fair to Dustin. This was his night, and she was here to support him. She would not ruin a night he was sure to remember the rest of his life by throwing herself at him.

"Camille is a wonder with decorations," she said in a rush. "Like I said before, she's really gifted as a hotel manager."

"Yeah," said Dustin, sounding dazed and confused. "Gifted."

The announcement that dinner would be served saved Isobel from further embarrassment.

Ever the gentleman, Dustin once again offered his arm as they weaved their way around the tables looking for their place cards.

Dustin pulled at his collar for the hundredth time, stretching his neck to both sides in an apparent attempt to ease his anxiety, and perhaps to gasp a quick breath of air.

Every movement he made was apparent to Isobel, who felt his anxiety so strongly and fiercely it started to become her own.

He shifted in his jacket. "Where are we supposed to be sitting?" he asked in a strained voice. "I've got enough to think about without having to sit on the floor to eat."

She was certain he hadn't meant the words as a joke, as tense as he was, but though she tried to restrain it, she couldn't help herself.

She burst into laughter.

"No matter what you think your brother thinks of

you, I doubt very seriously that he expects us to dine picnic style."

Dustin looked at her, his eyes glazed over as if he hadn't heard her at all.

"And if it is, hon," she said, still laughing, "I'm in a lot more of a pickle than you are. At least you're wearing trousers."

Dustin stared at her for a moment, the same glazed look in his eyes.

Suddenly, the clouds parted, the sun broke through and he smiled. The happy-go-lucky man she knew and loved appeared back in his eyes.

"Let's find Addison," he said. "Surely he knows where he seated us."

Dustin took her hand and led her to the head table nearest the raised platform. Addison was seated by a famous hockey player on one side and a well-known national politician on the other.

"It's about time you got here," Addison said, smiling at them. "I was about to feed your salad to my pet rabbit."

Dustin raised both eyebrows in surprise, but said nothing.

Isobel squeezed his hand.

"Well, sit already," Addison said, indicating the two vacant chairs opposite him. "I'm sure Isobel is hungry, even if you are not. It's really not very nice to keep your date away from the dining table, kid."

Dustin looked down at Isobel, panic in his eyes.

She knew what was bothering him. He had to sit

at the lead table and act like fancy banquets were something he did every day.

"You can do this," Isobel whispered. "It's just food."

He nodded, a smile pulling slightly at the corner of his mouth. "Right. Just food. I'm hungry. How about you, Belle?"

He held the chair out for her to sit and then seated himself.

With a flair that surprised her, he selected the right fork and gently dived into his salad, taking slow, small bites.

As the courses changed, Dustin leaned toward her. "Smile," he whispered. "If you keep looking like that, everyone is going to know I'm a fraud."

"You're not a fraud," she whispered back fiercely.

Dustin spoke frequently throughout the meal. Unlike Isobel, who had to force herself to be outgoing for the sake of her business, Dustin was a people person. He got along with everyone, and made easy conversation that would have been painful for Isobel to initiate.

After the meal and before dessert was served, Addison rose and moved to the podium on the platform. He turned the microphone on and tested it, then looked down at Dustin and smiled.

"Tonight is an important evening," Addison announced to general applause.

"As you know, tonight's event was to sponsor the cancer ward at the Children's Hospital in Denver. My company, Security, Inc., has asked you all here to generously match our donation of five hundred thousand dollars."

The guests roared with approval, and it was several minutes before Addison could continue.

"I am astounded by the giving hearts in this community, and am proud to announce that not only did you match our contribution tonight, but you surpassed it. Our total tonight is one million, ten thousand dollars. I'm sure the hospital will be overwhelmingly grateful for your generosity."

Dustin whistled under his breath. "I had no idea my brother was doing such philanthropic things," he said to Isobel.

"Philanthropic or Christian?" she replied, meeting his gaze with her warm chocolate eyes blazing.

"You may have a point," he said.

"There is another reason we've gathered tonight," Addison continued, cutting off their conversation as Dustin gripped her hand.

"As many of you know, in my father's will, he left me in charge of my baby brother's trust fund, with very stringent conditions."

"Some baby brother," a man called out from a rear table.

"Point taken," Addison said with a laugh.

The crowd laughed along with him.

"Anyway, Father left strict instructions on distributing the fund to my brother, and I am happy to say that tonight I have witnessed a major change in him, exactly what I had hoped for."

Isobel became ruffled.

What did he mean Dustin had made a *major change?* He hadn't really changed at all, except for the tuxedo he was constantly fidgeting in.

"I'm proud tonight to introduce you to my brother, Dustin, and to present him with his well-earned trust fund."

Dustin's whole body was shaking. He gritted his teeth, trying to control his emotions. This was the moment he'd been waiting for, when he would finally receive his trust fund.

All he had to do was get his legs to work, walk up to the platform and receive the coveted check.

The only problem was that he was completely frozen to the spot.

He couldn't move a muscle, except to pull at his ridiculous collar and his strangling bow tie, which felt like it was getting tighter by the moment, choking him to death.

He certainly couldn't stand, never mind walk.

He took a deep breath, trying to steady his nerves and pull himself together.

Suddenly Isobel was out of her chair, standing behind Dustin with her hands on his shoulders.

He had no idea what she was up to, but he could feel her hands shaking.

"No," she said so loudly her voice echoed in the big room.

Addison cleared his throat and tapped his fingers against the podium. "I beg your pardon?"

"I said," she repeated, emphasizing each word as if she were speaking to children, "no."

Chapter Seventeen

Panic rushed through Dustin.

What was Isobel doing? She was ruining everything they had worked for.

He could see the train wreck coming but he was helpless to stop it.

"Stand up," she whispered for Dustin's ears only, a command rather than a suggestion.

He complied, but only to turn and implore her with his gaze to stop whatever game she was playing and let things go as they were.

"Take it off," she said, once again in the loud, piercing voice that everyone could hear, even those clear across the room.

"What?" asked Dustin, in a daze.

"I said, take it off. Now."

He had no idea what she was talking about, so he stood staring at her, wondering if she'd gone completely mad from nerves or something.

"If you don't, Dustin, I'm going to," she warned in a low voice.

"Ms. Buckley, may I ask what you are doing?" Addison asked from the podium. The rest of the crowd was so silent they could have heard a pin drop.

Isobel made good her threat, and finally Dustin understood what she was doing, besides killing any chance whatsoever he might have to get his hands on his trust fund.

She started with his coat, yanking it off his shoulders and down his sleeves until she'd completely shed it from him.

Then she started on his bow tie.

She stepped back and looked at him for a moment, then reached her hand up and mussed his hair.

Dustin felt a good deal more comfortable, which he supposed was a good thing, as he was going to his own funeral.

Isobel stomped up onto the platform, her high heels clicking with every step. Addison yielded the microphone to her without a word.

She paused and took a deep breath.

Dustin was holding his breath, half terrified and half oddly interested in what she would say.

After a moment, she pointed at him.

He cringed and wondered if he ought to crawl underneath the table.

"This man, ladies and gentlemen, is Mr. Dustin Fairfax."

There was complete silence in the room as Isobel continued to point.

"I am a professional image consultant. Six weeks ago I was hired by Addison Fairfax to make over Dustin, to help him become something that would fit the terms of their father's will."

Dustin clenched his fists, unable to fathom what was going on.

"I admit I like the new haircut," she said wryly, and the crowd chuckled along with her. "However, I cannot let this farce continue. I am here tonight to tell you emphatically that Dustin has *not* made a major change that suddenly makes him worthy of the trust fund."

Dustin groaned quietly, seeing the end in sight. He could almost hear the chop of the ax.

"Dustin is not a person who likes to dress up and attend social functions," she continued. "He is most comfortable in faded blue jeans, old tennis shoes and a plain old T-shirt.

"He is more comfortable with his jacket off—it confines his shoulders—and his tie removed. Oh, and the buttons. Dustin does not like anything too tight around his neck."

"Ms. Buckley," Addison whispered frantically, urgency in his tone.

She held up her hand to him.

"Dustin has not changed," she repeated, looking out into the crowd, "because, ladies and gentlemen, he does not need to change."

Several murmurs broke out among the crowd as Isobel's speech began to make sense.

"Dustin Fairfax is the most honest, giving, hardworking man I know. He makes all kinds of contributions to society, and we don't need to know what they are. As the Bible says, he keeps his good works a secret, so that his reward is in heaven.

"Dustin is the best man I know. He should get the trust fund simply because he completely deserves it. He has earned my respect, my confidence and my loyalty."

As she finished, she lowered her head, tears in her eyes.

The crowd was roaring with applause, many standing in ovation to her speech.

Addison quickly moved to Isobel's side and put his arm around her, whispering gently into her ear.

Dustin was on his feet in a second. Something about seeing his brother with his arm around Isobel spurred him to action like nothing else could.

He was gone in a moment.

"Do you know where we're going?" Camille asked, excitement lining her voice as she turned a corner in the clunky, boxy old car Isobel had never been able to convince her to part with.

Isobel leaned against the cool window and groaned, holding her forehead in one hand. "I thought you said it was a surprise."

Camille gave her a quick glance and smiled

despite her friend's obvious agony. "It is a surprise. I just wondered—you know—if you recognized the neighborhood or something."

Isobel gritted her teeth. She didn't recognize the neighborhood because she wasn't watching where they were going.

She couldn't care less.

It had been three weeks since the banquet, three weeks since she'd seen Dustin, and she was miserable.

Addison had announced that Dustin would be receiving his trust fund, though he'd been gone by the time she'd finished her ill-fated speech.

She wondered if he knew he was getting his money.

Addison had given her a check, but she'd handed it right back, donating it to the Children's Hospital, the night's chosen charity.

It had felt like blood money.

"Oh, will you cheer up, already?" Camille chirped. "This is going to be fun."

Isobel begged to differ. Nothing was ever going to be fun again. In every man she saw Dustin's face, every voice, his voice. Every laugh, his laugh.

She wasn't sure if she would ever laugh again. The logical part of her argued that Dustin was a phone call away. She knew where he lived, for pity's sake.

But if he didn't want her, she wasn't going to go chasing him around, making a nuisance of herself.

And he obviously didn't want her.

It wasn't just that she didn't want to walk out of his life and never see him again.

It was that she wanted to be with him. She wanted to share every joy, every sorrow.

For richer and for poorer, in sickness and in health, her mind mocked her.

How had she only now figured out what must have been obvious for at least a couple of weeks, maybe since the first day, when Dustin walked into the deli with that awful haircut?

She was completely and unconditionally in love with Dustin Fairfax.

She had had relationships with other men before, but they had all been short-term and, in hindsight, rather shallow.

Stupid. Stupid. Stupid.

"We're here," Camille said, turning off the car. "Get out."

Isobel recognized where they were the moment she slammed the car door shut.

The church with the belfry and red doors.

She tried to pull on the door handle, but she had locked the door by habit when she'd exited.

"Camille, take me home. Now," she ordered, pulling on her friend's elbow.

She just laughed. "No way. Come on, girlfriend. Your future awaits you."

Then why did she feel as if she were going to a funeral?

She knew Dustin was waiting inside. She just didn't know why. And after three weeks?

She looped her arm through Camille's, and her friend patted her hand for good measure.

"Deep, slow breathing," Camille advised. "You can do this."

Camille had watched her mope about for three weeks. She knew the agony of unrequited love herself. Why was she drawing this out?

Camille was in cahoots with Dustin, that's what it was.

Then they were inside, and the real surprises were only beginning to show themselves.

The youths were there, milling about and chattering up a storm.

Dustin was at the piano. He appeared not to notice her appearance.

But then the tune changed, and suddenly the choir assembled, humming a background to an unsung melody. Addison stepped from one side of the church, her mother from the other. They were both smiling.

She was confused.

Stunned.

Elated.

In a moment she was in front of the piano, and Dustin was seated at the keyboard. His kind, flashing green eyes were on her as he stroked his fingers lightly over the ivories.

His expression was as serious as Isobel had ever seen—his brow furrowed and his lips tight.

"Hey there, Belle," he said as if they had seen each other yesterday. "How's it going?"

"I—uh," she stammered, unable to process what was going on.

She cleared her throat and looked around her. "Okay, I guess."

He nodded gravely. "Well, I—" he started and then paused, his gaze locking on hers. "I'm feeling absolutely terrific tonight."

He smiled just for her. "No, better than terrific. Fantastic. Wonderful. I can't put it into words, how I'm feeling right now."

He put his hand on his heart, still holding his earnest gaze with hers.

She tried to hold back her grin but couldn't.

"Stupefying?" she suggested, knowing her eyes were gleaming with the hilarity of the private joke.

"Mmm, yes. I was thinking more along the lines of *supercalifragilisticexpialidocious.* You know, the word you use when you can't think of a word?"

Isobel couldn't help it.

She laughed.

He smiled gently. "Well, Belle, do you remember the night of the Elway Foundation benefit?"

"Ha!" she said, letting out a puff of breath. "Do I remember it? As I recall, it was your midterm, and you flunked."

He nodded and winked at the crowd hovering around them and chuckling at the scene. "This is true," he said with a casual shrug of his shoulders. "I definitely didn't rank up to par."

"That's the understatement of the year," Isobel mumbled under her breath.

"Yes, well, anyway, I'm sure you recall that I was late that night."

"Very late."

"Very late," he agreed.

He paused for a moment, running his tongue across his bottom lip and looking deep in thought.

"I had a reason for being late that day, although I didn't tell you then what it was."

She was baffled. "Why not?"

"It wasn't finished yet."

"I'm sorry," she said, her forehead creasing as she tried to comprehend his words. "I don't think I understand. What wasn't finished?"

He looked at her then, long and hard, and yet tenderly. His expression was serious, but a soft smile quickly appeared.

"This," he said in almost a whisper.

Then his fingers ran over the ivories one more time, and he began playing the softest, sweetest song Isobel had ever heard.

She closed her eyes, reveling in the beauty of the music, and in the knowledge that Dustin had written this song.

It was so beautiful, and from the way he had phrased it, she was certain it was the first song he'd ever composed on his own.

But why hadn't he simply told her that?

Did he think she wouldn't understand?

She did understand.

She understood Dustin almost better than she knew herself. She felt inexplicably linked to him, but she knew that this was only her side of a relationship that would never be.

Suddenly, Dustin began to sing, his clear, rich baritone piercing through the sanctuary even though he had no microphone.

And he was singing about her.

When Isobel heard her name, a finger ran up her spine and gooseflesh covered her arms.

The song was about her!

She gulped down and tried to pull in air, but nothing seemed to work. She felt as if she were suffocating.

His words whirled around her, every note burrowing into her.

He was singing a love song.

A love song!

Could it be that he returned her affections, that he felt the same connection as she?

Was it true?

Dustin continued singing, but his gaze met hers, and in his eyes she could see all the love and affection and commitment that she felt for him.

He smiled and winked at her in that crazy, adorable Dustin way he had, and her heart flipped over, and then over again.

He loved her!

Oh, how she wanted to be alone with him right

now, to finally express all the feelings she'd kept hidden in the depths of her heart.

Dustin finished his song, clearly spelling out his love for her—by name.

And the next minute he was beside her, holding her hand. She was unaware of the crowd gathering closer to see what would happen.

She could only see Dustin, and the love beaming from his eyes.

Part of her screamed that it was too good to be true; that there was no way her dream could be becoming a reality.

And yet there Dustin stood, softly smiling just for her.

"This took me longer than it should have, Belle," he said, dropping her hand and putting both his hands in his pants pockets.

"For what?" she asked breathlessly.

"To figure out I'm in love with you."

Her breath rushed out of her body and she stood like a statue, his words having frozen her.

"And there was one more thing."

"What?" she whispered, all choked up.

"Your father."

"My *what?*" she screeched.

Her mother put her arm around her.

"Mom?" she asked.

"This should come from me," she said.

"What?" Isobel didn't know whether to be happy or sad—but she was confused.

Dustin answered. "Before I could make things right with you, Belle, for all you did for me, I needed to find out what happened to your father. I wanted to give that knowledge to you as a gift—so we could go forward with a clean slate."

"So you went to my mother?" Isobel demanded, adding a bit of anger to the cloud of emotion she was feeling.

"Not immediately, no. First I hired a private investigator. When I found out the truth, I went to your mother for confirmation."

"What do you mean *confirmation?* Mother? You knew what happened to Dad? Why he didn't come back?"

"He did leave your mother for another woman," Dustin said gently, placing a hand on her mother's shoulder. "And he thought a clean break would be better, at first."

"But then that other woman broke it off," her mother offered, a tear sliding down her cheek. "Your father wanted to come back home again. I wouldn't let him."

Isobel was stunned into silence. Dustin put his arm around her.

"I was angry, Isobel," her mother explained. "Angry and hurt. And then—" She broke off suddenly, closing both hands over her face.

Dustin cleared his throat. "You were about five years old then, Belle. Your father, he was—he overdosed on medication. The police believe it was an accident."

Isobel burst into tears, and then, as if a light

poured on her, she remembered the day her mother had gotten a certain telephone call, and what had come of that.

"Do you think…?"

But she didn't have to finish the question. Dustin nodded. "I do think. And now you can let it all go."

Still crying, her mother embraced her. "I'm so sorry for not telling you the truth. I was so ashamed of my own behavior."

Isobel hugged her tight, and they cried together. The others, besides Dustin, stayed back, letting the family renew their own vows.

After a while, Isobel turned to Dustin. She opened her mouth to speak, to tell him she loved him, to thank him for his heartfelt consideration. But the words wouldn't form.

She couldn't breathe, much less speak.

He smiled gently and put a finger over her mouth.

There was no need for her to speak. The love between them was almost a tangible thing.

Suddenly he pulled his hand from his pocket, a white velvet box clutched in his hand.

She might have panicked, with all these people around her, watching her every move.

But the look in Dustin's eyes calmed her, and she waited to see what he would say.

He flipped open the box to reveal a lovely gold ring with interwoven aspen leaves made from genuine Black Hills gold.

Gently, carefully, he removed the ring and held it up to her.

"This is a promise ring, Isobel," he said in a soft, smooth baritone filled with the richness of his love for her.

"If you accept this ring, you are accepting my promise to you—before God—to love you, care for you, be there for you, and when the time is right, make you my wife."

She stared at him for a moment, just letting his words sink in.

How she loved this man!

Slowly and with great regard, she lifted her left hand and accepted the ring, which Dustin quickly slid onto her hand, as if she might change her mind.

This, she knew, she would never do. And she realized she owed Dustin the same kind of vow he had given her. He needed to hear it from her.

As he started to move his hand away, she grabbed it and held it.

"Dustin," she said, her voice choking with emotion, "I love you, too. I accept this ring, not only as a token of your love, but of my love for you.

"I will—before God—love you, care for you, and when the time is right, I will become your wife.

"I look forward to getting to know everything about you, and to bond our love by our time together."

"Kiss the woman," a man in the crowd called.

Soon, everyone in the crowd was calling for the culmination of such serious vows.

Dustin grinned like a cat, amusement lighting his eyes. "What do you think, Belle?" he whispered for her ears only.

She grabbed the front of his shirt and pulled him to her, so their lips were mere inches apart.

"I think," she said with a sly smile, "that you'd better kiss me."

Dustin obliged willingly, closing the distance between them with a soft, sweet kiss.

"We're on it!" a man and a woman said. She thought it might be Addison and Camille, but she wasn't sure and she didn't really care.

A moment later, the bell was ringing, clear and loud inside the sanctuary of the church.

Around them, Isobel could hear applause.

She thought all the angels in heaven must be applauding at that moment, for the joy of a man and a woman who'd finally found each other.

Chapter Eighteen

Four and a half months later

Isobel heard the pounding on the door to her condo, but she was busy playing with her cat, Epiphany, and didn't want to move to get it.

"Camille, can you get that for me?" she called.

Camille appeared at her side, dressed, but with a towel wrapped around her hair.

"In any other circumstances, Izzy. But I think you should answer it this time."

With a groan, Isobel picked herself up off the floor and went to the door.

Not a huge surprise, Dustin was on the other side of it. What did astonish her was the man standing behind Dustin.

His brother—Addison.

She hadn't seen Addison since that time at the church when she'd received her promise ring.

It was only then she realized Dustin was holding a box with a ribbon—and it wasn't just any box, it was a clothes box.

She couldn't have been any more surprised. She felt as if he could knock her down with a feather.

"Come in," she said to the men, holding open the door. "Addison, it's great to see you."

He rubbed his hands together as if he were nervous, but then gave her the pearly-white Fairfax grin.

"You're looking as pretty as ever."

She smiled and shook her head at him.

She would have said more, but Dustin cleared his throat.

"Excuse me," he said wryly, "but isn't anyone interested in the gift I brought? The gift in the *clothes* box?"

She laughed. "You know I am."

He nodded. "Good," he said firmly. "Then you'll follow my directions to the letter."

She frowned at him, her eyebrows furrowing. Who had exchanged her sweet, carefree Dustin for a man who gave orders?

"It's important, Belle. Just do what I say, this once?" He was pleading with her now, his big green eyes like a puppy dog's. She couldn't resist.

"Okay, so what gives?" she said, giving in with what she hoped was a modicum of dignity.

Camille had wandered out to the living room, and

Isobel was surprised to see her hair was not only dried, but styled.

What was going on here?

Dustin handed her the box. "There are clothes in here," he said, as if it weren't obvious. "I want you to go in and change. You have to wear what's in the box today. Promise?"

She had a feeling this was a promise she was going to regret, but how could she say no with all these people staring at her?

"Camille can help you get dressed," Dustin suggested offhandedly.

As if she hadn't been dressing herself all her life?

But she smiled and took the box from Dustin, then allowed Camille to herd her into the bedroom.

"What did I just get myself into?" she said to Camille.

Her friend just laughed. "Why don't you just open the box and see?" she suggested merrily.

Isobel set the box on the bed, held her breath and untied the blue ribbon, gently easing the top off the box.

Blue jeans. It was blue jeans. *Faded* blue jeans, to be exact.

It figured. It just figured.

"Well, put them on," Camille suggested with a wave of her hand. "You know he said you have to wear this outfit today."

"Yeah, don't remind me," she groaned.

She picked up the jeans and found an even worse surprise.

"Oh, it's a T-shirt," she said of the carefully folded cotton material. "He knows I hate T-shirts."

"Well, look on the bright side," said Camille. "At least it's hot pink. You'll look really cute."

"I'll look really grungy," Isobel replied, but she pulled the jeans over her hips.

"Okay, okay, the shirt," Camille urged.

"All right, already. Don't rush me. I'm not in a huge hurry here."

"Well, it's not fair to leave Dustin and Addison waiting," Camille advised.

Isobel picked up the hot pink T-shirt and rolled her eyes at her friend. "So I'll get dressed, already."

She pulled the T-shirt over her head. "I'm ready. Let's go."

Camille looked at her strangely. "O-kay," she said, drawing out the word. "You first."

Isobel shrugged. "Whatever."

She stepped out of the bedroom and back into the living room to find both men smiling from ear to ear.

"Well?" asked Dustin, rubbing his hands together.

"Well, what?" she said, lifting her eyebrows.

Camille sighed loudly. "This woman cannot take a hint."

Isobel turned to her. "What are you talking about?"

Dustin laughed. "Come here," he said, leading her to a full-length mirror in the hallway. "Now, look at yourself."

She did, and then she screamed for joy, throwing her arms around Dustin and kissing him soundly.

Though the words were reversed in the mirror's image, she had still easily been able to read the words printed on her T-shirt.

Marry Me.

* * * * *

Dear Reader,

Change.

It's a six-letter word that draws fear in all of us, from the humblest to the mightiest.

We can't control many of the changes that happen to us—but sometimes we become obsessed with changing ourselves.

As Dustin and Isobel learned, and what Moses himself learned straight from God, maybe life—today's life—isn't about change at all. Maybe it's about being just who God made you—right here, right now.

God loves you just as you are, and has placed you just where you are—for a reason.

It's worth a thought.

I love to hear from my readers! You can write me at:
Deb Kastner
P.O. Box 481
Johnstown, CO 80534

Resting in His strength,

Deb Kastner